HONOR BOUND: BOOK TEN

ANGEL PAYNE

HONOR BOUND: BOOK TEN

ANGEL PAYNE

WATERHOUSE PRESS

For the wild boy who dared to love
this wild girl and gave her wings to fly.

Thomas, you make every day an adventure
full of our magic and our love.

You are my always.

CHAPTER ONE

"Hot. Really hot. And hard."

"No way. Slow and sexy."

"Girl, please. Look at his posture."

"*Looking.*"

"And that says 'slow' to you...how? That man likes being large and in charge."

"Can't we just wish he prefers both? *A lot* of both?"

"Maybe he'll let one of us explore the issue further."

"After we're done with the dog-and-pony show tonight."

"You mean after *Tracy's* done with it?"

That was it. The banter between her two closest friends finally made Tracy Rhodes choke on her "soothing" cup of tea. She set the cup down on the dressing table, swiveled in the high makeup chair, and unloaded two rounds of exasperation at Gemini Vann, aka her Chief Counsel, and Veronica Gallo, her Media Secretary. At the moment, however, they were distracting thorns, numbers one and two. "Not helping with the 'relax' segment of the schedule, girls."

Relax. If that were possible. Down the hall, an army of Las Vegas Convention Center staffers readied a hall that would soon seat thousands. In a little over an hour, all those seats would be filled—with people waiting to hear what *she* had to say. About a subject she knew all of three damn things about. Okay, two and a half. She needed all the help she could get.

That officially nixed relaxation.

Calm. Maybe calm was achievable—though that depended on getting five minutes of deep breathing. Time sure as hell laughed at that one. Sound check was in ten minutes, followed by half a dozen this-can't-wait phone calls and then a meeting with local schoolchildren. And space? Fifteen people in a twelve-by-twelve dressing room might be *someone's* idea of space, but she wasn't that someone.

There were a lot of "someones" she never thought life would turn her into by now.

Widow.

Single mom.

Entrepreneur.

Vice president of the United States.

Annnnd there went the possibility of calm.

Before her nerves could start their usual run with that, Gemini came to the rescue, holding out a bottled water. With eyes half a shade lighter than hers and the same somewhere-between-blond-and-brunette hair, many mistook Gem as her sister. Neither of them refuted the claims. Why bother when it might as well have been truth?

"Better to ask forgiveness, right?" The woman's blue-silver gaze sparkled. "So...errrmm...sorry, boss?"

Tracy took a second to think of a good zinger as comeback. It was all the opening needed for the strawberry blonde poised at the other end of the mirror. Veronica, actually *looking* like a Veronica instead of the shortened version of Ronnie she preferred, pointedly cleared her throat. "You mean *sorry, Madam Vice President*, right?"

Gem snorted. "She was my pinky-swear bestie long before she was DC's darling. She'll be the same long after they've moved on to the news cycle's next favorite flavor. Still"—she

8

nodded Tracy's way—"sorry, *Madam Vice President.*"

Tracy stifled a chuckle. "You're forgiven, Madam Counsel to the vice president."

Gem glanced across the room again. "Just for that, I'm ogling the new guy again."

"Not if I beat you to it." Ronnie sneaked in a long stare at the cluster of men near the door—"men" seeming the worst ration of a word for the sight. At least ten better definitions came to Tracy's mind for the dark-suited group.

Giants.

Fighters.

Leaders.

Alphas.

Rulers.

Annnnd that did it. She was now a member of the gawk-a-thon too. And that was a surprise...why? With the turn her life had taken in the last year, there'd barely been time for a little self-induced fun in the sheets, let alone activities like—gasp—a date. And if she could even find the time for that? What then? One couldn't trade small talk about the job over dessert and coffee when most of that information was classified. One couldn't invite a guy up for a nightcap when Secret Service was opening the car door and the street address was One Observatory Circle.

Even if that wasn't the case, she had to consider Luke.

Like she did in every decision she made. In every breath she took.

Well. Speak of the handsome devil now.

No. Not a devil. Despite the glints in his eyes and the cant of his grin, her son would always be her perfect gift from heaven. A little extreme? Of course. A thought process she'd have to revise one day? Definitely. But not today and not now, even if staring at Luke meant she had to keep looking at the suited hunks, now engaging him in caveman-worthy fist locks and shoulder bumps. The lump in her throat swelled bigger as she watched his attempts at reciprocation, all gangly limbs and fifteen-year-old bravado, clearly worshiping the warriors who joked around with him—

Until he locked gazes with the new arrival to the gang.

The one who made the others, even with their linebacker shoulders and towering thighs, look like his wimpy kid brothers.

The one who still had Gem's and Ronnie's tongues dragging on the floor.

The one who turned her kid into a speechless slab.

Especially the next moment, when he turned and gripped Luke in a thoroughly masculine handshake. With their hands locked, the man's fingers stretched halfway to Luke's elbow.

"Holy shit," Gem rasped at the sight.

"Holy *something*," Ronnie seconded.

"Sssshh," Tracy admonished. "He's talking."

And she didn't want to miss a second of it.

Because his voice was the most alluring thing about him.

Dear. God. That. Voice.

Deep as his dark, watchful eyes. Formidable as the shoulders straining at every stitch of his jacket. Warm as his caramel-colored skin but cool as his control. It was the kind of voice she could imagine in the front lines of battle—but also at the pulse points in her neck. And other places on her body...

Holy. Cow.

Well...holy *something*. Cows weren't exactly at the mental forefront at the moment. Stallions, maybe. Or mambas. Maybe even werewolves.

No, no, and no.

Pumas.

Dark ones.

Ding, ding, ding. *When the metaphor fits...*

She really did need to make a date with the electric boyfriend soon.

"It's Luke, right?" the hulk was saying. "Good to meet you, man. I'm John. How's it jammin'?" The query came with a nod at the phone into which Luke's ear buds were plugged, drawing her attention to the extreme skull cut of the guy's ink-black hair—another element of utter hotness. "Yeah," he murmured, stepping closer to study Luke's playlist. "That's some beatin' stuff."

Okay, forget about playing coy. Tracy escalated her gawk to an open ogle. John the hulk had to be part wizard or druid or sorcerer—whatever the hell Luke's video-game-of-the-month was calling them—to entrance her son into revealing the hallowed contents of his playlist.

Not a druid.

Maybe a god.

He sure as hell looked like one.

Moved like one too. She looked on, certain she added drool to her gawk, as he greeted Sol Wrightman, who'd entered and made a beeline for him. They clasped hands and then butted shoulders, making her notice John the hulk was taller than the agent in charge of her Secret Service detail, who was no small man. The bigger difference was in their demeanors. Sol was a constant dervish, full of jagged energy. John's movements were just as powerful but fluid in their force, flowing from one action to the next, backed by the strong surety of all those muscles. No, she couldn't see them. But she damn well knew they were there.

Sol was accompanied by another man, whom she recognized from their brief introduction from the day before. The guy's name also began with an *S*, but that was all she could remember, despite how his bold bone structure, expressive lips, and endless legs seemed better fitted for an underwear ad model than a top-shelf Vegas security advisor.

"Ready to go, champ?"

She swung her attention toward the source of the challenge, wondering how he'd sneaked into the room. Had the hulk smoked over her attention so thickly, she hadn't notice Dan Colton's own entrance?

Not a question to which she wanted a real answer.

"Well hey there, runt." She pushed to her feet and pulled the polished businessman into a hug that'd leave bruises. She was fully justified, especially since the man's wife, Tess, looked on with a laugh of approval. "Gah," she muttered, pulling back to slap his well-defined jaw. "It's so unfair."

Dan shook his head, freeing his penny-colored waves out of his piercing blue eyes. Since officially stepping away from the CIA to head Colton Steel, he'd let the locks grow into some trendy asymmetrical look, longer on top and shaved at the sides. "What's unfair? You don't like the dressing room? Is everything okay at the villa?"

"Everything's great at the villa."

"So says the girl who can make the nastiest news smell like roses. I don't give a crap about the roses, Trace. You're doing me a huge favor here, so if the Bellagio isn't cutting it, I can—"

"I'm *fine* with the villa." She chuckled. "It's gorgeous." A fold of her arms emphasized the point. "I'm *not* fine with the fact that you're hotter now than you were in high school."

She expected her friend's beat of discomfort. Dan *was*

hotter than he'd been at fifteen, but the only person who didn't get that was Dan at thirty-three, courtesy of the mottled burn tissue along the left side of his face. Because of it, his features would never be Ken doll perfection again, but he was still here after a mission that should've taken his life. Instead, it'd made him a hero. Regrettably, the man hadn't seen it the same way. His self-pity party had been in full swing until Tess came along and walloped well-needed sense back into him.

"Yeah, well," the man muttered. "Who's now just a schmuck trying to make a buck, and who's the fucking vice president? And fuck, there goes my mouth again. *Fuck.*"

"Guess what, runt? The fucking vice president has a teenage son. She's heard the word a few times before."

Dan snorted. "Don't remind me of *that*, either." His gaze swung over to Luke. "Who gave him permission to grow up?"

Tracy raised both hands. "Don't look at me, mister. I'm clingin' to the saddle and hangin' on for the ride."

"*Fuck.*"

Dan's encore of the word felt more like a new curtain rising. His cocky growl was gone, replaced by a rasp as if he'd seen a ghost. His expression conveyed the same thing—as his stare jumped from Luke to the hulk. In less than a second, her old friend jolted forward, tackling the man in a brutal bear hug.

"Well hello, beautiful." That caramel baritone sounded even better when infused with a laugh. "What's a pretty spook like you doing in a joint like this?"

"Not pretty *or* spooky anymore," Dan countered. "I could ask you the same question, ground pounder."

"Not pounding so much ground anymore, either."

The guy could've jammed Dan's finger into a light socket and shocked him less. That didn't concern Tracy as much as the hulk's open discomfort. He clearly didn't like the feeling and refused to wear it well. Nevertheless, he gave Dan a follow-up through tight teeth.

"Got back from the mission in Kaesong, and brass called me in. Said they 'thought it best' that I cash out early on my billion years of stored-up leave."

Quietly but quickly, Dan's demeanor turned as dark as his friend's words. "You have more than a billion, and they know it."

"*Knew* it."

"You also made the right call on that mission—and they know *that*."

The man grunted. "Right."

Dan chuffed. "Usually am."

"*Pffft.*" The man attempted a subtle shrug. Not easy with shoulders the breadth of football fields. "Somebody's gonads had to get smashed for it, brother. They went for the simple choice."

Dan shook his head. "Dragon, neither your name or family jewels belong in the same sentence with 'simple.'"

"On *that* note"—Tess's interruption, like her smile, was overly bright—"let's talk 'jewels' of different sorts? Perhaps the young entrepreneurs coming to see you two tonight?"

Tracy smiled, though her own look was forced. She'd hang by her toenails before admitting it, but the men's conversation was the most invigorating debate she'd witnessed in the last six months. The confession, though secret, also brought the guilt. Craig Nichols had bucked everyone on Capitol Hill when appointing her vice president after a golf course heart attack struck down Duane Sanford. Sure, she was the surprise darling on the Hill after arriving less than two years ago, refusing to leave until after everyone had listened to her case for foreign security reform, but besides her passion and persistence, she was also young and inexperienced.

Translation: a thoroughly unconventional choice to replace the elder statesman.

And yes, despite her fast friendship with the president and first lady, she'd nearly turned Craig down. In the end, she'd set up camp on the opposite end of that spectrum, determined not to let her leader down—even if that included a lot of boring meetings with a lot of boring old guys looking at a lot of boring vector charts. At this very second, it also meant she got the jollies from listening to her high school buddy and his chum, "The Dragon," invoke their guy parts as conversation reference.

But even as the vice president, she couldn't just order them to get back to the subject—even if the crowd for tonight's event *was* some of the good stuff. Despite her already-shot nerves about it, she was damn glad she'd come. Events like tonight, where she'd meet a combination of high-tech gurus and young innovators, made the job worth it. This crowd represented the private sector's investment in public education, especially programs blending the arts and technology. Luke himself was proof of the strategy's success, but she'd gotten lucky in finding teachers and schools open to the concept. When corporations across the country embraced the concept more, the results would be spectacular—a hope strong enough to make her push past the stage fright one more time.

One more time.

The mantra always got her through the ordeal—partly because she was stupid enough to believe it, partly because it was better than pulling her head out of the toilet long enough to get on stage and sweat through a bunch of rehearsed lines.

"Excellent idea, my ruby." Dan stroked a gentle hand through her lush red curls. He glanced to Sol. "You know if they have a private room around here? The vice president and I just need a few minutes to compare notes."

Sol nodded succinctly. "We'll find something, but first things first. Madam Vice President, we have to apprise you of a minor change in plans."

Minor? Was that why the man's face shifted into Bruce Lee mode? That was what she, Gem, and Ronnie called it when Sol went übertense. "Deep breath, Sol. Whatever it is, we'll handle it."

"Of course we will." He raised expectant brows at his friends, choosing to end with Mr. Mystery *S* Name. "Which is why I'll let Mr. Bommer take it from here."

Mr. Bommer.

Shay Bommer.

Tracy didn't let them see her exhalation of relief. *Better late than never.* "Good enough. Lay it on me, Shay."

Bommer's lips spread, exposing a boyish grin. Even he was pleased she'd remembered. All too rapidly, the look sobered into something more diplomatic. "I've come to apologize to you in person, Mrs. Rhodes."

Tracy frowned. "Apologize? What for?"

"As you know, Mr. Wrightman and I have been working in tandem, coordinating your heightened local security needs for tonight. I was slotted to take the lead on all operations but am afraid there's another lady who must take precedence for me."

Tracy tilted her head, already sensing what he'd say. "That's all right, Shay. I get it."

His face crunched. "You do?"

"Sure. Didn't I see Arianna Grande's back in town for a week or so down the street?"

Bommer chuckled. "She's sweet but not my style."

"Don't say." She tossed a defined glance down to the man's wedding ring. The band gleamed so brightly, she could imagine him polishing it every morning. That was all the invitation the guy needed. Out came his phone, and an image of a woman with large, dark eyes and a bigger, rounder belly.

"My wife, Zoe," he clarified.

"She's beautiful."

"She's also in labor." His expression sobered entirely too fast. "Two and a half months early."

As his face drowned under more troubled waters, Tracy instinctively reached for his hand. "And everything will be just fine."

His reciprocal grip was full of gratitude. "Yeah, I know. She's barely dilated, but this is our second, and delivery on our first was—"

"Difficult?" she filled in after a beat of tense silence.

"It was...an adventure. Let's say that much."

The word often came with a thousand nuances of meaning, especially when one spoke to ex-military operatives. Tracy didn't know a speck of Bommer's back story but was willing to bet he'd worn dog tags at some point in his life. "An adventure with a happy ending, I hope?"

Bommer's grin returned with wider emphasis. "Damn straight." A slide of his thumb across the screen revealed a baby barely older than twelve months, with golden eyes like her father and sable curls matching her mother's. "Her name's Selene."

"She's beautiful too." She meant it.

Shay gazed at the screen with soft eyes. "She is, isn't she?"

"And she needs her daddy right now." She meant that even more. Though Luke had been nearly ten times Selene's age when Ryker died, there were more times than not that it had already felt like he was gone—none of it proper preparation for when he was. "*Go*, Shay Bommer," she urged. "Kiss your daughter. Be with your wife. Those are direct orders from your vice president."

Bommer pocketed the phone, looking tempted to follow up by full-on hugging her. He held himself back after a quick glance from Sol, though his exuberance remained palpable as he scooped up her hand again. "Thank you, Madam Vice President. *Thank you.*"

Tracy returned the tight squeeze of his fingers. "Thank me by sending me a picture of your healthy new baby."

"Roger *that*," he replied with gusto before centering himself with a long breath and continuing. "But first things first. I'm not leaving you and Sol in the dirt here."

Of course he wasn't. Which was why, as soon as the words left him, nervousness tapped a delicious dance up Tracy's spine. This was it. Time to play the part of the land's second-in-command, when all she wanted to do was twirl hair around her finger like the swooning teen inside—

Especially as Bommer motioned John the hulk to stand directly in front of her.

Manna of heaven. Up close, he was even more formidable. Had she expected anything less? Perhaps she had. A slight slump. A schism of ugliness in the crinkles at his eyes' edges. A soft spot *anywhere* on his body. Instead, his fierce force engulfed her harder, matching the nickname Dan had referred to him by. *Dragon.* She half-expected mighty wings to unfold from his back.

"I'm honored—and damn lucky—to be presenting Captain Keoni John Franzen," Shay declared. "Captain Franzen, the vice president."

"Mrs. Rhodes. It's my pl—"

The baritone cut short as soon as their hands clasped—and their gazes locked. As much as Tracy reveled in his voice, she secretly celebrated his hesitance. Thank God she wasn't alone in the feeling. No. *Feelings*, plural. So many, colliding all at once. Feathers of fire through her hand. Radiant heat up her arm. The awareness, now coursing through her whole body, of *his* form. Of even more than that. For a moment, just one blissful moment, the rest of the room disappeared. The noise of the world stopped. All was a haze of golden energy... the same shade she could now glimpse, in tiny perfect flecks, at the very edges of his dark-brown irises.

What would those rings of light look like from inches away? What would *everything* look like, smell like, feel like with the man pressed close instead of at arm's length? And why was she tempted to use some of Dan's four-letter words when realizing none of those fantasies were relevant, much less possible?

And why did she want to tell Shay Bommer to shut the hell up when he spoke again, shattering the gold haze?

"Franz is the gold standard, Madam Vice President. You're actually getting an upgrade, but I won't say that too loudly in front of him." He chuffed, pointing to Franzen's severe haircut. "His dome gets too big, we worry about the doorframes becoming sawdust."

"Yeah? And if yours gets too big, they turn into forests."

Tracy giggled before she could help it. She attempted an apologetic look at Shay. "You do have a lot of hair, bucko." It cascaded around his face in artful negligence like a young Jared Leto or an old John Lennon, usually inspiring appreciative female glances—though not hers. The etched elegance of Franzen's look, though? Her fingers itched from the thought of those black spikes jabbing into them.

Who was she kidding? Her fingertips only carried the start of the itch.

Behave.

Focus.

"Bucko." Franz snort-laughed it, exposing the hint of a smile. Holy hell, the man had dazzling teeth. "Dude. You're a bucko."

"Yeah, well, *you're* a—" Shay interrupted himself, seeming to remember they stood in suits in a convention center, not BDUs in a jungle. "You're a good friend, man. That's what you are."

"Ohhh, boy." Tracy mock-groused it. "There's the pregnancy hormones talking now." She cocked her head, encouraged by Franzen's smirk. "Save the boo-hoo for the delivery room, Bommer—and just tell me what I need to know about this one. 'Dragon,' was it? Do I dare ask where *that* came from?"

Like a kid waiting at Dairy Queen, she couldn't wait for the man's bigger smile. Instead, he started resembling *the* Hulk, eyes stormy and lips tense, before muttering, "It's just a name. Doesn't mean anything."

There was more to that. A lot more. Tracy read that much in the ensuing expression across Bommer's face, debating a reaction somewhere between a *fuck you* and a full throat punch. He eschewed both to state, "As soon as I called with the SOS, John graciously hopped his backside onto a plane from Seattle. He's been based there for the last eleven years—at least the few times he's been stateside—out of Joint Base Lewis-McChord. Headed the Spec Ops team my brother was on, or at least that's what it says on paper. What it *doesn't* say is—"

Franzen chopped him short with a grunt. "Don't start."

Tracy tapped a toe. "Oh, come on. Humor me. What *doesn't* it say?"

Shay smiled.

Captain Franzen looked ready to bust out of his clothes and turn green.

A dozen earpiece radios squawked.

The intrusion made Tracy start. Rarely could she actually hear her security team's comm links since they were hooked into tiny ear pieces for each member, but the blare quashed the silence after her dare, all but ensuring she'd never be answered.

"Roger that," Sol said into the mic beneath his shirt cuff before circling toward Tracy. "Main hall's been checked and secured, ma'am. They're ready to run your sound check."

"Of course they are." As soon as the grumble spilled, she mentally smacked herself for it, despite feeling like she'd earned it. That just once, she could take a break and indulge some harmless interest in a hotter-than-hell man...

No. She was more than interested. She was drawn. Like some damn molecule depicted in one of Luke's Chem lessons, she was helpless about it too.

And she had no idea why.

And *there* was the crux of this frustration.

Keoni John Franzen. There was something about him. Something deeper than the muscles and the confidence and the powerful grace. Something beneath all the one-liners and the smack talk with his buddies. A darkness...but not one cowering in shadows and shame. He liked his darkness. Took refuge in it. Was more than happy in it.

Alone.

So why was she so hot to climb his tree?

And she *was* hot. More than she wanted to admit, even as the light caught the gold rings in his eyes again. As he rolled his head, cracking his neck. As he readjusted his stance, looming and large, before moving into place near the dressing room's door.

Hot butter on a damn biscuit.

Her heartbeat doubled. Her libido flared. Everything between her thighs thumped in time to her escalated pulse rate.

She wanted him to stride back over to *her.*

As she lay on a massive bed, waiting for him.

Her body totally naked.

Her legs completely spread.

"Tigress is en route to the stage. I repeat, Tigress is en route to the stage."

Nothing like Sol barking her code name into the comm link at his wrist, along with a mention of the damn stage, to land her pussy back on ice. Even if it *was* a kick-ass code name.

Shay eased the sting a little, letting her pull him into a maternal hug on her way to the door. "Off with you, Daddy Bommer," she ordered. "And no fainting in the delivery room either."

As he pulled away, a laugh lightened his lips but weariness darkened his gaze. Sol had said Bommer had "covert ops" experience. *Not* special ops. Suddenly, the difference hit her between the eyes—a difference she was all too aware of as vice president. The man had been black ops, likely some of the blackest.

Still didn't prepare a guy for the birth of his own child. Even the second one.

She spent one last second to clasp his hand, using the contact to zing him with the energy of the prayer in her heart, before turning toward the door with fresh resolve.

She could do this. It was just a sound check.

She could do this.

As soon as she could move again.

As soon as she accepted—somehow—that John Franzen now waited, his stare missing nothing and his power filling the air, to become the back end of her security sandwich all the way to the stage.

As soon as she remembered—somehow—that the man was focused on her physical safety, not how huge her ass looked in this clunky skirt suit.

As soon as she acknowledged—somehow—that his arrival might even be a blessing in disguise.

For the next twelve hours, she suddenly had something to be more nervous about than being onstage in front of ten thousand people.

Thank God, after it was all over, she'd be boarding a plane back to Washington.

CHAPTER TWO

Thank fuck she'd soon be back on a plane to Washington.

It was brutal, but it was the truth. Best way to face this kind of shit. To remember that no matter how stunning the package, there was still a politician under the ribbon.

Politicians made policies.

Policies dictated a lot of bullshit.

John Franzen had learned that one the hard way.

Trouble was, he wasn't supposed to be alive after learning that lesson. That one should've killed him. Wasted him in a blaze of glory thousands of miles away and then shipped him home in a box—if there were any of him left for that. Not that it mattered. His soul would've managed fine, surfing on clouds and flirting with the angels...

Instead here he was, looking at thirty-three next month, his ashes nowhere near a blissful resting place beneath the swaying palms of Kaua'i. He was alive and too fucking well, sweating in a monkey suit and blasted by dusty air conditioning, losing one of the nastiest skirmishes of his life.

A fight with his own dick.

What the hell?

Rhetorical question. His brain already had the answer— another truth gained the not-so-easy way. Living through a lot of crap that should've killed him by now.

Fate was a fickle little shit.

And took a lot of delight in being so.

Example? Twenty-four hours ago, he'd been bench-pressing through bitterness and boredom. One phone call and a few hours later, he was on a plane for Vegas, texting suit measurements to the buddy calling in a panic, begging for his help in guarding the vice president. Not the worst distraction he could think of, even with the whole politician aspect of the thing...

Except Bommer had left out one key detail.

The shithead never said anything about that VP being hotter than hell.

Okay, so he'd noticed the...finer points...of Tracy Rhodes's beauty when he and the guys watched the newsfeed of her being sworn in last year. Who hadn't? She was gorgeous, making a guy steal second and third looks because the physical shit was just the start of it all. Not that the outer stuff wasn't worth the effort. Her classic doll features, complete with a button nose and a kittenish mouth, were covered in skin the color of the morning sunrise over the sands of Waimea, peach and gold blended too perfectly for an actual name. Her dark-gray eyes widened whenever she laughed or smiled, fringed by lashes a shade darker than the waves of her hair. At least it looked wavy. He could only guess by the little parts breaking free from her meticulous twist of a hairstyle.

Oh, he hadn't stopped looking there.

He'd tried, damn it. He might not officially be on the US government's payroll anymore, but she was still due his respect, and they'd dressed her in that boxy outfit for a reason. She was the treasure to guard. The asset to protect. The *high value* asset.

That shit, he *could* do—and *had* been doing—until he'd shaken her hand.

Until she'd matched the clamp of his grip with the soft surety of her own. Pressed the warmth of her presence into his very pores. Met his gaze with the brilliance and awareness of hers.

Awareness.

Yeah. That shit.

Changing everything.

When she looked at him...and saw into him. Beheld him as no woman ever had. Not just as a soldier, bodyguard, or conduit for her safety. Not just as Dominant or lover, an avenue to her orgasm. Sure as hell not as a son, brother, or cousin, unless she had some long-lost genetic tie to Samoa he didn't know about. Her stare was none of those things—but strangely, wonderfully, all of them. As if he could be all of it and more for her...

No.

He'd been tired. Really tired. And fuck, she had to be too. It was the only explanation. He didn't do melodrama like "being everything" for someone. That was the shit he gave to his country. His essence sacrificed for the good of the many...

Had sacrificed.

Way to let that *thought go sideways, asshole.*

"Captain Franzen? Is something wrong?"

And way to let it tromp across his features too. Shoving both into the mental shredder, he turned and forced himself to confront those wide doll eyes staring at him from the other side of the Escalade's back seat—in which, through a bizarre string of circumstances, he'd landed with her.

Alone with her.

Hell.

"No." He clamped his teeth harder, jogging the edges of

his lips higher. "Everything's fine, Madam Vice President. Don't worry."

"I'm not worried." Her auburn brows crunched, as if weathering an internal chastisement. "All right. That's a lie. I'm a little worried. This isn't protocol. Is Luke going to be okay?"

"He's in the car right behind us. I'm sure he's doing great. His usual detail is being backed up by Sam Mackenna. He's a good man."

"The red-haired Goliath? Looks like he should be hacking and slashing his way across a moor in a kilt and nothing else?"

Soft chuckle. "He actually owns a few of those. Nellis has him on loan from the RAF for a while. Has a day job training the jet jocks out there."

She smiled. "Luke'll be in heaven about that."

"But you're still worried."

Her pensive gaze out the window confirmed what he'd heard in her voice. "This isn't the way we normally do things."

"Vegas isn't a normal city."

"I'm well aware of that."

"Which is why you can't stop stressing."

"I'm a mother, Captain. Stress is my middle name."

"I could just order you to stop."

Had he really gone there? Referencing her and "orders" in the same sentence—and then letting his libido fill in the rest of that erotic scenario? She went to work in the White House. He spent his days in the gym—and before that, made his living in swamps, forests, and third-world ghettoes.

But damn it, something about her called to every Dominant bone in his body—which was just about *every* bone in his body. No. She just...*pulled* at him, period. Brought instincts to the surface of his blood, primal and feral and needing, especially with her new reference. *I'm a mother.* Like that was the most important burden on her shoulders, not being second-in-command of the free world. She didn't mean it, of course. She couldn't. But for the few moments he let himself believe it, he was entranced. Captivated. Ensnared by the Tigress...

Her gaze flared—as if she'd been able to read his mind. Or maybe she was just as enticed? And if so, how deeply? Did her imagination burst to life with the same dream as his? The same whispered words between them?

Get on your knees, kitten.

Yes, Sir.

Now worship me with your mouth.

Oh yes, Sir.

Shit.

Shit.

Shit.

"Well." She angled more fully toward him, setting down her phone and folding her hands in her lap. "You clearly know what you're doing. And if Sol also felt the protocol break was necessary—"

"For him to head up the decoy motorcade as a masquerade? Yeah. It was necessary."

Really necessary, but she didn't have to know the extent of that. Remarkably, it was easier to maintain the façade about that instead of his growing attraction to her. Sol had received the intel while Rhodes met with a group of local elementary kids who'd won a writing contest, *The Adventures of Barry the Bald Eagle.* While she'd listened to the first-place winner read his piece aloud, Wrightman took a call from the Vegas PD, with Franz listening too. The cops played back an untraceable message in a computer-generated voice, about how the vice president would soon be "sinking into the pit of hell, along with the other oppressors pretending to better the world with their corrupt leadership."

Fucking wing nut.

One this gorgeous woman with eyes like the Milky Way did *not* need to know about. She was already skittish as—well, a kitten—about having to give that presentation with Colton tonight. Sound check had wrapped over an hour ago, and tension still tangibly crackled over her. He only wished it didn't make her even more mesmerizing to study. To desire.

To fantasize about.

You're tense, kitten.

I know.

Perhaps I can help take that edge off.

Perhaps you can.

Lie back. Spread your legs. And let me feast on you.

Oh yes, Sir.

"Well." Her repeat of the word, even more businesslike, gashed through his erotic haze. *Idiot.* His ass was sitting here, rather than in the lead car where it belonged, because a tangible threat had been logged toward her—and all he could think with was the wrong head?

Focus, dipshit.

He started by echoing, as nonchalantly as possible, "Well?"

"*You* tell *me*, Captain." She dropped her head to the side, dropping the doll face for the incisive perception that'd surely played a big part in catapulting her to the VP's office. "I like surprises as much as the next girl, but only when it has to do with flowers, chocolate, or a foot massage. Or all three at once.

I'm not picky."

He nodded toward her feet. "You mean those pointy things aren't the height of comfort?"

"Hey." She lifted a leg by a few inches. He didn't miss the action's effect on her skirt, hiking up her thigh a good inch. "Don't diss. I refused grandma flats and secretary pumps, though the stylists have confiscated my platforms until I'm out of office."

"*Not* the platforms."

"Hey," she mock-rebuked. "No dissin' on the platforms."

He noticeably smirked. "Wouldn't dream of it."

"I joke about a lot of stuff. Shoes aren't one of them." She scrutinized her lifted foot. "I'm still in platform DTs...but at least they allowed me kitten heels as the compromise."

"Kitten heels?" He hoped his gulp looked casual. "That's really what they're called?"

Her response, a snorty giggle, gave him all the answer he needed. Of course they were.

"Back to the surprise." She lowered the leg. A good thing, because she had damn distracting legs. Her love of bicycling was public knowledge, and that fitness showed in the well-defined quadricep he'd glimpsed—and instantly yearned to see more of. "What are we looking at here? Fully verified threat? Terrorist radio chatter? Run-of-the-mill crackpot with an ax to grind against the establishment? Maybe a posse of Luke's groupies, just to make things interesting?"

His forehead creased. "Luke has groupies? Don't answer that." Only took him another second to do it for himself. "Of course Luke has groupies."

She glowered. It was fucking adorable. "Mama Tiger did *not* want to hear that."

He chuckled. "But she probably needs to."

"Yeah, yeah. Add it to the list." Her gaze turned watery as she redirected it out the tinted window. "He's fifteen on the outside and an old man on the inside."

For a long moment, as she propped her chin on curled fingers, nothing filled the air but the rush of the tires on the asphalt. John didn't change that, sensing she needed the quiet.

"So much upheaval in his life," she finally went on. "He's rolled with it better than a trained SEAL. First when his dad was...taken...from us, and now experiencing a lot of life from the road or DC..." The moisture evaporated from her gaze. A firmer look replaced it, though her chin remained planted against her hand. "All of it would've turned *me* into a basket case at that age."

"You originally from Texas?"

"Yeah. Corpus Christi. I moved to Austin for college and just stayed."

"'Keep Austin weird.'"

"I've logged a few decent efforts to the cause."

They shared a quick laugh.

It was...nice.

Even...easy.

So damn easy.

John's limbs fought the feeling. *No, no, no.* There was only one place on the planet where life was "easy," and it was nearly three thousand miles away, in the middle of the Pacific Ocean. Other than that, *hard* was the mantra of his life. Hard was the missions of his job. The rigor of his fitness. The pace of his hobbies. And yeah, the Dominance he gave to lovers who begged for it.

What would Tracy Rhodes beg from him? How would

that sweetly musical, lightly accented voice of hers sound, husked with lust...

Sharpened by pain?

And there he fucking went again.

At least the moment wasn't easy anymore.

"All right, let me guess." He prefaced his response with a slide of snark for good measure. "I'll bet your parents set you up right. Pink bedroom? Canopy bed? Bucket for the cheerleader pom poms, and teen idol posters on the walls? And who were *you* a groupie of?"

She lifted her head fully. Slanted a narrow stare that he felt all the way into his cock, tempting him to already pump a fist in victory...

Until she said, "Sorry. Just doing a quick tally of the steers you roped right, cowboy. Oh, wait. Doesn't take too long when the answer's zero."

He audibly choked.

She hid her laugh behind a hand.

"You *lolo*, woman?" His arched brows and tilted head translated the word for him, judging from the lip she pulled between her teeth.

"I'm probably *lolo* about some things," she murmured, "but not this." After a short sigh, she explained, "My mom disappeared when I was a baby. It was always just Dad and me."

He took a second to process that. Still, his mutter was confused. "Disappeared?"

"Yes." She rapidly sobered. "As in, left. Dad overcompensated by spoiling me, though from girlhood, my idea of indulgence was always a little skewed from normal."

He was fascinated before—and captivated now. "How so?"

"Dad actually *is* a rocket scientist," she explained. "So my idea of childhood 'fun' was usually a hike in the woods, a trip to the lab, or an afternoon at the science museum."

John grunted. "Takes care of the posters and the pom poms."

"Takes care of *all* of it."

"Oh, come on. You didn't still jones for pink walls and a canopy bed?"

"You mean when I could be convinced to get *in* the bed?"

"Huh?"

She nodded. "Hated the whole idea of it." A little shudder claimed her. "Still do, though I have to do the adulting thing now."

No camouflage to her laugh meant he could hang his gape. "So where *do* you prefer sleeping?"

Crap.

There was shucking cover and then there was just inappropriate. Army regs would *not* encourage asking the vice president about her nocturnal habits. But for the first time in a long time, he could also tell those regulations to make like besties with his ass. Silver linings. *Fuck yeah.*

"You want the truth?" She finished the challenge by biting her lip again. Christ. If she kept doing adorable shit like that, he'd forget the word "inappropriate" even existed at all. Did her lips taste as good as they looked? Some company should sell the color and make a goddamned fortune. It'd be named something just as good too. *Tracy's Temptation. VP's Vice. Lips of a Goddess.*

"Truth." He grabbed the chance to steer his brain away from her mouth. "Always a good thing, when you can swing it."

Humor flashed in her eyes. "I liked sleeping on the floor."

"The floor?" It didn't shock him. It *did* make him curious. He watched her pick up on that, her composure loosening a little more. She settled herself sideways against the cushion.

"Used to really settle me." She flashed a searching look across his face, as if trying to see beyond the surface of his reaction. With a finger, she traced a nervous figure eight over her knee. "Kind of silly, I guess, but—"

He made her stop by grabbing that enticing finger. Pulled the rest out too, curling their tips toward him. Her fingernails were perfect and polished, coated in a pale pink, so different from his dark, nicked-up paw.

"Butts are for smokes and rifles," he murmured. "And anyway, I get it."

"You do? Really" The clutch in her voice twisted weird heat around his nerve endings. What did he do with this shit? Give him a lying terrorist or a wise-ass recruit, and he could deal with the energy. But this woman's brave, bare honesty? He was in the weeds without chicken plates on his brain's armor, surrounded by an enemy of his own making. His fascination with her.

And his lust.

Yeah, that asshole too.

"Yeah," he finally managed. "I really do. But I'm a well-trained grunt who's used rocks as pillows more times than I can count." He looked away, unsure again. Her stare had gotten intense, gaining incredible silver lights. What the hell *was* that? If it was her version of pity, he preferred staring at his own shoelaces, thank you very much. "Sometimes it's easier to sleep with dirt in my hair and Sondheim in my ears than drowning in a sea of puff pillows and comforters."

"Right?" She disconnected their hands by flinging hers

up, giving him a full what're-you-gonna-do. "You get too comfortable, you can't think things through. And if I don't think things through, I'm sure as hell not going to sl—" Her features scrunched on a frown. "Did you say *Sondheim*?"

His smirk kicked higher. "You like Sondheim?"

"He's a genius."

"Damn straight he's a genius. Though I'll likely go to my grave wondering whether *Company* or *Assassins* was the best."

"Pardon the hell out of me? *West Side Story*, anyone?"

"Doesn't hold a candle to *Company*." He chuckled. "Guess my cosmic dilemma just answered itself."

She tilted her head and smirked too. Impish. Delicious. "Now you can die happy."

"Suppose I can."

"Just not at the moment, please."

"That an order, Madam Vice President?" He couldn't help jumping on her little taunt with one of his own. If that were the only thing he was tempted to jump right now, things would be a lot easier. Wasn't in the cards, especially as she tapped a finger to the side of her chin, pointing his attention to her enticing dimples.

"Hm. I suppose it *is*, Captain." Her cat-in-the-cream tone sent a matching vibe through her posture. "Well, what do you know. Executive rule has an *up*side, after all."

He grunted—only half teasing this time. "Don't get used to it."

A pout plumped her lips. "Killjoy."

"Just doing my job, ma'am."

Killing.

A lot more than joy, at that.

Only now, the Big Green Machine didn't need his

"services" anymore. Not like that. Sure, there'd been the obligatory offer of "alternative" duty—some on-base, paper-pushing gig banishing him as far from missions and field training as they could possibly maneuver—but they might as well have suggested a one-way ticket to hell. The same pasty walls, soft-ass chair, and lukewarm coffee every day? No fucking way. He'd leave this dimension the same way he'd been born into it. Suddenly and brilliantly. If he were lucky, he'd save lives in the process. Special Operations had been the perfect means to that end.

Only the end had never come.

Hundreds of rockets. Thousands of grenades. Millions of bullets. How many had been aimed at his sorry ass in the last eleven years—and not had the courtesy to take him out in the process? Goddamn them.

There were no more blasts now.

And he was lost in the silence.

Except when the explosions came again.

In his dreams.

Rescuing him.

Haunting him.

Taunting him.

With the life he no longer lived. The purpose he no longer had.

A noise, high and sharp, vibrated through his head. An ice bucket of salvation in radio hail form. He swung his wrist to mouth level, efficiently answering Sol Wrightman's buzz. "Dragon here. Go ahead."

"Franzen, what's your twenty?" Wrightman sounded irked by Franz's use of the call-sign. Not that he could be blamed—but John sure as hell wasn't going to waste time with an apology. If Sol couldn't deal with a slip like that, he was in the wrong damn line of work.

"Little over a mile from home," he responded. Yeah, more code. Wrightman would deal and thank him for it. No security specialist in their right mind, especially one brought on by the Secret Service themselves for extra expertise in a city like Vegas, would openly name the hotel at which the vice president was staying. For someone planning an attack, the information was findable in a dozen other places, but he'd be damned if they found that success from listening to her security detail.

He confirmed the estimation with a glance out the window. The driver, an easygoing dude named Shep who'd seen a lot of action in the Marines, had followed his instructions to the inch. While Sol and the decoy motorcade took Paradise and then Harmon, crossing to the Bellagio's back entrance off Sinatra Drive, John had insisted on taking this smaller group, with just one lead vehicle and four scattered incognito behind, straight up the Strip.

Unorthodox? Not really. It was the oldest trick in the book. Hiding the target in plain sight. And sure, it added several minutes to their trip since traffic on the Strip was a zoo on the best of days, but the delay was a good thing. Wrightman would arrive at the villa first, flushing out any real threat before Tracy was anywhere near.

To that end, it felt safe to add, "Confirm Tigress's destination is checked and secure?"

Sol's comeback quickly had him sitting up straighter.

"Negative."

"Negative?"

Three syllables on his lips but a dozen queries in his mind. What the hell? Was there a problem? He didn't pick that up from Wrightman's voice, which held steady at annoyed not alarmed, but Sol was still as readable to him as tea leaves in milk soup. For all his manic energy, Wrightman clearly kept his deeper shit to himself. The man could have a gun to his head or simply be constipated.

John scowled. Deeply. He was used to knowing his team inside and out, down to the nuances in their voices.

He checked their location. They were nearly at the light for Tropicana. A left could take them right out to McCarran, where her plane waited on the tarmac, but if security had been compromised, he'd advise a right, toward I-15 and Nellis. It'd take a minute, maybe less, for Sam to hook them up with proper clearance and then transport back to DC.

First things first. "Clarify." The Escalade's interior echoed his growl back, a leather-and-wood slap in the face. *You're not in charge, and this isn't war.* Through gritted teeth, he added, "Please."

Sol's reply was prefaced by a weary sigh. "Itinerary change. We need you to head back."

"Back where? To the convention center?"

He watched the reflection of his frown in the vice president's narrowed gaze. "What?" She snapped. "Why?"

"You heard the boss. Clarification, please." Repeating the politeness was the easy part. Enduring the increased tension in Tracy Rhodes's gaze wasn't, even as he got busy disconnecting the audio jack to his earpiece, instead jamming it into the car's patch.

"Some idiot over here slugged too much juice into one power box," came Sol's voice through the car's speakers. "They blew out the whole building, which crashed the drive on the sound system."

"Peachy," John muttered.

"Damn it," Tracy layered atop that.

"They're out getting a whole new laptop to reprogram now," Sol continued. "Sound levels have to be recalibrated, and we only have an hour until they let the crowd start to line up. Once that happens—"

"Loose threads are more likely," John finished for him. Yeah, even at a high-profile event like this. Even with a hundred pairs of eyes on the building's exterior and a matching number on the inside. As circumstances went, the scenario wasn't awful—and on a normal day, they might even be able to discuss a slight variation in plans—but this wasn't a normal day. Paranoia had to be everyone's middle name.

Maybe it was time for Tracy Rhodes to be apprised of that too. John strongly weighed the risk of coming clean with her about the anonymous phone call, especially as she glowered at the speakers, standing proxy for Sol, as if she longed to punch the damn things in. "Sol. *Damn it*. Are you kidding me?"

"I'm sorry, Mrs. Rhodes." To the guy's credit, he sounded like he really was. "I wish I were. You know that. I wouldn't cut into your daily time with Luke if it wasn't important. If you want to walk onto that stage tonight with confidence—"

"All *right*," she snapped. "Fine. I get it, I get it."

Securing the comm line back into his headpiece, John sent a quick wrap-up to Wrightman. "Confirming itinerary change. Tigress on return."

Good thing he'd logged eleven years of disguising frustration. Intrinsically, he felt where the guy was coming from—Sol cared about his boss beyond simple security, invaluable for a political staffer at any level—but concern about what she did publicly had to start with the person she was privately. The woman needed a break, no matter how small. He observed it in the creases of exhaustion at the corners of her lips and the heavy dip of her shoulders. Tension vibrated through every significant line of her posture. But most importantly, it drenched her gaze in raw, unguarded pain—emotion so stark, he doubted few had ever seen it.

It sliced into him, cold as a steel blade. Humbling as a lead bullet.

Making him react with equally honest instinct.

He reached out. Gathered her hand inside his now. Once more, marveled at how small she was. Even struggled with the recognition, which was bizarre. This wasn't new. Compared to him, most women were small. He'd spent most of his youth on surfboards, either Maki or Nani balanced on his shoulders, followed by competing on the wrestling teams in high school and college. After that, boot camp. Eleven years later, he was verifiably huge. None of it explained why Tracy Rhodes felt extraordinarily tiny—or why he was suddenly consumed by the need to shelter her with more than a hand. Then maddened by the recognition that he couldn't. Not in the way it mattered most right now. By giving her back even a fraction of that private hour with Luke.

No.

Hold the fucking phone.

He was special ops, damn it. Maybe not wearing MultiCams and slogging the swamp anymore, but he could still make the impossible happen. Most importantly, he *wanted* to make it happen. For her.

Franzen pushed forward. Smacked a determined hand against the right side of the driver's seat. "Hey, man. Change of plans again."

The guy tossed a smirk over his shoulder. "That so?"

"Yeah. That's freakin' so." Before his spine hit the leather cushion again, he'd opened the line back to Sol. "Wrightman, this is Dragon again. Come in."

A measured pause, in which Franz swore he could feel the man's agitation from across the miles. *Get ready, sugar pie. Here's where you earn your paycheck.*

"Wrightman here. Go ahead."

"Minor change to route. We're proceeding to the hotel for a brief stop."

Another pause, undoubtedly filled with any number of cuss word combinations from the man at the other end. Franz was almost sorry to miss it. Sol struck him as an impressive cusser.

With a blast of static, the line reopened. "Negative," Sol barked. "That is a large *negative* on the request."

"Isn't a request." His ass would likely be torched and booted back to Seattle within the hour, but the sedition was worth it. After a hit of the gorgeous, grateful tears in Tracy Rhodes's eyes, he was sure. Yeah. *Worth it.* "It's a necessity."

"Clarify. *Now.*" Not a second of downtime prepped the command this time.

"The vice president has...uhhh...spilled...*coffee.*" The word was practically a shout but not a lie, thanks to the woman who popped the lid off her drink and dumped the contents on her luxurious skirt. "Yep," he declared, spurred by the truth, "coffee. *A lot.* Everywhere. She needs to change, unless you want her rocking some weird new modern art on that stage tonight."

"Someone can bring her new clothes," Sol snapped.

"Uhhh, sorry. Repeat, please. Lost you on that?" He forced

his gaze ahead while stammering it. No way would he pull off the charade if he even glanced at the softly giggling woman a couple of feet away.

"Franzen!"

"Still not getting anything, man. Damn, what's wrong with this thing?"

He pulled the earpiece out. And left it out.

"Franzen."

Sol's bellow was drowned in the magic of Tracy Rhodes's laughter.

Worth it.

The conclusion smacked him even before she did. Damn good thing, since he didn't expect or see the force of her sudden embrace.

Or maybe it wasn't such a good thing.

He and surprises had never been on the best of terms, even when they were "good" ones. *You want too much, Keoni.* Hell. If he had a buck for every time Mom had repeated the mantra to him... *Because you give so much,* keikikāne. *But expecting the same in return, it shall only bring you pain.*

So he'd grown up and learned how to control the surprises. All of them.

Until Tracy Rhodes.

Who gripped his neck with unbridled trust. Who pressed herself against him with fervent intention. Who flooded his nostrils with the scent of her citrus shampoo, along with a perfume blended of ginger, jasmine—and coffee. Like he needed a damn drop of the stuff, after the adrenaline spiking his blood, the alarm twitching his muscles, and the reaction taunting his instincts.

Fight or flight? Evaluate the adversary. Assess the risk.

Then retreat or retaliate. Contain or exterminate.

What if the answer was neither?

What the fuck did he do when the answer was as unpredictable as her—as all the incredible effects she had on his system? When all he could do was lift a stupid hand to the middle of her back, returning her grateful grip as if he patted a damn dog, when he craved a lot more.

So much more...

You like it when I pull your hair like that, kitten?

Yes, Sir. Thank you.

You want me to pull on other things too? Like these pretty nipples?

Ohhhh yes, Sir!

Fuck.

Fuck.

Fuck.

Saved by the beeping security gate.

As the Bellagio's ornate gates swung in for the car, Franz dropped his hand and eased his body back. The woman fitted so perfectly to him, from the waist up anyway, relaxed her hold too.

But not all the way.

She stayed close enough for him to catch the silver flecks in her pupils. To watch the dimples-inside-the-dimples appear beside her expressive lips. To stifle a groan as those lips parted, displaying a smile that somehow bridged the gap between girl and woman. Between friend and—

What?

Did he want to know?

Hell fucking yes.

No, goddamnit. *No.*

"Thank you." Magically, her two words saved him from that Purgatory. They were soft but casual, dragging them solidly back into the friend zone. For her strength, *he* was tempted to thank *her*.

"You're welcome," he said instead—finishing with an arched brow of warning. "I can't guarantee you'll get a full hour, though. Sol won't believe you took that long to change your clothes."

"What? A gal can't linger?"

A multitude of things came to mind as a comeback to that—but not a damn one that would help either of them. He simply let his gaze narrow enough to show her that if she "lingered" anywhere in his vicinity, it wouldn't be to primp for an arena of up-and-coming entrepreneurs. It'd be for his eyes—and cock—alone.

After he hit her with the look for two seconds, her breath snagged. That sparkling gaze flared.

And he glanced away.

Because you haven't pulled enough cards out of the dumb shit deck already, that you have to go making Dom-guy eyes at the fucking vice president of your country?

Like that would work out—never.

On that heartening note, he resquared his shoulders. Raised his stare back to her, snapping on the mien he'd always saved for officers way above his pay grade. She sure as hell met that qualification.

"If you change fast, you and Luke can probably get in a good twenty minutes," he issued and felt good about it. Yeah; he'd stuck that landing solid, with authority but not arrogance. Okay, maybe a little arrogance. He skewed toward Deadpool, damn it, not Captain America.

Rhodes jumped herself to a new level of his esteem by respecting that. As exciting as it had been to dance at the edge of flirtation, it was time to back off. Not wise to waltz on a precipice when the canyon was as big as DC politics. "I can work with twenty minutes. That's enough time to check homework and catch up on his girl problems."

He narrowed his gaze again. Way different motivation. "Girl problems? What about the groupies?"

"Hello?" she parried. "You think the groupies are *puppies*?"

"Point to Rhodes." He ticked the air with a finger. "But he's a good-looking kid. Seems smart too. And has kick-ass taste in music."

She slid a wry look. "Says the guy who argued *Sondheim* with me?"

"Says the guy who also jams on Green Day, U2, and hip-hop. So...*American Idiot*, *Spiderman*, and *Hamilton* for the point?"

Her lips quirked. "Given, renaissance guy."

John shrugged. "Or a guy who's spent a lot of downtime waiting on orders for the last eleven years." But sure as hell not in digs like this. Just the private portico entrance to the villas, with its ornate tiled fountains and marble statues, was luxury he'd never seen. This was a long damn way from sleeping on rocks.

Wasn't tough to observe how Rhodes barely gave it a second glance. Was the princess feigning indifference, or had she gotten used to the high life after a year in office?

He didn't have to wait long for an answer. The first half of it came as they approached the entrance and her glances grew more impatient. By the time Shep set the Escalade's parking brake on the Italian stone driveway, her agitation was tangible.

Not uncaring. Or jaded. Just a mother desperate for twenty minutes of solitary time with her kid.

Shep remained where he was while the agent in the passenger seat, a stocky Irishman named Donald, exited the car. As he stopped, hand on the backseat door, Tracy twitched like a shopping addict on Black Friday.

Donald didn't budge. He knew not to until Franz gave the all-clear.

John wasted no time unfurling all six-and-a-half feet of himself from the car. As he did, all five senses jumped to high alert. Every moment of the trip before this was left behind, his energy funneled into instincts that'd kept him alive since joining the elite corps of Special Forces Group One.

Sight was his strongest ally. He swept keen eyes over the driveway, up to the rooftops, through the clean-trimmed Cyprus trees and lavender bushes, even into the depths of the fountains. All seemed peaceful.

Too peaceful.

He opened his ears next. Received nothing in return but the soft trickles of the fountains and the distant rush of Strip traffic.

Calm. Too damn calm.

What *was* it? What was out of place?

He'd studied the villa's layout during the plane trip down from Seattle, along with mentally updating himself on the schematics for the convention center. He'd also reviewed the extra intel Bommer forwarded. These villas had dedicated housekeeping, butler, and food services. Why didn't he see or hear any of those personnel? Shouldn't they be out here to greet one of the most "VIP" guests they'd ever had?

He extended his hands out a little, palms down, fingers extended. The air itself was still. Too still.

"Franzen?" Donald's brogue was gruff but soft. "We all cl—" He clipped it short when John raised a hand, fist closed tight. *Full stop.*

He took measured, nearly silent, steps toward the front of the car. Heel-toe, heel-toe; distributed weight; ninja silence. When Donald locked him with a significant gaze, he flung back a battle spear of a stare, forged with a solitary message.

Something's not right.

Donald jerked a nod. Shep repeated the action when the spear stare hit him.

Franz looked over to Tracy again. Her face was distant, pale, and troubled—but trusting. Filled with complete reliance on *his* instinct...

Which still conveyed just one thing.

Something. Is. Not. Right.

More tires sloughed onto the driveway. *Shit.* The Escalades bearing Tracy's two girlfriends, a slew of other staffers...

And Luke.

Who, like the fifteen-year-old being led by his small head instead of his big one, ignored his security detail to bound like a boss from his vehicle. Wasn't tough to decipher Luke's confidence. Popping her head out in his wake was a little blonde, freckles across her nose and a lopsided grin, who gasped upon glimpsing the private backyard and swimming pool.

"Luke! Ohmigawd! This is where you're staying?"

"Only until tonight, when my mom's done with that thing at the convention center."

Smooth. The kid pulled off humble yet confident in the same line. John made a note to commend him—as soon as he murdered him. "Luke. *Damn it.*"

The teen rolled his eyes. "John? Seriously?"

"*Seriously.* Get back in the car."

"Gah. Dude, I thought you were cool."

"Lucas Levane Ryker Rhodes." The charge, louder than it should've been due to a suddenly unrolled window, seized Franz's gut like it clearly did the kid's. "Get back in your car, or this week's allowance doesn't happen."

Franz stomped to the open window. Flung a glare inside the car. "Know what else won't happen if this window isn't closed in ten seconds?"

Thank fuck the woman filled the rest of that in. She wasn't stupid—most of the time—but her blind spot was definitely her son. That much was proved as she hit the button, raising the bulletproof glass back up.

If only her offspring would be as smart.

Not in the cards, even after the threat of allowance deprivation. "This shit is so lame," Luke huffed.

"Hey." Franz jabbed a finger. "*Language.* Especially in front of a lady."

"But *you* just—"

"You're costing everyone valuable time," John bellowed. Irretrievable, perhaps priceless, seconds. "Get back in the car, Luke."

"And don't move your arse until *I* say so." The order, issued by a brogue thicker than Donald's, came from the guy now surging out of that car. Though his ginger hair turned to fire in the sun, the brilliance didn't touch the enraged blazes in Sam Mackenna's eyes. "Do ya have a brain to claim in that thick skull, ya hormonal numpty?"

Luke kept up the fume. Franz almost began to feel for the kid. Sometimes a guy had to choose what won, their good sense or their fury. Rarely did the two blend well. "Sam! *Shit.*"

"Language." Sam helped on the growled repeat.

"What*ever*," Luke retaliated. "We were just here a few hours ago, yeah? You think the boogie men really snuck in between then and now, and—"

"*Stop.*" The Scot's jaw emulated a cliff from his native land. "Before I'm tempted to show ya what a boogie man really looks like. Now both of ya, back in the car."

Luke jabbed his own jaw. Okay, Tracy had been right. The boy had it bad for his little girlfriend if he was openly defying orders from a guy like Sam, who now really looked ready to pull out a broadsword for the cause. But as Mackenna jumped to the ground, locking the teens back in behind him, he swung an expectant stare back over to Franz...

Exposing the deeper knit in his brow.

John had no compunction about copying it.

Something still didn't feel right—but a feeling was all it continued to be. Nothing his senses returned as hard evidence was adding up to anything but confusion.

Sam steeled his posture, silently agreeing. Shook his head slowly, mouthing three words to John. *What the hell?*

John added another syllable to his wordless return. *No fucking clue.*

At least they were on the same wavelength. A good thing in the middle of a jungle or the outskirts of a village full of hostiles—but standing on a driveway with marble insets, gawking at a villa that made the high-roller suites look like the ghetto? He had no damn idea, and it freaked him the fuck out.

Anything can happen...in the woods...

"Not a Sondheim moment, asshole," he gritted under his breath. Far under.

Another long moment passed. Another.

Sam didn't let him down. Helped him listen. Watch. Even smell. Damn good thing, because the tendrils of Tracy Rhodes's scent still teased, blatantly reminding him of the precious cargo under his watch. A duty he seriously struggled to keep objective...

Who the hell was he kidding?

He'd lost half his objectivity before they passed the waterfalls at the Mirage.

Not. Acceptable.

Unlike Luke Rhodes, he didn't have the luxury of letting his dick guide him here.

He fired up the *big* head, joining Sam in sweeping sights around the whole area once more. What were they missing, damn it?

The answer came in a blast of horror.

As Donald began stepping toward the villa's front door, drawing Franz's attention to his feet...

And the thin blue filament stretched just inside the front entry, at calf height.

A thread of light—barely discernible, especially in the sun.

The incandescence of a laser trigger.

"Fuck," he choked.

"Fuck," Sam gritted.

"*Shit*," Shep gasped. "Reverse. *Reverse.* This shit is genked up. Reverse!"

All the drivers throttled the Escalades back down the drive like hornets bolting a nest. Shep gunned his engine so hard, the front passenger door whumped shut by itself. The sound of it was a lead punch to Franzen's gut, emphasizing the absence of the man who'd just stood next to it.

The guy who, a second later, crossed that damn blue thread—and was swallowed whole by the explosion he set off because of it.

CHAPTER THREE

"Stop the car."

Tracy didn't blame Shep for his stunned glance. The composure beneath her words *was* bizarre, not anywhere near the shock sweeping her mind, the dread fisting her stomach, and the terror icing her veins. But if she was going to get Shep's attention, this was the way.

And right now, she *needed* his attention.

Because right now, she needed John Franzen back in this car.

Knowing what to do. Knowing where to go. Knowing how to calm the tremors conquering every inch of her form. Replacing her fear with his strength and her uncertainty with his experience.

Yeah, this was her. Yeah, admitting she needed a man. But in this suspended moment, with the clarity only brought by crisis, she saw the synchronicity of everything that had happened up until now—and the certainty of knowing the captain still had to play a part in it.

Some would call it fate, destiny, or even God's purpose. At the moment, she wasn't picky about the labels, especially when all the events led to the same cosmically correct result— starting from the second Dan had called her about this event. The hole she'd actually had in her schedule for it. Sol recognizing they needed extra support from local experts. Sol finding Shay Bommer to assist. Bommer backing out because of his wife's early labor. Shay calling on help in the form of flying in John Franzen.

Who'd stepped into that dressing room this afternoon and then stomped on the axis of her world.

In the very same moment, restoring every millimeter of its balance.

It sounded crazy. It *was* crazy. But her life was a whole lot of crazy.

A lot of survival too.

Reliance on her gut and never doubting the rightness of what it spoke to her.

Just like it spoke to her now.

Telling her to set her shoulders, steel her jaw, and repeat, "Stop the damn car, Shep!"

"Ma'am, with all due respect, I don't think now—"

"Received and acknowledged, Agent Cary. Now pull the hell over. We're waiting for him."

The agent emitted a sound rougher than the gravel they churned on the side of the road. As soon as the three drivers in their wake copied the move, they instantly laid on their horns. Knowing she'd piss him off more but unable to help herself, Tracy unbuckled and then flipped over, shooting a stare backward.

Fervently, she scanned the other Escalades. Her breath escaped in a relieved whoosh. In all the reverse-gear chaos, they'd taken out the Bellagio's back gate and then skidded onto the street like a *Fast and the Furious* scene gone wrong. But a thumbs-up from the burly driver of the second car back told her he'd gotten Luke out. A glance to the driver's seat of the car directly behind them, and the Taye Diggs doppelganger commandeering Gem and Ronnie's car, confirmed they were all safe too.

Her lungs gave permission for one full breath.

One.

Aside from the distant wail of fire engines, the street was eerily quiet. Tracy peered up and down the block, fighting the need to bolt out of the car. But the stress lent her strange insight. If this were a movie, the audience would be screaming only one thing.

Don't do it.

Don't do it!

Screw the audience. And her better sense.

And Shep's gritted use of the F-word as she unlocked the door, cranked the door handle, and then pushed out of the Escalade—

Only to be shoved back in.

By a really pissed John Franzen.

"Shit on a shingle!" It was her own version of the F-word, as furious as Shep's growl, as Franzen piled back into the car. Before the captain could shut the door again, she received a full view of the scene he'd just run over from. A billow of smoke curled up from what was the villa, dancing like a wraith against the clear blue sky. The thing was angry and black and huge, likely visible for miles now.

Holy hell. This wasn't a drill. This was a real-life, real-bad situation.

Making her doubt what she wanted to do more to John Franzen right now.

Kiss him or kill him.

He was alive—*alive*, thank God—enticing her not to waste another moment on merely dreaming of running her hands, mouth, and other things all over him. The psychobabble experts were right. Fear *was* a heady aphrodisiac, and every cell in her body confirmed it like a lit firecracker.

"What the fuck?"

Then there was his pissed baritone. Attached to his snarling face. Backed by his arrogant hands, digging into both her hips, slamming her back down against the cushion.

"Franzen," she bit out. "For the love of—"

"Not. Now." He spat tacks along with both words—a prelude to the nails he shot into Shep. "What. The. Fuck?"

"Down, Fido," Shep snapped. "I was following orders."

The captain's glare flared darker than the soot on his cheeks. And yes, Tracy was close enough to tell, since he pressed against her while yanking at her seat belt. "*Drive*," he ordered Shep. "Now."

As he rammed the buckle into its housing at her hip, the car lurched into motion. Once more, gravel pelted the Escalade's undercarriage—Shep understandably taking his tension out on the gas pedal—and then they were speeding along the road, the freeway on one side and the hotel on the other, the other cars in the caravan racing to keep up.

After he was done locking her in, Franzen stayed unusually close. As in, he loomed. As in, he resembled a huge orc protecting his—whatever it was orcs protected; she couldn't ever get that part out of Luke when he spoke of the menacing monsters from the fantasy games he played online with the friends he only saw every few months now, instead of every few days.

Because of *her* insane job.

The job that had almost taken his very life.

As the comprehension set in, her anger drained. And as a tremor convulsed her whole body, she'd never been more grateful for orcs in her entire life.

"You okay?"

Or for copper-skinned hulks who tamed their bold baritones into tender murmurs—and then emphasized with a silken brush of a thumb across her cheek.

"I—I don't know." It was the most weak-willed shit that'd left her mouth since Ryker's death, but Vice President Rhodes didn't have to be "on stage" right now. It felt damn good to have an orc on hand, issuing a soft grunt as if to tell her that was okay.

Not that he gave anyone else the same leeway.

"Whose orders?" he barked, addressing Shep's initial defense.

The guy behind the wheel jutted his jaw, taking the shout as if he'd expected it. "Higher pay grade than yours, man."

"*Whose?*" Franz twisted, burning a glare into the back of the driver's close-cropped head. "Goddamnit, Shep. I don't care what the flow charts say. If Sol Wrightman thinks he has the right to dictate what's going on here, from across the fucking city, especially after what just happened—"

"You mean after the detour *you* insisted we take?"

Shep's retort dunked Franzen into thick silence—and Tracy into a bathtub of guilt. The man had flown from Seattle for the priority of her safety. Had defied Sol for the sake of her happiness. Had tolerated Luke's arrogance for the "privilege" of nearly getting blown up in his place. For what? To weather that kind of insinuation?

That was *not* going to happen. Not when she could do something about it.

"Mine."

Like issue that declaration.

Franzen scowled. "Yours...what?"

"My orders." She straightened. "He ordered the route

change for me." Shoved Franz over to lean toward Shep. "And we all know it—which is exactly how we'll tell it."

"Won't matter," Shep huffed. "And with all due respect, you know that, ma'am. The others will—"

"Screw the others."

It took just a second for Shep's startling response—his hearty snicker. "Received and acknowledged, Madam VP."

Franzen's reaction wasn't so easy to watch. His face, still as fiery and fierce as a pissed-off bull, darkened into something harsher. Harder. A creature with gritted white teeth and eyes as black as fresh lava.

Something a lot like a dragon come to life.

A dragon wanting to bite into *her*.

And not in the good way.

"You," he gritted, baring those teeth a little more. "*You* ordered the pull-over, not Wrightman."

CHAPTER FOUR

She was going to make him wait for the answer.

And damn it, he was going to let her.

For five seconds. Ten. Fifteen. Seconds they didn't have. Time they couldn't afford. But he let the little rebel have them because she fucking blew him away, sitting there as serene as a queen even while smoke coated the sky behind them. *Lots* of smoke. The very real evidence of what could have been her very real death. The comprehension hadn't escaped her—he saw evidence of that in the tremble of her fingertips and the brightness in her eyes. She simply chose not to let it daunt her. She decided to reach for courage, even if it meant dragging herself from the pit of fear.

He began to understand why Craig Nichols had tapped her for this job.

Even if she maddened the hell out of him while doing it.

Even if she tempted him to tear the remaining spikes of his hair out as she jogged up her chin and then stated, "It was me. And I'd do it again in a heartbeat."

John's nostrils flared. He knew that because he consciously made them do so. He had to borrow sanity in the form of oxygen to prevent himself from telling the vice president of the fucking country that the "heartbeat" she referenced might have been her last. Actually, that part was fine. It was the other phrases he longed to jab in with it—like "idiot call" and "damn fool" and "what the hell were you thinking" that stopped him, fuming and flaring...

Up to the second his ear was blasted with furious sound.

"Home base to Dragon. Home base to Dragon. *Fuck.* Tell me you hear this!"

He slammed the comm link so hard his ear drum was likely in shards, but his brain thanked him. No more of Sol's berserk blaring.

"Dragon here. Go ahead." No sense in adding to the fireworks. He'd had enough of those today—to the point that even squeezing his eyes shut couldn't erase the image of the item flying from the blast at Sam and him, landing with a sick *clink* at their feet. They'd both skidded to a stop, hoping for the impossible...

It had been Donald's badge. Fried so badly around the edges, it was still smoking.

Yeah. The impossible.

Fuck.

Donald.

He didn't even know the guy's last name. Couldn't tell Wrightman which form to look up, to contact the people who'd come after Donald's potato chip of a badge and some goddamn answers. Something other than "he was a hero, and he died serving his country."

Had he?

What the hell purpose had that just served?

What the hell *was* that?

His teeth locked harder as he prepared himself for the same demand from Sol Wrightman.

Somebody, somewhere, had to have briefed the man already. Using an internal reverse clock honed from years of experience, Franz backtracked the timeline. It felt like fifteen seconds since the explosion, but it had been more like fifteen minutes. Nine hundred seconds. Precious time. More than ample for word to reach the guy in charge of the VP's security detail.

Translation: in charge of keeping Tracy Rhodes alive.

A goal he'd gotten pitifully sloppy on.

No.

An objective he'd completely kicked to the curb—for the sake of what her smile could do for his dick.

So yeah, he braced himself for the shit storm.

For the command to deliver her sassy ass back to Wrightman and then get his sorry one on a plane back home.

For the confirmation that maybe the brass up in the Army Head Shed were right all along.

That making responsible field calls was no longer *his* calling.

That he had to figure out a way to be useful to the world without a mission plan on his smart pad, a SIG in his hand, and a comm line in his ear.

But for now, none of that had changed—especially the comm link. He could make the firearm happen too, but Wrightman's snarl served as perfect proxy for at least twenty bullets.

"Sit-rep, goddamnit. Now."

No. Not bullets. The guy's voice was like another round of C-4. John frowned. Wrightman had struck him as a spaz but not a panic pusher. The shit fraying the edges of his voice now?

That was panic.

"Franzen! Did you get that?"

"I'm here." His own response was as silken as foam on a wave. Hardening his nerves into lead in the middle of crisis had been his stock-in-trade for a decade. This time, gods willing, it wouldn't let him down. "I'm here," he echoed, stronger and clearer. "Go ahead."

A rush of relieved breath roughened the line though Wrightman rushed on, "Tell me you have Tigress. Tell me you are actually *looking* at her and confirm she's alive. For the love of fuck, tell me she's alive."

"Confirmed." He gave into a puzzled frown. While he understood a lot of Sol's conniption, the melodrama pushed the envelope. "We followed protocol." At least he knew *that* as the truth. "To the letter—despite the tiger cub and his Nala having other ideas."

He waited for Wrightman's empathy, at least on that angle of things. Instead the guy volleyed, "Those kids and their antics probably saved your hide—and Tigress's too."

"No. Your team member Donald did."

A leaden pause answered him. Wrightman finally broke it with a rasping sound, as if scrubbing a heavy hand down his face. Finally he muttered, "Damn it. Reese was a good man."

"Yeah. That was my impression too." *Divine spirits of the afterlife, please watch over the soul of Agent Donald Reese, now in your safekeeping. Guide him to the afterworld with care and patience.* With the weight eased on his chest, he was able to add, "He took one for the whole t—"

"No." Another hard grunt from Sol. "He didn't."

So much for tossing aside the bricks on his sternum. "You want to fucking clarify? Because there was a laser trip wire—"

"Likely put in place as a backup, just in case the first charge didn't go off."

John stiffened. Once more fixed his gaze past the front windshield, ramming a mask of neutrality over all his features and words. No way in hell was he alarming Tracy Rhodes before he had to. Not yet. "The first charge?"

"Affirmative. A timed bundle."

"Timed?" There was neutrality, and then there was sounding like a moron—but Wrightman's allegation was getting harder and harder for viable logic. "Are you positive?"

He needed to be positive. A timed charge leapfrogged this shit to a different level of dangerous. It was one thing for some half-cocked section-eight to sneak, climb, bribe, zip line, or wing it on a bell cart to get in here—all possibilities in the fun-filled Oz of Vegas, explaining why Wrightman brought in extra help from the locals to begin with—but it was another to purposely figure where to park a block of explosives and then preprogram the blast for when Tracy was sure to be in the villa. If it hadn't been for the sound check delay and their detour, thanks to the mysterious tipster, that would've absolutely been the case.

A scheduling detail only known to the vice president's inner circle.

The focus on this camera shot—and Sol's paranoia about it—suddenly made a lot more sense.

In the most disgusting ways.

"Yeah." The guy's response to his query held the timbre of commiseration. "Yeah, we're sure." He let John hear his long huff, a vocalized version of that deeper message. *I know exactly what you're going through, man. Passed it by about three minutes ago.*

But if that were the case...

"You're sure...because you know something else already."

More silence. This time, a pause so dense and deep, Franz swore he heard scuba pings even through the comm link. He swallowed hard. It really hurt. His throat was so dry and constricted, even breathing was agony.

"Because you know *what*, Wrightman?"

Sol took even longer to come back.

Too damn long.

"Where you at right now, Dragon?" he asked quietly.

Too damn quietly.

"I-15." He was too irate—and yeah, scared—to bother apologizing for the snarl. "We're playing it safe this time. Coming up and around back to you. Looping back in via Sahara. ETA is ten to twelve mikes and closing."

"Negative. Do *not* return to home base, Dragon."

He nodded, if only to push the emphasis into his response. "Acknowledged." And no, damn it, he hadn't forgotten the man playing hide-and-seek with pertinent intel, but more important questions now had to matter. "We'll reroute to Baby Star Base." As soon as he used the agreed-upon code for the private charter tarmac at McCarran, Shep tapped a pair of fingers to his temple in a pseudo-salute, confirming the route change. Franz ticked a fast nod of thanks. Thank fuck the juju with *him* wasn't wonky. Thank double fuck for the equally capable driver of Sam's vehicle, making sure they stayed nearly on the back bumper even as congestion worsened with their approach to the Strip. "Has the ground crew been notified?" he directed into the comm. "They're ready to launch the bird when we get there?"

"Negative."

"Also acknowledged." Though he didn't leave the implied question mark out of it. What the hell was going on? Wrightman was starting to remind him of a *Hamilton* understudy who hadn't learned all the main raps. "So you need *us* to contact Star Base?"

The prelude for Sol's response was so tight and rough, it sounded like static. "Negative," he finally said.

"Pardon the hell out of me?"

"I said negative on the reroute to Star Base as well, Captain."

"I heard what you said. Now clarify, damn it."

At the same time, Tracy twisted to fully face him. The afternoon sun, though a dim glow through the tinted window, added an ethereal amber halo to the top of her head. Her eyes, wide and curious, were lush collections of gold flecks and gray velvet. She shook her head in jerky little spurts, a nonverbal version of *what the hell?*

Should have been the question he directed at himself too. She was clearly agitated, edging toward stressed, and all he could ponder was how that searching stare of hers would look atop her naked body—and how that naked body would look straddled across *his*. Moaning into his chest. Slicking his cock with her aroused juices...

Thank God his frustrated growl fitted the situation. He channeled the fury tighter, biting into the comm mic, "That's not clarification."

From Wrightman's end, silence.

Then more silence.

What. The. Fuck?

The man finally came back on, after a pause long enough for John to run down a shitload of scenarios as well as their bizarre repercussions. Number one on the list? That the lunatic who'd called truly hadn't been sitting around whacking off to the concept of blowing up the vice president of the country. That maybe he had a few friends helping him out... friends who'd compromised both the convention center and the hotel.

"Dragon."

"Still here." Truly feeling like his call-sign now—ready to spout fire but trapped in a rolling steel cage on Sahara Avenue—like Wrightman was ready to notice or care. But hell, wasn't like he'd never had experience with this shit before. Any Spec Ops soldier who'd waited on "orders from DC" knew this restlessness. But damn it, he'd left his iPod back home, so no show tunes playlist to help allay the agitation. He was even with a "bunker mate" who'd appreciate the songs. Fate had a sick sense of humor sometimes.

"Pocket."

And maybe he should have just wished for more silence.

"Rocket?" he snapped. If the man wanted to play cryptic word association, he could sure as hell do—

Something buzzed inside his suit jacket. The speaker in his ear was filled with the buzz saw of Sol Wrightman's repetition. "*Pocket.*"

He *had* asked for clarification.

Sure enough, the window on his cell displayed an incoming call—from a number composed of all zeroes. Instinct revving at full throttle, Franz clicked his comm line off. Only then did he swipe the screen on the cell, heeding his inner voice once more to keep his outer one as succinct as possible.

"Yeah."

"Your comm line's completely off?" Sure enough, Sol wasn't jingling to shoot the shit about the World Series.

"Yeah," Franz confirmed.

"Is Tigress still with you?"

"Right here." He looked over. Tracy's gaze hadn't left him. If anything, she gaped more intensely. Nervously.

Fuck it.

He reached out. Wrapping her hand in his once more. *So small.* And trembling.

He meshed his fingers with hers. Squeezed hard. *It's going to be all right.*

He had no business forcing that message to his gaze but didn't care. He'd given more impossible promises in his life, in the last year alone. To a rebel-ravaged village in Thailand, he'd ensured new internet connectivity. To three desperate kids in Aleppo, the safe return of their missing puppy. To a group of half-starved North Korean scientists, the chance to live their lives in freedom.

Two out of three wasn't bad.

If only unlucky number three hadn't nearly dragged his country into war with North Korea.

He gave his head a harsh shake, freeing it from the past. Weirdly, Sol's paranoid grunt was a good helper for the cause too. "All right," the man said. "That's good; very good."

"Good for what?"

And why did his gut already knot, preparing for the answer? Regrettably, he could fill in *that* part. Wrightman's energy had surpassed normal crisis mode settings. The man was skittish, frantic, freaked the fuck out—and he was a trained professional in the world of "freaked out,"

"Good for *what*, man?" Okay, he'd admit it. His own case of paranoia instigated the re-do on the snarl. Good thing. Wrightman wasn't into dawdling about the comeback anymore.

"You need to get her out of here, Franzen." Nope. Definitely not dawdling anymore. "Out of the *city*," he stressed, biting out each syllable. "Her and anyone else who was supposed to be in that villa with her. Nobody can know they all survived the blast—is that understood? Not yet. Not now."

"The...fuck?" He twisted Tracy's fingers tighter into his own. "Wrightman, what are you—"

"Do you *understand*, Franzen?"

"Yeah, yeah. I copy. I understand. But—"

"Good. Make it happen. Coordinate with Mackenna and Cary if you must, but *only* if necessary."

"Getting the vice president, her head counsel, her press secretary, and two horny teenagers out of Las Vegas?" Harsh grunt. "Yeah, I'll need Sam and Shep." And a team of at least eight or nine more guys, but he could sense Sol's hissy about just the two from across the miles.

"Fine." Yep. Hissy pegged it. "But if you involve them, you take them too. Nobody who knows your destination can be left behind."

He felt like dragging a hand down his own face. Shit, he felt like taking off a whole layer of skin while he was at it. "Sure, and let me make the whole Statue of Liberty disappear while I'm at it. David Copperfield's in town; I'm sure he has a few seconds to teach me."

"You want to involve David fucking Copperfield, you go right ahead. You'll just have to kill him after you're done with him."

"Fuck." Maybe more than a layer of skin had to go. "Wrightman, this isn't an episode of some damn TV show—"

"A little affirmation you and your 'wild boys' have conveniently forgotten on a few occasions, yes?" The man's voice climbed, clearly picking up on the blood of Franz's shock in the water. "Did you think I didn't research you before greenlighting Bommer's decision to call you down here? So yeah, Captain, I know about your wild boys pack and how you enjoy a quiet but robust reputation for *off books* missions that would make television creators cream their jeans. Likely factored into the big brass's decision about cutting you after the Kaesong gig too—but I don't give a shit. You know how to cross lines, and tripping *that* kind of terrain requires more than just steel balls."

John sucked in a burning breath. "While my junk appreciates the appraisal—"

"Your junk doesn't get a say in this, Franzen, any more than the rest of you." The man's grunt was dark and impatient. "You have resources, fucker. Now use them."

His jaw jutted. His nostrils flared. "It's not as easy as—"

"I don't care."

"Goddamnit. She's the vice president of the United States!"

"*I don't care.*" But the way he sliced the end of each word spoke the exact opposite. Sol cared, all right. He cared to the point he was scared. Not a let's-get-this-right kind of scared. It was deeper. Bigger.

Armaggedon-style bigger.

What the *fuck* was going on?

"Just make shit happen, Franzen," the man rasped as if facing his own gallows. "Take them all dark. Do it now, and don't tell anyone. Do you copy me on that? Nobody. Can. Know. Not even me. Christ, especially not me."

"*Kanapapiki.*"

Son of a bitch.

That part, he stowed under his breath with the phone against his chest. With the device back at his ear, he growled, "You going to feed me a scrap of what's going on here?"

"It's our only chance."

"A bigger scrap than that?"

"*You're* our only chance."

The guy's breaths were now harsh slices through the line. Franz envisioned him tearing through the convention center at a full sprint.

Shit on a shingle.

It was a good one, so he borrowed it. Not that he wanted to. He liked his melodrama performed on a stage, thank you very much, not plunked in his lap and open for insane interpretations.

"Just get them out of here," Wrightman dictated again. "While they all still think..."

"What?" John sliced into the man's deliberate pause. "They all still think *what*? And 'they all' who? What the *fuck* are you talking about?"

The man let out a strange sound, grunt and groan mixed, before uttering, "Wish I knew the full answer to that, Franzen." A rough inhalation. A harsher breath out. "On the other hand, maybe I don't."

"Christ." He rammed the top of the phone against his forehead. "You seriously pulling an *X-Files* on me? I'm not in the alien baby business."

Wrightman snorted. "Just promise me you'll get her out of here. Luke too. I need to know I can trust you on this. There's no one else right now *to* trust. I know you'll stay this course. You do the right thing, Franzen—even when the fine print orders you to do otherwise."

Wasn't that the candy treat moment of the day. Shiny compliment as it went down; fucked-up stomachache as it became reality. "Yeah," he muttered. "The fine print." Grinded the phone into his temple again. "So you've done your homework."

"And damn glad I did." From his end of the call, sirens swelled louder. "I have to go, man," Sol stated. "And so do you. *Quickly.*"

"Sol—"

"You have to *move*, Franzen." The sirens were shrill and close, nearly drowning his words now. "Take them," he shouted. "Hide them. Get someplace nobody will think of. Once that's happened, contact me—but use deep-cover protocol. Do you understand?"

For a long second, he didn't respond. Just sat unmoving, thankful for the shell of the car for once, feeling like the mortals from *Ghost* after something from the other side had barreled through them.

"*Franzen.*"

"What?" It stumbled from the ice cavern of his senses. Chunks of the frozen stuff broke off into his stunned senses, making his head jerk.

"Do. You. Understand?"

In a hot blast, the ice melted away. Strength surged over him, as ingrained as the blood in his veins, a default mode eleven years in the making.

Mission mode.

So yeah, he did understand. Could do this shit in his sleep—not that a lot of that had been happening lately. But maybe even that was a good thing. Sleep wasn't going to be a luxury on an assignment like this, perhaps the craziest he'd ever been handed. He was leaping into a bottomless black hole, dug by the man to whom he was speaking, who wasn't even handing him a flashlight for the trip. Why not? And did Franz really need to know? He was just the guy who made the mission happen. The bigger picture didn't have to be his concern. *Couldn't* be.

Hadn't Kaesong taught him that?

Kaesong. The mission that had changed everything.

That, in no small way, had made it possible for him to be here right now.

That, if he believed more in such things, might have him dialing up the gods for a little chat about their twisted version of humor. He enjoyed a good joke as much as the next dude, but this was *not* funny.

A point backed up in grotesque detail the very next moment.

"What the fuck?" His whisper layered atop Tracy's stunned gasp. Considering the context, she was fully entitled to it—along with the death grip she wrapped around his hand.

The metaphor fit.

Too damn well.

They were stopped at a light just after clearing the Strip. A sports bar sat to their right, a coffee shop to their left. Both were packed, but not a single person in either was laughing, drinking, or caffeine-ing. Not even the wait staff and baristas moved, riveted along with their customers on TV screens filled by somber journalists.

At first, the sight was confusing. Even if the media had arrived at the Bellagio on the heels of the fire department (highly likely), then connected the blown-up villa to the vice president (also highly likely), and then formed a "theory" she'd actually been *inside* the villa (moderately likely), they had to lock the story down with confirmation from someone in Tracy's camp—highly *un*likely.

Or was it?

Because there, prominent on the monitors before those crowds, was the professional head shot of the woman by his side. Her birth date *and* death date—today's date—were listed underneath.

But that wasn't the most shocking thing about the broadcast. That came with the next "update" across the screen.

The announcement so shocking, John couldn't summon a reaction for it in English.

"*Kefe.*"

His brutal growl didn't make translation necessary—though Shep layered the word on the air anyway.

"*Fuck.*"

Tracy emitted a tight, stunned choke. "Th-That can't be right."

"Maybe it isn't." Shep's voice was vicious with hope. Normally, Franzen would shut that shit down. He'd done it enough times in the past—talking the brutal truth into a desperate soldier after watching their buddy get blown apart—that it was second nature by now. But this time, he yearned to believe too. This time, as he yanked down the small TV screen from the ceiling console and then jabbed the power button, he prayed the bar had opted for some trash TV network instead of verified news...

The news every channel on the planet was now carrying.

Shit.

Not that it amazed him—though to really convince himself this was real, he ceased his station surfing on the Golf Channel. They were apparently a subsidiary of the larger cable news outfit so had spared their anchors the task of having to break this kind of a story. Those guys, still in their polos and checkered pants, were probably as frozen and stunned as the rest of the world, listening to the main news anchor speak with visible strain.

"We're still waiting confirmation from the office of Vice President Tracy Rhodes—but it appears the vice president has joined her leader and mentor, President Craig Nichols, on the casualty list of this bleak, black day in our world's history."

The newsman couldn't keep his shit together the whole way. He stumbled over the last few words, his emotion cracking through, now seeming to pour from the monitor. As the light turned green and Shep guided the car down the street, it came as no wonder that all the passing sights seemed different. In one day, the world had changed.

"Nichols and his wife, First Lady Norene Nichols, were pronounced dead after a preprogrammed explosion tore apart half of the White House residence. The first couple were enjoying a rare lunch break together. Six members of their Secret Service detail were also killed by the blast. It is still unknown how the explosives escaped multiple security scans."

Tracy clapped a hand over her mouth. The move barely muffled her anguished moan. "Craig. Norene. Oh my God."

"We'll bring you updates about the tragedy in Washington as they are received, but as most of you know, it is just the beginning of the shocking stories we've been forced to confirm over the last two hours, from all around the world."

John leaned over to turn up the volume. The position secured her head into the crook of his arm, but damn if that didn't feel ideal right now. The inches responsible for taking her out of the politician box, into the space of being simply *woman*. The woman *he* was responsible for, despite what looked to be even weirder news than what they'd already heard.

Something strange...is happening in Oz...

"We now have validations from the United Kingdom, Germany, France, Canada, Australia, and Japan. As we suspected and reported at the top of the hour, every one of their leaders, including Prime Minister Azkan, Chancellor Pfeuller, President LeBon, Governor General Ontario, Governor General Long, and Prime Minister Shoju, as well as the King and Queen of England, have been officially pronounced dead, taken out in blasts similar to the attack that killed President Nichols—and, we presume, Vice President Rhodes."

"Holy. Fuck."

Shep's oath mixed with Tracy's sob. As she twisted, burying her head against John's chest, her outburst intensified. He clutched the back of her head, keeping her close, absorbing her grief—in more than one screwed-up way, even thankful for it. She poured out the shock he couldn't allow himself to feel— had been trained *not* to feel.

When feelings got involved, he made stupid decisions. Caused missions to go sideways. Nearly got people hurt—or worse.

Not this time.

Because this time, he gambled with the lives of Tracy and Luke Rhodes.

Existences he had to hide from the world, even if that meant tossing his feelings down the garbage disposal. He'd dig the remains out of the pipes later—if there was anything left to salvage. If there was anything left of *him* to salvage.

And wasn't *that* a fun way for fate to come knocking at his consciousness again?

He could practically hear the little fucker giggling. Watching in glee as realization took over, shining on his psyche like a sudden blare of light...

Was this why his remains hadn't become Kaua'i fertilizer yet?

Was this the mission his sorry ass had been saved for?

To save her?

The irony of the recognition was subtle as a Skrillex riff. John freakin' Franzen, sidelined from the job he loved because of politicians and their machinations—only to be tasked to save one of them. One of the most prominent players on the field.

No.

Technically, she'd just become the *biggest* player on the field.

Yeah. Skrillex was sounding pretty fucking perfect by the minute.

The newscaster on the monitor clearly played the same soundtrack. He jolted up so violently, his chair was upended. Every viewer confronted his incensed gaze into the camera and watched his trembling hands fist atop the stainless-steel desk.

"Okay, people. Listen to me. The world is a changed place, which means *we* have to change. We have to be better than we were when we woke up this morning. Braver than we were; stronger than we already are—not just for our country but for the whole world. Right now, we have a couple of black eyes, but we're not down for the count. We're not—"

John shut off the feed.

Silence again.

But not peace.

A stiff desert wind buffeted the left side of the car. The rumble of the road was a taunting lull.

As they went where?

The guy's gaze, glancing expectantly to Franz via the rearview, conveyed a silent repeat of the query. Aloud, the guy muttered, "Fuck me five ways."

"Not now, honey." The quip thinned the tension for half a second. Franz enjoyed it while he could, having to switch back to cold mission mode. "We have more important things to focus on."

"Like what?" Tracy beat Shep to the response. Not surprising, since it was backed with a stare of a thousand more questions—and shoulders weighted by the very huge world just dropped upon them. With his hand dropped to her nape, it was easy to detect the tension. Not so easy? Resisting the craving to rub his touch outward, to help ease that massive load on her.

She was so small.

She was so devastated.

And he was about to make it worse. But waiting "until a better time" was *not* an option.

He took a deep breath. Secured his hold on her a little tighter and then simply got the damn words out. "Like accomplishing what Sol Wrightman mandated me to do."

She searched his face again with those miss-nothing eyes. For a second, seemed confused. "What? Get me back to Washington in the middle of this shit storm?"

"Get you off the damn grid in the middle of this shit storm."

She went weirdly still. Finally rocked her head, pushing back against his fingers. "Excuse the hell out of me?"

John dipped his head. Settled his gaze more directly with hers. "They think you're dead—and you're going to stay that way. Completely dark. And I'm in charge of getting you there."

"Where?"

She still didn't understand. Not completely. And that was okay. He was trained for this playbook, but that didn't mean the thing was written yet. "I'm not sure yet," he muttered. Too many things had to fall into place—starting with getting

Sam back on the horn and lining up air transportation in an "invisible" plane or two.

Yeah. He'd seriously gone there. Conjured *that* image, fueled by the jacked adrenaline in his blood and the survival-of-the-fittest-let's-procreate thing going on in his dick, of the female next to him clothed in Wonder Woman garb. Went right ahead and parked her hot ass in a Plexiglass plane too...in which he was the willing copilot...

Feel like focusing on the situation that matters *here, dickwad?*

"I don't understand." Tracy's interjection, husky with urgency, was an odd aid for the concentration cause. If he had to hone on something besides fantasies of her body in red, white, and blue spandex, her near-bedroom voice was a damn good alternative. "I—I *really* don't understand." Clearly, she said it to convince herself as much as him. "I mean, if Craig is—"

"Dead." Franz supplied it as gently but firmly as he could. "He's dead, Tracy. Start saying it, because you have to start accepting it." *Hypocrite.* He could barely wrap his own mind around the horror—manifested by the adolescent visions of Tracy Rhodes as a daughter of Zeus.

"Then they're going to need me." Her head rose. She set her lips into a purposeful line.

He braced her jaw in the V between his thumb and forefinger. "They're doing all right so far."

"Because they have to." Her eyes sizzled with silver fire. "Because they think I'm dead too!"

"Which is our biggest advantage right now."

"Our...*advantage*?" She pushed his hand away. "The country needs guidance—"

"Which they're getting from Speaker of the House LeGrange."

"That's your idea of an advantage?"

There was the official buzzkill for the spandex dream. The woman's code name *was* Tigress, for a number of reasons—including what had to be a killer political pounce. She wasn't the youngest vice president in the history of the country because she'd written nice things in everyone's yearbook and brought the best brownies to the prom decoration party. Clearly, she was chomping to get back to the Hill, especially at a time like now. Political legacies—hell, a permanent place in world history books—were established at moments like this.

The conclusion hit his gut like a rotted fish.

He pushed back, to the other end of the seat. "The *advantage* here is called staying alive," he gritted. "Excuse me if that messes with your plans for grandeur, Mrs. Rhodes."

She had the grace to frown, apparently confused, before a veneer took over her face, hardening everything but her eyes. In those gray worlds, lagoons of hurt still lived. Or so she wanted him to believe. The hard gulp she tossed in was sure a convincing touch.

"Because whoever just tried to blow me up...might attempt it again."

Shep covered the honors of getting a response into the air. "Smart lady."

She grimaced, though John had trouble interpreting the look. Was she pissed, chagrined, frustrated? "You think they'd really try? Even now?"

John grunted. "Especially now."

She flashed a new scowl. Correction. A full glower. But the pained glint in her eyes flashed doubly as brilliant. "Your paranoia is duly noted, Captain."

The stab emulated its razor of tone. Quick, clean, and slicing deep—at least enough to keep him from retorting something just as glib. *Damn it.* He'd always been the king of the one-line comebacks. Not now. Not when the only way he could think of conquering this woman was by *conquering* her—

By bending her over his knee.

Yanking up her prim skirt.

Getting his hand on her full, plump bottom. Soundly. Repetitively.

"Paranoia." Thank fuck Shep's sarcasm was still in working order. "Ohhhh man. Where you going to start with *that*, Franzen?"

Took him all of three seconds to go with the set-up. Another three, weighted and determined, to slant a steady scrutiny across the car. "No place to start. We're already at the end."

The woman in his sights arched both chestnut brows. "The end?" she drawled. "What; as in 'happily ever after'?"

He hitched a shoulder. "If that's what you prefer."

She shrugged too—though the sentiment was only casual on the outside. Her gaze was now dark as thunder clouds. "You saying I still get a choice?"

He rocked his head. The statement, and its underlying anger, were legit. In the space of half an hour, her world had been blown apart on every fathomable level. It was a fair question, deserving an honest answer.

"No. You pretty much don't."

Even if that honesty was fucking shitty.

"And you don't have a choice either, I take it?" she finally snapped. "Because you're just following orders, right? You're just here to save my precious little life?"

Once more, frustration to which she was rightfully entitled—though delivered with such an edge of brat, he wondered yet again about the cat turd. Or if her adrenaline was starting to crash.

Or if she just craved the same thing he did.

Her. Over his knee. Counting out the swats until her ass was pink and her mind was mush...

But at this rate, he was going to beat her to the mush department.

Not. Acceptable.

So he took command back in the only way that made sense. Swiftly. Forcefully. Pushed back across the gap until he had her by the nape again. Locked her face just inches beneath his. The soft snort from the front seat was all the approval he needed from Shep on the action. The woman in his hold clearly didn't agree. Her mouth popped open. Resistance stiffened her body. Franz didn't relent his grip. He didn't care if she was pissed anymore. She'd pulled the brat card. She was going to get brat treatment.

"I'm not here to save your little life, *kitten*." Departing from the fantasies that'd birthed the nickname, he deliberately ground it out. "I'm here to keep the new president of my country alive. And oh yeah...her son too."

In a rush, the fight drained from her body.

In a flood, guilt crashed through Franzen.

Yeah, he'd gone *there* too. Played the Luke card. Aside from tying her down and making her listen—not an option right now, despite how certain parts of his anatomy screamed for it—this was his best and last resort. Something had to get through her gorgeous but thick skull. To get her past the shock of everything that had just happened and cycling through the processing stages as fast as possible. Mentally healthy? Fuck no. Completely necessary? That would be a hell fucking yes—for which he'd logged the years of real-life experience as justification.

He just always forgot how much he hated this part.

Especially when the danger was so goddamn real.

That the bad, *bad* fuckers who rigged that explosion at the villa were still out there somewhere. No. Out *here* somewhere—ready to slap that huge target on her back before blinking again. Their reasons? Not important to him. Not yet.

Their intention, deadly and powerful and still in play, did.

So he hit the Tigress where it hurt the worst.

Didn't mean he had to like it. Didn't mean, with her sharp huffs hitting his lips, he didn't dream about her actually begging him for pain. Didn't mean he breathed in her soft scent and didn't imagine its difference with the arousal from her pussy blended in. Didn't mean he locked gazes with her and avoided thinking how magical those gray depths would be, wrapped in a subspace fog.

It only meant one thing. That he made her get to one end result.

Her resigned rush of surrender. Before she finally muttered, "Fine, damn it. You win. Take me away to Neverland, Captain Hook."

For a long second, disguising it beneath the mode of double-checking her sincerity, he kept watching her. In truth, he just enjoyed watching her fume. Probably too damn much. But as she'd just said, he was the captain now.

Finally, *the captain* countered in a drawl, "Neverland?"

Shep cut in with a snort. "I liked the Captain Hook part better."

Franz shrugged without turning his head. "Fine. That just makes you Smee."

"Wait. Huh?"

The woman beneath him burst with a small laugh. Franz watched her, captivated. For one moment, as if fate really had dumped pixie dust on them, Tracy Rhodes became simply the same woman with whom he'd first clasped hands, locked gazes, and shared enough electricity to light all Sin City just an hour ago. The same perfect connection clicked. Once more she lifted that adorable little grin, as if to call complete bullshit on his he-man swagger.

Feisty little Wendy. Perfect little challenge. Beautiful little brat.

"You have a problem with Neverland, Captain?"

John slanted his head forward. Then a little more, until his forehead almost pressed against hers. He could almost hear her heart pounding. Or was that his? Or did it matter? Not with the comeback he yearned to give her.

"Not sure you can handle my idea of Neverland, *popoki*."

The challenge he went ahead and whispered.

The dare she went ahead and took him up on, working a hand around the blades of his tie and then pulling...until he came close enough their skin *did* touch...

"Second star to the right, Captain. Then straight on till morning."

He swallowed. Hard.

Pushed back once again. This time, by inches.

Excruciating ones.

Somewhere in the gray matter he was hopefully still calling a brain, his comm line crackled again.

"Braw Boy to Dragon," demanded a thick Scottish accent.

"What's going on? Who the hell's calling the ball on this circus now?"

With a tight groan, making the brat-kitten next to him softly giggle, he straightened in the seat and then spoke into his wrist. Yeah, the one still pounding with his pulse rate. "You're talking to him," he barked. "But I'm going to need your help, man. In some big ways."

"Go big or go home, Franz. Ask away."

Be careful what you offer. But John knew better to add it aloud. Sam Mackenna was the kind of friend who'd sprawl across railroad tracks for a friend. This plan wouldn't come to that—hopefully.

Which meant it was time to set the gears in motion.

To do what his government had trained him best for.

And in doing so, to protect the most valuable asset of his life.

"The circus is hitting the friendly skies," he said to Mackenna. "And we're taking the Tigress completely dark."

"Well." Sam inserted a rough chuckle. "Guess you *did* come to the right source."

"I've been known to do that from time to time."

He took heart in that truth—and in the instinct he was going to have to trust again, despite everything his own government had done to discredit it—and most of all, despite the alligator of self-doubt still snapping at his gut, an alarm clock gleaming in its gullet with every greedy new bite.

Tick...

Tock...

CHAPTER FIVE

Tick.

Tock.

Tracy had always had a love-hate relationship with time.

As a teenager, it had been her worst enemy, pushing back against the plans she'd carefully laid for her grown-up life. But after early high school graduation and an accelerated pace through college, it became her biggest ally—especially after meeting Ryker. She'd begged time to stop, for as many days and nights in the man's arms she could get. For a few years, time had really listened...

Until the phone call from Iraq that had proved the extent of the bastard's true evil.

Throughout it all, she'd never not been conscious of time. Nor, especially for the last few years, not cared about it.

Until now.

She dragged a hand through her mussed hair, lifting from a bed piled with pillows and blankets. It was centered in a cozy bedroom with polished wood paneling extending halfway down the walls, where alabaster wainscoting took over. The theme of European-style elegance continued in a cherrywood armoire with mother-of-pearl insets, leading her gaze toward a sunken sitting area with a Victorian-influenced fireplace. Natural logs burned on the grate, their warm light flickering over matched furniture with modern lines, two chairs and one love seat, upholstered in burgundy velvet.

Though the man sprawled on the love seat made the thing look more like a piece from a doll play set.

Or a dragon sleeping on his turret.

Just waiting for a young virginal princess to seduce...

How she wished she could fill even one of those categories now.

Young cooperated with her sometimes, especially after longer sessions on Capitol Hill. She was the first to admit she didn't know everything, but after a day trying to soak it all up from people twice her age, young was definitely how she felt.

Virginal? No tricking anyone about that one anymore. Duh.

Princess was the trickiest. She could pull it off if the inspiration was bad-ass, like Elsa, Leia, or Eowyn. She had to have Eowyn on the short list. Luke would have her head on a platter otherwise.

Luke.

Panic knifed through her belly and didn't stop there. Her legs shot out, kicking the covers free, helping her out of the bed despite a wave of crazy dizziness. She blinked, temporarily stunned at the pink tank and sleep shorts she wore, until remembering a sweet-faced brunette offering her the ensemble after they'd gotten here last night. Nothing would've changed even if she was buck naked, though. Nothing else mattered when it came to her son. Especially after yesterday.

There were three exits to the room. One obviously led to an *en suite* bathroom, and another, covered by vertical blinds, was obviously the portal to an outdoor space.

Meaning she sprinted for door number three.

She'd gotten halfway to the door, off a landing near the fireplace, when a rumbling voice halted her.

That voice.

"He's safe."

Lava turned into words. A dark, growly crust crackling over dangerous liquid fire. Turning her body to magma. Turning her senses even hotter.

Making her *very* aware of what she was wearing—well, *wasn't* wearing—as she pivoted, attempting to look as graceful as a Bond girl about it.

Who the hell was she kidding?

Bond? She felt more like the newest clown spilling out of the funny car, especially standing higher than him. Okay, two steps' worth, but that was enough. She wasn't naked but might as well be, despite how the man gazed at her with nothing but patience, silence, and only slightly widened eyes. Her sights quickly adjusted to the dimness, letting her observe his own change of clothes. The dark suit was gone, replaced by black track pants and a gray, nearly painted-on T-shirt.

Hel-lo, Mr. Bond.

She could sure as hell dream of saying it now—though Keoni John Franzen was, without a doubt, hotter than Sean Connery, Roger Moore, and Daniel Craig combined.

"Luke," he finally murmured, seeming to sense she needed another yank from the mental fog. "He's safe. Sleeping in the guest room, down the hall. Sam's with him."

Tracy nodded. "Of course. That's right. Sorry."

As she stammered, the memories of their whirlwind arrival returned. Yep. Whirlwind. No exaggeration. Sam Mackenna, surely put into place by the hand of the Divine, handled their Vegas exit plan with one phone call and a lot of aviator ju-ju—resulting in their arrival at the "Whirly World Vegas" tarmac, disguised under purchases from the seedy tourist trap around the corner. With bling-covered caps, sunglasses, and neckerchiefs in place, they'd scrambled into a couple of helicopters to take them on a "sightseeing flight" to see the Grand Canyon at sunset.

Instead, less than an hour after she, Gem, Ronnie, Luke, and their security details had "died" in the blast at Bellagio, they were all flown northwest, Shep at the stick of one helo, Sam at the other. They hadn't stopped until the lights of the Seattle skyline twinkled below. After swooping past the distinctive spire of the Space Needle, they'd touched down atop one of the city's tallest skyscrapers.

"Why are you sorry?" Franzen's query sliced into her reminiscence. But the tone wasn't angry. It seemed more like... chastisement. The protective masculine kind. Or maybe that was *her* senses reacting...from a place of everything inside that was purely woman and feminine...hell, perhaps even a real princess. One who could think of wearing satin and silk instead of body plates and chain mail all the time.

On that ridiculous note—back to the situation at hand.

"To start with," she retorted, jerking up her chin, "how about the fact that I forgot where my own son was?"

"For two seconds," he countered. "*Gasp.* Someone revoke the woman's mom card."

There went another chunk of her body armor. Through the chink, she let a little laugh spurt. "Sorry. Think I left the mom card in my other purse."

He notched his head to the side, nicking his tongue to the back of his teeth for a sexy little *tsk*. "Damn. I hate it when I leave shit in my other purses."

Another laugh. She couldn't help it. "Do that a lot, hmm?"

"It's a problem." He pushed to his feet, though once more

his movements were so fluid, she looked for the hidden cables helping him out. The man *had* to be using one of those cable systems they used for sci-fi movie stunts. "Between them all, I must have a dozen fro-yo punch cards with only one hole."

"You get out for fro-yo a lot?"

"More than I used to." The words were there, but the humor wasn't. Wasn't hard to connect that observation with the new shadows across the man's face—but deciphering them wasn't an option as soon as he reset his composure and began approaching her.

With every step he neared, her awe grew. It wasn't just his physical majesty. It was his sheer fortitude. At the push of some internal button, the man was able to toss his personal shit into a mental basement and lock it down tight. She stood there, watching as it happened, impressed but daunted. The trick was an invaluable asset in a soldier and protector...but did he ever get a chance to pull the stuff back *out* of the dark? Did he have anyone to help him dust it off, look at it, process it, be okay with it? What happened when the dragon wanted to climb off his spire and be just a lazing lizard for a while?

And why the hell did she care so much about the answer?

Time to clear some room in your own basement, Tracy.

Didn't mean she had to feel great about it.

"So." Her shoulders straightened as she got the word out. "Sam's with Luke."

He'd gotten up the two small steps to her level. There, he stopped before settling into a parade rest stance. The move was probably habit—though she couldn't say the same thing about her own body's reaction. There were men made to look great in military mode...and then there was *this* man, who transformed into a damn demigod. Every bulging inch of his body, from the mounds of his shoulders and arms down to the formidable swells of his calves, was beautifully displayed even through his clothes. *Dear, sweet God...*

Into the thick stillness of her gawk, he finally answered, "Yes. Mackenna's been texting me updates every thirty minutes or so. Since your boy's head hit the pillow, he's barely moved. That's...*not* good news?"

Tracy's head jerked up. "It's great news. Luke's slept like the dead his whole life, except for the three or four months after Ryker passed."

"Your husband?" he asked quietly.

She nodded. "It happened just after Ryker came home for Luke's eleventh birthday. I tried to shield Luke from a lot of it—the violent parts, at least—but as you've probably figured, the kid's wired like his dad. Smart and sneaky. He waited until I went to bed and then waltzed into our home office and read everything for himself. Didn't know a lot of the bigger words but pieced enough together that he realized his father, an independent contractor who'd gone overseas to help rebuild a war-torn country, was in a group mistaken as the bad guys... and got killed because of it."

Though his posture didn't falter, Franzen's face darkened. His lips twisted, as if debating choice profanities. She wouldn't have minded—hell, Ry and his team had spent so much time with the military, they could trash-talk in six different languages—but it was solacing to have a man hold back for her. For *her*, not his vice president. At least she hoped so. Maybe he still *did* see nothing but her rank, even as she stood here in just a very small tank and very teeny shorts. She couldn't tell, even as he tactfully steered them back to the subject at hand. *Thank God.*

"Well, it's good to know the shit from yesterday didn't seem to disrupt the kid that much," he stated. "But I'll alert Sam about the situation, just in case."

"Thanks."

Her distracted tone wasn't lost on Franzen. The bold slashes of his brows dropped over his eyes. "But there's something else."

She didn't even try to deny it. "Sam's been updating you every thirty minutes?"

The slashes didn't budge. "Affirmative."

"So neither of you have had any sleep."

He chuffed. "We've had plenty of sleep."

She refolded her arms. "Oh?"

"Every thirty minutes means we both get twenty in between."

"And *that's* what you've been using for sleep?"

His head ticked to the side. Weird excuse for a shrug, but it worked. "Some of the best sleep I've gotten recently, actually."

Her attention riveted on him again—not that it'd strayed far—but the resurgence of that basement-deep darkness across his face...and the blades of pain in his gaze...and the new clench of his jaw, as if beating himself up for letting the confession out... A person had to be a damn robot to ignore it. Or to not want to hold him because of it. Or even just ask why twenty minutes of sleep was a "good" thing for him.

Reactions, one and all, that would be like cutting the man's balls off. To him, anyway.

For that reason alone, she pretended he'd merely commented on the weather. "Okay, soldier. Since you're so bright-eyed and bushy-tailed, how about a few more personnel updates?"

Yep. Definitely the right decision. The surge of his new confidence, fortifying his posture, blasted warmth through every inch of her body. Of course, that meant a fresh kind of torment. Refraining from holding the man was tough enough. Now that he was back to looming and formidable again, she fantasized about jumping him.

"It would be my pleasure, ma'am."

Though if he insisted on keeping up with the "ma'am," she'd revise that desire to decking him.

First things first.

"I'm most concerned about Luke's young lady friend. Is someone with her?" She shook her head, overcome by a moment of remorse. "Her name is Mia Hemingway, and I believe she lives in Henderson. She and Luke were in an online chat group for fantasy book fans. They'd been looking forward to meeting in person for months." She twisted her arms tighter together. "What her parents must be going through, thinking their daughter was killed..."

Franzen nodded—one movement conveying a volume of empathy. "Understood but unavoidable at the moment. I have, however, contacted Sol about reaching out to the Hemingways via deep-cover field agents."

She copied his nod. "And that'll take time."

"Yes, ma'am."

She scowled. What place on his face would hurt the least to smack? When getting the answer seemed as hopeless as head-butting a brick wall—or his chest; same thing, really—she focused on easier things.

"Ms. Vann and Mrs. Gallo haven't left her side," Franzen assured then. "Currently, all three are out cold on the pull-out futon in Z's office."

Her frown deepened. "Z?"

"Zeke Hayes," he supplied, going on when she returned just a blank stare. "The big, semi-scary dude you met last night?"

The description helped. "Ohhh. Right. Nicked right temple. Tortured superhero stare. Grizzly bear voice." *In short,* she added silently, *could pass as your brother.*

He smirked. "Pretty good, considering you passed out so hard in the helo, I had to practically carry you in here."

"*That* I would've remembered."

And *there* was her foot. The one she wouldn't miss, now that it was solidly shoved down her throat. Franzen, trying to help, quirked a glance to the side as if she'd spilled a tampon from her purse. If only things were that easy and she could just scoop the damn thing back up—but she'd dropped something much worse. Words. Telling ones. Cheek-reddening, air-thickening, blood-heating ones.

"Yeah, well. I wouldn't have forgotten it either."

Nope. Wrong. *There* was the line transforming the air to soup. Delicious, smoky, sensual puddles of the stuff...

He swung his gaze back to her face. His irises were like chocolate decadence, perfectly complimenting the smooth coffee of his skin, which stretched over the incredible swells of his muscles. Damn, how he made her mouth water...and her blood heat...

She *had* to get back under control.

Now.

Okay, so they had chemistry—but after the fireworks were just smoke trails again, she was just another assignment to the man. Sure, a temporary gig that had ballooned into way more, but in the end, she was just another body for him to guard.

Another target to deliver. *Get your head together and focus on the fundamentals, girl. Like he is.*

"Okay." She spoke it as confirmation to the pep talk but also as a kick-start to the conversation. "So this Zeke guy..."

"Can be implicitly trusted," Franz filled in. "And his wife, Rayna, too."

"Rayna." She nodded as more memories pierced her haze. "Yes. Right. The gorgeous brunette who gave me the sleepwear."

"Affirmative."

She frowned. Why was his stare beating feet for the floor again? "It was a lovely gesture."

"It was."

"I'll have to thank her." She peered at him harder. "Though I'll probably be doing it alone, won't I?"

He tossed back a swift glance—before noticeably shifting his weight for the first time. "Oh, I'm thankful to those two for a great many things," he rumbled. "But those pajamas sure as hell aren't one of them."

"Huh?" She bent forward in the name of giving herself a thorough once-over. When the exam yielded nothing too horridly out of place, she rose back up—only to freeze when her gaze reached the level of his crotch.

She sure as hell wasn't confused anymore—or doubtful about his attraction matching hers. The ridge between the man's thighs answered both quandaries with clarity she hadn't imagined.

He was beautiful. Long but thick, filling the black nylon until it gleamed from the strain, nearly making her wonder what he'd look like if freed from the fabric. And damn it, the bastard didn't even try to hide the evidence—clarified by his next response.

"Now that we're clear about my...issues...with the pajamas..."

"Right." Tracy straightened, taking her own turn at the skittering gaze game. She took the chance to move everything else away too, retracing the path she'd just taken...

Back toward the...bed.

Detour. Now.

A large window took up the center position on the other side of the U-shaped landing. Vertical blinds led her to believe it was a full slider, perhaps to a balcony or backyard. Fresh air sounded damn good right now.

As she walked over, Franzen supplied, "We're safe here—for now. Zeke's been one of my go-to guys for years. He's had my back in some hairy three-ring circuses, even when the pucker factor was off the charts. Plenty of times, we thought we'd be shipped home in matching boxes."

Well, that got her to stop. With arms tucked tight to her sides again, she squeezed her eyes against the vision he induced. Instantly castigated herself as a child for it. It was normal for guys in his line of work to turn death into circus metaphors—it was necessary for getting the job done—but with all the tears in her armor already, it was all too easy to let him reach in and jab at the wounds beneath. The spots which never truly healed...nor would again.

"Fuck." His terse mutter, slicing through the air as her shoulders slumped, betrayed his come-to-Jesus moment about the point too. "Way to go with my moron social skills. May as well have tossed a dagger into your back while I was at it, yeah?"

She pushed up a hand. "It's all right, soldier. Don't break out the cello and pathos."

To her astonishment, he complied. As he followed her route, his steps were defined and sure. For long seconds, *she* didn't know what to do. Between days of politicians with endless agendas and nights of a fifteen-year-old with layers of angst, she wasn't used to having a sentence simply mean what she said. He came from a world of the polar opposite, with concepts squeezed into acronyms and hand signals communicating whole novels.

She liked it. And now, she took advantage of it to get this subject changed for good.

"What time is it?"

There. Perfect. No way to maneuver that one back around to her pajamas, his crotch bulge, *or* matching coffins with his SOF bestie.

"Somewhere near midnight. *Don't* open those."

His warning was two seconds too late. Tracy already parted the vertical blinds, peeking outside. Sure enough, it seemed like midnight—though they were definitely on a higher floor of the building, so it was hard to tell. She let the slats fall again, smacking against each other and giving her intermittent glances at the cute balcony with a view to the bay. The area had a little arrangement of plush patio furniture, walls of hanging plants, and even a fully stocked wine cooler. It was all so inviting. So *normal.* A normal she longed for, now more than ever. When was the last time she'd just sat and relaxed with a glass of wine? Enjoyed a social event without worrying about entertaining a snooty dignitary to her left and a windy politician to her right?

You mean the politician you *are now?*
And technically, the snooty dignitary too?
No.

Not yet.

Right here, right now, she was still officially dead.

And God, it was nice.

Nicer than she'd anticipated.

Much, *much* nicer.

Especially when she turned from the window to damn near run into the granite slab of Franzen's chest. He'd stepped even closer now, bringing his size and heat right along too. She could smell him now, like exotic spices, adding even more incredible heat to the sensual slam of his presence. She reached for him, using the inner crooks of his elbows to steady herself, even as she doubted the wisdom of it.

Ohhhh, God.

This was...

Good.

This was...

Hot.

This beat the hell out of being dead.

So much so, she sagged, giving him all her weight...maybe even the first edges of her self-control. She was again conscious of him...*all* of him, even the swollen and pulsing parts...a recognition re-sparking the air between them. Well, what was left of the air between them. Not that she minded that either. As he countered her hold by bracing her waist with both huge hands, she dug her nails into the sinew of his biceps and let the spice of his scent invade her senses. She dragged her gaze up, only to get lost in the hot, hooded concentration of his.

The centers of their bodies throbbed as one. New arousal flared, promising bigger flames. Their attraction sparked like the beginning of a bonfire. It was beautiful. So damn beautiful.

But so damn dangerous.

Because right now, in the anonymity of this moment, the fire looked so pretty.

But when the night was gone and the world became real again, there'd be scorched fields.

"Okay. Got it. No windows. I'm terribly sorry, Sir. It won't happen again."

Yet the thing was...

She'd been burned before.

Making it all too easy to curl more smoke than regret through her syllables.

All too simple to let him grip her tighter...to press himself closer.

All too addicting to let the flames in his gaze sear straight through her.

"You're...sorry?"

All too wonderful to smile at the heated growl of his retort.

"Doesn't it sound like I am?"

Holy hell, his skin was warm. And taut. Her fingertips traced the veins standing out as he coiled his arms.

"You really want me to answer that?"

As his voice dipped lower, so did his gaze. He raked it over her whole face, finally fixating on the center of her lips...igniting even more heat in the most illicit parts of her. Tracy raised her hands, splaying fingers against the massive mounds of his coiled arms, reveling in every damn second of his smoldering attention.

"Probably not," she finally murmured.

A breath left him, taut but sensual. As he pulled air back in, he dragged her closer too—half an inch that carried a world of meaning. The new proximity meant she had to tilt her head back to keep gazing at him. It implied deeper surrender...

greater trust. Every plane of Franzen's face conveyed the pleasure he found in that.

Nevertheless, he uttered, "Well then...what *do* you want me to do?"

"Hmmm." She cocked her head, attempting to channel mystery and mirth at once. Chita Rivera ala *Kiss of the Spiderwoman*, maybe even Catherine Zeta-Jones in *Chicago*. Yes. He'd probably like that one more. "That depends."

His gaze intensified. "On what?"

"On whether you want me to answer as 'ma'am' or 'kitten.'"

Take that, Catherine Zeta-Jones. For a moment, basking in the new intensity of his stare, she was no longer a dork in borrowed pajamas. She was a temptress in a slinky black dress, garter stockings, and a hot ass. The imagery helped with her shock. Had she really just said that out loud? This wasn't her— yet he made her feel beautiful enough to believe it.

Especially when his fingers found their way under her shirt and a rough, low sound emanated from the depths of his chest. "You like kitten, do you?"

She tightened her own grip. Traced the veins standing out against his muscles. "A hell of a lot better than ma'am."

"Hmmm."

How come his version of that sounded *so* much sexier than hers? And how come, as he worked his hands to the small of her back and fitted their bodies tighter together, all she could think of was a train picking up speed? One of those modern electrical versions, speeding on polished steel rails, silent but mighty, into the station of her personal space...

"I want you to repeat something for me...kitten."

She heard the words—as well as the command beneath them. Trouble was, she could barely manage a sigh in response, let alone words. At least it vibrated with meaning, high but heavy, telling him all too clearly what she thought of him slotting his crotch directly into hers...notching the heated length of himself against all the most illicit parts of her...

"Oh," she was finally able to rasp. "Okay."

His grip twisted, bordering on admonishment. "Why don't you try 'yes, Sir'?"

More shock, as a sultry laugh rolled out. "Like *that*, do you?"

"I like it a lot," he murmured. "Especially when you say it."

"Oh." For a moment, it was all she could reply to his openly sensual snarl. "All right." Then only that, as she tried out the rest of the words in her head. The syllables were delicious and salacious, unfurling tingling tendrils through her bloodstream. She accepted the awareness of how vulnerable they'd make her...and yet, how desirable. "Yes. Of course. Yes, Sir."

"Good." His praise warmed her hairline. "Very good. You ready, kitten?"

"Yes...Sir."

"I want you to repeat this so you really know this."

"I—I understand, Sir."

"'I'll stay away from the windows because it will keep me safe.'"

She didn't rattle it back right away. For a few seconds, debated if she would. Of all the lines she expected from him, that certainly wasn't one—and yet, once she considered it, made the most sense. The man clearly enjoyed being a warrior, but only because he was an instinctual protector. Every move he made, nearly every breath he took, was in the name of safeguarding others.

Even if he had to seduce his way to the point.

But maybe, this one time, that was okay.

Better than okay.

It boxed things in. Framed in his force. Made him easier to comprehend, knowing he was using his magnificent form just for the sake of his important point. Hell, it even elevated his erection toward a noble cause. Who was she to deny a warrior his nobility?

"I'll...I'll stay away from the windows..." *Nobility. Remember nobility.* Nope. Impossible. She felt everything except noble as he dropped his hold to her thighs and then backed her against the wall. Heat spiraled from every point he touched, sizzling all the way into her toes. "Be-Because it will..."

"Come on. You can do it. Now the rest."

She quivered all over. This time, the shiver starting in the depths of her womb. She wanted him there. Could nearly imagine what it would be like, having his body fill her in those trembling depths. "Are—are you *kidding* me?"

His deep chuckle vibrated along her collarbone. "Not in the least."

Devastating dragon. Beautiful bastard.

"Fine," she snapped. "All right, *fine*. I'll—I'll stay away from the windows...because it will keep me safe."

Along with his approving growl, he nipped at the corner between her neck and shoulder. "Outstanding."

She audibly seethed. "Says the gloating victor."

He leaned back so their stares met again. His face was still a stunning picture of patience, considering the persistent erection at her center. "I wasn't aware we were keeping score."

"Weren't we?"

He dipped his head in again—close enough for her to spot

the russet specks in his irises. "I'm not being a hard-ass for the hell of it. Right now, especially with what's happened across the globe, everything outside this condo has to be considered enemy territory."

Tracy gave him an even nod. "That makes sense."

He nodded back. "Thank you for understanding."

"But..."

She let the rest of it drop—into air that thickened inside three seconds. Just like that, she knew it was back. The intangible, incredible awareness...beyond the intimate positioning of their bodies. The pull surpassing just the physical. The longing to touch more of him...the lust for him to touch more of her.

And beyond.

The beyond of here and now. The possibility, in the solitude of this midnight moment, that their spark could combust into so much more.

Dare they...?

Would he...?

Should *she*...?

Too many questions. So many answers that loomed and crowded and daunted.

So she let the silence stretch on.

Until, with a taut grunt, he persisted, "But...what?"

"But...what if I hadn't understood?" *Shit, shit, shit.* Why did this feel so much like now or never? Like her libido stood on the edge of the high-dive board, with her psyche back on the ladder, goading her forward?

Now or never. Now or never.

Because yesterday, she had nearly been blown into *never*.

It was *now*. And she didn't wait any longer, going for it

with a brazen reach between their bodies.

"Fuck," Franzen rumbled.

She was tempted to echo the sentiment. Holy...wow. Her fingers stretched around his bulge, even wider as he swelled for her. "Well, Captain?" she managed in a saucy murmur. "If I hadn't been so *understanding*, would you have used this to make me...obey?"

Despite the oath, his face barely betrayed its angles of control. The tense brackets at the corners of his mouth hardly counted. "You have your fingers on the pulse of how much I like that idea, woman."

"But...?" She copied his word with a deliberately coy injection.

"But not all ideas can always be actionable." The brackets tightened. His jaw visibly clenched. "We both know that."

She let her brows knit. "We're also both grown-ups. Adults who recognize we both had...a few *thoughts*...from the moment we first touched, then endured a crazy-as-hell day together, and may now need to let off a little steam."

"Steam." He laughed it out. "Grown-ups."

Tracy smiled. "Last time I checked, at least."

"Yeah, well...sometimes, grown-ups have secrets." His shoulders sagged, as if the message was directed as much at himself as her. He pulled a hand free, flattening it instead to the wall. "Dark ones...that aren't appropriate for other grown-ups to know."

Since her frown had already started, she let it descend to her mouth. But as her lips twisted, the same effect took hold in her belly—though down there, it gathered from a different force. A tension radiating upward...

From the tissues of her pussy.

Secrets.

Dark ones.

Why don't you try "yes, Sir"?

Her heartbeat skipped. Her blood danced.

Her gaze reached into the shadows of his. Seeking his secrets...

But finding none.

He'd locked them tight.

With a determined huff, she gripped more of his cock. As his flesh pulsed, Franzen hissed...

But his gaze remained closed.

"Franzen," she whispered. "John." Squeezed again. "Please."

A heavy gulp expanded his throat. "You don't know what you're asking."

"The hell I don't."

"You're the goddamn vice—*no*, you're the goddamn *president*, and—*fuck.*" The last of it was a groan as she changed her hold to a stroke. She damn near echoed the sound, discovering black really was one hell of an optical illusion maker. His sex was longer, mightier, and hotter than she'd dreamed. Only gritted willpower helped to pull her hand away. The man was going to need...further persuasion.

"You done yet?" she charged, starting to tug at the hem of her tank. "Because that's a really short list, mister." She jerked an edge over one shoulder. "You want to know what *else* I am? A mom. A friend. A former small-business owner. A crossword puzzle freak. A weirdo who likes anchovies in my salads but not on my pizza. The sole person on the planet who hasn't seen *The Walking Dead.*" Up over the other shoulder. "And oh yeah"—she yanked the whole thing over her head and then let it drop to the floor—"a woman. Just a woman who's been through a shitty day and really wants to enjoy the attention of the warrior who got her through it alive."

To his credit, the man's jaw barely dropped. But his gaze did, pupils dilating, fixating on her bare breasts. She embraced the tiny victory, skin suffused in warmth, senses high on his attention.

"Ma'am."

Shit. A tiny victory, indeed.

"It's not that I don't—" His sinewy neck vibrated with his rough swallow. "But ma'am—I—"

Her seething snort cut him off. "Franzen, if you call me *ma'am* again, I'll come after your penis with my flattening iron." Which was technically nothing but cinders now, in the rubble of the villa, but the man wisely didn't point that out. Even more prudently, he let his continued stillness, as well as the steady smolder of his gaze, do the significant talking for him. Both mesmerized her like a puma baiting its prey. She knew it as she stepped closer, letting her breasts pillow against the hard magnificent of his chest. She felt it while lifting her hands to the shoulders above it, spreading fingers along the molded perfection of his delts and traps. She reveled in it as his stare thickened, turning dark umber from the force of his own attraction.

Upon her own face, Tracy fixed lines of determined attention. "I'm also a person, Franzen. Just like you, a person who's logged a lot of heartbreak in my life. However 'dark' you think your secrets are, I guarantee I'm strong enough to handle them."

How easy it would be to push the point even further, but the strict line of his jaw told her differently. His body might be churning with tangible desire, but his rigid brain and his unflinching pride would never let him consider the idea of fulfilling those needs—not with her, anyway. As if she needed to be stabbed further with the point, he emphasized by taking a slow step back, almost a Samoan Jesus resisting Satan in the wilderness. Nice. Just the role *she'd* wanted to play tonight.

As if her Jezebel of a body was going to make it any easier to forget.

Screw you, she silently railed in return, grinding her fists harder into the wall, force-feeding her lust into a kiln of fury instead. Better. Much better. At least more recognizable. And controllable. And usable.

Especially as the man shuffled back by another step.

Fine by her.

Tracy took advantage of the extra space, shoving off the wall and then wheeling back toward the bed. On her way, she grabbed the tank and jabbed her way back into it. "I'm going back to sleep."

Liar. Like she and sleep were going to be anything but sworn enemies tonight. Her blood was roaring. Her nerve endings felt like lit sparklers. And oh yeah, there was the not-so-tiny issue of her burning, throbbing sex, especially with her vibrator in the same pile of ash as her flattening iron—and that man likely returning to dragon mode on the couch. Could she dare hope he'd change into cutaway tails, drag her to an underground lair on a boat, and then sing sweet music of the night while she fell into romantic slumber? No? She'd have to put up with being pissed and sleepless—

And now, listen to him hiss rapid-fire Hawaiian beneath his breath. At least she had a good excuse to ignore him.

"Tracy. *Damn it.*"

So much for the ignoring thing.

"I think we should leave it there, Captain."

She might have underlined the last word with a little more rebellion. She might have hoped he really noticed.

More of his whispered island profanity came back, before a gritted, "You understand, that in any other time and place—"

"Sure."

Lip service. She didn't understand—and she wanted to wallow in that ire. It was the middle of the night, after one hell of a day—which had included the indisputable, inaugural spark of their intense mutual attraction. And technically, to the rest of the world, she didn't even exist. So what exactly *was* he asking her to understand?

For a second, just one, she listened as he shifted a step back toward her. One single sound, filled with so much conflict...causing her hands to freeze around the pillow she was plumping. Would he finally get it? Be brave enough to?

"Yeah. Maybe you're right. Sleep's probably the best thing for you right now."

Then there was Box Two. The jerkwad exit.

Back to the basement.

The darkness she let him escape to, no matter how mad it made her—or how scary it was to think of the hours ahead without him right next to her.

Stupid lamenting.

Ridiculous moping.

She was *thirty*-five, not five. She helped shape the character of a nation. More defining than that, she was the mother of a teenager. She could handle *one* enigmatic ass, even if it meant lying here and *pretending* to sleep for the next five or six hours.

Powered by that fortification, at least for the moment, she flashed a look over her shoulder inspired by all the blithe, bold, rejected-by-morons heroines who had ever been in this position before her. "Right, then. Good night."

Yes. Perfect.

It was all over but the middle finger—from which she forced herself to refrain because she couldn't skip completely off the vice-presidential reservation—but gave room for a preening smile to wield at the captain as she settled against the pillows.

And wield she did.

No matter how thoroughly Franzen's counterstrike of a stare blew through her. Penetrated her as if time had folded on itself and *this* was suddenly the first moment they'd ever locked gazes—and exchanged their energy. *That* energy. The silent, potent connection she'd never experienced before with someone...the link of awareness she knew *he* felt too, no matter what kind of crap lines he fed her about the other aspects of their attraction. *This* part of it was real. *This* visceral bond would never go away.

He knew it too. She saw him accept it, though he sure as hell wasn't happy about it, as his brows tightened into new slashes, matched by the parallel line formed by his lips.

Before he pivoted to make his way back to the couch.

But then stopped...

And bounded two steps her direction.

Before he stopped once more.

Retreated yet again.

Back to his damn dragon's cave. His emotional basement—into which she was *not* invited. Nor would beg to be asked back again.

It was time to let him go back through that door—and then to shut it soundly behind him. And yeah, to let a little hope go along with him too. The man had brought something back to her world that she'd honestly given up on knowing again. The feeling of being the center of a man's interest...and desire. Just simply, wholly, appreciated as a female...

It had been good. Really good. And giddy. And freeing.

For that gift, she would be forever grateful to Keoni John Franzen.

For that reason, she owed him a decent attempt to be her best in the morning. Which meant taking a stab at some sleep.

Or faking it super well.

CHAPTER SIX

"Holy. Shit."

The gritted syllables of Ethan Archer's reaction were nearly as brutal as the watery afternoon sun, sneaking past the blinds of Z's kitchen. What the hell? It was October, and this was Seattle. Sunshine was supposed to be outlawed.

Normally Franz would be happy about the breach, but right now, his sleep-deprived system craved some old-fashioned Northwest gloom. In the meantime, his dragging blood begged for coffee, while his throbbing head urged him to give in to Zeke's offer of a Pike Stout in a frosty bottle.

Fuck, was he tempted—but the beer would help his headache and little else.

Least of all, the painful quandary he now had about Tracy Rhodes.

The woman he'd given his word to protect.

The new president he had to keep alive.

The spitfire with the breasts of an angel.

Fuck.

And he knew breasts. He was, when all was said and done, an island boy. He'd grown up appreciating women in all their glorious curves and angles, on an island where coconuts, bathing suit tops, and the all-natural look were interchanged often and freely. By default, he'd become a connoisseur of everything from swell to areola to nipple—and his expert's eye savored the paradise of Tracy Rhodes's offering to the trove.

There was only one hitch to that joy.

Hashed yet again by the two guys on the barstools opposite him.

"Tracy Rhodes is still alive." Archer still looked like he didn't believe it.

"So we've been saying," Z supplied.

"And right in the next room."

"Ding-ding-double-ding," Franz filled in.

"I'll be a monkey's bastard uncle."

Z huffed and took another pull of his beer. Archer tapped a couple of agitated fingers over the top lip of his. Not the way to enjoy a good stout, but Franz was far past dictating to the guy. Ethan was almost out of the service himself, having put in for early discharge months ago, to no one's surprise. As Ava, his wife, ascended through the elite ranks of Hollywood power stylists, Ethan attended a load of TV and film premieres—and eight months ago, one of those events had resulted in a lucrative modeling gig. Since then, Archer had been juggling the modeling assignments between missions, but now his agent was sending him movie scripts too. Archer was a perfect pick for global film stardom, since he fluently spoke eight languages and could get by in half a dozen more. Between the demands of his new career and the requirements of his old, dude spent most of his life on airplanes these days—and frankly, Franz had been shocked to find him stateside when he'd called. Nevertheless, the pretty boy hadn't hesitated to cash in some flight miles and get himself here in a matter of hours—and Franz was damn glad of it. He was gathering the perfect team to help him keep Tracy safe—and, technically, dead—until things calmed down and she could take her rightful seat as the nation's leader.

If things calmed the hell down.

He had to believe they would. Had to fight the frustration of not being on the front lines of figuring out what the hell had gone so horribly wrong, spurring a global act of violence on a scale nobody had ever seen before. His nerves turned into new minefields every time he contemplated the audacious move, as well as what terrorist group had that kind of reach and those kinds of resources...

Okay, maybe it wasn't just terrorists who'd gotten to his nervous system lately.

Maybe, goddamnit, he still couldn't dismiss that woman's brass, as well.

More accurately, what she'd done to *his* brass.

Leaving him with one giant muck-fest of a dilemma.

How the hell was he supposed to safeguard her, when all he could think of was fucking her? After tying her down, of course. And blindfolding her. Yeah, that would definitely be part of it. Maybe clamping those gorgeous strawberry nipples of hers too. She'd moan as he sucked them to stiff peaks and then scream for mercy as he closed the clamps around each stiff bud...

"Franz? Dude?"

He jerked his head up, refocusing on Z and Runway, before snapping, "What?"

Archer's stare, too lush a blue for a guy, focused on him. "You all right?"

"Yeah."

No.

And it was *her* damn fault. Filling his imagination. Consuming his every other thought. Engorging him, every second, from his screaming blue balls to the throbbing head leaking against his zipper...

"You don't look all right."

Steaming glare. "Yeah? And there's leftover makeup on your neck, honey."

Z spat a laugh as Archer actually checked his jaw. The big guy finished with a "Zsycho brow" in Franz's direction. "So what's the plan, at least for now?"

The last part of his statement earned Archer's refreshed attention. They'd both logged enough hours under his leadership to know mission ops were often switched up by the second, especially ones like this. Off the books? Hell, this one was off the damn reservation. No wonder they both looked as somber as characters in a GI Joe movie but as eager as two kids clutching the Target-exclusive action figures.

Franz leaned over, planting both elbows on the counter. Regarded the bottle of Perrier between his knuckled hands. Shit. He should've flung some crack at Z about the joys of domesticated life—*water*, with *bubbles*, from *France*?—but he was the pussy drinking said water, and Z would always be one of the finest soldiers and Doms he'd ever known. He was more than willing to give the guy a bye on the foo-foo water.

After taking a swig of the stuff—which wasn't half-bad—he started with what felt like the obvious. "The plan is, we do this as by-the-book as we possibly can. So right now—"

"We need intel." Runway supplied the obvious. "I'm all over it from the tech side."

"And I can supply eyes and ears on the ground," Z stated.

"Well, neither of you will be going at it alone." Franz hit them both with the surety of his gaze. "Sam Mackenna, one of the guys who helped get us all out of Vegas undetected, put in for emergency leave with his RAF commander. He's able to stay on here in Seattle for about fourteen days. Runway, you're going to find him damn helpful to you on systems, as well as eyes from the air. And Zsycho—"

Zeke straightened, cutting him short. "If you tell me Hawk is coming home early from Thailand, I'll kiss you on the lips."

He grimaced as if the bastard had farted instead. "Nice try, Z, but you're still not my type."

Archer tossed a confused smirk. "You have a type?"

Z snorted. "Hell to the yes, he has a type."

Franz pulled out the visual version of a broadsword, killing the subject there. Wasn't because Z was wrong. The bastard was scarily *right*—and had been Franz's wingman at enough playrooms and kink clubs, from here to Bangkok and back, to know those definitions. It didn't boil down to physical requirements. Fuck, if it were only that easy—but he was a male with a reverence for the female form in all its magnificent expressions, from curvy and petite to willowy and sleek. His personal demands were more specific...much deeper. Things he required from a woman's spirit. Surrender he needed. Trust he demanded. Passion he longed to stoke.

Like all the things you were offered by a stunning brunette bathed in midnight moonlight?

The things you turned down—like the royal idiot you are?

All because it felt too easy with her? Too right?

Too vanilla.

A flavor he hadn't tasted in a very, very long time.

A sexual restraint he couldn't promise to heed with this woman—that he'd been craving to toss away every half hour throughout the morning, every time he peeked in on her in the next room over with her girlfriends, her son, and the Hemingway girl. They'd enjoyed a movie before the kids discovered Z's video game arsenal; now the women chatted in the corner while the kids faced off against each other. Her hair was pulled into a messy ponytail; he longed to grab it and yank her head back, opening her lips for his hard kiss. Rayna had lent her soft sweats and a loose sweater; he fantasized about peeling them away and then burying his nose in her naked pussy.

Eating her until she gasped.

Taunting her until she screamed.

Pinning her and fucking her...until she came.

And came.

And came.

Shit, shit, shit.

But what the hell was wrong with any of that? Last time he checked, wearing a woman out with orgasms still qualified as pure vanilla fun. Nothing hardcore there. Not even a soft spank in the scenario...

Said the alcoholic, fantasizing about "just a sip" of booze.

He'd already had "just a sip" of Tracy Rhodes.

And wanted more. So much more.

A *more* he craved like a goddamn vampire and blood. A *more* he'd keep seeking...returning for, again and again, no matter how damn unhealthy it was.

Abbie. I'm so sorry.

The words were useless. He made his mind say them anyway—as he stared into his designer water bottle and saw the woman's big eyes in the green glow of the glass. Abbie's stare had possessed a strange sheen as he hugged her for the last time, his apologies dueling with hers. She'd thought herself the "stud submissive" in refusing to safe word; he begged forgiveness for—

Everything else.

Letting the scene go as far as it did. Letting *himself* spiral out of control. Bleeding his impatience with the world into the chemistry of their dynamic—using her open surrender as his permission for unhinged anger.

It was fucked-up on an entirely new level.

He could *not* afford to be fucked-up with Tracy Rhodes.

No matter how stunning the silver of her eyes, as the word "please" whispered off her lips. No matter how mesmerizing those actual lips were, inspiring a thousand fantasies of how they'd feel around his cock. No matter how perfect her luscious little body, down to the tips of her damn fingers...knowing exactly how to grip his pulsing dick...

He gritted back a groan as laughter ripped him back to the present.

Two baritones, joining in sarcastic reverie. Z and Runway, to his rescue once again.

"Fine," Zeke declared, smacking his hand on the counter. "No making out with my CO tonight."

Franz emulated the action, adding a grunt. "Not your CO anymore, big guy."

And on that note, it was *really* time for beer. He turned, closing in on the fridge and securing a stout for himself.

"Yeah," Zeke grumbled. "Fine. Whatever."

"I mean it," he snapped. "I'm just Franz, okay? Not your CO. Not the head of your team. Not the guy riding your ass about everything. I'm just the buddy with a few friends in higher places on this one—"

"Ya think?" Archer inserted.

"—who's damn grateful for how you've both dropped your lives to do this for me."

"Awwww, honey." Z pushed out a pout. "You *sure* you

don't want to make out?"

Before Franz could spin up a comeback, Archer countered with, "You want to talk gratitude, man? Okay, I can go there. Wasn't too long ago you guys all dropped your shit to save *my* bacon from a full-board lunatic intent on nuking this coast down to San Diego."

"Outstanding point." Zeke fist-bumped him. "And six months before that, how 'bout the crazy times with the *other* nut job who implanted me with a neurotoxin?"

"Then there was Shay and his Dr. Moreau mad scientist."

Z snorted. "We had to go after *that* fucker twice..."

Archer chuckled. "Damn. If I saw all this shit in a movie script, I'd wonder about the sanity of the writer."

Franz and Z joined gruff laughs to that—though as they all took new pulls on their stouts, Franz sobered again. *Fuck.* He needed to tell them more, words better fitting a Rodgers and Hammerstein score than what they normally jawed over, but these two were worth it. All his guys were. They weren't just the best of the best by the army's standards. They were good men, period. Someone would be lucky to call even one of them his friend. Fate had given him that gift eleven times over.

"Movie deal or not, I appreciate the hell out of you guys." He abandoned his beer to give them simultaneous shoulder claps. "You're *ohana* to me. Family. Always."

At once, Ethan returned the gesture. "Ditto, brother."

Z did the same, only ensuring they both saw his addition of a broad smirk. "Just remember that *ohana* shit when I want to borrow your place for family vacations."

Archer's black brows lowered. Jumped right back up again before he repeated in a rasp, "Holy. Shit."

Z's lips quirked. "Warmer..." he teased.

"For...*family*..."

"Waarmmmer."

"As in, a bigger one?"

"Red hot, sugar lips."

"Fucker!" Franz barreled into his buddy with a full embrace.

Zeke snickered. "Yeah. I *am* that, huh?"

"Congratulations, man."

Ethan moved in, repeating the gruff hug. "Well, *this* shit should be fun to watch. Ezekiel Hayes, proud papa man."

"Yeah, well." Z raised both hands as if being robbed. "Slow that roll for now. We're not telling the entire world yet. Rayna's only five weeks along."

"Understood," Archer replied. "But she's doing great so far?"

"Knock wood." Zeke dropped one of his hands, bonking it on his head. "Aside from some mild morning sickness, which is why the fridge looks like a Perrier ad, we're so far, so good."

"The gods just help the little *keiki*." Franz couldn't resist the jibe. "Especially if it's a girl."

One of Z's brows arched. The hand he'd knocked to his noggin flipped around, middle finger extended. "That so, dragon jizz?"

Ethan tossed his head back on a loud laugh. "Hey, this Franz-ain't-the-CO shit is kind of fun."

Franz let his shit-eating grin serve as his agreement to that. "Sorry, Z. But if the shoe fits..."

"Yeah, well." Zeke gave the counter another smack. "Just remember, you and I are the same shoe size."

"Only now, we'll be able to tell the boots apart." He pointed at his friend's feet. "Green poop in the soles..." Swung the finger back at his own. "Not a drop of green poop."

"You're wearing flip-flops. *My* flip-flops, I might add. You're welcome for the loan on *all* those clothes, by the way."

"He looks better in them than you," Archer cracked.

"Yeah?" Z parried. "That'd be harsh—if I gave a shit." He slung back some more beer. "I *do*, however, look forward to the day I take green poop recompense on you both."

Ethan's response was surprisingly serious. "Soon as I have a couple of movies under my belt, you may be doing exactly that, my friend."

Zeke grinned. "Outstanding!"

As soon as they both swung gazes to him, John joined the laughter—with a bitter bark. "Don't look at *me* for more of that happy-joy-joy."

"*Psshhh*," Zeke volleyed.

"*Please*," Archer protested at the same time. "You'll make a great daddy-o one day and you know it, Franz."

He set his beer down so hard, the slam reverberated against the stainless-steel appliances. Into the uncomfortable silence that followed, he softly snarled, "Fuck off, okay?"

Great. Who needed infant shit to mess up the floor when there was his psychological baggage to do the job? Nothing like a great cue for getting the hell out—only the second he turned for the door, Archer's angry voice chomped on the air.

"That's not an order I have to care about." Shock of shocks, the guy just got prettier when he was pissed, resembling a Renaissance oil angel as he stalked over. "So too bad, so sad; no fucking off for Runway today." He halted the approach but braced his stance, balled hands at his sides. "What the hell is up with you?"

He relented, stopping as well. Dropped a shoulder but

lifted a stare, the listen-because-I'm-only-saying-this once kind he usually saved for the thick of missions. *"What's up?"* he fired back. "Not a damn thing, except that I'm running on fifteen seconds of sleep after nearly having my balls blown into my brain by a mystery terrorist yesterday afternoon." He tilted a sunshiny smirk. "What's up with *you*, guys? Long as we're standing here shooting the shit."

Ethan gave back nothing but a gruff grunt. "You live on sleeplessness the way the rest of us live on oxygen."

Translation: he wasn't buying the bullshit. Zeke, with ass parked on the counter and hands spread atop his thighs, clearly concurred. "Sleep is for sheep, not dragons," he pronounced. "It's one of my favorite Franz-isms."

Archer chuffed. "Because it's the only one not borrowed from Sondheim?"

"There *is* that." As Z pushed all the way to his feet again, his stare remained intent—to the point of unnerving. "But this isn't just about the dumb creeds, is it?" He stepped over too, though his movements weren't as fired up as Archer's. He was full of stealth—of more unnerving attention. "What *is* this about, Franzen?"

John almost laughed. Did the bastard think the Batman shuffle and the ominous gaze would vet him a full gut spill? "I just told you, damn it. I'm on an empty tank."

"Okay...yeah. An empty tank." Z's face tightened. "And a cracked engine block."

Franz gave in to the laugh. "You're just getting that *now*?"

"No," Z stated. "But *you* are."

"Pardon the hell out of me?"

"*You* are." The guy emphasized it with such a determined nod, his head led the way into his next pair of steps. Slightly ahead of Archer now, Z stopped, letting the direct alignment of his gaze do a little work too. His eyes favored their copper tint more than the green—his ready-to-rumble color. "You're not just acknowledging those cracks, buddy. You're putting them to good use. They're your goddamn fox holes. Your hiding places."

Breath rushed up from his lungs. Exploded from his nostrils in incensed snorts. "And you hate it when *I* go off with the metaphors?"

Zeke might as well have not heard him. "But hiding...from what?"

"Christ." He backed away. "Do you hear yourself right now? Is your wife juicing her pregnancy hormones for you to chug too?"

"Welllll, then." Archer took a hard swig of his stout. "Is that *Smash Bros* I hear coming on line in the den?"

"It's not the mission ops." Zeke's intent didn't falter. "You've got Sol Wrightman on secret speed dial, and we've all performed these duties a thousand times."

"Zsycho." John gritted it from thinned lips. "Back. Off."

"So if it's not the mission—"

"*Goddamnit.*"

"Fuck me." Z blurted it with an oddly blank stare. He didn't need to worry, since Archer's gape conveyed enough shock for them both. "It's the package."

Franzen widened his stance. Dipped his head. If it made him look like a bull about to charge, all the better. "She has a name."

"No shit." Archer found his voice again. And, weirdly, another laugh. It stuttered out of him, bracketing his follow-up. "Tracy Rhodes. This is so epic. Our Dragon Man has a crush on Tracy Rhodes."

Half a beat passed, nobody's gazes wavering, before Zeke uttered, "Hey, Runway?"

"Yeah?" Archer's voice was still edged with mirth.

"If you still want to make a living off that flawless nose of yours, now would be a good time to join that *Smash* game."

The air went quiet for half a beat more.

"Don't start without me!" Archer disappeared into the den, calling dibs on playing Lucario. Shitty choice. Charizard would've been the better way to go, but Franz believed in letting his guys make stupid mistakes if it didn't maim or kill anyone, Nintendo characters excluded.

Besides...he still had Zeke to contend with.

The guy who stood there, watching him with nearly surreal calm.

Okay, it was a façade—but a fucking troubling one nonetheless. In many ways, John knew Z as well as he knew himself. Composure could be a good thing and a bad thing. Good when it was there to prevent beasts from getting out; bad when it kept them in for too long. And yeah, Z had beasts— different from John's, because they'd been born and bred during a childhood on the streets of Seattle, but they were sure as hell there. They were what made him a good soldier as well as a sought-after Dom. Zeke Hayes had entered the army *and* his first BDSM dungeon as means of escape...to become a better person than when he'd walked into the joint.

Franz wished he could claim such noble purposes.

Perhaps they had been, at the beginning. Not that he'd been a complete Pippin about things. Life wasn't an ideal existence, but if he could give other people even a boost toward that, he'd leave the planet better than when he arrived on it, which was a hell of a lot better than renting out surfboards or pouring pineapple whips all day.

That philosophy lasted until the end of his third tour, when violence and disillusionment started taking heavier tolls. His attitude changed about the D/s dynamic, veering away from the selfish immediacy of the sex. He began to see what he could give *back* to a submissive, including the acceptance, approval, and higher purpose he'd been seeking for himself...

Until the disaster with Abbie.

Dark times...shared a very few.

Zeke Hayes just happened to be one of those few. The weight of that knowledge made the man's shoulders slouch as he re-crossed his arms, quietly venturing, "Is it true?" He pushed out a violent grunt when Franz returned nothing but a stubborn glower. "Is it *true*, asshole? Do you have a...*thing*...for Tracy Rhodes?"

Franz hauled in a heavy breath. Scuffled both feet while glancing at his watch, hoping he'd luck out and see it was time to fire up a new burner cell with which to contact Sol. "She's the goddamn president now."

"That doesn't answer my question."

"The hell it doesn't." John reared his head back, letting his face contort sharply. "And what the hell is a 'thing'? You in fifth grade, man?"

"Apparently, I have good company." Zeke's gaze darkened. "You've dodged the issue with everything except *my dog ate the homework*."

Franz welcomed new steel to his stance and fresh grit to his jaw. He planted both hands on his hips. "I think there are more important issues to address than my attraction to the vice—the *president*. According to some polls, half the nation is attracted to her."

"You *trust* the polls?"

"Now who's dodging the issues?"

"Fine. I don't think you can address the issues until you deal with the attraction."

A laugh barked out. He ignored the burn churning up his throat at the same time. "Deal with it, huh? Just like that?"

Zeke cast his gaze toward the ceiling. It was going to be a good look for his daddy-o arsenal. "I didn't say you have to flog her and fuck her. Go meditate it off if you have to."

"*Meditate* it off?"

"Or pray to the island gods. Or take a cold shower. Or cut your goddamn balls off." He unfurled his arms and tossed up both hands. "I don't care what you do, asshole; just get your shit together about whatever you're feeling for the woman. Though for the record"—he wheeled around, grabbed his beer bottle, and knocked back the remaining gulp inside—"don't blame you for the caveman urges. She's a gorgeous woman, and you did just save her life."

"And then there's the polls..."

"And there's you with the dog eating the homework again."

For a long second, his fixed stare felt like the best choice of reaction. If he moved right now, he'd either hug or deck Zeke. Neither was acceptable; both were lame extremes; completely blamable on the relief of coming clean with at least one person about this crazy...

Thing.

Fuck.

Fine. He admitted it. Even knowing what kind of a damn dilemma came skipping along in the wake of doing so.

The conflict of knowing Z was right. About all of it.

He had to clean this shit up. His conflict was collecting

on his cracked engine like used motor oil, meaning he risked making everybody else on the team crash and burn too. Not cool when there were lives at stake. Important ones.

In short, if he wanted to keep his big head on straight about protecting Tracy, he had to take care of the issues in his *little* head. Somehow, in some impossible way, he had to.

Damn it. You're Special Forces, asswipe. Suck it up, buttercup, and make this mission happen.

His brain two-by-foured it into his senses.

But where the hell did the *other* voice come from, fronting its retort like an emotional I-beam?

Easier said than done, fucker. And my name isn't "buttercup."

Worst of all? The way Z's gaze bounced with amusement— as if the jerk were actually listening to his internal dialogue and finding it as amusing as a *Who's On First* reboot.

Franz narrowed his own glare. "You're enjoying this, aren't you?"

Z's lips twitched. "Immensely."

Deep breath. Another. They didn't help much, except for fortifying his posture. Better than seething here like a stooped old man.

"Glad to know you're entertained."

"Immensely," Z echoed.

"All right, then, smartass." He jerked up his chin, an unwritten version of paying deference to the guy who'd once been hailed "The Dark Night of Seattle" because of his own damsel-rescuing exploits—most notably with the woman who now carried his child. "You've been in these moccasins a little before, yeah?"

Zeke's expression sobered by a few degrees. "You could say that. A little."

"So how the hell did *you* fight it?" Franz demanded. "You know what I'm talking about, so don't pretend you don't," he pushed. "When wanting to protect the girl so badly, you fantasize about just tying her up yourself..." He stopped. Exhaled hard. "And then doing other things..."

"While she's still tied up?"

"Fuck," Franz grated. "Yeah."

A look of commiseration fell over the guy's face. After seeming to make an inner decision, Z wheeled back toward the kitchen. Grabbed a new beer from the fridge and popped the cap by leveraging the edge of the counter. Before lifting the thing for a swig, he shrugged and tapped the bottle's neck in the air. "Word of advice? Don't."

"Tie her up?"

"Fight it," he countered. "I'm serious, Franz. Just don't fucking fight it."

Franz growled softly. "I was afraid you'd say that." *I was hoping you'd say that.* "You know what you're advising me to do, right? And to whom?"

Z plunked down the beer. Spread both hands along the counter. "I only know that you asked me how I fought the craving to have my woman beneath me, as opposed to protecting her behind me. I'm assuming you're talking about my Ray-bird and what I had to do when that asshole Mua came after her." His head dropped for a second. Still shaking it slowly, he went on, "That was a crazy couple of weeks—that probably would've got a lot easier if I'd trusted my instinct about Rayna to begin with." Strangely, a serene smile worked its way back onto his face. "And straight-up truth? You're able to think much clearer about guarding them when you're not preoccupied about getting inside them."

John blew out a long breath. Scraped a hand over the top of his head. "Wasn't exactly what I wanted to hear, man."

"But it's what you asked for," Z rebutted. "Same as what you've always asked me for, my friend."

Franz slid his hand to the back of his neck. Murmured dismally, "The truth."

Zeke shrugged. "Sometimes it really can set you free."

"Not what I wanted to hear either, assface."

His friend's teeth were a brilliant crescent as Z burst into a hearty laugh. "I love you too, honey."

CHAPTER SEVEN

"You are so dead."

"Says *you.*"

"Peachy go...peachy go...yessss."

"Whaaaa?"

"Score! Princess power!"

"That was intense."

"Darn right. And the girl owns your guts—*again.*"

Tracy closed the book she'd been attempting to read as a distraction after six hours of cable news binging. With Ronnie and Gem handling all the latest from the internet feeds, she'd been left to listening for carefully couched clues in the broadcasts about the investigation's progress. After one hour, the duty could be qualified as tedious. After two, as enjoyable as babysitting snails. After six, the existence of usable gray matter was dubious—evidenced by the fact that Mario and Princess Peach were suddenly more interesting than getting lost in a moonlit French garden with a French princess and the Versailles viscount assigned to protect her.

Mia started a new game, including Ethan on the challenge this time. He picked Donkey Kong as his avatar, launching the teens into a meme quote war—and blasting Tracy a cue to dive back into the book.

The viscount and his lady were the last of her options, perhaps her sanity. No way could she sit in Zeke's office and watch another second of talking heads, but Gem and Ronnie were also on break, so entertainment options were limited at the moment. Franzen tossed her phone before they left Vegas, adding to the ruse that she'd died there—and to be honest, she hardly missed the thing. A break from being tethered to the device had been heaven, though she couldn't claim the same for all the other restrictions the dragon put into place. No eating too many Nutter Butters, her go-to comfort food, because somebody might notice the boxes in the trash. No doing her daily round of jumping jacks, burpees, and high-knee jogs, because Rayna and Zeke had confirmed they were gym rats when Z was stateside, and the neighbors would get curious about their "odd behavior."

None of it made her as crazy as the windows.

No peeking from one, let alone opening one. No sky. No clouds. No treetops. Not even any panoramic city views, which she'd only guessed at by the distant traffic sounds she could pick up—through the *closed* condo windows.

She hadn't even been dead a day, and she *really* missed windows.

"La la la la...smash!"

"*Seriously?*"

"Luke. Dude. You keep leading with the same move."

"Because it's a good move, Ethan!"

"The definition of insanity is trying the same thing and expecting different results."

"*More* Franzen wisdom?"

"Errrm...that's Albert Einstein, kid."

"Huh. Just sounded a lot like Franzen."

And there it was.

Again.

Franzen.

The subject making her more restless than the window ban. The man who wouldn't leave her memories—and her imagination—alone. Not since he'd stepped through those midnight shadows, shattering the lustful tension between them. Fitted his huge cock to her thrumming cleft. Filled her senses with his exotic scent. Drenched her every breath with hot, illicit craving for him...

Restless?

No.

This wasn't "restless."

This was a fever she couldn't bring down. Fire, licking at her skin, she couldn't douse.

Desire she just couldn't write off.

She gulped down a breath. Slid her eyes shut. Prayed the black curtain over her vision would conquer the flashbacks as easily as Mia kept pounding Luke in their game.

Fail.

The darkness simply allowed the man better access to her mind. Let him invade her mind's eye like he'd annihilated her personal space in the bedroom. Silently. Dangerously.

A torment she could no longer ignore.

"I need to grab a shower."

Gem cracked a sleepy eye open from her end of the overstuffed couch. To her left, Ronnie was curled so deeply under a blanket in the recliner, only a poof of her strawberry strands showed. She didn't move a muscle as Gem mumbled, "Didn't you already do that today?"

Leave it to Gemini Fiona Vann to remember something like that, even half-comatose. Plus side? Her best friend really was half-comatose.

"I'm jittery." Not a lie. Not one damn bit. "I'm hoping it'll help take the edge off."

Also not a lie—just probably not in the way Gem assumed. And that was fine. If either of her friends knew how Franzen had gotten under her skin like a million fire ants, they'd corn-feed the critters until they were the size of centipedes and then try to convert Franzen into a centipede enthusiast.

Wasn't going to happen. The man was already clear about how much "enthusiasm" he was willing to commit to their attraction. To her at all. His flesh was willing but his stubborn, baggage-bearing mind was certainly not weak. She'd seen the weight of that baggage in his gaze—along with the obvious conclusion to that. A "casual" roll in the hay with her would drag all that bullshit out of his psyche again. He'd have to look at it all again...

She understood that. In a normal world, could even be okay with it—because in a normal world, they'd have time to develop a normal relationship...

But this wasn't a normal world.

She was like Mia's peach princess. Running into an impassable wall. Knowing there was treasure on the other side but trapped, unable to get to it.

Trapped...

Sometimes, the princess had to opt for a cold shower instead of the treasure.

"Hummm." Gem's sleepy moan brought her sights back down. Her friend squeezed Tracy's fingertips and then used her free hand to muffle a yawn. "Okay, honey. Have fun."

With a smile, Tracy tucked Gem's hand back under her lap blanket. Sweet, exhausted woman. There was a damn good chance she and Ronnie had slept as little as Franzen last night. The evidence of their nocturnal activity was still strewn all over the dining room table. Armed with only a bunch of legal pads and short spurts on the deep web, they'd managed to learn little beyond the information already carried via the TV networks. The hits on seven different world leaders, across just as many cities, were as horridly unexpected as they were meticulously planned—by a web of operatives deeply embedded in each country's government. The individuals who'd turned traitor on their lands were in tight connection with each other and had been for a very long time.

Encouraging each other...as they watched every move their targets made...

For how long?

The question was a specter in her mind, haunting every step she took down the hall toward the master bedroom.

In how many ways?

Did they know that Craig took ten minutes out of every morning to keep up a handwritten journal? Did they know he tried to keep Wednesday nights free so he and Norene could maintain their pizza night tradition from college? Did they know that every day when he called or came by Tracy's office, he brought a new Broadway trivia question to try to stump her?

What if they knew all of that?

What if they knew even more?

By the time she entered the master bathroom, a shiver defined her steps. Thankfully, there was a switch for a wall heater. She pushed it on before even activating the lights. As soon as all those were on—the set over the shower stall, as well as the main overheads and the vanity illumination—she finally turned and shut the door.

Staring, for a very long time, at her trembling hand against the knob.

Ordering herself to let it go.

Wondering why the hell she'd even come in here.

Franzen.

Yes.

That was it.

What he'd done to her. What he *hadn't* done to her. The needy, hot mess her mind and body had become because of obsessing over it, to the point she was nearly crawling out of her own skin...

To the point she'd fallen prey to fear like this.

Let those bastards, whoever the hell they were, take her *into* this hell again. A trembling, terrified zombie, trapped in a torment she swore she'd never enter again. She'd served her penance here already—starting on the day she'd had to tell her son his father was never coming home again.

Fate had noted her vow. And honored it.

Until yesterday afternoon, when the bastard screwed the entire planet at once—a catastrophe she'd accepted with surreal serenity, even to her own mind, until just now, when looking at Ronnie's frantic notes, and recognizing the delayed reaction shock had kept from her.

Not anymore.

It was all sinking in.

Completely.

Ruthlessly.

Shooting down the vortex of her exhausted mind, directly into the core of her consciousness. Reminding her, inside one freezing minute, that hell wasn't brimstone and flames. It was ice—and fear.

And solitude.

Isolation that claimed even more of her in its frosty fist.

Choked the air from her throat. Yanked her down, sliding against the wall, until she curled to the floor in a ball of shivering aloneness.

No.

No.

She couldn't do this.

She had to get through this.

Had to fight her way back...

To what?

To what?

She crawled across the floor, dragging herself to the shower and popping the stall door back. A weak laugh broke through—that was a good sign, right?—when she saw the embossed letters for the temperature controls. This had all started with her actually thinking she needed a cold shower. Her only obsession now was cranking this shit as hot as it would let her.

She had to get through this.

She was stronger than this.

But even as the spray hit her, warming every second, her legs didn't reinvigorate to stand. Her body wouldn't cooperate with her will. The heat just seemed to open more vortices now, into which her heart melted...and her grief poured.

Beneath the pelting heat, she curled into a new ball. As the water soaked her clothes and then her body, she let the pain drench her defenses...

And topple them.

CHAPTER EIGHT

Still frothing with irritation at Z, Franzen kicked off his flip-flops—*Zeke*'s flip-flops—and then barreled across the master bedroom in full target lock mode.

Cold water. His body. Right now.

It'd be a shitty excuse for how he normally handled stress—in Special Forces leadership, the skill was as essential as reading a mission or stomaching ration packs—but right now, there wasn't an ocean to swim in, a gym to pump in, or a dungeon full of subbies ready to give him an hour or two of Dominant escape. There was only the shower and the restart of sanity it would give in the form of ten freezing minutes.

He hoped.

If not, this day was going to get a hell of a lot longer. And more painful.

As if he needed a reminder of exactly that, he took a recharging breath and instead got a lungful of one distinct scent. *Tracy.* The woman with the sassy, sexy name and the huge kitten eyes smelled like ginger and jasmine and vanilla, filling his senses with a spring he wanted less than the sunshine—but couldn't desire more.

So the spring turned into summer. Suffusing him. Centering, as always, on the part of him craving her the most.

"Fuck." He gritted it as his dick punched his sweats. Again. He needed that cold shower five minutes ago.

The purpose drove him across the last few feet of the

bedroom, throttling him through the bathroom door...

Where he entered a bank of solid steam.

"What the—"

He pieced his mind together long enough for two possible conclusions. One, he'd somehow fallen asleep and now dreamed of some jungle-based mission. Two, Z and Rayna had installed a bathroom sauna and it had somehow been turned on. Admittedly, he'd started leaning more toward option two...

When the reality of option three set in.

The shower was on. And there was someone inside it.

But why was the door open?

More importantly—why was that person sobbing?

More urgent than that—where was she? And *was* it a she?

The answer to the last was as certain to him as his own heartbeat. Yes. It was a woman. More definitely, even without having a visual on her, he knew exactly which woman. As soon as the shock of the steam wall wore off, he'd known. Had felt her down to the marrow of his bones, an awareness begun in the sizzle of his blood, the burst of his senses...the fullness of his cock. It was the same jolt she'd given him yesterday, before they'd even met. Then again after the sound check, when they'd been briefly separated so he could discuss the driving route changes back to the Bellagio with Sol. And now—God, especially now. The air was different with her in it. His entire body was different.

Even now, with the force of her presence carrying her distress. Sorrow that clenched his gut, vise-gripped his muscles, and redirected all the pain in his groin to the plain of his chest. It choked up to his throat, turning talking into a torment.

"Tracy?" he forced out while clearing the space to the

shower in two critical strides. By the time he got to the lip of the stall, his feet were soaking wet. No way had she just turned on the spigot—

A fact verified as soon as he saw her.

Still fully clothed. Huddled against the stall's wall, her head leaned against the wall. Her eyes were vacant, but her face was crumpled in a sob.

"Tracy," he croaked again. "Kitten. Shit."

Without second thought, he scooted in next to her. Leaned over but stopped short of touching her. Aside from laying a limp hand on his knee, she didn't acknowledge his arrival in any way. Didn't look at him. Still didn't speak a word.

"Tracy." He intoned it more firmly, in service to the field commander he allowed to take over his psyche. Franzen the man was still in there, only running around like an idiot gaping at a spreading fire with a dead phone and an empty bucket. Thank fuck for Dragon the captain, ordering the lunatic to take a seat so he could speak to the shock clearly claiming her from head to toe. "*Ku`uipo*...can you hear me?"

She blinked. Just once. He accepted it as progress.

"Okay. So try to hear me some more."

"No."

Okay. More progress. He wasn't sure he liked it better than the blinking, but he'd take it.

"No?"

"No." She pushed it out louder. Used the hand she'd placed on his knee to shove at him. "Not going to listen. Not to you." Her face twisted again. Harder than before. "*Not* to you."

He pushed back to his haunches. Commanded a breath in and then out. Yeah, fuck it, this was progress too. Progress like gaining ground by stomping on a wasp's nest, but yeah, progress. She was talking to him. Now if he could get her talking *with* him...

"Okay. Then maybe I can go get someone you *will* listen to." He visualized where he'd last seen Gemini Vann and Veronica Gallo. In the den, relaxing with the kids and their stereophonic video games—though something had clearly, finally triggered her to cave like this from yesterday's shock. The delayed emotions didn't surprise him, though what she'd done about them did.

"No."

She gritted the retort this time, intensifying his concern to the point that he reached out again. But the second his hand formed over her shoulder, she flinched and seethed.

"No! There's no one you can 'go get,' damn it."

He pulled back, watching his hand curl on itself in midair. He thought of all the damage that fist had done, to so many shitheads and losers over the years, but was now a symbol of utter helplessness—inches from a person he was aching to help. Fate was getting in all its best taunts today. His spirit hadn't agonized this much even when the news about Nichols had come out.

And the pain in this stall is about you...how?

Easy answer. It wasn't.

But no way in hell was he leaving her in here, all but drowning herself in several senses of the word. If she ordered him all the way out of the shower, then he'd abide—and simply sit on the tile outside. One puddle for another; no difference to him physically—but he *would* stay here for her, whether she asked for it or not. Even if it fucking killed him.

For now, he chose to simply settle back on his haunches. Nearly as an afterthought, reached and cranked the spray off. In the eerie silence after, Tracy joined her quiet sniffs to the heavy drops of the draining water. John re-balled both his hands, hating even the inches between them. To not even touch her, let alone resist the baser need to clutch her close...

Fuck.

Waterboarding had nothing on this shit.

And the worst part hadn't even sunk in.

She's just following your lead, asshole.

That was the worst part.

In protecting her from his secret side, he'd been locked out of her secrets too. In shielding her from his darkness, she'd made sure he stayed right there—in the dark. Away from the ability to even give *her* some light...

Moron. You. Same sentence, Keoni John Franzen.

Finally, she snuffled with more determination. Jerked up her head a little, long enough to slide him a furtive side-eye but nothing more. She pulled her hand all the way back in, tucking it beneath her chin as she settled her head against the wall again.

"I want to talk to Craig."

A brutal exhalation left him. His throat tightened. His chest compressed. Hell, nothing was comfortable. Nor was it meant to be.

"I know you do," he murmured.

"I'm...scared."

Screw uncomfortable. Everything was agony—especially when she wouldn't even let him do anything about it. No. When he'd pushed her away out in the bedroom, letting her walk away with the impression that he *wouldn't* do anything.

"I know you are."

At least he had words. Paltry proxies, but they'd have to suffice somehow.

"I have no idea what to do."

"But you don't have to figure it out alone, *ku`uipo*."

Her face contorted again, though not with impending tears. Her eyes flared with irritation. "Don't call me that."

He barely repressed a grin. "You're gorgeous when you're hissy, kitten."

"Yeah? Well, I have Tigress claws, remember?"

"Fine, fine." He held up both hands. "Maybe you just want *ma'am* again?"

"And maybe you just want me to hunt down a flattening iron."

His chuckle was impossible to tame. Her glower went from simmering to smoky. He had no idea there were so many nuances of gray. In her eyes, they were all fascinating.

"Maybe you can just close your eyes and pretend I'm Craig." The offer was sincere—he was up for any creative solution here—but her laughter, high and biting, was nowhere near a vote of approval.

"That's *so* not going to happen."

He frowned. "Why not?"

"Because I'd know the difference."

"How?"

"*John.*" Her laugh mellowed to a watery eye roll. He suddenly knew how Luke must feel when a test wasn't studied for. "I'd know the difference between you and *any* other man."

And just like that, no more feeling like her teen kid.

Feeling everything like the jerk who'd probably made the biggest mistake of his life with her earlier and would spend the rest of his mortal days cussing himself out for it. "Fuck." Might as well start now. "*Ku`uipo.*"

Her Tigress side flared in a swift snarl. "What didn't you

understand about *not* calling me that?"

"And what don't you understand that I'm only here to help?" The backlash, his higher ground pick of a reply, was still better than choice two: smashing one hell of a kiss on her feisty lips. "It slipped. So skewer me."

Her regard softened. "It's okay. Just...be careful."

Now he was the one clinging to his scowl. "You don't even know what it means."

"I can guess by your tone."

"And that's a bad thing?"

"When your voice alone makes me want to come over there and maul you? Yeah." She lingered her stare longer—to his intense pleasure. More intense than he wanted to admit but couldn't deny. Not when the heat from his skin met the wetness of his clothes and created a new experience for him. *Steam Bath—in SenSurround.*

"Tracy." He heeded her request—the tone was new; perhaps the first time he'd ever used it outside a bondage dungeon before—though its replacement was just as merciless. Perhaps more so. He issued her name as a declaration...a command. Nothing he'd ever use on his battalion members because this asked for a different kind of obedience. No. Demanded it.

"What?" She dropped her head but lifted it again. Her eyes were as huge as a pair of London moons.

"Do you...*want*...to maul me?"

For the first time since he'd crawled in here, her body loosened. She opened up a little, still staring with the moon in her eyes—only now, joined by the comets in her energy. Untamed rogue comets—all aimed his direction. "*Want* isn't the word I'd use."

Flames licked the edges of her voice—and now the length of his cock. Fuck, how this woman got to him. How her spirit and sass challenged him. How her desire affected him...

"Tracy." He didn't hesitate about wielding the dungeon command now. Doubly deep, three times as severe.

"Wh-What?"

Oh, yeah. He also liked it when her defiance wobbled a little. What would it be like to make it shake a lot?"

"Get over here and maul me."

CHAPTER NINE

Every inch of her body screamed yes.

Craving the strength of him. The authority of him. The hard, burnished heaven of him.

Every neuron in her mind blared no.

Remembering his rejection. His confidence about it. His surety of exactly what she needed from a man—relationship, stability, commitment—and his inability to supply any of that.

But right now, she didn't need a freaking commitment.

She needed an escape.

A way out of the insanity tumbling down on her. The world that felt too big. The fear, closing in like a forest under a dark spell...

She needed the sun. The fire. If only just this once, the perfect incineration...

Of him.

She leapt at him with desperate, driving force. Grabbed his wet shirt with one hand and the meat of his neck with the other, using both to slam her body tighter against his. *Yes.* So blissful, straddling him. So hot, feeling him. So stretched, and she was only riding his pulsing bulge through their clothes...

A situation needing to be changed.

As soon as damn possible.

If his taut groan was any clear communicator, Franzen was on the same perfect page. He finished it by croaking, "*Fuck*. Kitten." More words tumbled out in his island tongue, and she didn't ask for a translation. His raw granite voice turned it all into filthy temptation, and she didn't want to think any differently. She succumbed to his erotic call with sighing abandon, exactly how she'd wanted to since meeting him.

"Meow," she uttered into his ear before sinking her teeth into the lobe. His hands, gripping her thighs, dug in to the point of pain. Together, they released aroused hisses.

It was awakening. Arousal. Explosions so electric and erotic and new, but a connection she also recognized already, in places even deeper than her womb...as if it were always meant to be.

As if *he* were always meant to be.

Nothing confirmed it more than the moment he coiled a hand in her hair, twisted her head back, and then plunged his mouth over hers.

She had half a second to mewl in surprise before the man stole even that from her. His tongue lunged and conquered, swept and ravaged, taking every part of her wide, willing mouth. Gone was the carefully reined warrior, even the diligent dragon guard, bringing on the understanding of why he'd backed off before. He'd known, even then. He'd known it would be like this if they gave in to their attraction...if they gave even one spark to their fire.

Too late now.

And Tracy wasn't one bit sorry.

She melted for him. Sighed and groaned, succumbing to the brutal mastery of him. Let her fear tumble free as her passion thickened, becoming the putty of his desire.

Mold me, her mind begged.

Take me, her pussy pleaded.

Free me, her spirit screamed.

John released her from the kiss only to impale her with his stare, the mocha of his eyes stirred with liquid gold—and the intensity of new insight. He'd heard her. Not in the clumsy rudiment of words but in the fabric of his own mind, soul, and body. *He'd heard her.*

But more than that, *he'd listened.*

So why did his grip loosen against her scalp? Why were his brows knit so tight, they nearly veed at the center of his forehead?

He released a tight breath from locked teeth, as if hearing those queries just as clearly. "I can't promise sweet and sultry, woman. I'll try, but—"

"But what?" she managed to murmur, despite how he interrupted himself with a growl radiating beneath her skin, through every cell of her blood.

His hands, now clutching her by the nape and waist, curled tighter. "But I want you too much." His head dipped until his mouth shoved aside her T-shirt, nuzzling at her neck. "I want these goddamn barriers gone. I want..."

"Don't stop." She implored it like a desert wanderer led to a waterfall. Wound her arms around his neck. Spread fingers through the brutal needles of his hair. Yes. *Yes.* He was so much...*so much.* Water flowing over a burnished dagger. Dark, smooth skin over ruthless power. A man wielding the force of ancient gods. She needed more. So much more. "*Please*...don't stop..."

Franz yanked her body harder against his. "I want to strip every thread of this shit off you. Make you lie back, legs spread, while you watch me strip too—knowing what my body is going to do to you next."

Holy. Shit.

Had the man taken some course in verbal foreplay? *How to Make a Woman Gush in Fifty Words or Less?*

And did she care?

Not one damn bit.

She only had one reaction—sheer, ecstatic gratitude—as she scraped both hands forward, bracing the formidable angles of his jaw. With that grip, she pulled him close for another kiss. She only touched the surface of his broad, full lips, but within a second the man took over, pushing at hers. No. He forced his way in, ramming her wide once more, drawing her tongue out to give exactly what his demanded.

Everything.

It was rapidly becoming a theme around here—proved by its resonance in her consciousness, fed by the surety of it in her soul.

Everything.

It was what he'd demand, in the form of her consent to his desire.

It was what she'd give anyway, because there wasn't a "half power" switch in her psyche when it came to this man. Not from the moment he'd first taken her hand. Definitely not now.

It was the mode she wanted to experience this in. To experience *him*. To be taken and consumed and claimed by him...

It was the way she gave up as he gathered her close and tight, jerking her legs high around his waist before he stood. His muscles bunched like physical poetry, as if they were on thick grass instead of slick tiles, handling her weight with powerful ease.

"Hang on tight, kitten."

God. The new gymnastics he taught her stomach with each new use of that naughty endearment...

In the next room, he tenderly lowered her to the bed. Not so softly, plunged his own body down next to her. Her heartbeat sprinted as soon as their gazes locked again. His eyes glittered, alive with a predatory heat she'd never seen before, as he gripped her waist and twined their legs. That animalistic energy moved across his whole face, shifting it into angles of primal intention...and open lust.

A gulp thudded down her throat.

His chivalric move might have been the last she'd see of his civility for a while.

She was terrified about the creature that would replace it.

And had never been wetter in her life.

CHAPTER TEN

Franzen had never been harder in his life.

And faced the fact that the torture wouldn't be over anytime soon.

Every muscle in his body clenched and strained, ordering the urges of his instinct to instant stand-downs. At least for now. Yeah, the woman still wanted him in return—thank fuck—and yeah, she didn't want to wait long, either—thank *fuck*—but just giving in to all their base lusts still wasn't an option. Tearing off her wet clothes meant an explanation to Rayna later. Spreading her wide and fucking her until she screamed? Not even a remote option, despite the volume at which Mario, Princess Peach, and Lucario virtually pounded each other in the next room.

He had to plan this through.

He had to think like a Dom.

Not the most helpful angle here, however. The one he kept defaulting to. The perspective at which she was his willing, eager little subbie. His kitten in all aspects of the word...taking whatever wicked treatment he could dream for her beautiful curves...

Stow those bullets, soldier.

None of this was about what *he* wanted. This was about the healing and escape *she* needed—and he'd bestow, with the command she clearly craved, without subjecting her to the full Dragon Dominance buffet. He wasn't a goddamn nug. He

RULED

recognized his mistake from earlier. Denying her—denying them *both*—of a fulfillment of their attraction, just because he hadn't settled for vanilla sex in nearly fifteen years, had been messed up. He could pleasure a woman without all that shit. Without even the words.

Though holy hell, did "Sir" sound so right with her subtle Texas lilt...

"How do you want me now, Sir?"

Just. Like. That.

Fuck.

He sucked in a deep breath. Swallowed hard before letting it back out, all the while leaning over her with one knee on the bed. "I think you already know the answer to that, kitten." He ran fingertips up the outside of her thigh. "So I'm going to let you get to work on that while I take care of the logistical shit."

"The...huh?"

He dropped a forceful but fast kiss to her lips. "Just take off your clothes, woman. Every fucking stitch. I'll be back before you're done."

He kept to his word, all but sprinting across the room to ensure the door was locked, the kids were *really* preoccupied with their game, and the room's lighting was turned low. A golden glow persisted from the midday sun beyond the blinds, for which he was now—unbelievably—grateful. The ambient lighting reminded him exactly of the wall sconces at Bastille...

Damn. Bastille.

It had been too fucking long.

And how incredible would it be to break that absence with this gorgeous woman on his arm?

And what kind of a planet have you moved to, where you can think of parading Tracy Rhodes right into your local dungeon—

even if you are half owner of the place?

Not the time for philosophical breakdowns.

Not with the softly smiling female on the bed, damp hair splayed on the pillow, already satisfying so many of his hottest fantasies about her.

She wouldn't fulfill all of them. He accepted that. But cake was still cake, even without the buttercream roses. After all this was over, when she was moved into the White House and he was back to figuring out his life, he'd be able to search for someone else who appreciated the thorns instead.

So what if that thought nauseated the fuck out of him right now?

So what if he wished that "right now" could just be the end of all the "right nows"?

That she could be the end of all his searches...

Yeah, and Transformers actually existed. Superheroes too. With invisible planes, webs like steel cables, and levitation cloaks.

The truth was, he'd always be searching.

How could he know a woman was right for his life when he had no idea how to define that life?

Even if he had *that* part figured out, one truth would remain glaringly clear.

His world. Her world. Two separate things.

But right now was only about *this* world, golden and right, that they would create together. No boundaries. No titles. No ranks. Just her beauty, waiting nude and perfect for him. Just her arms, lifting in welcome to him.

Just his passion, plunging him down to her again.

Just their lust, bursting as their mouths collided again.

Exploding as if they hadn't just done this minutes ago.

Arcing...crashing. Pushing...pulsing.

Searing...then tearing.

Demolishing what he'd been clinging to in the name of decent foreplay. Shattering through him, turning his muscles to flames and his skin into the cage now fried by that blaze. A groan left him as the hellfire spread, only soothed when his body spread hers, fitting tighter against hers. Tracy's answering moan was a vibration of validation, driving him to spread his knees out, opening her wider for him. The ridge in his pants slid against the sultry seam of her pussy, swelling in recognition of the heaven it sought...burned for...needed.

In the other room, Archer let out a bellow of victory.

Beneath him, Tracy burst with a high cry of wonder.

"Oh," she rasped. "Oh...my *God*..." Her pelvis jerked and thrust, reminding him of the sleek, hot escape she offered. Her hands, braced to his shoulders, turned into urgent claws—then nails of piercing demand.

John formed his mouth over hers again. Though Tracy had calmed, her lusty breaths intensified. They were sharp and high, finished off by tiny eruptions matching the passionate points of her nipples. The sight of those stiff berries, along with the pain she kept digging into his shoulders, worked to whip his own mind to the brink of its limits. With every new scream into his mouth and fresh stab into his shoulders, his dick filled with another surge of arousal. His balls made out like horny teenagers. His shaft was swollen, seeping with precome, beyond the point of pain. Even rocking the length along her cleft wasn't assuagement anymore—no matter how thoroughly the little kitten herself loved it.

"Don't...stop," she begged, moving a hand to the back of his head, locking him in her luminous, lusty stare. "Don't stop, John. *Please*."

He forced her to confront the regret in his eyes. "Have to."

"What? Why?" She bucked against him as she whined it, and the heat of her juices warmed the length of his crotch. By the gods, how delicious she smelled too. Musk and cream and sex. He wanted that scent on the inside of his nose...as his tongue fucked her cunt.

Not before his cock.

Bringing him full circle in this erotic shit storm.

"Can't...just can't...do this. *Fuck*." The exclamation was his ineffectual protest to her heels at his buttocks, shoving hard enough to propel him against her again. The friction alone nearly unraveled his control. But her hot, plump nether lips, cushioning him like waves of raw fire...

It was rapture.

Torture.

A limit he couldn't fathom.

A boundary he couldn't take.

A temptation he could no longer deny.

"*Tracy*." It was a buzz saw in his throat, shredding everything on its way out. If it sounded like a yak puking, he didn't care. The edges of his vision dotted. His cock screamed in need—even as he shoved down the front of his sweats, freeing the glistening length.

"Franzen." Her breath fanned the front of his neck. Her nails twisted into his skin.

Sending lightning to his cock.

Heat that could no longer be denied.

"*John*."

"*Shit*." His brain turned to fuzz as his dick sought her body. One thrust did it, consuming him...killing him. He pulled out and fought like hell to stay there, until the wet cushions of her channel sucked him back in. Another lunge, twice as blissful—and terrible—as the first.

"Oh!" She pressed it into the underside of his jaw. Her lips were hot and wet, just like the convulsing walls of her sex.

"Fuck. *Ku`uipo.*"

Not a single rant at him for the word now—when he really, freaking needed one. Instead, she locked herself tighter to him, whispering into the underside of his ear, "You're so—*it's* so—"

"I know."

She scored both sides of his back as her fingernails of wonder torture slid down to his butt. Yeah, because driving him into erotic insanity with the pain in *one* spot on his body wasn't enough.

"So...good."

"I know."

"So...tight."

"I know."

"Yessss."

"*No.*"

He backed it up with a growl of torment but purpose, pushing the sound through his body until he was able to shove back—and all the way out.

CHAPTER ELEVEN

"No!"

Tracy shivered uncontrollably. He wasn't there anymore. Not inside her, not even next to her. The walls of her core clenched from the loss. Her inner thighs ached, needing his to spread them again.

Confusion hit—followed at once by indignation. She drilled him with the force of both, finally propelling up and then leaning on her elbows.

"John? What the hell?"

"Don't. Move."

He bolted off the bed before she could process the command. Not that he made it easy, suddenly shucking all the way out of his pants.

Holy. God.

In a life full of jaw-dropping moments, Tracy was certain this one was already on the Top Ten list. He was more magnificent than she'd anticipated, with toned hips dipping in before the flare of his taut ass and bold thighs. They weren't "gym thighs," either. The striations in his legs could only have been developed from years of brutal training and fierce team missions. But all of that was just a prelude to the main focal point. His penis, broad and proud, was the color of rich bourbon, supported by balls in a taut sack. The tip bobbed toward the rippled perfection of his abdomen, exposed in all its glory when he crisscrossed his arms and then peeled away the T-shirt as well.

Before she could help it, Tracy profusely wetted her lips. "Not. Moving," she managed to rasp in response to his order—and meant it. Especially if this was the view she received as her obedience reward.

"You will be in a minute." Franz faced her again. His gaze turned to smoke as it roamed the length of her body. Wetting his own lips, he fisted his gorgeous erection. "You'll be moving in ways you never thought of, woman."

Breathe. Breathe. Breathe.

It became a necessary mantra in response to his Scotch-smooth voice. The tone completed the whisky spectrum of his sexiness, and now she couldn't wait to get batshit drunk on him...

Meaning she nearly moaned aloud as he disappeared into the bathroom.

What the hell now?

Her answer came quickly—in the form of distinct sounds. The opening of a cabinet. His rustling hand. His rough snort of victory. The rip of a foil wrapper.

He swooped back around the corner like he'd actually sprung dragon wings and was coming in for a landing. A cocky smile now curled his lips—and an unwrapped condom was perched between two of his long fingers.

"Thank the gods for dudes who use rubbers for more than one purpose."

Tracy cocked her head. Sneaked a wry glance up at him. "Do I even want to know the details about that?"

A small tic vibrated his jaw. "Depends."

"On what?"

"On whether you like to play with clean toys."

She dropped her gaze—while her heart bypassed a few beats. The subtle pause he took before his last word, and then the way he emphasized it with a vat of sensual intent, didn't exactly fill her vision with alphabet blocks and Tinker Toys to mind.

It *did* give her inspiration for a comeback feeling just as sexy—and a little scary.

"All kittens love toys, don't they?"

The good kind of scary.

Franz's nostrils flared. His lips parted, setting free a heavy hiss. The moment the sound hit the air, Tracy's nipples tightened again. She sat up, using the motion to scissor her legs, granting pitifully little relief to the pressure pulsing anew between her thighs. He only worsened the ordeal with his sudden lunge over, securing her by one of her wrists and yanking her toward the edge of the bed.

Holy hell.

How this man could go from flirty rogue one moment to fierce conqueror the next... It was as crazy as contemplating Texas weather changes and just as idiotic to fight. As if she even wanted to. The weather always gave her an excuse to just accept. To just embrace. To just surrender...

As his hold, his stare, and his stance commanded of her right now.

And then his movement—

Pressing the rolled condom into her hand.

"All right, sweet kitty. Make *me* your toy, then." He curled a knee up on the bed, angling his swollen length closer to her. "Get it on me, *popoki*. As incredible as it was to ride you bareback, we've got to be responsible. You deserve the important shit."

Important shit.

She smiled, unable to help it. She was likely making too much of nothing, but it felt damn good to be "important" just because she was a woman. A lover. A person. *His* person, if only just for now. His protected kitten.

Who now felt about as clumsy as one too. "I—ummm..."

He pressed a hand to her cheek. "What? It's all right. Just say it."

She drew in a breath. While letting it out, she fitted the cap of the latex around the top of his cock. "I— It's just been awhile for me..."

"You're doing fine, *ku`uipo.*" It rolled out on a deep groan. "Ahhh...*yeah.*" His head fell back. "Better than fine." He tunneled his hand into her hair. "Roll it on, nice and tight. Your fingers...they're so perfect..."

"*You're* so perfect," she whispered.

She finished sheathing him but didn't want to let go. It wasn't the first time she'd done this—she and Ryker had been all about condoms for a few months—but either her memory was fading or this simple act had never seemed so sexy. *Ever.* The way Franzen moaned, deeper and deeper, as her touch advanced down his erection. The way his hips convulsed and his ass tightened. The tension in his whole body...even the way his masculine nipples jutted as his head jacked back...

"Damn, woman. *Damn.*"

She smiled again. Soared her gaze up all his incredible muscles. "I want to make you feel so good."

He choked out a laugh while bringing his head back around—though his smile was gone. His face was harshly hewn by just one element now. Lust.

"Then do it." He brought his other knee up, centering his

beautiful body in front of her...guiding her mouth to the base of his engorged length. "Take my balls in your beautiful mouth. Worship them with your tongue and lips."

Forget about weather change worries. The air was a steam bath, coating her whole body in aroused dew, as she leaned in to comply with his filthy request. As if his hand, now bracing the back of her neck, would allow anything else.

She sighed, sucking him in by one orb and then the other.

Franz groaned, curling his hold tighter.

Beneath her lips, his balls pulsed and squeezed. His skin stretched and trembled. "Damn. *Yes*. Take them both at once, kitten. Make them fill your mouth."

He pushed at the corner of her lips, prodding the joint to open wider. Tracy closed her eyes, focusing on every tender tongue stroke she gave him and the powerful shudders of his body in return. She'd never done this for a man before—and recognized that dearth as a mistake. Serving him like this... meant she actually owned him. Every jerk of his hips, snarl from his mouth, and coil of his muscles was because she made it so, with the pressure of her mouth and the flicks of her tongue. Never had she felt more powerful. More alive.

"*Fuck*. Just like that." He palmed her cheek with his other hand, cupping the bulge of himself there. "Feel that heat? That's my come, and you're heating it up—so I can fuck it into you." He slid his hand in, stroking his sheathed cock. "I won't be able to hold back much longer. You're driving me crazy with that nasty mouth of yours. Making me want to get this dick deep inside you..."

His words faded into a snarl as Tracy suctioned his balls with force. As they trembled on the back of her tongue, the man himself tensed. Even his hand stilled along his shaft. The moguls of his abdomen contracted, and the logs of his thighs turned into sleek striations.

After several brutal breaths, he finally uttered, "Little. Minx." The words intoned enough vehemence that she looked up, eyes wide—

But not as wide as they got as he pulled her head away from his body and then flipped all of hers over.

Astonishment shot through her veins as her breasts smashed to the coverlet, her head landed to the side, and her legs were fiercely kicked open. "Oh," she finally blurted. "Oh... my—*oh*!"

Her stunned cry came with the clench of his hands around her wrists. He used the hold to flatten her arms next to her head.

"Gorgeous." His dark puma growl roughened the shell of her ear as his fingers laced with hers, pushing hard at her hands. "Keep them here, *popoki*. I need my own hands for... other things."

Hurried gulp. "Other...things? Like what?"

His hands were already back at her shoulders. Along her spine. Kneading the small of her back. She swallowed again, in hopes the action would help her breath return. Dear *God*, how his touch enflamed her. How his fingers thrilled every inch of skin they covered. How her body became the lava that had coated her from the depths of his penetrating, nearly punishing, stare.

"Like...this."

His second word was emphasized with a slap.

On her left ass cheek.

"And maybe...this."

Another—to her right.

Lava wasn't the right way to describe anything now. "*Oh*," she rasped again, using the position of her arms to push up, twist, and cock a look backward—

As the man smacked her again, left and then right.

Her stunned stare dropped from his rugged face to the pinkened spheres where his hands rested. *Holy shit.* The sight was...pretty damn hot. Much more arousing than she'd expected, especially as he began massaging the skin he'd just struck. The sensual sweeps, radiating heat through her hips and upper thighs, drove her gaze back up to his face. Most importantly to the black darts of his brows and the need all but glowing from the gaze beneath.

She felt her lips move apart, letting out shaky air. She'd intended words to accompany it, an incensed "what the hell" at least, but her brain couldn't fabricate a damn syllable. She was mesmerized. Melted. And, in a strange, unexplainable way...

Changed.

"I...see," she finally succeeded in saying. Well, in whispering, but semantics were definitely not a priority right now.

Franzen's stare climbed slowly up her body. With equal deliberation, he countered, "Do you?"

"I..." She licked her lips. "Well, I think so. I—"

"Tracy."

"What?"

"Do you want more?"

She pulled in a puzzled breath. There it was again. The same feeling she'd known when he was in her mouth—only now, the man was handing her the power under different circumstances.

Now, he was asking her to give it right back.

If she said yes...she had a feeling he wouldn't be asking anymore.

Her mind whirled. What would that feel like? To be relieved of that choice? To be freed from having to decide about anything, if only for a little while. To even think.

Being commanded...only to feel...

"I..."

"Tracy."

"Huh?"

"There isn't a right or wrong answer here." His hands parted, sliding to the outside of her hips. "I'm still going to fuck your beautiful body, kitten. You only have to tell me if you'd like me to hurt it a little too."

The bottom fell out of her stomach. But not with nausea. With sensations she never could have imagined, racing each other for possession of her thoughts, her will—both seeming to fly somewhere outside herself right now anyway.

The anomaly felt...

Really good.

"Hurt it," she finally repeated. Her voice wasn't hers either, a soft and strangled sound. "You mean...spank it again."

"For now? Yes."

"For *now*? What do you—"

A harsh sound punched from his chest, cutting her off. "Thoughts back to here and now, *ku'uipo*. We're not negotiating a long-term contract."

She scowled at the subtle inflection of his last sentence. "Because you've done *those* before, for this kind of thing?"

She almost wanted him to say yes. To magically produce a pair of handcuffs from somewhere, lock them around her wrists, and then force her to sign the damn thing while he spanked more of that incredible heat into her backside. He accommodated her on half the fantasy, at least. As his hands landed two more blows to her cheeks, both at once this time, she let out a censuring yelp—mellowing into a savoring sigh.

Shit. Shit. Shit.

The kitten had let her cat out of the bag.

A fact *not* missed by the man in bed with her.

Who, just as swiftly, turned the kitten back into his prey.

She'd barely blinked before his hand invaded her hair again, twisting in the damp strands and yanking her head back—for the merciless plunge of his mouth. There was no polite pause to part her lips or testing to see if she was ready for his kiss. He invaded her with it, leaving no part of her untouched by it. He was inside her mouth, sweeping and ravaging, taking even the particles of her breath—and certainly the threads of her rational thoughts.

It was just short of an attack.

It was one step from heaven.

Minutes passed—maybe hours, she didn't care—before he released her. Tracy descended, limp and gasping, back down to her original position on the coverlet.

"All right, then," the dark predator murmured, somewhere above her. While his voice trickled into her mind as if in a fog, his touch registered in her senses like piercing blades of sun. "I'm going to make this ass as pink and plump as the cunt I'm going to fuck. Think that'll take at least ten more swats, kitten—on each side."

Belly flip time again. Only this time, accompanied by a slice of fear in her heart...and a clench of arousal through her pussy.

From the midst of that crazy chaos, her mind managed to

push words to her lips. "Yes...Sir."

The predator rumbled, making her think of a pacing puma in those shafts of sun. "Oh, that's so nice. Such a pretty little sound, *popoki*." His hands soothed across her buttocks, spreading and rubbing, gradually easing her legs farther apart. Tracy moaned and shook as he neared her quivering center, taking teasing sweeps over the flesh around her intimate core. How did he do this to her? How did he simply *know* the exact places to caress her, tease her...control her? "Oh, sweet woman. You *are* ready for the pleasure, aren't you?"

"Yes." Wasn't necessary to think or hesitate about that one. Ready? She'd leapt past "ready," hovering somewhere in the ether between needy and nearly passing out. Her sex hadn't missed one tantalizing second every time he'd deftly passed, her clit perking for his fingers like a flower sprouting for the spring sun. Only inside, she was a flood. A rainstorm of arousal, drenching everything between her womb and her clit. "Yes...please!" she panted. "I—I need—"

"Say it all." He drew one finger in a tiny circle at her dripping entrance. "I want the pleasure..."

Her hands fisted the bed cover. She forced her mind to push through the forest fire of arousal, twirling the flames into words. "I want...the pleasure."

"But I also want the pain."

"But I also want—"

Holy shit.

What the *hell* was she agreeing to?

"I also...want the..."

She was interrupted by a ruthless crack.

The blow of the man's first real spank on her bottom.

"Shit!"

It spilled before she could even think—when she did, weirdly thanking God for Luke and his loud video games— and process the hot stings now radiating from her ass to her hip and thigh. A second later, he delivered the same agony to her other side. Two more spanks followed to each side before Tracy could even remember this was just the start. Seven more swats loomed ahead.

Hell no.

No matter how much her skin now felt like strands of glowing, turned-on heat...or how her senses rejoiced in his deep, satisfied snarl...or how every nerve in her body danced, antsy with anticipation for his next commanding smack...

Hell, no.

She didn't want this. She couldn't...

But she did.

Because as number four came, then number five, her skin still smarted...but her brain began doing something different. Something freaky, fuzzy...a haze of warmth and arousal like nothing she'd ever experienced before...

The man didn't just bring the sun anymore.

He *was* the sun.

Dazzling her. Drenching her. Burning her.

And then, sizzling into her once more. Stabbing through her soft folds, into her weeping tunnel, edging his heat inside, as he delivered the final swats to set her ass fully on fire.

"Can't...wait," came his desire-filled grate. "Need inside you. Need to...fuck you. Now."

A moan answered him, shrill and submissive, but she wasn't sure where it came from. Her responses weren't her own right now. Her damn *mind* wasn't her own. And her body? Long past obeying what she craved—or thought she did.

She'd let the man spank her. Many times. Had lain here and gasped as he burned each blow into her skin—and now, rejoiced as he parted her pussy lips, making way for his cock to fill her body in a single, brutal slide.

At last.

Everything quaked as his flesh took over hers... recalibrating her body to the hard demand of his. Her tissues wept and clenched around him. Her ass burned as he lunged deeper, stabbing his cock in long, brutal strokes. Her consciousness was a smoky mist, latticed by the brilliance of his sexual sun.

"Hang on." He enforced the order by sinking his teeth into the back of her neck. "Can't help it. I'm going to take you so damn hard, kitten."

Tracy groaned. He wasn't doing that already?

Took him just another thrust to supply that answer. He secured her head with one splayed hand while ramming so deep, she felt his balls trying to squeeze into her passage too. Before she could recover enough from the shock to react, he glided out—and then did it again.

"Holy..."

Words left her then.

And the sobs took over.

Primal. Carnal. Born in a part of her truly incapable of thought or logic or existing beyond the visceral heaven and hell of this moment. Her mind left her, turning her body into a plank of pure feeling, accepting all the brilliance and boldness her predator had to give.

And he gave.

Fire, in every driving, dominant slide of his cock.

Rain, in every hot gush from her tunnel and wet quiver of her clit.

Air, in the completion they reached for together. The crash of passion, as her world finally welcomed his sun...

And was incinerated for it.

"That's it." His lips burned the words into her ear as his body surrounded her, slick with sweat and hard with desire. "Give it to me, woman. Every drop of it."

The tremors started, hot and searing, from deep inside. Shot to her sex like sun flares, scorching everything they touched, until everything was a bursting, blazing tongue of fiery need. She hissed from the urgency, arching her head back, needing exactly the contact John waited with. His mouth caught her, saving her. His tongue pulled her, clinching her—

Before his lips gave the words to deliver her.

"Scream," he ordered in a soft snarl. His breaths pumped into her in the same rhythm as his cock. "Let it go. Nobody will hear. I'll make sure of it, kitten." He dipped in harder, ravaging her mouth in brutal command. "Scream," he commanded again against her lips. "*Scream for me.*"

Her breaths faltered. He'd plunged so deep inside her body, but how had he found his way into her psyche too? How had he known about the tiny corner of composure to which she'd clung, hoping he wouldn't see or notice once his own pleasure had come and gone? The man had to be close. She wondered if the condom was even holding together, he'd swollen so huge inside her.

Big enough to punch into her soul, as well.

Then seeing it.

Then demanding it.

Commanding her to give him even that now.

Knowing she'd no longer be able to resist. Especially if he angled himself down into her a little higher...then pushed extra hard, pinning her pelvis until her clit smashed against the coverlet—

She screamed for him.

She screamed *into* him.

He latched their mouths harder as soon as the orgasm hit, keeping her grounded even as her body shot like a rocket into an ether of white-hot bliss. For every wave of her pleasure, John had another trio of savoring growls—until one overrode them all, mighty and masculine, as he pounded her so hard, the smacks of their bodies were almost as loud as his punishing foreplay.

Oh, God.

His foreplay.

Thoughts of it all—the spanks, the ferocity, his commitment, his command—washed another climax upon her, toppling the first. But there was no scream this time. There was only the silent, intense, straining surrender...the surety that everything she once was had just been demolished, and somehow, in some way, she'd have to resurrect a new Tracy from the pile of those sated cinders. Even if she didn't want to.

Which was why, the moment Franz rose to get rid of the condom, she forced her muscles to work once more. With a tight groan, she rolled to her back—but was only pushed back to her elbows when the man reentered from the bathroom.

"Well, isn't *this* a nice dessert." He crossed the tattooed masterpieces the rest of the world knew as his arms. To her, they had entirely new definitions—especially the hands and fingers into which they tapered.

She swallowed, pushing those thoughts back. *Way* back. With a soft huff, she rolled toward the end of the bed—

Until her ankle was seized by one of the hands she'd been fantasizing about.

"Hey!"

"Hey?" How had he moved with the same measured calm as his voice? He was like a damn ninja...

"What are you doing?"

"Where *you* going?"

"John."

"Tracy."

"Let me go."

"Answer my question."

She expelled a long breath. At least he hadn't used one of those nicknames, infused with the island accent capable of melting her like sugar in water. Right now, she'd take any scrap of strength she could get. "You know where I'm going. This—you—were—"

"What?" His voice was like his hold. Gentle but ready to clench if he had to. Strangely, it made her feel...safe. Secure enough to preface her answer with a soft laugh.

"Truth? I was trying to think of a better superlative than *incredible*, *amazing*, or *mind-blowing*."

He twisted his hand, moving his thumb in order to stroke the curve of her ankle. "Which is why you're trying to leave before your blood pressure returns to normal?"

Humor, exit stage right. Arrogant god who knew he'd just fucked a woman's mind into next Tuesday? Enter stage left. "My blood pressure is fine."

"Tell that to the pulse in your neck. And the flush on your face."

"Tell *that* to my *life*, Captain Franzen."

He slid his hand away.

Leaving a gulf of silence behind.

Silence bearing a weird mix of shit for her. Regret but

indignation. Flinging out the formality, when her body was still flushed from sex she couldn't find a descriptor for? Not so copasetic. But neither was his clingy act, when all they'd done was find a great way for relieving a little tension.

Okay, a lot of tension.

In a *really* great way.

"Your life?" Though he'd dropped the hand, he remained close to the bed. Too damn close. His voice persisted with the intimacy too. *Damn it.* "You mean the life that officially doesn't exist right now?"

Double damn it.

She rocked her head back on her shoulders. Tore the man's own page from his own playbook, crossing her arms and steeling her features. "For an island boy, you sure as hell know how to skate on thin ice."

If the guy was smart, he'd recognize that as the Zamboni truck on his ice and clear off.

The guy was *not* smart.

His own head shifted on its shoulders—to lean over her with lips all but snickering. Even more stupid, as he fitted those lips atop hers. The *king* of stupid, as he caught the hand she raised with intention to shove him the hell off.

"For an island boy," he murmured, as soon as they pulled apart, "I'm also being pretty *lolo* for a mainland *wahine*."

Tracy twisted free from his grip—but her hand didn't drop. It was drawn, like a damn electromagnet, toward the muscled slope between his neck and shoulder. "But she can't be *lolo* for you." She dug in with her nails, underlining the ache of her retort. "Because her life *will* have to exist again one day... and she'll be somewhat of a working mom."

Franz laid his chuff atop her watery laugh. "Somewhat."

He drew a hand across his chest as if pledging an allegiance, only his fingers ended atop her hand. The pressure in his hold was the physical form of the new texture in his gaze. Quiet reassurance...penetrating attention...as if he were trying to memorize her...

Though she already knew *she'd* never forget *him*. Tried, probably in vain, to tell him with her deeper grip into his neck. She didn't even care about marking him now. Perhaps even wished she did.

"John..." Leaden swallow. *Why* was this so hard? They'd had fun. He'd even been a big boy, ensuring that was all it could be. "I'm—I'm sorry."

"Why?" The query was sincere.

"You deserve..." She looked away. "More than this. So much more."

He unpeeled her hand off his neck. Dragged it forward so he could press lips to the inside of her wrist. The whole time, the dark certitude of his stare didn't falter. "But right now, this is all I want. So..." He hitched the top of his head toward the artistically arranged pillows against the headboard. "Let me have just a few minutes more?"

Tracy giggled. Couldn't be helped. There was plenty of cocky arrogance left in the silken words, but they were also husky...in all the right ways. Grating just enough to nick at the edges of her heart, exactly as he'd tempted the fringe of her libido...until there was nothing left to resist him with.

As she nestled with him under the covers, she mitigated her actions by knowing Luke was, for the moment, safe and happy with Zeke Hayes and Ethan Archer nearby. Gem and Ronnie were probably still passed out where she'd left them, with nothing left to do but wait until Sol contacted them through the dark channels he and Franz had established.

So in several ways, the smug bastard was right.

For all intents and purposes, her life was still pretty much a giant blank.

Which was kind of funny...considering she couldn't remember the last time she felt this perfectly sated.

And finally, *at last*, exhausted.

Recognizing, as she yawned and settled her cheek against a warm, hard slab of pectoral muscle, that sleep was a lot like Keoni John Franzen. Best when simply surrendered to.

CHAPTER TWELVE

She even mesmerized him when she was asleep.

Especially when he was the one who'd exhausted her like this.

Yeah, that probably turned him into fifteen kinds of a creeper-stalker bozo dork, but right now, Franz was ready to let that freak flag fly. He hadn't been able to help a bunch of lingering gawks even when they weren't in the same bed together, and now with her just inches away, he flipped a mental middle finger at the resistance.

It was time to indulge because it would soon be time to give this up.

Yeah, even the gawking.

He noticed the things that always turned him crazy caveman for her, of course. The wild tumble of her brown-sugar hair. The sleek curves of her mouth, expressive as hell even as she slept, twitching as if even her subconscious was dictating to-do lists. The determined line of her jaw, turning into the elegant line of her neck, becoming the beginning of her slender shoulders...

A sight drawing him to all the details he didn't know yet.

The sprays of light freckles across both those shoulders. Her really long fingers. Her really big ears. The fact that he'd never believed in heart-shaped faces before confronting the truth, beautiful and breathtaking, in hers.

He looked longer, determined now. He wanted to discover

it all—but at the same time, knew he never would. The woman was going to be his president yet still looked at so many things about the world, and people, as if they were brand-new. Many people mistook that as naiveté, discounting her because of it. Many others were captivated by it, as he'd seen firsthand in Zeke and Rayna when they'd arrived last night. He wondered how the crowd in DC split on those spectrums, though from what he knew of politicians, he guessed the former—and barely muffled a snarl of outrage because of it.

Not that the heavy huff with which he replaced it any better, proved by the restless twitches of Tracy's lashes. She interrupted her dreamtime list-making with a harsh shake of her head, a move Franz recognized at once. He'd made the same move himself, having to haul his brain from sound asleep to wide awake in seconds. Most days he still woke up the same way, only to be pissed he couldn't break the habit.

The woman's face contorted with the same frustration. He didn't know whether to be delighted or aggravated about it. She was still so gorgeous, even in her ire, he almost expected cartoon birds to flit in and help with little ribbons in her hair—which made no sense at all, considering he hadn't seen a cartoon in a long goddamn time.

"Oh." She murmured it as if answering a question to herself, also a move he understood. After realizing she wasn't in the bed of her mind's default—for him, it was always the futon on the back-garden lanai at home—she'd likely wondered where she was and then fast-tracked the memory up to now. That'd explain her sudden flush as well as the embarrassed flicker of her gaze around the room.

Anywhere but at him.

"*Aloha, ku`uipo.*" He went on, answering the query in her

eyes, "It translates to something like *sweetheart* or *adored one*."

She accepted the information with a thoughtful smile. Shot him a tiny side-eye before murmuring, "You have an interesting way of 'adoring' a woman, Captain."

He nestled his head on a bent elbow. Contemplated the woman with a look of raw fascination. How had this happened? She'd thrown out the formality as a conversational spike strip, but it had failed. Though he saw through her ploy, he wasn't pissed by it. He was challenged. Captivated. And hard as a damn rock.

Why?

Was it just her voice? The ribbon of it, like sleek satin on one side and a wild animal print on the other, was a great start but not the whole story. Not by half. It was her. The more he learned about her, the more he realized he *didn't* know—but craved to. Like the covers tucked under her arms, exposing enough to make him lustful for more, he longed to pull back what she still concealed in her heart, her soul, her spirit. He wanted to know it all...

"I receive a lot of interesting feedback too."

She laughed softly—and kept her gaze averted. "I imagine you do."

"What about...yours?"

"My what?"

Screw it. He couldn't resist reaching to her anymore. That blush, flowing down her neck, enticed him to stroke in its wake. He ran his knuckles down her carotid and across her exposed collarbone, submersing a growl as he brushed the rose of a lingering bite mark on her shoulder. *His* bite mark.

Damn, yes.

"Your feedback." He flowed the touch over until capturing

her opposite cheek with his thumb—and tugging her gaze his direction. "How are you doing?"

Her brows knitted. Her stare centered on his nose. *Damn it.* "Why are you asking?"

John grunted. Wasn't the first time he'd encountered avoidance, though he'd never been in a position where he couldn't simply command it out of a woman. In so many ways, this wasn't what he was used to after spanking, biting, and then fucking a woman.

Well, shit.

He was going to actually work at this.

To...communicate.

How hard could it be?

He pulled in a deep breath. Where did this shit usually start?

Finally he ventured, "I pushed you...a little."

"A little?"

"All right. A lot?"

He didn't know what to do when she broke out in a full laugh. While the sound was gorgeous, winding its way around his cock like a longer length of her verbal ribbon, it was perplexing as hell.

What the fuck did she mean?

At least she didn't make him wait long for an explanation. "Been at this Dominance stuff awhile, mister?"

If that could be called an explanation.

Instead of deciphering her sarcasm, he decided to call her bluff and go in with the truth. "Actually, I have."

Target acquired.

Three seconds, and the full solemnity of his assertion hit her between the eyes. Her mirth faded though left a lingering spark in her eyes as she uttered, "Well, you're damn good at it."

"Thank you." He was serious about that too—bringing a hit of shock. He hated compliments. Distrusted the majority of them. Empty words for empty feelings. Why not be more plain about it? *Manners. Etiquette.* Why not just be kind to each other? Why did people have to do it while picking up the right fork at the same time?

He refocused after the rumination, to find an interesting sight waiting. His *ku`uipo*, finally gazing into his eyes. Hers still possessed silvery flecks, turning them into gorgeous lightning bolts of interest.

"John?"

He smiled.

John.

"Yes?"

"Are you really—" She stopped, visibly gritting her teeth. "I—I mean—"

"Am I really what?" He bumped up to his elbow, leveraging his position to loom over her a little. Yes, it was on purpose. And yes, it felt damn good to be repositioned for command. And *hell* yes, it felt good to watch the change in her own mien... the velvet welcome in the depths of her gaze.

Despite her physical response, Tracy sucked in a determined breath before confessing, "A Dominant." She rushed the rest out. "I mean, in *that* way. Okay, not that way bad, but that way just in...well, *that* way."

He embraced his turn to laugh. "You mean, in the way that I can tie knots seventy ways though I'm not a squid? And how I like the word 'play room' for more than video games?"

"Uh, yeah." A breath burst from her, sounding a lot like relief. Or perhaps...excitement. God, could he really hope

175

for the latter? Or did he dread it? "That'd be...exactly what I mean."

He scooted closer to her. Cocked his head, making sure he still had her full focus. This was probably the first time he'd just blurted the shit to anyone.

"I've been interested in the lifestyle since college," he began. "Researched it there a little too, though I was too young to visit any clubs and too scared to try it with girlfriends."

She waved a dismissive hand. "Consider yourself spared. Women are messes in college anyway."

"And us *kānes* are any better?"

"Valid point." The corners of her mouth curled up. "So... how'd you get *un*-scared?" She tugged teeth at one of those delectable corners. "Asking for a friend, of course."

"Sure." He smirked. "For a 'friend.'" He held her gaze despite her deepening blush, determined to soak up as much of its double meaning as he could. The good girl in her, still unwilling to accept all she'd let him do, fought for a peace accord with the filthy woman who wanted to let him do more.

He could only hope.

"Okay." She smacked his shoulder. "Stop gloating."

"I'm *not* gloating."

She huffed. "Sure. Because you just look like the Dom who ate the sub's lunch *all* the time?"

He pushed in closer over her. Palmed the side of her face. "Your lunch isn't what I'm hungry for, kitten."

Her breath caught. Her lips parted. Only as he inhaled, scenting the honey of her arousal even through the covers, did he reconsider the pass on the gloat. The need got worse as she swallowed, clearly pushing her mind back to rational thought again. "Stop it."

"Stop what?"

"Trying to change the subject."

Franz cocked his head. Tried to go ahead on the gloat but instead, muttered with total sincerity, "What *was* the subject?"

Funnily, his bafflement seemed to soothe her anxiety. Maybe she just needed to take back some control of the discussion. Rebalance things.

Or maybe...

This communication stuff was as just much an ordeal for her.

A thought not bringing half the shock he expected.

A conclusion actually making a lot of sense.

The same way Franz had been insulated in his world, she'd been cushioned in hers. Yeah, she'd only been at it for a few years as opposed to eleven, but everyone knew Capitol Hill time was like dog years. Out of whack and mysterious to explain. Maybe he really wasn't the only one trying to hike unfamiliar territory here.

"We were talking about you," she finally prompted. "And being...scared." She paused to insert a puzzled pout before the last word. "And I still can't believe I just did that."

"Did what?"

"Mashed *you* and *scared* into the same sentence."

He let out a snort. "I'm scared all the time, woman."

"The hell you are."

"We *all* are." He shifted his hold, gliding his thumb up to her brow line, giving him an excuse to lock his gaze with hers again. "Fear is part of the human experience. What turns the experience into triumph is what a person does with their fear... how they channel it." Sure enough, as her eyes glittered with comprehension, he turned his hand over to stroke the side of her cheek. "Like everything *you* did after your husband was killed."

A tiny sound clucked up her throat. Tracy shook her head, looking as bored as a socialite as a charity ball. "Ohhhh no, no, no. We're not making this about me."

Franzen hummed. "Right. It's about the 'friend' you're asking for."

"The friend who wants to know more about Dominance and submission, *not* listen to the violins backing my damn life story—*again*."

"Because she already knows it as if she's lived it?"

"Because she's as sick of it as me." Her hands twisted into the top of the blanket. "In another time or another world, it would all be a bad Sunday afternoon TV movie anyway." She jabbed two fingers into air quotes. "'Widow of slain engineer becomes activist for foreign aid workers; ends up getting appointed vice president. Tune in at two for all the excitement.'"

"I see what you mean."

"Right?" If she saw or heard his irony, she wasn't admitting to it. "All that's missing are the stalker ex-boyfriend and the secret baby."

"But that doesn't mean you—errmm, your *friend*—shouldn't look to all that for her inspiration."

"For understanding BDSM?"

"For understanding fear."

She was as lost with his explanation as she was with the irony—only this time, realized it. "Huh?"

Her gaze jumped at him, open and questioning. Franz answered her with equal frankness and an answer he hoped would make sense.

"Your husband...he was killed in Iraq, right?" He kept the words crisp but his hold tender, hating himself for bringing even the tiny shards of pain in her eyes. Dredging up her grief wasn't his purpose but momentarily necessary in proving his point. The second she got out a shaky nod, he went on. "And I'll bet, after all that went down, you were a thousand kinds of terrified, yeah?"

Tracy swallowed. Twisted the blanket tighter. But her new nod conveyed the weight of her trust in where he was taking this—and filled him with such deep warmth, he wondered how he'd accepted a life without it for so long.

"But instead of wallowing in the fear, you chose to turn and face it."

She snorted. "*Chose?*" A wry smile formed. "I was running a small business and raising a ten-year-old boy. Nothing was a choice for me, John."

"*Ku`uipo.*" He underlined it by grabbing one of her hands. "Getting up in the damn morning became a choice for you." Her twisting lips wanted to argue, but her tearful eyes confirmed his allegation. "But instead of retreating into your grief, you picked breaking out of your shell. *Way* out."

The grimace made its way up her face, except for the trust she continued in her gaze. He was doing what she'd forbade, all but writing the script for the straight-to-cable movie, but for now, she was willing to follow him. "I couldn't *not* do anything. Everyone justified the decisions of those indie contractors by the buckets of cash they got paid. They were being painted as mercenaries. Many, like Ryker, would have done it for half the money."

"And you wanted Washington to know that."

"Damn straight I did."

"Why didn't you just write a letter?"

She shot a shrill laugh. "Yeah, that's a good one—just like the response I got to the *eight* letters I *did* try."

"So you chose to take the fight to DC's door."

She winced once more. Scooted herself into a sitting position against the headboard. "You keep saying I 'chose' to do those things. But—" Her own huff interrupted it. "Fine. I guess I see it now. I did have a choice. But at the time, it sure as hell didn't feel like that."

"Of course not." He readjusted his own position, angling an arm across her body. Because of that, he was able to lean a few more inches into her personal space. "You were compelled by a power higher than you—in that case, your allegiance to Ryker's memory—and it motivated you to push beyond your fears, all the way to Capitol Hill."

She huffed softly. "But I wasn't afraid."

He grunted louder. "Liar."

"I'm serious!"

"Remember who you're talking to, gorgeous?" He tipped his head forward. "The guy who watched you break out in a cold sweat before a sound check in front of twenty staffers and a lame-as-hell sound crew?"

Who, now that he really thought about it, weren't the seasoned union guys who should have been hired for such a high-profile event. Curious...

"Fine," she finally muttered, adding a hard enough *mmpphh* of punctuation, the blanket lost its hold on her breasts. If she noticed the slip, she was too irked to care—and Franz sure as fuck wasn't going to complain.

Still, he plunged on with the point. "You were scared, Tracy. It's not a mortal sin. I've spent the better part of the last eleven years being scared."

She was probably the third person, outside the team, to whom he'd ever offered the confession. First, there weren't a lot of people who knew exactly what he did in the army. Out of the people who did know, like Maki, Nani, and Lino, no way would they accept their "Big John," ready to take on everything from ten-foot snakes to twelve-foot waves, had a fear-filled moment in his life. But when a guy specialized in unconventional warfare for a living, fear came in shapes and sizes that also broke the rules.

But if any civilian was going to get that, it would be Tracy Rhodes.

A gamble she proved worthy of, with the gentle hand she lifted to the center of his chest. "But you've had another power pushing you too?"

"Yeah." He inhaled deeply. Exhaled the same way. "A lady I love deeply." Before the troubled glint in her eyes got too intense, he clarified, "Her name is America."

Her stare softened, turning the shade of morning mist, even as her fingers pressed his chest with more purpose. "So fear isn't always such a bad thing."

The warmth she'd begun, augmented by the gift of her touch, was too good not to reciprocate. He hoped his fingers spread the same magic back through her. "Fear can be *good*, kitten." Then, because he couldn't help it, he slid his fingertips toward her cleavage. "Even exciting." Slipping lower still... "And...explosive."

"Explosive?" Though her rebuttal was sultry, the pulse at the base of her neck was a wild tattoo against her skin. "That too, hmm?"

"That too." He nudged the blanket down, exposing one

gorgeous, rosy nipple. His kitten didn't protest. With their gazes still fastened, he trailed his fingers over, tugging lightly at the tip. "With the right power pushing the choices."

His voice faded into a seductive hiss as she began breathing harder. The motion, pushing her breast deeper against his hand, inspired her telling gasp. "I think I'm beginning to understand."

"Yeah?" He murmured it with a slow smirk—while pushing down the other side of the blanket. It fell to her waist, forming a fabric puddle around the creamy perfection of her torso. *Fuck*. New blood rushed to his dick, as he envisioned tasting every inch of skin he could see. But first things first. He moved in, closing his whole hand around her breast this time. "Feels good, doesn't it? Leaving the choices to a power you trust? A Dominant who only has your pleasure as their priority?"

Though her body was all but undulating in his hold, her gaze captured his with its stunning clarity. She asked, not shy about her curiosity at all now, "Are you speaking from past experience, Sir?"

"You'd know the answer to that if you felt what your sweet 'Sir' just did to me, kitten."

"Errr...sorry?"

"Like hell you are," he drawled, when her demure grin and dancing gaze betrayed her delight in having grabbed him in the balls. "But we'll discuss that in a minute."

To back it up, he tightened his muscles and focused on the overture of *Cats*. Cats on their own merit? Coolest animals on the planet. But people acting like cats on a stage, in linty costumes through a nonexistent plot? Excellent dick limpening stuff—especially when her query deserved a fuller answer.

"When I first fully dove into Dominance and submission, I explored the idea I might be a switch." When her brows furrowed in a new question from *that*, he explained, "Someone who enjoys power exchange from both ends of the spectrum."

Her head jolted back a little. "Why the hell would you even consider yourself a submissive?"

So much for matted cat fur replacing what she could do to him. Her unflinching vote in his Dominant box was all it took to roar that part of himself back to the surface. Still, she deserved more of an explanation from him. An assurance he wasn't some creep hiding behind a uniform but a guy who believed in the beauty of the BDSM dynamic.

"When you're young, you're already confused," he began. "I mean, I knew I was into women a lot like my mom and two sisters, who were smart and strong-willed—and all but worshiped around our house. My pops wouldn't allow my brother and me to get away with anything less."

Tracy brought her head back down. Fingered the ends of her auburn waves. "So you had a substantial male role model as well."

"Hell, yeah."

"So you freaked when discovering you wanted to dominate women."

He chuffed. "That's one way of putting it."

Her brows drew together. "What's another way?"

"How about, I all but wrote off my chances for getting accepted into Special Operations?"

"Whaaaat?" She half-giggled it.

"Truth." He held up two fingers, scouts honor style. "I was certain they'd rout it out during the psych eval and toss me out for being a Class-A, sadistic perv." As he lowered his fingers, he cracked a smirk. "Quickly learned if that were the case, half the world would be tossed out too."

"Now that *doesn't* surprise me."

"Well, it did me," he returned. "Enough to keep learning about the lifestyle as well as the elements about myself that were drawing me to it."

Tracy's face changed. While the elegant angles softened, the interest in her gaze got bolder. Wow. If this was half the ju-ju she threw at the guys on the Hill, no wonder she already enjoyed a reputation for getting things done. "That was a pretty brave decision," she told him with matching intensity.

He attempted a shrug, but the action was all wrong, a casual write-off for a significant moment. She was right. It *had* been brave, only he'd been trivializing that until now. Until speaking a truth he'd never really put into words for anybody before. "Those months of learning about kink, beyond just the sex, were probably some of the best self-prep I gave myself for Spec Ops."

Her hand dropped out of her hair. "*Beyond* the sex?"

He smirked. "Surprised?"

"A little." She huffed and then conceded, "Okay, maybe a lot."

"Not a sin," he assured. "And a normal vanilla reaction—where we all started at some point."

He steeled himself for what she'd do with that. Everybody loved vanilla, but few liked to be identified by it—though the definition was a damn accurate fit for what the rest of the world seemed to many kinksters. Didn't stop vanillas from acting like they'd just been wrongfully tagged as something close to terrorists.

To his pleasant shock, the woman simply shrugged, spread

her hands, and offered, "Everyone has to start somewhere."

Franz submerged the craving to scoop up both those hands and press awed kisses to their backs. Yeah, even right now, with her naked chest still begging him for a lot more than kisses.

Instead he replied, "In kink, that place is usually discovering the whips, chains, and spreader bars aren't the point. They're helpful in *getting* to the point, but they're only tools, like paint brushes to an artist or guitar strings to a musician."

That secret weapon of her attention went full ju-ju on him again. No; the force of her gaze was beyond that. She looked fascinated. Rapt. "So what *is* that point?"

He splurged a little, lifting one of her hands and bestowing that kiss, before answering, "Connection. Honesty. Moving past the normal bullshit so you can be open for relating to a person on a deeper level."

He kept their hands clasped. Her fingers twined tighter into his. "Pushing past the fear."

"Sometimes," he hedged, "yes. And sometimes, the dynamic helps people just figure out *what* the fear is." A deep breath went in and out before he clarified, "Taking off your clothes, getting tied up, or even being the one wielding the flogger... That's all outward delineation for what's happening on the inside. Shit on both sides of the dynamic gets broken down, stripped away, exposed for its truth. It's beautiful, but sometimes it's messy. And lots of times, yeah, it's frightening. That's why safe words exist and why many kink clubs won't allow people to drink and then play."

The statements, clearly sinking in with her, also spurred a dreamlike expression. "Kink clubs," she finally echoed. "So...a lot of those around, hmmm?"

"Oh, yeah." Other than a small chuff, Franz focused on modulating his own expression. As if it did any good. The way the woman could delve to his soul with just a touch, he was certain she'd see straight to the truth this time too. *They exist, and they thrive—and they're owned by guys like me.* Aloud, he confessed, "It was in one of them, actually, that I finally found the answers to a lot of my questions."

"The reasons why you were drawn to all of it."

Not a note of judgment colored her tone. She simply held his hand, truly interested in knowing this about him—and while the subject matter wasn't the usual, he sensed she'd be just as interested if he'd admitted to being a Mount Everest Sherpa in his spare time.

Damn.

It felt...nice.

Better than nice.

He finally scraped out of his amazed gawking to scrape out a response to her. "Yeah."

The corners of Tracy's lips hitched. "And?"

"And what?"

"The reasons?" she reminded. "Everything that drew you to BDSM?"

"Ah." He whooshed out a breath. "Yeah. That."

She squirmed, backing up the new edge of dubiety in her stare. "Messy?"

He shook his head. "Long."

"Highlights reel?"

He set a smile free. Her verbal shorthand, always knowing what to pull out of his soul's narrative and notate, was on point again. Scarily so. But as he'd just admitted to the woman, fear had been his middle name for eleven years—sans the last six months.

It felt pretty good to be frightened again.

Because of her.

For her.

So for her, he sliced through the fear—and yanked up the truth.

But not before slipping his hand free and moving it to the creamy valley between her breasts.

With knuckles stroking that warm vale, he said, "It all boils down to the fact that I'm an arrogant piece of work." Too much of it was the truth to even think of diluting, so he maintained his rhythmic strokes over her flawless flesh. "I'm ignited, in my spirit and my body, to know I can help another person open up to new parts of themselves. I'm happy, seeing the beauty of a submissive's pleasure by my hand...watching them come undone and then find their sanity again."

Her chest rose and fell on her own full breath. "Like an alternative therapist," she ventured.

"More like an alternative conductor," he countered. "In therapy, only one side benefits. But submissives give back to me like instruments in a concerto. The more beautifully they play my notes, the more I'm fulfilled too." Instinct, deep and sure, turned his touch into a more circular motion. He spread his fingers until they flowed over the sides of her taut swells. "The further she follows me and the more she trusts me, the more powerful I feel...and the more she rockets me to a high I can never get enough of."

Beneath his touch, Tracy quivered again—only he was damn certain he joined her in the quake. *Damn.* Just putting it all into words was the beginning of a crazy epiphany...a step back into a mental space that felt so much like home. A home from which he'd exiled himself after that horrific night with Abbie...but the home he'd desperately been seeking since returning from Kaesong.

And while he still couldn't wrap his head around the idea of moving all the way back in...

A visit would sure as hell be nice.

He swept his hand farther up. Brushed his fingertips over her nipple. Her breathing hitched and her areola puckered, luring him to repeat the sweep—pinching it this time. Her sweet, high wince was his incentive for repeating the move to her other stiff peak. As soon as he did, she unspooled into sensual languor, sliding back to the pillows...right underneath him.

The blanket all but slipped away. John kicked it back completely, twisting to settle between her thighs. *Holy gods.* She was already slick and soft and hot for him. Only through a clenched effort did he resist plunging his cock all the way inside her. Yeah, even bareback. She drove him to the edge of *that* stupidity.

As he moved in tighter, flattening their chests together, Tracy unfurled a Tigress's sensual snarl. Her nails scored his shoulders. Her legs parted farther, wrapping higher around his waist. She made him crazy with need, burning hot with desire—and that was before their gazes locked again, subjecting his senses to the full lightning force of her magical stare.

He gazed down, echoing her primal rumble.

She stared back up, hitching her hips a little.

His rumble became a groan. Her sex was sweet, wet, and tender—and his mental moorings were nonexistent. She did him no favors by nudging her chin up, taking him in with equal parts curiosity and challenge, stirring her kitten side back into the mix too. *Goddamn. His* self-control went into the drink when her eyes went that huge and her mouth got that plush.

"Thank you."

And her voice turned that husky.

"For what?" he managed to murmur back.

"For sharing all of that." Her hands slid in, wrapping around his neck. That, along with the new searches of her gaze, had her reminding him of a swimmer clinging to a dock. "For sharing...all of *you*...like that."

He liked being her dock.

A lot.

He slipped one hand up, rubbing a thumb along the pillows of her mouth. "Well, thank you for listening—and hearing—all of it."

She had more to say. John discerned it in the questing flickers in her gaze and the continuing tension around her mouth. He didn't press her, though. Sometimes, patience was its own reward.

"John?"

"Yeah?"

"I want to get you high too."

And sometimes, patience gave a guy other rewards too.

Huge ones.

With another long, low growl, he worked his crotch against hers. Shit. After just sermonizing about the mystical higher purpose of D/s, all he wanted to do was give her some of the filthiest commands in his arsenal before sinking himself inside her to the balls and screwing them both into hot, heavy, lava-style climaxes that stretched into tomorrow...

He started by taking her mouth under his. Explored her

thoroughly with his teeth and tongue until she shuddered, mewled, and writhed for him. Pinched both her pretty tits again, until the tips were hard as cinnamon candies. Rolled his hips and bunched his ass, massaging her equally stiff clit with the aching, throbbing tip of his agonized erection.

Until finally, it was time.

To heave up, pushing away onto his haunches, leaving her sprawled against the sheets, shiny with sweat and shaking with need...

And pissed as hell.

"What the—"

"*Kitten.*" He was quiet but commanding. Already shifting his mind to that space where the dragon could take over, focusing the fire all on her, transforming the power he could already feel in his blood.

"*What?*"

He arched a brow—effective for hiding his delight at her sass. Gods, did he love it when the takeover got interesting. This was going to be fun.

"*What?*" He sent her word back with a challenging jump of brows. "Or did you mean that to be 'what would you like me to do now, Sir?' If not, that's cool too. I'll just bug for the couch again, let you get some more rest, and—"

"No!" She sat up. Slammed a hand to the center of his chest. "I—I mean no, Sir; please don't go to the couch." As her hand lowered, so did her gaze. "I'm ready. Just...please...tell me what's next."

He ran a hand over the top of her head. He always cherished this moment, when a submissive first dipped her toe into the pool of his control, but this occasion was better than all the others combined. Logically, he wrote it off to the length of his self-imposed banishment from the dynamic—but instinctively, he confirmed it as more. This woman, with the will of a wildcat, the soul of a survivor, and the fighter's spirit so much like his own, wasn't just another submissive. She'd ignited his blood from their first clasp. Had entrusted him with her life and now yearned to give him her body—as his *partner*, not just his sub. She heard what he'd said, really heard it—and clasped that knowledge in, turning it into a beautiful offer...

Of herself.

I want to get you high.

Christ.

Did she know how totally she already had? Just a tiny mental touch on the memory of fucking her a few hours ago, and he was as hard as a goddamn bull again. Thank fuck, when he'd sneaked out for five minutes to check on Luke and the others, he'd thought to stash a couple of fresh condoms in the nightstand. Wishful thinking could sometimes be the universe's cue.

Meaning he was more than ready for *this* cue.

Drawing his hand to her chest and then filling his palm with her breast, he instructed, "What's next is...you lie back, lift your arms, and spread your legs for me."

Eagerness defined her face, as well as the moves she made to comply. Franz focused on keeping his breaths even and his cock under control as she transformed from being delectable to irresistible. Holy *fuck*. Her ripe nipples pointed toward the ceiling. Her thighs were creamy and perfect, begging to be marked by his bites. And her pussy, a palette of rosy pink, was the most erotic sight he could think of...sprinkled by the milk of his precome.

"Ohhhh." She moaned it from a tight throat. Her hips

jerked, betraying how the drops from his cock taunted the most sensitive parts of her pussy.

"Be still, kitten."

She tensed, exposing her clenched teeth. "Easy for you to say."

He let a smile ghost his lips. "You want my lube worked onto your clit?"

Her gasp was thick with grateful arousal. "Yes. Holy shit, *yes.*"

"Like this?" Two syllables for two digits, swirling across her quivering button.

"Ohhhh! Yes, Sir!"

"Or perhaps...like this?" He turned his fingers over. Smacked them sharply across her flower.

"Ahhhh!" How quickly her sighs became sharp gasps. How dead-on they hit the bulls-eye of his Dominant spirit... and wound around his aching, stretching cock.

With a dark groan, he twisted his fist up his length. Pushed at the base of his swollen head, where more white essence leaked from the hot slit.

"Don't move, *ku`uipo.*" That, ordered as he pushed aside her lips, letting his milk trickle over her exposed bud. "Grab the pillows if you must—but keep your arms up."

She took him up on the suggestion, though eyed him with open apprehension. "You say that like you're going to—to—"

"To what?" he asked mildly.

"You *know* what," she huffed. "I can see it in your stare. You're going to spank me...*there.*"

He kicked up one side of his mouth. "Is that what you're afraid of?"

"Would it turn you on if I said yes?"

"Oh, yes."

"Then I'm afraid."

"You just saying that to turn me on?"

"I'm saying that because I like you making me afraid." If her direct gaze wasn't enough to nail that home, the tautening tips of her breasts certainly did. By the *gods*, she had great tits. "And then I like you pushing me past it." Her mouth pressed into a determined line as her hips bucked upward again, offering herself to whatever treatment he chose for the glistening folds at their apex. "If I can get past these fears, it helps me think I can handle all the others too."

All the others.

Three words, representing a thousand more apiece. In Tracy Rhodes's world, they weren't things like workplace drama, girlfriend squabbles, or the kid's school grades—even before everything that went down yesterday. More accurately, had been blown up yesterday. But here she was, surrendering her spirit, confident he'd give it back to her in a stronger place to lead the whole damn world out of this chaos.

He probably should've been daunted.

Weirdly, maybe even stupidly, he wasn't.

He was honored. Invigorated. And like the "arrogant piece of work" he was, turned way the fuck on—a truth he showed his little subbie, inch by swollen inch, while repositioning himself between her thighs. Tracy's tongue flicked out, nervously moistening her lips, as she watched every move he made, clearly trying to predict what he had in mind for her gorgeous cunt next.

"Hell, woman," he finally growled, bending over to learn how her clit would like his *teeth*, "this is going to be fun."

CHAPTER THIRTEEN

"Are we all having fun yet?"

The line, a tried-and-true favorite from the days when Tracy didn't have to speak to her security team leader on a burner cell, induced the man to at least a lukewarm chuff over the miles.

"How are you holding up, Madam President?"

"*Sol.*" She rolled her eyes, but the gesture was wasted on the reading chaise and soggy plants in the small atrium attached to the condo's office. Though everything outside was painted in dreary late-afternoon light, she wasn't picky about the view. It contained a square of honest-to-God sky—the chunk she'd finally persuaded John to let her glimpse, so long as she didn't actually go into the atrium to do it.

A step in the right direction.

Dear God, she hoped.

For two days, hope had become a steady diet staple around here. For everyone.

She just wondered when hers would morph into insanity.

Not just because she couldn't see enough sky.

Because she'd been flying to too many stars.

Courtesy of one amazing, rippling, passionate, powerful star captain.

Even now, as Franzen let himself into the room, her gaze went to work on undressing him. Already she envisioned the burgundy Henley stripped away, revealing exotic island

194

tattoos emblazoned across his bulging shoulders and mighty pecs. Took even less effort to remove his track pants, exposing her imagination to his sleek hips and massive thighs, centered by his thick bronze stalk.

That cock...

It had transformed her into a creature of so much lust, she was certain the terrorists knew she was still alive and now tried to finish off the job with some erotic supervirus.

If she *had* to go...

And now, his morbid sarcasm officially rubbed off on her too. She punished herself for giving into it by turning back toward the atrium, denying herself his beauty. Sometimes the humor was fun, but even teasing fate about her death just wasn't. The country would get along fine without her, but Luke wouldn't.

"What?" came Sol's defense in her ear. "'Madam President' doesn't have a nice ring to it?"

"It doesn't have *any* ring to it." She hoisted her chin, more out of defiance to the hulk skirting the desk and then sitting in the chair behind it. "Because it's not the truth."

"Yet."

Sol's volley coincided with John's raised gaze. His eyes, gone that expensive chocolate shade, dipped over every inch of her form. Her skin turned to electricity and her womb turned to magma, not making it easy to accept Sol's follow-up.

"You'll be back here and in the Oval soon. The rightful heir in the rightful throne."

A laugh spilled before she could stop it. "Thanks for the time travel to the Middle Ages, my friend—but I don't want a damn throne." At the moment, she wasn't certain she even wanted the chair behind the *Resolute* desk, in that icon of an office. She'd just gotten used to the layout of the vice-presidential digs. "I just want to work hard, serve the people, and do some good."

Another eye roll almost took over—directed entirely inward. She sounded like a fantastic campaign slogan, if the occasion were Luke running for his high school class council. Sincere intention or not, "working hard" and "doing good" weren't viable platforms for running the hugest democracy in the world.

When Sol's steady silence confirmed as much, she forced her tone into a combination of conversational and professional. It was tricky but not unpracticed. She used it all the time on senators all over the Hill. "So tell me what excitement I'm missing. How's LeGrange handling everything?"

Blake LeGrange, the Speaker of the House, had been sworn in as president before the embers at the Bellagio were doused. The haste of the act chafed Tracy like going braless in burlap, despite accepting that it was necessary for the nation's morale. She and LeGrange stood apart on issues more than together, but she found it hard to reach middle ground with a dude who had sideburns like silkworms, a Henry VIII swagger, and a gaze fonder of her thighs than her face. When she did insist on sticking to her ideals, even with Craig's support, LeGrange had favorite write-offs like "You're so cute when you're feisty, Little T." But she could've had it worse. His wife, Lucille, got the honor of being "Little LuLu."

Yeah. The nation's first lady really went by "Little LuLu."

Tracy didn't care if the woman called herself the Czarina of Russia, as long as her husband was doing his job. She couldn't imagine LeGrange not diving right in, especially under the circumstances, but she needed that reassurance from Sol. If the man was still lazing by the figurative pool, she didn't care if a thousand lunatic terrorists were still on the loose; she'd order Franz to scoot her ass onto the next transport to the capitol. The country needed stability right now, and that shit had to be flowing from the top down.

After a pause extending to worrisome length, Sol finally rendered an answer. "LeGrange is...LeGrange." He stuck in *his* first laugh of the call, though the burst hardly brimmed with mirth. "Let's just say he's got the bull by the horns."

Tracy felt her brows bunch. "Which means exactly what?"

"That everything's running smoothly—as long as the bull lets him lead."

"Okay." The way she drew it out clearly captured John's attention too. As he peered harder at her, she continued to Sol, "That's a good thing, right? As long as we know where the bull is?"

Sol released another chuckle—this time, actually stirring warmth into the sound. "Damn. You *are* missed around here, Mrs. Rhodes."

"Oh yeah?" Her smiled spread into her tone. "Unbelievably, I miss you guys a little too."

"Hmm." The reaction shot out with his normal Sol efficiency but was clipped with more nuance. For a second, it seemed as if her confession really was a surprise. "Just a little?" he added, making Tracy aim a bewildered glance at the phone. Who was this guy, and what had he done with the friend who always helped her make fun of Capitol Hill antics like it was high school with more money? Right now, Sol sounded like the epitome of achy-breaky-needy bestie. It was annoying—another truth she didn't mind meshing into her tone.

"I'm sure as hell not hiding out across the country for my

health, bucko." Though thanks to the man still so focused on her from across the room, she'd been rocking the best sleep of her life the last few nights. Falling asleep with the big dragon wrapped around her was better than a couple of glasses of wine and fifty pages of committee reports. "So let's make a deal, my friend. Push on your friends at the FBI and CIA to find out who the hell masterminded the blackest day in world history, and *I'll* come back to DC to help you all throw their asses into the deepest, blackest, piss-filled prison cells we can find."

The phone turned into a ball of static from the rough exhalation from across the miles. The sound ended in Sol's low, appreciative whistle. "Well, shoot my pretty horsie in the foot," he added to it.

"Excuse me?" she retorted.

"The sweet widow from Texas really does have a few fireballs in her arsenal."

She snorted. "Fireballs are just the start of my secret powers, Sol. But like every good Texas dame, I wait for the perfect moment to whip them out."

He released another chuckle, though once more it walked the weird wilderness between humor and gloom. Still, she could hear the echoes of his typical hurried footsteps, even over the line. Maybe this was Sol's usual tone, and she'd simply always been too busy to analyze it in full.

Finally he countered, "Well then, get a stack of those flamin' pups bagged up and ready to go."

Her face must have reflected the jump of her interest. John straightened, dropping his hands to the ends of the chair's armrests as she prompted, "Why? What's up?"

"You mean who's going *down*?"

She plunked her hip to the side of the desk. "Are you kidding?"

"Kidding is for the playground." It was another of their shared one-liners—only for the first time, Sol invoked it without a single lilt of laughter.

She twisted, glancing at John. "Can I put you on speaker, Sol?"

There was a half second's pause. "With who?"

"Franzen." She let her tone add the *Duh, dude* to it.

"He's with you? Even now?"

She let her own telling moment go by. Not for Sol but for her. For just a few seconds, she let the question stream through her with a different meaning.

He's with you, Tracy?

Taking care of you?

Giving you everything you need...as a guardian, a person...a lover?

"Yeah." For just one more moment, she pretended all those questions were still on the line too. She gazed at John as if they were. Sure as hell reached for him like it. Her fingers looked so tiny against the back of his hand. "Yeah," she repeated softly. "He's with me."

She refused to feel guilty for it, either. For once, it felt good to say it like that. To have someone to say it about.

For once, it felt good not to be completely alone.

"Well." Sol didn't waste a second getting it out. "He's taking the detail seriously. That's...good." Though he sounded more like the drama geek praising the quarterback for freakishly landing the lead in the school play.

Tracy pushed aside the metaphor, telling her imagination to calm the hell down, while locating the speaker button on the unfamiliar device in her hand. "Okay," she said, back to business once she did, "you're on the air, Wrightman."

John, raising a curious glance to her while leaning forward, greeted, "Long time no talk, man." Such pure sarcasm, it didn't even need the dry tone. There'd been a pile of burner phones on the dining room table when they got here; the pile had been depleted to three. The two men had been in constant contact—which further explained John's open inquisitiveness. "You got something you're holding out on me?"

Over the line, there was a shuffling sound. "I've got something requiring a higher security clearance than yours, Captain."

Tracy shoved up from the desk. John, trying to hold her back, was too slow on the uptake. "And you're throwing *that* out at a time like this?" Her head started to throb. She ticked it John's way. Sol couldn't see the action, but it sure as hell informed her tone. "What part of his eleven years in SOF are you forgetting? He's used to receiving more high-level intel in one mission than you get in a year."

"You mean *received*."

"Tracy." Franz nudged his left foot behind her right calf. "He's right." He looked professional but grim. "If this is high-level shit, then trusting me—"

"He's trusted you with *me*." Making sure the whole building felt her stomping retreat, along with the seething tone, might have been overkill—but the show wasn't just for John. Sol's brain was a bucking bronc of weirdness right now, and she was tired of wondering where he'd throw her next. "Think that might change your mind about getting your head out of your ass right now, Mr. Wrightman?"

John didn't move.

Faint static *shoosh*ed out of the phone. Sol hadn't ended the call—though obviously wasn't happy with it.

"All right," he finally uttered. "I'll tell you what I know. But then I really might have to kill you, Franzen."

The man tied it off with a wry chuckle. Tracy wasn't sure whether she wanted to thank him or borrow his figurative gun and shoot him. Her goals weren't so fuzzy when it came to the big warrior sitting before her, leaning in to add his own laugh to the exchange before jibing back, "Promises, promises, asshole."

★ ★ ★ ★ ★

Twenty minutes later, she and Franz had barely moved physically—though everything about the world, including the planet's axis, felt inexorably shifted.

Felt?

No.

The planet literally had to have jumped off its rotation, for what Sol had just shared as conclusive truth. A viable enough theory, at least, that the FBI and CIA were playing nice about pursuing it together—and because of that, scooped up three suspects who apparently hopped back onto the *right* axis and started talking about the plan that stalled seven world governments in the exact same day.

But now, seventeen minutes after Sol turned the surreal into the real and the impossible into words, Tracy couldn't do the same. Letting the stillness stretch on felt more...right. Respectful. The memorial she hadn't been able to speak for Craig. The sadness she'd been sucking back, perhaps hoping it had all been a dream and they'd find her friend miraculously alive in some bunker even she didn't know about, below the Residence...

Craig would know what to do about this insanity.

But Craig really wasn't coming back.

Words she couldn't wrap her heart around—and never would.

Words she somehow had to beat into her mind.

Just...not right now.

Which was why the stillness felt better.

Which was why, the second John rose from the chair, she seized his forearm though said nothing. Her tongue was a slab of glue. Her throat was a desert of despair. But he stared down, seeming to know that too.

"It's okay, Tigress." He deliberately used the name, despite how it clearly clenched his own throat, before wrapping his long fingers beneath her elbow. "I'm not going anywhere."

"Don't you fucking dare."

The words hardly made him flinch. The only change she noticed was the hue of his gaze, emerging from shadows to a caramel tint as he shifted closer. "It really is going to be okay."

She gave at least an effort to believe that. Pulled in a deep breath, praying his conviction permeated her, but it was like throwing open the freezer door instead. She gripped him harder as a shiver conquered her, full of fear and dread and rage.

"Keep living that fiction, buddy," she finally gritted. "You're not the one who has to deal with a world where a dozen paramilitary organizations, led by a huge cell in the US itself, decided to form their own terror cartel."

He moved his grip to the back of her head. Tucked her close to his body, her cheek against the ridges of his abs. "And you're not going to do it alone," he countermanded. "You have a *cartel* of your own, already working together to fight back.

Remember what Sol said? It's only been two days, and they already have three assholes in custody—colluders talking *without* coercion or pressure. They're crumbling from the inside already. They know what an insane plan they signed up for. Order *doesn't* come from chaos."

Tracy wrapped her arms around the tree trunk of his waist. Rubbed her cheek into the firm warmth of him, letting his words soothe her like autumn leaves drifting from mighty branches. He smelled the same way, oaky and savory, and she indulged in another deep breath just to appreciate that rich scent.

"I believe you," she finally whispered, pushing a new level of trust into each word. "I do."

"I know, *ku'uipo*." His other hand rose, setting a comforting rhythm up and down the length of her spine. "But that's not the important issue here."

She stilled. Noticed he did the same. "You mean the one about figuring how we can just stop time right now?" If the technology existed, she would've seriously considered it. Here, surrounded by the heat of his body and the calm of his touch, she could float in surrender, be centered in herself.

He laughed quietly, a nearly imperceptible sound to the outside but a calming vibration in her ear. "No." He lifted the end of the word in gentle reprimand. "The issue of *you* believing in *yourself*."

Tracy huffed. "You're kidding, right?"

His hands realigned, palming both her shoulders. "Kidding is for the playground."

"Oh, *gawd*. And now you're forbidden from any more unsupervised calls with Sol."

He gripped her tighter. "And you're forbidden from

skirting the issue, kitten."

She snapped her head up. Franz was ready, capturing her chin under an equally fast-moving hand. "*Kitten?*" she echoed in an incredulous bite.

The man only smoothly dipped his head and calmly arched a brow. *Damn it.* "You heard me," he answered—with a voice growling to lower octaves. The gritty cadence to which he defaulted when they began leaving reality behind...for the world of their Dominant and submissive alter-egos.

There was just one problem with connecting Point A to Point B this time.

"I *did* hear you, *John.*" She wasn't leaving any meaning to chance. "But this isn't about just getting me to try a new ice cream or making me take swats for biting my nails." Though for the record, she'd loved the pint of maple hickory, even topped with crumbled bacon, and was all but broken of the nail-biting thing. "This is—"

"I know damn well what this is about."

So much for him fielding her ire like a dragon with a kitten scratch. The dragon had stayed, all right—but the big lizard had been poked now and wasn't effing happy about it. Not one damn bit.

Tracy scooted back a little on the desk, taking the blotter with her but not daring to correct the mishap. Not daring to look away from him, period. When she first met Franzen, he was in stealth protector mode. During the flight from Vegas, he became a lethally focused warrior—then here, in their urban hideout, he'd peeled back the layers on the man beneath both... and then the Dominant lover beneath that. She'd never lie; every phase made her fear him in strange new ways. But every time, she'd somehow known she only feared the *fear*, not the man.

Now she knew the truth.

None of that came close to fear.

None of that compared to the frantic pound of her heart as she watched the fire flare through his eyes—and knew she had to get off that desk.

Scrambling backward on her butt wasn't going to do it. She swiftly rolled, gaining a little more purchase on her stomach—

Until his hand came down on the small of her back, pinning her like a bear paw.

"John—"

His other hand came down on her ass, making her yelp despite the barrier of her new yoga pants. She was the same size as Rayna Hayes, which had made it possible for the woman to get out and purchase some fresh clothes for her.

"Try again, *popoki*."

"Sir."

No damn way was she admitting how easily it spilled out. The story right now, and she was sure as hell sticking to it, was that he was being an overbearing ass and she was going along with the game—but only until she maneuvered to a perfect angle for jamming her foot into his crotch. No way was she letting the jerk wad in on how his caveman act did something wholly hot and new to her blood...or how the knowledge that he had her trapped here, at least for now, already made her senses spin toward the blissful mist to which he always led...

"Sir." She repeated it with gritted sweetness. "If you'll let me up, we can talk about this like rational—*ahh*!"

Two more swats on her bottom, hard ones, were followed by the gentle but sure pressure of his fingers, stroking in wide arcs, redistributing the stings into brilliant heat. A gasp escaped, high and uncontrollable, as waves of warmth suffused her thighs and lower belly...and yes, all the way into her awakening, throbbing core...

"*I'm* rational, madam." He kept rubbing as he shifted, kicking out her knees so he could step between them. "And we *will* discuss this issue, here and now. Keep your hands there. That's perfect."

"Shit." Tracy fumed. She had to go and entertain the notion of gripping the lip of the desk, both hands over her head, thinking to push off into a new resistance at his iron hold. Or so she told herself. Kind of. Part of her, a huge part, still didn't believe he was initiating this, here and now. It wasn't the desk—the man's stare alone wielded a magical force, capable of turning *any* piece of furniture into a possible support set for their sexual magic—but his approach was an entirely different issue. He meant business. *Real* business. Their torrid chemistry had a distinctive new ingredient. *Her* real life. Nothing should have murdered her arousal faster—but as he spread his hand against her hip with the force of arrogant ownership, her body answered at once with a gush of new arousal. Then another, as he did the same to the other hip.

It was just the preface to what happened when he shoved her pants down.

"Oh!" she got out—before he stepped in, catching the crotch of the stretchy fabric beneath his foot and stomping down. "*Oh!*" The repetition popped out as her pants hit the floor—and every corner of her womb tightened like a bow.

Then tighter when she realized he wasn't backing up. And she recognized how much that terrified her.

Because if he wasn't backing up his body...

"We're going to talk about a few things, Madam President."

...he was definitely not yielding on his original intention

for this discussion. If that was what they were still calling it. Not that the label mattered. At the moment, she didn't care if they were having afternoon tea in the Oval Office—which would have made the defiant lift of her head, coinciding with his assessing squeezes to her ass cheeks, an even more interesting move.

"Okay, Franzen. Seriously—"

"Completely where I'm coming from here, Madam President. Glad we're in agreement."

She snarled a protest through her teeth. "We are *not* in agreement. Not as long as you keep calling me that."

"What would that be..." His voice mellowed, though his touch roughened. "Madam President?"

"*Damn it*, Franzen!"

He waited several seconds, still kneading at her bare flesh, before responding. "Indulge me a question." It was something between request and demand, though he hadn't invoked *those* dreaded words yet, so she went ahead and dipped a short, agreeable nod. "How many times did you have to rehearse that presentation for the entrepreneurs' crowd in Vegas?"

She snorted. Damn near laughed. "Ohhhh no, you don't. Comparing that to *this* is saying Barney's ready for *Jurassic Park*."

"How many times?"

"Not relevant!"

"How. Many?"

Another harsh huff was finished by a frustrated grunt. "A lot," Tracy finally spat. "Okay? Happy? Gem ran it with me until I could nearly recite it backward. But it was *necessary*. I needed to know that shit in my sleep because—"

"Having to present it to all those people was...what?"

She dropped her head back down. Fought to infuse the hard, cold wood of the desktop into her head before injecting it straight down her spine. Useless. This man...what he did to her with his voice, that baritone coated in the richest chocolate... how he turned her bloodstream into a strand of melted taffy... how she became his damn candy counter of submissiveness, giving up exactly what he wanted, when he wanted them—

Like right now.

"It was...terrifying." The words themselves were easy to spill. She only wished the same were true of what her mind went through to retrieve them. What her heart endured, beat by horrifying beat, to reach this surrender.

Because she knew that wasn't all.

Because she knew it was only the start...

"Just like the idea of your presidency is terrifying?"

Just. The. Start.

"John—"

"*Tracy.*"

"Sir." She autocorrected for herself more than him. The tension in his tone hadn't stemmed from her breach in protocol, and they both knew it. She could've resorted to calling him SpongeBob SquarePants right now, and his purpose wouldn't waver. She already saw the ocean to which he dragged her and knew he wouldn't stop until she dove in and swam to the other side.

Without a boat.

Without a life ring.

Only with him. Period.

But the idea of even dipping her toe in...

A shudder took over, from her hair follicles to the ends of her toes. The ocean was freezing. And there were ice floes. Big ones, layered by years' worth of emotional layers. Insecurity. Inexperience. Even ignorance. All the what-ifs. *So many what-ifs...*

What if I'm a failure? What if I blow everything up? I can't figure out my son's math homework. How am I supposed to run a whole goddamn country?

Two sharp smacks exploded on the air, whipping her mind back. Her body was only two seconds behind, once the recognition set in. His hands. Her ass. At the same time. An answering gasp tumbled out as the stings set in, shooting toward her hips and then back again—

Though by the time the sensations boomeranged back in, they'd become pure heat. Flames through her inner thighs... the crevice of her ass...

...then deeper...

"Holy...shit." She all but moaned the last of it as the man magnified the sensual torment...in all the best and worst ways. Skimming his hands down to the back of her thighs and then swirling his fingertips in waltzes of seduction. Pushing his legs out another couple of inches, forcing hers apart in the process... opening the wet folds of her most intimate self to a rush of cool air and the blast of his aroused snarl.

"How is that for you, Madam President?"

He wove the rough sound throughout the words, which shouldn't have made a difference in how she took them—but did. Braced by that wolfish, roguish grate, the title was no longer the petrifying curse she'd been damning. The words were a shameless caress. An irreverent come-on.

A filthy dare.

A challenge in which her body had been laid on the table as the betting pot.

"Holy shit." There was a whine in her reiteration, and she didn't care.

Because now, she was scared all over again.

Behind her—and now, leaning over her too—Franzen strung out a deep growl. "Wasn't the question," he taunted. Oh yes, that was the perfect descriptor too. *Taunted*, as if this was more than fun for him—his little party gaining momentum as he glided his hands back up, higher and higher, joining his middle fingers directly over her pussy. As he teased the tips of those powerful digits along the tingling tissues around her entrance, he emphasized, "I asked how you're enjoying this, Madam President."

"Ahhhhh..." It was more a sketchy breath than the beginning of a word. The way he'd deepened the sex track of *his* words...as if his instinct were tuned to the exact frequency of her body and now broadcast his most erotic intent into every listening outpost of every wilderness of her system...

She was ready to go up in flames.

"Dear God." The rolling, languid warmth started taking over. Her hips jerked. Her hands slipped. A pen cup and a paperclip holder went flying as Franzen whipped up a hand, slamming her wrists back over her head.

"Keep. Them. There," he intoned. "Or I won't be so gentle about this."

"Gentle?" she returned. "About wha—*ohhh!*"

As both his middle fingers returned to her pussy, his index fingers stretched up—

To prod at the opening of her ass.

"Damn. John. We need to—"

"Ssshhh." He wasn't exactly "gentle" about *that*, turning the soft sound into everything short of another growl. "This is going to happen. And you're going to be open-minded about it."

She almost jabbed up a middle finger. *Open-minded.* It was a favorite expression of hers, used regularly on her petulant son during fourteen occasions on any given day, and the fucker standing over her clearly knew it...openly using her own words against her in his seductive gamble.

Damn him.

And once again, his point was Barney and Jurassic. This had to be a violation of some cosmic law. Dragons didn't get to use lizard legends for their purposes like this, did they? Where was his karmic payback?

Inspiration struck, despite how his caresses to both entrances had begun to fray the edges of her logic. "Wh-What if I choose to safe word?"

He'd actually given her one of those. *Ice cream.* Technically it was two, but on that occasion, she also hadn't been thinking straight. A girl had a tendency to get that way when a Dom decided to spread maple hickory ice cream into her sex and then lick it off to the tune of five orgasms for his writhing submissive. He'd demanded to go for number six. She'd threatened to go on a new flattening iron hunt.

This was a much different situation than that.

Much different.

She could deal with washing ice cream off. Even attempting to walk on nonworking legs after five climaxes.

She couldn't deal with having her ass invaded.

No matter how naughty and forbidden it felt.

No matter how sensitive her back rim seemed to be as he spread her wider there.

No matter how thoroughly he knew how to work all the

nerves up and down her other tunnel, offsetting the discomfort of having him invade where no other man had before. While Ryker could be passionate, he'd been conventional with a capital *C*...

And now, she was truly beginning to learn how many other ways the alphabet could be arranged. With this man, who taught her how to see the world in so many different languages...

"*Hemolele. Kamaha`o.*"

Like that one.

She really loved that one.

Especially if she could capitalize on it to distract him. Perhaps entice him to do something with body parts other than his fingers...

"I'm not sure I've heard that one before, Sir." She nudged her hips a little higher, knowing her kittenish moves were his sexual Kryptonite. "What does it mean?"

Franzen stilled. His significant pause caused her to glance back. One of his brows was dipped low, the other hiked in assessment. His expressive lips were compressed to a harsh line. A pulse ticked in his jaw.

"It means you're not going to safe word."

She let him see the challenge in her own stare. "That so, hotshot?"

He smirked through a snort. "That's so, Madam President."

"You're really sure of yourself."

"And you're really wet." A hint of his teeth showed, brilliant and straight, through the arrogant part of his lips. "Sopping with juice, my little subbie. And so goddamn sexy because of it." As if he planned it, his middle fingers slipped free from her pussy with a slushy sound. As Tracy sweat onto the desk from the force of her flush, his savoring moan drenched the air. "Perfect. This cream is so damn perfect."

For what?

But she already knew the answer—and let the fresh tension of her body do the talking as he slid those moistened digits out to the tiny aperture now spread open by his other hand. As Franz worked the cream of her arousal into the hole, using tender but steady pressure, one word finally made its way out.

"Shit."

"Ssshhh." He repeated it with the same deep authority as he breached her deeper with one finger. "Be still and accept your lesson."

Tracy grimaced. Worked her hands tighter around the desk's lip. "Which would be what, exactly?"

"That some things in life aren't comfortable at first." He pulled the finger out—but joined another to it on the way back into her tight hole. At once, her hips jerked as her instinct kicked in, trying to escape the new pressure. John pulled her back, firmly locking his free hand to the bottom of her spine again. "But if you stop trying to fight the forces, they often bring incredible things." He pushed in harder. Stretched her in ways she'd never imagined. "Beautiful things, *ku`uipo*." His thrusts came with subtle rolls of his body, his banked fires turning into physical curls of smoke, flowing against her...inside her. "You have no idea how beautiful."

His voice was gruff with pleasure...perhaps some pain too. She almost snorted again. And what, exactly, would *he* be hurting about right now? But something in his tone tugged at her—and the words now swirling out of her, almost as if one person occupied her aching, invaded body and another controlled her soaring, racing senses.

"Tell me," one of those women whispered. No. Pleaded. "Tell me how beautiful. Please, Sir."

Several seconds stretched by, filled only with her Dominant's soft but gruff breaths. He changed nothing about his treatment. One hand pinned her down by the small of her back. The other maintained a strong rhythm, pumping two fingers deeper and deeper inside her back hole.

"You ask so prettily," he finally murmured. "But are you really beseeching more as the kitten who wants poetry or the Tigress who wants the truth?"

For long minutes, she only moved to work her forehead against the desk's surface. Like that was going to help her with an answer—the definitive reply he was demanding, to a question that meant more than its words.

So much more.

Does he get a kitten or a tigress?

Her answer was going to change some things. Major things. If they had just two days, two weeks, or two *months* left with each other, it wouldn't make a difference. Franzen was making that clear, here and now. If she wanted more with him, more *from* him, he'd exact more in return. There was an admission cost to his basement, beyond the spank-and-cuddle "playtime" they'd had so far.

Now, he wanted something more.

Wanted to lead her farther down the steps.

Into the darkness where his cravings dwelled...

If she followed, it wouldn't be easy. Or comfortable. Or fear-free. And yet, God help her, she yearned to follow. Perhaps needed to. She craved more of that scorched dragon lust beneath his voice...and yes, the raw desire turning his touch into blazing brutality. Even now, knowing what that touch was doing to her...where it was going inside of her...

How deeply it would violate her...

But she wanted it. Throbbed and pulsed for it.

Right. There.

And everywhere...

For the first time in such a long time—perhaps the very first time—she wanted to give a man the fullness of that trust. A man who wouldn't let her fall off the wall.

Hell. A man who was going to barrel right through the wall.

All she had to do was hand over her doubts and let him guide her through the rubble afterward.

As his Tigress.

Looking out for him too.

"I want the truth, Sir. You know I do."

A rough hum emanated from him, conveying his dark pleasure in her submissive tone. "Very well, then. Here's your truth, *madam*." He adjusted his big body, seeming to re-secure his stance behind her, before continuing in a low growl, "The sight of my fingers fucking your ass is so incredible, I've soaked my pants in precome just thinking of putting my dick there instead." As he leaned forward, the weight of his body pushed his fingers tighter inside her. "And I'm not even going to ask if that makes your pussy wet, because I already know it does." He worked himself in, twisting until the pressure became something else. A strange, sizzling, invasive pleasure, turning her into a ball of needy mush beneath him.

"I—I think I'd be okay with that, Sir," she somehow managed without interjecting a hundred moans.

"Of course you'd be." His soft snarl vibrated the back of her neck, raining delicious awakening down her back, connecting to the mix of pain and pleasure he gave her ass. "If I said that was how you'd be taking my cock."

"Yes, Sir."

And there it was. Spilling from her without thought, almost as if called out by the universe, though changing everything inside two seconds. The point of no return. *The bridge is crossed, so stand and watch it burn.*

Just not forever.

As soon as all the terrorist network was shattered—and it would be, with suspects talking and a global deployment acting on the intel—the bridge would be erected again. She'd cross back, leaving her service to John Franzen's dominance behind, restarting her service to her country. And she *would* serve, because she'd sworn to do so. And she'd hate the damn title at first—John was right; it was a discomfort she'd likely never get used to—but most days, she'd forget about it completely. The work would matter most. It had to.

So for right now, she chose to burn the bridge. To give over the surrender.

To know the freedom, right now, of giving in to all the heat. Of surrendering to her burnished, beautiful Dom.

"Yes, Sir. Let me take your cock, as it pleases you to give it."

CHAPTER FOURTEEN

Why the hell had he made that dumbass promise not to take her ass with his cock?

Well. Not right now.

But right now, her flawless rosette was all he could see, taking every plunge of his fingers with tight, trembling welcome...with suckling, searing seduction...

With submissive beauty speaking straight to his cock.

While her words whispered straight to his soul.

As it pleases you...

By the gods. He'd met presidents and kings. Gotten naked with sirens and goddesses in at least a dozen different countries. But none of them, anywhere, had given him a gift like those four words, their beauty heightened by her honesty, her sincerity...

Her submission.

"*You* please me, woman." It was the only response to give. The only words he *could* give—

Followed by the command he was destined to give her. He knew that now, down to the very fabric of his being.

"And it's going to please me, *very* much, to bury my cock inside your tight, hot body..."

"Yessss," she hissed.

"...as soon as you give me the executive order to do so."

Tracy, who'd started to writhe her ass in time to his illicit attention there, fell into stillness. He saw her surprise turn into shock, clutching the whole upper half of her body, before her head twisted enough to give her the angle for a pronounced side-eye.

"Excuse. Me?"

Holy gods. This little wildcat, especially when summoning her claws to the surface, scratched him up in all the right ways. He loved bleeding for her. Stinging for her. And making her hurt for him in return...

Felt like a fucking miracle.

How he adored her. Craved her. Basked in the glory of doing this for her.

"You heard me, Madam President." He had to be going to hell for this—invoking the highest office in the land, even in the name of getting this lesson into her thick, beautiful skull—but goddamn, what a way to go. He now knew, whenever he saw her on TV in her prim presidential suits and crisply styled hair, all he'd think about was having her like this, fiery and feisty and half-naked, with his fingers in wicked places and his cock straining to fuck her... *Hell.* No. *Heaven.* "I want to take you so fucking badly, Tigress. Push my dick into that soaked, sweet cunt of yours and fill you until you feel nothing *but* me anymore. At the same time, I'm going to ram these fingers deeper into your ass, until I touch parts of your body you never knew existed. I want to make you come from the inside out, until you scream so loud I'll have to fuck your tongue with mine just to quiet you."

"Shit," she broke in, moving beneath him again. Undulating like an exotic dancer as waves of arousal clearly claimed her. "Holy...shit. *John.*"

Her high sigh had his cock weeping again. He forced himself to leave the damn thing covered, gritting his teeth to continue his ruthless torment. "Not the words I'm after, *ku`uipo*. Maybe you just want to think it over a little more? Maybe you just want to get out of here and deal with your empty pussy in some other way?"

"No. *No.*" She panted heavily between the protests. "Please. *Please.* I—I need—"

"You mean I'm *ordering* you, Captain Franzen, as your president..."

"Yes! Fine! All right!"

"All right...what?"

"What you said. Just—damn it—fill me. Fuck me..."

"Uh-uh." To be sure she got the point, he punctuated by lowering the hand at her back to the fullness of her ass and raining sharp smacks to both sides. "From *your* lips, not mine."

"What difference does it make?"

"It's going to make a shit ton of difference when you're in the Oval. Now give me the fucking order, Tracy, or we'll both walk away now."

"You're a bastard."

"Hmmm. True."

"And I'm ordering you, as your fucking president, to get that cock out of your pants and inside me."

"*Fuck.*" There was the official stunner of the day. The order heard across his body—and deep inside his balls. "Yes, *ma'am.*"

"You going to talk or act, soldier?"

Her sass gave him a deep chuckle and a harder dick, despite the pinpricks of regret sneaking in with both. In another time, in another place, his imagination would already be filled with the anticipation of making her truly his. Locking a collar around her neck while publicly claiming her and fucking her before all his friends and fetish family at Bastille. As a submissive, she'd never let him get complacent or bored. As a woman, her inner beauty would only get more gorgeous with the years. Most importantly, as a person, she'd be his willing partner, helping him figure shit out—even this crazy entity known as a life after Special Forces.

But they didn't have another time or place—and he was hell-bent on forgetting exactly that as he jerked the front of his track pants down, finally freeing the angry red length from beneath.

After indulging two seconds of a clenched groan, he exhaled roughly but responded with sure silk, "Madam President, haven't you learned by now that I'm a man of action?"

"Thank God." Her sigh fluttered the air as he yanked the condom packet from his pocket—wisely, he'd started carrying them everywhere—ripping the thing open with his teeth, and then one-handing it for the latex roll-on. No time for pulling out the Don Juan moves right now. He needed her like air. Hungered for her like an animal scenting its mate on the wind and then finally finding her in the forest, ready to be rutted. If he didn't get inside her *right now*—

One lunge and he was home.

No. Not home.

Paradise.

"Sir! Yes!"

"*Fuck.*" Okay, beyond paradise. Where the hell was that? He didn't care. Wherever this was, he wanted a full fucking tour. Needed to fly higher into this Shangri-La with her, where they rode winds made of fire, drank from rivers of lust, and twisted themselves so tightly into each other, he literally had no idea where the force of her ended and the power of him began.

They were meshed. Woven.

One.

He'd never experienced anything like it.

He'd never begged destiny more to make a moment last forever.

He'd never begged destiny for shit, period.

Destiny was supposed to have taken him out a long damn time ago. Destiny was supposed to have been a grenade at his feet, a bullet to his head, a knife in his gut. It was supposed to have been quick and ruthless, a flash of pain and then a forever of noble nothingness.

Well, this shit still had the pain right. And the flashes. The agony of the throbs in his balls, the strain in his cock, and the thunder of his heart, all screaming to fuse tighter with her, to push deeper inside her—to let her climb deeper inside *him*. And the flashes? They hit with every single one of her racing breaths, heavy and hard, keeping time to the rhythm of her cunt's pulls on his dick and her ass's clamps around his fingers.

Christ.

What she did to him.

How she stunned him.

How she submitted so much more than her body to him.

In every push of her hips and gasp from her throat, he felt it. Knew it. Had no choice but to accept it. The raw power of her passion. The pure honesty of her spirit. The fierce beauty of how she opened herself to him, filling the air with the brutal force of her energy and fire and light...

She was a revelation.

An illumination.

A surprise so intense, he was incinerated to his core.

A blast so brilliant, he could no longer keep his restraint from getting torched too.

He bent deeper over her. Slid his free hand up until wrapping it around the base of her throat, pressing in hard enough that she damn well knew he was there.

"*Yes,*" she rasped, filling his grip with the vocal vibrations as his cock swelled into every corner of her channel.

"Yes," he echoed against the hollow of her ear, lust enflaming him in equal measure, cutting everything in his mind down to sparse syllables—primitive words from the wildest, most untamed part of him. "Yes. *Yes.* Tigress mine. All of you. Pussy. Ass. Body. Mind."

"Yes...Sir."

Despite her hard breathing, the acquiescence was a perfect pair of soft sighs. The liquid texture of her body gave him the rest of that story. She'd given him everything and now soared in pure surrender. Disconnecting, only to reconnect. Becoming a ball of her most basic needs, her animal-level desires. God*damn*, he knew the feeling. Was nearly there himself. It roared in the center of his balls and then chased the white-hot pleasure up his shaft. Pumped into her impossibly tight tunnel until he was nothing but a beast himself, sliding his hand up, clamping his palm over her mouth.

"With me, submissive. Come with me. Squeeze your cunt around my cock. Scream your pleasure against my skin."

Her breathing doubled. Her lips opened against his palm.

Her sex convulsed around his dick.

As her climactic cry fired into his hand.

Holy. Fuck.

He was done.

Broiled.

Scorched.

And now, spilling with heat belonging only to her.

Only to her.

What the *hell* was she doing to him?

No orgasm, with any other lover, had brought him even close to this inferno—so intense it imploded his mind, destroyed his logic, consumed his body. He was the core of a bullet, exploding from its casing. The heart of a volcano, awakened to blue fire by the gods. A flood bursting past a dam, taking down giant chunks of control in the unstoppable deluge.

He was...changed.

He was terrified.

A truth not letting up, in clarity or intensity, even as their climaxes mellowed to dull roars and he rose, gliding carefully out of both her entrances. A psychic glare only growing as he leaned and grabbed a box of tissues from the office's credenza, wiping his hands and cock as best as he could, before making himself decent again. A pressure turning his chest to lead as he peeled her off the desk and then rolled her directly into his arms, sitting in the leather chair again, using its mobility to gently rock them both.

An ache in places deeper than that lead, as Tracy curled herself into him with sighs that were nearly songs. Soft. Grateful. Happy. The siren to his serpent, appeasing his soul with the magic of her music.

But not easing the terror.

Terror he'd just been preaching at *her* to embrace, to move through, to confront and conquer.

Hypocrite.

He grunted softly.

Guilty as charged.

Though if the universe wanted to pursue a trial, he was tagging a coconspirator. Fate wasn't getting out of taking some of this blame. Nor, damn it, from helping him shoulder the consequences—namely, the impossible task of figuring out where his life went from here. Three days ago, *here* had been a lot less complicated. Daunting yet doable. Now, doable had disappeared behind enemy lines, and he had no rescue helo in sight.

Doable was gone.

Leaving only one entity behind in the bunker with him.

Impossible.

He fought the verdict even as he dipped his head, locking his gaze with the searching fervor of hers, tightening his hold around every inch of her—recognizing the byzantine dream of her. Further than that, realizing why her job had nothing to do with the unworkable paradox of them. Harder issues were at play here. Huger issues. Walls having nothing to do with her and everything to do with his jammed-up mind...

A conclusion invading him so hard, it was a no-joy battle to keep it from invading his composure. As he'd feared, Tracy's radar went up at once, jerking her as sharply as if he'd spanked her again—making the list of shit he'd be taking up with fate soon, since he hadn't gotten the actual pleasure of delivering said swat.

"Hey." Though she tenderly palmed his jaw, her voice was a hardcore mandate.

"Hey." He released it atop a long exhalation, banking on the casual but professional approach to diffuse her. With a little more affection, he asked, "How are you doing?"

Damn, that felt good. Aftercare was right up there with

fuck swings as one of his favorite aspects of the dynamic. The chance to be close to a submissive again, knitting what their bodies had done into a deeper mental bond, was a high like no other—and one of the prominent reasons why he liked playing hard. Breaking down walls, getting to guts and honesty, took fire and courage—and sometimes, if one was lucky, sheer magic. While he'd tasted the first two with other submissives, he'd all but given up on truly finding it with anyone in a real sense. Maybe—probably—making his living in all the most un-magical places on this planet hadn't helped either. Very likely, he'd given up on magic, not the other way around.

Or so he'd thought.

Until Tracy Livia Rhodes.

Until the one woman he wanted to aftercare the crap out of but couldn't, thanks to this stockpile of bullshit in his brain.

Only it wasn't bullshit.

Which made this suck even worse.

Especially as she huffed so adorably, he almost considered throwing her back on the desk and simply pretending it was a fuck swing—even as she followed it by snipping, "Don't change the subject."

A grin formed. Holding back a hurricane would've been easier. "*Popoki,* how you're doing *is* the subject."

Her lips pursed. "Beguiling me isn't going to work."

He surrendered half a shrug. Denying she was right would've been a lie. She could insist on being his Tigress everywhere else, but in these tender moments, his Hawaiian version of "kitten" melted her every time.

Mostly.

"I was hard on you," he finally stated. With fingertips flowing along the back of her arm, quietly added, "And I'm just making sure you...liked it."

Her tongue darted along the seam of her lips. "Yeah," she whispered. "I definitely..."

"What?" His hand stilled. His brows narrowed.

"Liked it." Her gaze followed the trail of her own hand, down to the center of his chest. "What I mean is...*shit*." Obviously, her gray matter was spinning up a few theories of its own. John pulled her closer, securing her in with a determined hand on her outside hip.

"Tracy."

"I'm not trying to be coy!" She snorted. "This just isn't easy."

"If it were easy, everyone would be doing it."

"Everyone *isn't* doing it?"

He lifted his stare, using it as admonishment. Her whip of a wit lashed his libido in all the right places, but that shit got locked back when she brandished it as diversion.

"Okay." She straightened her posture—not a help for the situation in his crotch, already responding to the nearness of her perfect ass cheeks again—and took in a full breath. "I'll at least give it a try."

"*Mahalo*." He softly kissed her forehead before settling back, determined to listen to her with his ears and hear her with his soul.

"So...I liked it. We're clear on that."

He dipped his head a little. "We are."

"But the thing is...I..."

"Didn't *want* to like it?"

"Oh, I wanted to like it." She worried her bottom lip. "I just didn't feel like...I should." Her fingertips played at the buttons on his Henley. "But you..." A sigh left her. This time, it wasn't such a sublime sound. Shiny droplets appeared on her lashes, each like a Karambit blade in his chest, but he remained still through the torture. She needed to process, to sort this shit out for herself, and he needed to shut the hell up and let her. "*You*, Keoni John Franzen," she finally rasped, fingers sliding to his jaw again. "You took me into the shadows, and you made all of it okay. The darkness, the pain, even the fear... You commanded me to look at it and then embrace it. You turned my most wicked thoughts into something..." She swallowed hard, shaking her head. "Well, something I never imagined could be reality."

So much for holding back.

Franz's hand, just finished with a caress up her arm, swept over her shoulder and into her hair. With a gut-deep moan, he twisted his fingers in. Yanked the strands hard—and then captured her squeal of pain with a brutal crash of his lips. Invaded her even deeper, diving his tongue along hers, forcing her jaw wider so he could taste even more of her hot, wet cavity. *Not deep enough.* He could never be buried inside her enough...

"I never thought you'd be a reality for me, either."

He gave her the confession as she'd surrendered hers—rasped and rickety, from the center of his gut. Listening to the words, bumping and pushing from him, caused his fingers to follow suit. He watched, amazed, as they started trembling in her hair. He spread the tips out, seeking her cheek...gathering the drops there. No. Hoarding them for the mental scrapbook he'd begun to keep of her...realizing that at any moment, the memories would be all he had left.

Besides, his words had effectively taken care of any new rainfall down her face. In place of the tears, she now wore an openly skeptical scowl. And damn it if *that* didn't look five kinds of adorable on her too—until she issued the words to justify it.

"Okay, hold up a second."

He ticked up one side of his mouth. Added a defined thrust of his hips. "I'll hold you up anywhere, ma'am."

"Thank you, *Sir*"—her succinct scowl clarified the title was now a term of ire instead of endearment—"but I need a little elucidation here."

"And I'd like to help you out." He calmed his cock and settled his smirk. "By all means, let's elucidate."

Her scowl tightened. "That should *not* turn me on so much."

His own brows hunched. Couldn't say the same thing about his dick this time, but that was all on her. "What shouldn't?"

"You. Saying 'elucidate.'"

"You know elucidate just became my favorite word, right?"

She took a hand to his chest again—with a chastising smack. "Be serious."

"I am. Completely." He tightened his hold, nestling her closer. "I'm ready for your elucidation."

An eye roll and a huff later, she turned her touch at his sternum into a pattern of hesitant swirls once more. As he looked on, the apprehension made its way up her face too. "What did you mean...that you never thought I'd be a reality?"

He chucked a soft choke. "I don't understand." Dipped his head, attempting to catch her downcast eyes. "I don't fuck around with symbolism, woman. I meant exactly that. You're..." His shook his head, dazed for a second. He really didn't fuck with words—but right now, even finding any of them to shoot straight was a huge damn problem. "You're..."

"Not your first ride at the rodeo?"

"Huh?"

"*John.*" She thumped his chest again. "Come *on.* You're pretty damn good at this stuff—"

"In case you can't tell, *ku`uipo*, 'this stuff' takes two."

"*And* a hell of a lot of experience. *A lot* of other rodeos."

He grunted. This had to be the strangest aftercare he'd ever been a part of. "And?"

"Are you telling me there's never been a dream pony for you before this?"

His brain skidded, nearly cartoon style, to a halt. Like the rider in that little movie, his logic slingshotted ahead, only to snap back into the saddle, gaping and dazed. "Should I be troubled that I understood every word of that?"

"Of course not." She patted his sternum with feminine ease, yanking him from the saddle again. For a woman who worked in a world of hard facts and gritty details, she was scarily peaceful in accepting the depth of their connection. "But that doesn't answer my question."

The lungs beneath her fingers filled with air. Franz slowly released it. This was ridiculous, talking about "ponies" who came before her, because the woman was his fucking unicorn—but she'd also just bared herself to him on a dozen different levels, and that alone earned her an answer. But how much of an answer? Honesty, even in its brutal and painful forms, was as essential to his world as purpose and goals—but how many of the gory details did that mean he had to share? Not that this woman, so brave and bold and real, couldn't handle any of the shit.

The pussy here was him.

He couldn't handle it, forcing *her* to handle all of it.

He wanted to keep being her hero.

But that meant clarifying how *she* was his heroine.

And that meant supplying her with the perspective of his past.

And yeah, that meant he was going to have to bust out with the strange shit again.

Communication.

Careful communication.

CHAPTER FIFTEEN

Be careful what you ask for.

Should've been the lesson she'd learned thoroughly by now, right? Turn a crafting hobby into an online store, end up with a hundred employees and two warehouses. Take on Congress about security measures for foreign contractors, be appointed vice president of the country. Push John Franzen when the man had you bent over and writhing atop a desk, and the words "executive order" gained meaning beyond the wildest imagination.

But keep pushing the man, even when the desk wasn't a factor, and get the strangest result of all.

A reaction, despite the sienna shade of the man's face, feeling a hell of a lot like a Kansas prairie snowstorm. Unreadable. Impenetrable. Eerie, even in the middle of the afternoon.

She forced down a deep breath for herself. Crazily, took heed of what she liked calling her "Capitol Hill Swami": the inner voice responsible for keeping her grounded when she most longed to pummel herself into that ground. She usually only invited Swami out after putting her foot in her mouth during committee meetings or pulling a dork move in front of the press like wearing different-colored shoes. Swami was most fond of telling her life really *was* going to be all right, no matter how she felt she'd just mucked it up.

Like right now.

No.

This wasn't a muck-up, damn it. This wasn't a sudden attack of needy, even if it looked exactly like that—though it occurred that maybe the man couldn't read *all* her thoughts, and "clingy crazy" was exactly where he'd gotten busy slotting her in his mind.

"Okay, just—" She pushed away from him. It was *not* easy, damn it—as a matter of fact, it was agonizing—but she succeeded at getting a few inches between them. "Forget I asked, okay? I was really just curious, and—"

And really just a huge, freaking liar.

Because when she managed to push out another inch, it was beyond agony.

It was scary.

She shook, battling not to throw herself back against him. Forced down a sharp breath, opening her mouth from the effort to prevent her teeth from chattering. Less than five seconds from tearing herself from the sun of him, and the galaxy was already a cold, lonely, empty place.

But soon, the space suit would be waiting.

And presidents didn't get time to alter any of the gear—or the course of the journey.

They were expected to latch in, hang on, and fly, no matter what the damn sun did. Or how beautiful he was doing it.

Or how glorious it felt when the sun flared, reaching out arms so forceful and knowing, and dragged them right back to his searing, soul-dissolving heat.

And rumbled a sound of warm satisfaction as soon as they sighed against the breadth of his chest.

The plane of such perfect light and heat, they could forget the space suit even existed.

Okay, maybe she was a little crazy clingy. And maybe she just had to be okay with that—for just another moment longer.

Then maybe another.

One more couldn't hurt.

As if she needed another affirmation of that, aside from his heartbeat under her cheek and his arms wrapping her close, Franz's kiss brought a rush of wonderful heat on the top of her head. He kept his lips there while finally murmuring, "I like it that you asked, *popoki*."

She started, but only by a little. No way in hell was she giving up his closeness this time. "You do?"

He nodded. Kissed into her hair again. Began stroking the strands near her ear, which were still damp from how hard he'd worked her. The subtle reminder of their passion, along with his rhythmic combing, drenched her in a hazy languor. "I just want to give you an answer not involving ponies."

She pouted. "What's wrong with ponies?"

"Not a damn thing. I simply prefer felines over equines."

She laughed softly. "Well-played, Captain Franzen."

"And I do enjoy playing, kitten."

"You mean blowing a submissive's ever-loving mind?"

"Yeah. Something like that," he chuckled back.

"You're still avoiding the question, but keep rubbing my head and I'll let it pass."

"Hmmm." He expanded his touch, massaging deeper. "Well-played yourself, Tracy Rhodes." He pulled in a long breath, raising and lowering her head along with his chest. "And still another reason why I never thought someone like you existed."

She let out a breath on a hum before burrowing tighter against him. Hopefully, it demonstrated how thoroughly she absorbed the confession into her heart. It was more than just the words. It was the walls he smashed through to speak them... the basement he had to push out of.

"It's really been that hard for you?" She tilted her face up so he could see the sincerity of her gaze. "I mean, I get it, John; a life in public service doesn't lend itself to a lot of Netflix-and-chill. On top of that, you usually can't talk about your day at the office."

"And there's the small issue of not being able to leave the orders on the battlefield. And the handcuffs. And the rope. And certain blunt instruments capable of leaving interesting marks on a bare ass."

His rejoinder made her frown. "Wait. Has that seriously been an issue for you?" Because just the idea of him, wielding any or all that stuff on her, flipped about a dozen new switches of arousal between her thighs.

"At first, yes." A frisson of something strange took over his face, especially his eyes. After a couple of seconds it was gone, though Tracy still felt the tense twitches in his body, indicating an inner battle. "But not since I partnered with my best friend to open a club of our own."

Aha. The war of the psyche, explained. She'd seen enough internal skirmishes like it, sitting across conference tables from people debating what truths to reveal in the name of political gain, to peg the behavior. But in this case, he was willing to lose—doubling her esteem of him.

That felt...

Really nice.

Even nicer, when she was able to lift an impish smile and dancing eyes, enjoying the new flare across his face as she purred, "Well. Just when I thought you couldn't get any hotter."

He grinned. Not just any grin. It was his look of supreme, sexy pride, curving his lips into curves more enticing than she'd seen on him yet. "Lighting it up *is* a favorite specialty."

"You mean like fire play?"

His smirk gave way to a new gape. "*Shit.*"

"What?"

"You know about that kind of kink?"

He was being honest. She had to do the same. "If you must know, I've dreamed about that kind of kink."

He blinked. Stared as if she'd just slapped him—to the point she reached up, spreading fingers across his jaw. "Have I officially freaked you out?"

He snorted. "In about seventeen ways." After sliding his tongue between her lips for a brief but searing suckle, he ensured, "All the best ways."

The words, and *that kiss*, spread tingles through every extremity of her body—to the point she almost ditched the conversation just to have more of that contact. She forced herself to focus on words instead. Essential ones. "So at your club, surely you had a line of subs waiting to get beneath you."

A line. *Ha.* Who was she kidding? The queue had probably wound out the door and down the block—a conclusion she was so certain of, it pitched a damn tent in her mind despite Franz's rough laugh.

"Bastille isn't McDonald's, kitten," he chided. "One just can't drive in, order their Dom or sub with no pickles and extra mayo, and then get busy. There are nuances. Variables. A lot of them."

She mulled on that for a second. "I get that, I think." Tilted her head in deeper thought. "I guess, the way I always perceived it, was that BDSM had gradients...lighter play to the hardcore things...and as long as you met someone with the same tastes, you were pretty good."

He dropped his head the same direction as hers, lining up their stares once more. "True, if one is only in it for the obvious surface benefits."

"And you're not a surface-benefits guy." She was damn glad she could issue *that* as a certainty too—but even more joyful about his matching conviction of an answer.

"Never was. Never will be."

For all the surety of his statement, there was another blatant ingredient. Sobriety. Resignation. And yes, sadness. A double dose of the last—slapping Tracy with a solid stunner.

Well...hell.

For as much of the man as she already saw—*thought* she saw—she'd committed the same sin as a lot of others, considering only his exotic beauty, boulder vista muscles, and hypnotic baritone, and then assumed he simply "picked from the line" at the club, like a superstar selecting groupies to accompany him behind the velvet VIP rope.

She'd been a moron.

She'd looked at the beyond-the-surface guy and painted him with her just-the-surface assumptions.

Her brains. Back pocket. Yeah, the one she'd just sat soundly on.

Not anymore.

She'd look deeper, damn it. See him for more.

The universe was all about insta-rewarding that—and she sure as hell didn't complain—with a rush of new insight. A hunch she was so sure of, she went ahead and spoke it aloud.

"So what was her name?"

John took his turn to jerk with surprise. His eyes

narrowed, but his lips smirked as he returned, "So it's no longer what were *their* names?"

Tracy arched both brows. "Oh, I'm sure there were plenty of those too—likely anywhere your team stopped for more than a few nights—but I'm not after those gory details."

"Why not?"

"Because they're not the goriest." She held up a finger. "Rephrase. They're not the detail that matters." Lowered that finger to the center of his sternum. "The one woman who got closest to this."

Which was also the closest *she'd* get to actually labeling that shit, as well. Unfair? Possibly. Probably. Neither of them were fresh-faced and dewy-eyed anymore. They'd both had lives before this moment. The evidence of the one she'd lived and shared with another man filled her days in the miracle of her son. It was petty and silly of her to think he'd gone that long without the same thing, but she did. Her guilt about it grew when thinking of him returning from his dangerous missions, only to have no one home to greet and comfort him.

"There's never been anyone...steady," he replied at last, clearly pushing up a few more basement stairs to do so. "Not a girlfriend or wife, if that's where this is going."

Tracy hooked her finger into the V of his Henley and pulled lightly. After they finished their soft kiss, she didn't let go. "It's not *going* anywhere, Sir." She slipped in the honorific, sensing he needed it. "I just want to know more about you."

He pressed his forehead to hers. "I know. And you deserve to be told."

"*You* deserve to tell it," she countered. "Everyone needs safe ground for their secrets, and you sure as hell have been mine for the last few days. So let me reciprocate a little—but only if you choose to. I'm not here to make you reopen old wounds." A teasing quirk sneaked across her lips. "Unless, of course, they're oozing green pus and need to be cleaned out, in which case—"

"Christ." He reared back, laughing and grimacing at once. "How'd we go from surface benefits to oozing green pus?"

"Fifteen-year-old son, dude." She tapped a playful finger to his forehead. "Remember?"

"You mean that grinning hellion who beat me four straight sets at virtual tennis last night?" He caught her hand before she fully lowered it, dragging his firm, full mouth across her knuckles. "Yeah, I remember," he added, his words and his gaze now infused with sobriety. "And yeah...it's about time I told you about Abbie."

And here it was. The brick she'd been relentlessly chipping at in his wall, finally loosened by their rapport—only to feel like it had dropped a hundred feet into the center of her head.

The brick had a name now.

"Abbie." Somehow, she managed it without gritted teeth—and a small smile. A *small* one. "It's a...pretty name."

"It is." His voice was a murmur, but his gaze was a miss-nothing radar. Tracy identified the mien at once. All the best diplomats she knew had it mastered. "And it's a special one to me. Probably always will be."

Okaaaayy.

Tracy schooled her reaction, going for pleasant but neutral, positive she failed on both fronts. Was this "Abbie" still an important part of his life? If so, how long had she enjoyed that status? And why? Not like the man was giving her anything to go on here.

Enjoy Vague Booking much, Sir?

And wasn't she just trivializing his truth, hoping it diminished her jealousy about it too?

A truth you've been pushing for, missie.

A trust you've been begging him to give you.

Put on your big-girl panties, and prove yourself worthy of that trust.

"Did you meet her—Abbie"—she could do this, she could do this—"at your club?"

He nodded evenly. "In a way, yes."

"In a way?"

"We met at a munch." He went on, as soon as she questioned that with an open frown, "Fancy term for a kink community event at a vanilla venue."

Welcome, deeper scowl. "And that works out for everyone...how?"

"It works out just fine." An authentic smile twisted his lips. "Because it gives everyone a chance to connect without the possibility of clothes coming off." He paused thoughtfully. "The best power exchanges start from the space over your shoulders, not beneath your waist."

"Yeah." Her lips curved into an answering smile. "I understand that now."

His fingertip traced the edge of her face. "I believe that."

She leaned her cheek toward his touch, cherishing the infusion of his energy from the simple contact. If anything proved the truth of his assertion, this was truly it. They were both fully clothed, but every fiber of her body acknowledged how easily he could claim governance over it again, if he so chose. "But I didn't get it, before now. I guess I just saw what a lot of the world does. The wicked toys, the shiny furniture, the kinky costumes..."

"All fun in their own right," he offered. "But not the main point of the dynamic."

God, how tempted she was to follow him further down that tangent trail. She longed to talk about toys, torments, and "all the shinies" with him for hours—and to definitely do something about where their libidos went because of it—but that wouldn't honor the path they were supposed to be on. She'd specifically pushed him for this information, and he'd climbed out of his basement with his honesty about it. Shoving him back into the darkness because she couldn't handle anything more than a name was *not* cool.

"And Abbie? She comprehended that point too?"

A wistful smile began in his eyes and crinkled the corners of his lips. "She did." His lips parted as if to add more, but he reined back the initial thought, seeming to change direction, before attesting, "Probably a little too much, now that I look at things with a little room."

A little room.

An inner victory dance about that certainly wasn't mature. Or diplomatic.

Maturity and diplomacy were overrated.

While her psyche cha-chaed around its private bonfire, she calmly said, "Well, there's an opening for about a thousand stories."

"Maybe not a thousand." The reply was as reflective as his gaze, now directed across the room. "But we had compatible needs, in and out of the dungeon, and it worked out well for a lot of years."

"Dungeon?" She repeated the word out of bafflement—or so she assured her inner dance party, quickly changing from a cha-cha into something more exotic. And erotic. Something much better suited for a dungeon run by a Dominant like John Franzen. If that was even what he meant...

"Another kinkster Easter Egg." He glanced quickly to her, as if trying to gauge her reaction as he finished. "A way of saying play room, for those of us into fire, whips, and chains instead of pads, rope, and ticklers."

Though he was casual about the innuendo's tone, his watchfulness intensified—*not* helping her newest desire to just kiss him. Or strip for him. Oh hell, why not both?

Because that option would advance them nowhere.

She had to settle for jerking her head up and whispering, "Then I guess I'm a dungeon kind of girl."

Franz's groan, emanating from deep in his chest, almost changed her mind about the kiss-and-strip plan. She sucked it up for both of them, clearing her throat as if simply moving on to a new agenda item in a committee meeting.

"So tell me why Abbie was so..." *Special? Remarkable?* "Compatible." In the end, his own term was truly the most tolerable one, driving her to yet another inward kick in the figurative ass. Since when had she settled for simply tolerable? The green monster in her psyche was more disgusting than her weight in pus, and she wasn't proud of it.

"It's pretty simple to explain." John spoke slowly, as if the statement were a new revelation. "I mean, the libretto fits the score about how things matched up in our dungeon sessions— and aside from a few hours of aftercare, she was firm about not wanting anything deeper in a relationship with me."

"So she was crazy?" The rejoinder spilled without a second thought, though she stood by it. The man was smart, funny, protective, and passionate. Then there was the whole body of a god and cock of a stallion thing too...

John chuckled as if reading *that* particular thought. "No. She was a psychologist—a leading one in the city, actually—with a couple of books about healing from your past, as well as one of those psychobabble call-in radio shows."

Tracy brought up her head and shoulders, tacking on a crisp little nod. "And she wrote the stuff from 'experience'?"

He nodded again, clearing his throat. Her new position, while lending professionalism to their upper bodies, fitted their crotches tighter. She could have—should have—rectified things by getting up and walking away, but maybe she'd just ask him for the call-in number to Abbie baby's show. Clearly, she needed psychological help. She was growing addicted to this man and his incredible body.

"She had a rough deal growing up. After her dad was hauled to prison for embezzlement and fraud, her mom turned to drugs, and the story goes downhill from there. Abbie ended up as a foster care kid at the age of twelve. Her angle is that bad shit can happen to anyone, at any time, and can be survived. Her whole reputation's built on it."

"And dating a guy who's part-owner of a BDSM club doesn't jive with the I-am-woman-hear-me-roar rep."

"Give the lady a prize." He lightly nipped the end of her nose with two knuckles. In the wake of his touch, Tracy wrinkled it with irked emphasis.

"Have you tried telling her that's bullshit?" She didn't explain herself. She didn't have to. He got it. He really did. He knew that a person's strength was greatest when they were at their most vulnerable. And dear God, how *she* knew it. Had learned it, over and over again, to the point it was nearly a theme in her life.

"A few times," he replied to her charge. "I *did* try. As her

Dom, I had the responsibility to. I mean, I knew there were parts of her I could help with the pain..."

"And the sex?" It hurt like hell to fill it in, but she ramrodded it through her lips. If not, she was no different than the woman to whom they referred, refusing growth just because it hurt.

"Yeah," John concurred quietly. "And the sex." But his gaze, swinging to her, was a blare of volume. His irises, the shade of polished brass horns, consumed her psyche like a whole orchestra. "But on both levels, we never totally connected. She wanted the heavy play and always verbally committed to giving it her all, but she kept parts of herself held back no matter how hard I tried to open those doors." His face tightened. "She had the keys and wasn't giving them up."

Tracy quietly rested her chin on the ball of his shoulder. "Maybe she couldn't disconnect from her public persona?" she suggested. "I've seen that one happen over and over again. The fame validates the public face more than the truth—but the sands under that foundation are constantly shifting."

His stare sharpened. "Shit."

Her head lifted. "What?"

"You sure you're only thirty-five?" He pushed questing fingers into the back of her neck. "Come on. Where are you concealing the zipper?"

"The zipper to *what*?"

"You're not really the young, hot VP, are you? You're hiding some older wise woman in there, instead—like Dolly Levi."

Her eyes bulged. "*Dolly Levi?*"

"No! I got it. The Reverend Mother from *Sound of—*"

She gasped. "Don't you dare go there!"

He laughed. "Fine. Maybe you're that cool bald chick from *Doctor Strange*..."

She twisted away from him, giggling. "Finish your story, island boy."

As much as she wished he'd get snarly and choose to spank her for the impudence, the man sobered swiftly. "Like I've said," he murmured, "not much of a story. Abbie wasn't interested in conventional dates outside the dungeon, and her schedule only left her opportunities for 'play dates' every few months—"

"Making her the perfect fit for a Special Forces team captain spending more time out of the country than in," she supplied.

He confirmed that with a defined twist of lips. "Which was why I committed one of the biggest Dominant fuck-ups in the book." His eyes slid shut, staying that way until he drew in enough breath to grimace from that as well. "I stopped paying attention."

Tracy lifted a hand to trace the creases bracketing his eyes and mouth, letting her own frown tighten. "You stopped seeing her?" She didn't pull punches on her confusion. "Things like that happen, John. All the time. People grow apart."

He peeled her hand away, finally releasing air on a ponderous growl. "I didn't stop seeing her, damn it. I just stopped paying attention. Do you get it now? She became just another fuck, Tracy. I tied her up because that was what she wanted. Flogged her because she liked that even more. Screwed her because she liked that the best of all. But it was all just actions without meaning, words without context." He grimaced harder. Gritted his next words out. "A sham of a connection."

Since he kept a tortured clench around one of her hands, she pressed the other to his chest once more. For long moments, simply let her touch be filled by his furious heartbeat. She'd known him less than a week, still unsure about everything from his birthday to what he liked on his pizza, but if there was anything of which she was certain about the man, it was his dedication to the truth—to being as real with people as possible. It seemed as ingrained in him as being raised in a large, loving, honest family, but perhaps had come about only recently, as a consequence of his subterfuge job. Life in the shadows meant one craved the sun—

And perhaps, sometimes, forgot what its warmth felt like.

"I'm sorry," she finally murmured into the silence. "That must have been strange for you."

He erupted in a short, sharp laugh. Dropped his head into *his* free hand. "You'd think, right?"

"It wasn't?"

His shrug was more of a terse jerk. "It was easier just to... let it be, I guess. I'd come home from missions, strung out and jet lagged, and just craved that last rush of adrenaline to fully drain me so I could sleep for days." He lifted his head, glancing to her with bleak eyes. "I became the Dom I swore I'd never be. Just in it for the flogging and the fucking."

Tracy took a second before nodding. She let him—and perhaps herself—know that the words had truly sunk in. It wasn't an easy task, realizing she had to yank him down from the stars, where he'd been existing as honor-bound warrior and lover, down to the earth of a human man, warrior nonetheless, who had issues to overcome after dealing with the uglier side of protecting his country.

But once she did...

He was even more beautiful to her.

Because he was more real.

All of that clamored in her throat, begging her for freedom, but she kept it back with a careful swallow and instead asked, "So what happened?" And yes, forced the remainder of that out too. "Or...has it? Is she expecting you to call her for another round of things soon?"

"No." He snapped it so swiftly, she knew it was the truth. "*God* no," he reiterated, confirming her belief. "Not after... everything that finally *did* happen."

She bundled an inch closer to him. "It's okay." Squeezed his hand and pressed his chest. "I'm right here, and I'm not going anywhere."

Though he flung a taut gaze, all but disbelieving her, he ticked out a fast nod. "It was about ten months ago. I was awaiting word for a mission; knew I could be called out to JBLM for deployment at any minute, but the waiting was driving me nuts."

"So you called Abbie," she filled in.

Another brusque nod. "We chose to meet at Bastille, as always." That was the last of anything easy about his expression. His jaw hardened like magma hitting ice. His gaze turned just as black. "But I was restless, tired of everything being 'as always.' I told Abbie as much. She actually seemed excited about the idea—which sure as hell gunned *my* rockets."

Tracy fought for a patient smile but failed. "Please tell me I don't have to like this part." Progressive and objective only went so far. The idea of any other woman "gunning his rockets," and Miss Sweetness-and-Light officially took a hike.

Franz shifted his hand, cupping her chin, before coaxing her up for his savoring kiss. "I'll skip to the relevant part."

"Correct answer." She initiated a kiss, just to let him know she approved of his answer on *all* fronts. "So...what happened?"

He exhaled once more. "I played her hard—that's what happened. Probably harder than I ever had before. It was...an intense session."

Her brows crunched. "Well, that sounds pretty damn nice. Unless..." Something pinched her mind and refused to let go. "Unless she safe worded?" There was more to the conclusion, but she couldn't summon the words to her lips. They consumed her mind though. *Unless she safe worded...and you ignored her?*

Franz's face expanded with shock, exposing how he'd taken her lead and run with it anyway. "No," he pronounced. "She didn't safe word." His grip coiled tighter. His eyes slammed shut again. "Though damn, it would've been so much easier if the little fool had."

Icicles stabbed her spine. "What...do you mean?"

He gulped hard. Reopened his gaze, only to hurl his focus across the room again. He was lost to memories.

Dark, difficult ones.

"No," he muttered then. "She wasn't the only fool in the room. I knew better. I should have been paying closer attention. Watching for the signs."

"What signs? John?" Tracy tugged on the front of his shirt, forcing him to face her again. "What signs?" She bit out both syllables through her teeth, continuing their painful clench when he glanced down, blinking as if barely recognizing her.

Just before a wave of fresh rage claimed every inch of his face.

Through his own clenched teeth, he uttered at last, "Abbie's diabetic." He took another long pause, obviously searching for words. "It was never an issue because we always made sure she was at an acceptable blood-sugar level for her submissive duties. Before a stitch of her clothes came off, I made her take a reading and show it to me."

"And you didn't that night?" The question was a welcome distraction. Nearly every cell in her brain, and tissue in her sex, had stopped back at *submissive duties*. Where could she sign up for some of that...whatever it was?

"Of course we did," he returned. "Her readings weren't negotiable."

"But something went wrong anyway." Talk about a subject to calm the libido.

He shifted. Again. "Like I said, the session got..." A massive breath heaved through his chest. "Well, it was powerful shit. I was keyed-up about the mission; she'd just gained some massive market share for her show...and in the places I'd normally stop to let her rest or rehydrate, she yelled at me for more."

Tracy's eyes bulged. "She *yelled* at you?"

"Submissives being denied orgasms often *do* do that."

"Oh," she stammered. "I—uh—see." And hello, dancing pygmies of arousal through her pussy again. "And...so...you..."

"Gave her what she wanted." His jaw jutted. Tracy sensed he couldn't tell whether to tack on a grin, a grimace, or both. "Hell, what *I* wanted. Trouble was...it wasn't what she needed."

"Which was what?"

"A fucking break." No smirk there. Nor even the frown. When the man was angry, especially at himself, his composure went beyond the realm of standard expressions. If only that aspect of him didn't fascinate her as much as his other sides... "By the time I realized something was truly, physically going on with her instead of the standard submissive head space, she was close to passing out from her blood-sugar imbalance."

"Holy shit."

"Yeah. Holy shit."

"But you helped her? She was okay after you realized..."

"After I realized what?" he retorted. "I didn't know what the hell was happening—whether her sugar was spiking or dropping or a roller coaster of both." He breathed in violent bursts now, as if his inner bullwhip was tearing his body open, thrash by bloody thrash. "Thank fuck for Max and Delphine."

"Who?" she pressed.

"Max Brickham," he elucidated. "He's my business partner. Bastille's co-owner."

"And Delphine is his girlfriend?"

He shook his head. "His Jag XKR-S."

"Whoa." She swung her own head back. "Yep. Car like that needs a name."

"She was our heroine for the night too. Got Abbie to the hospital in five minutes flat. They processed her fast. Balanced her levels out right away."

"And all was well that ended well." Which had her stomach hurting and heart twisting all over again. The hideous green monster wouldn't stay away, even if *she* was the one currently mashed on the man's lap, feeling the bounty in his pants between her ass cheeks.

"Sure. Let's just say that." But a Tardis dropped in the middle of the room would've been easier to ignore than his caustic overtone. "'All was well that ended well.'"

Tracy huffed. "No saying it if it wasn't true." Grabbed the V of his Henley and tugged again. "So *was* it?"

The man's luscious mouth opened. Clamped shut again.

"John?"

Another moment. Obvious deliberation in the sienna shadows of his eyes. "Yeah. Sure," he said, like a father relenting on a candy request to a relentless kid.

Tracy released his shirt. Curled her finger in with the others in order to form a full fist—quickly pummeled into his sternum. "Yeah, sure?" she retaliated. "How about *yeah sure*, you're full of bullshit?"

Humor pursed his lips and sparkled in his eyes. "Well, well, well, Madam President. Bossy is kind of sexy on you."

"Don't change the subject." She dug knuckles into the closest slab of pectoral. He humored her by wincing, but his demeanor sobered by several degrees.

"Fine," he relented, rocking against the chair's headrest so his stare pierced up at the ceiling. "You deserve the truth about the last part too."

"The last part?" She sounded five kinds of nosey, probably ten in suspicious. Inwardly puking about both accounts, she stroked a hand to the side of his neck and reached—*reeaached*—for a light laugh. "You mean there's more than a close call with a diabetic coma?"

"Oh yeah." He snorted, though didn't borrow any of her humor. "A close call with a much bigger risk—at least to Abbie." His gaze darkened as his voice softened. "Her reputation."

Like a congressional budget finally balancing, so much began to make sense. "Oh," Tracy blurted. Repeated it, drawing the sound out with the light of comprehension, before stating as the fact she was so sure of, "So someone in the ER recognized her. Maybe more than *one* someone."

"Both her nurses." With the affirmation, Franz began gently rocking the chair. The man and his Adonis thighs were making it damn hard to stay focused on the subject. She kept it together as he went on, "They were both huge fans—meaning neither missed the subtle marks still left on her waist from the flogging or her cagey answers about what we'd been doing on our 'date' earlier in the evening."

"Oh." The syllable got extended once more, though this version was lighter in her throat and on her psyche. Didn't mean she couldn't feel awful about it. Embarrassment was never fun for anyone. "So what did she finally tell them?"

"She didn't," Franz answered. "*I* stepped in, basically letting them know it was a private matter between lovers. But as soon as they left, Abbie turned and dropped the hammer. She was adamant about never seeing me, or a kink dungeon, ever again." He evened his gaze with hers again. "I drove her home, even called her the next day. She didn't pick up. Day after that, I hopped on a plane for North Korea."

Of course he had.

Because that was what soldiers did, even after women pushed them aside like used toys.

That was what heroes did, protecting the land those women lived in even after that kind of shit happened.

That was what warriors did because they'd been called by fate to make the world a better place, even if that meant sacrificing their lives.

But he didn't see all that, even now. He didn't have time for self-pity because he still saw only his duty. He didn't even have room for anger at Abbie because he was too busy spending it on himself. Fighting so hard to control the situation, he even took over the mental floggings. Because if *he* controlled the pain, it would hurt less, right?

The thought alone made *her* heart crack—and her vision

open wider. She brushed fingers over his intense face, seeing so much as if for the first time. The line of his jaw, always fixed at the same ruthless angle. The constant tension behind his temples. The perpetual darkness in his gaze. Restraints, she now realized, not there to keep himself in check...

But to keep the pain at bay.

It wasn't just the mental games Abbie had played with him. It was the tremendous toll of his "day job," the profession he gave over ten years of his life for, only to be abruptly ordered to step down and figure out his life all over again. It was the loss of himself, beyond what his battalion mates or even his family could help with. That shit had to come from deeper...a corner in his soul even he didn't know about.

She knew about that corner.

From firsthand experience.

The knowledge provided at least a little balm to her heart. She let it seep in through a long silence, knowing Franz filled the minutes by sorting through his own thoughts and memories. Finally, she broke the stillness by murmuring, "And when you got back from the mission? Did you try to contact her again?"

She hoped he'd say no but knew he'd say yes. The single dip of his head confirmed the latter without words. "Nothing was different. We tried to see if it would be, but...we just talked. Not for long. About the weather. About her show. About how my last mission was crap but I couldn't talk about it."

You can talk about it to me.

But now wasn't the time or the place. Now, all she wanted to do was clutch him close, sealing the fissures in his spirit with the passion of her kisses. She started with one, offering her mouth in open surrender, letting him softly take whatever he needed, for as long as he wanted. God knew, it was what *she* needed. His heat. His power. And yes, even his pain. Everything about this man—his chemistry, his biology, his energy—felt so perfect, so right, to all the corresponding parts of her.

Holy hell.

She'd fallen for him.

Maybe even a little more. Maybe even...a lot more.

Yeah. She had. And would pay for it later.

Joyfully.

Right now, even as he lifted his lips away from hers, the resolve sealed itself to her spirit, her heart. *Later.* The fine for this would come later—meaning she was damn well going to enjoy every magical drop of it now.

"So," she whispered. "Captain Franzen."

"Madam President." One corner of his mouth hitched. "May I be of service?"

"You may." She wrapped a hand against his skull, savoring the feel of his harsh spikes between her fingers. "I'm issuing a new executive order."

"Well, shit." He went on, underlined by her soft laugh, "Should I be scared?"

"Hmmm. Scared is a good thing, remember?"

"Ahhh." He kicked up the end, adding that mix of cocky and sexy deserving its own trademark. "Indeed I do."

Tracy let a smile burst across her lips. Framed the back of his head with her other hand, just to ensure she had his full attention for this. "From now on, the ghost of Abbie stays in the graveyard of the past."

His stare turned the shade of a smoky sunset. He pulled in a sizable breath. "Now that's an order I like." But as he released the air, another piece of him seemed to drain out too.

His arrogance. Tracy blinked. It was so much a part of him, she almost didn't recognize the man left behind: a person gone raw—and beautiful—with vulnerability. "I just can't promise I'll be good at delivering."

She dug her fingertips into his scalp. God, the man even had a perfectly shaped head. "Of course you will...because you'll have a new submissive to keep you focused." She joined the whisper to more determined tugs, guiding his face down again. "A kitten, here to give you all her trust and surrender."

A deep groan escaped him in two seconds before he took her lips once more. Tenderly, he suckled on her. Sighed into her. Captured so much of her heat while giving the fullness of his own.

Finally, with their breaths still merged and their foreheads locked, he rasped, "Christ, *ku'uipo*. How you honor me. Humble me."

She brought her hands forward, spreading them to the sides of his face. "And now, let me *help* you."

He warmed both her palms with kisses before dipping back in, coating her in the chocolate perfection of his stare. "You already have."

Her eyes slipped shut for a moment. The words meant so much, and she took the time to make sure they were stitched into the permanent fabric of her heart. "Not nearly as much as you've helped me."

"*Pfffft.*"

"Truth!" She opened her eyes and whacked him on the shoulder, secretly glad to welcome his cocky bastard side back. While she was moved, in ways she'd only started to fathom, by him stepping from the basement and then completely lowering his shields, she also knew that wasn't the way he preferred "getting naked." It was also much easier to drawl out her follow-up. "You think I ever would've gotten used to 'Madam President' without you?"

When one of his brows leapt, it took her libido right along with it. The smolder of his half smirk ensured the bundle went up in flames too. Holy shit, the man was good at mashing discipline *and* reward into the same hot look.

"Not a bad point at all, ma'am." He added the other half of his mouth to the grin, knowing damn well how his full smile affected her. Enflamed her. Know-it-all bastard. Gorgeous warrior.

Sure enough, she had to fight past the million butterflies in her belly and the flying fire in her blood just to shove at him again. "Yeah, well...find a way to get me used to the whole public-speaking thing, and I'll tell Luke to let you win a few tennis matches."

His gaze flared. "You *do* like seducing me."

"What?" She flattened a hand to the base of her neck. "Little *moi*?"

He emitted a sultry hum as his gaze drifted once more to her mouth. "*Oui, petite chat. Toi.*"

Damn it. Not the best time to forget that, as the Spec Ops stud he was, he knew how to say "kitten" in at least ten different languages—and sound that gravelly, gorgeously sexy in all of them.

Regardless, she managed to feign haughty sneer and a prissy pout. "*I* am a woman of integrity, John Franzen."

"*Pffft.*"

"I beg your pardon? *Ahhh!*"

Her saucy act went the way of her T-shirt, deftly whipped off by the man—at the same time he swept them both down to the floor. Before Tracy could process the surprise of *that*, the rogue filled the space over her, his mouth circling the erect areola of one newly naked breast. At once, she was a writhing mess. The rasp of his stubble across her sensitive nub... Holy *hell*, so good, but so much...an intensity doubled as he attended the other nipple with masterful pinches and tugs. Instantly, her whole body writhed, only to be stilled as he swept his hand down, palming her hot mound. A gasp finally broke free when his fingers went to work, circling between her wet folds, sliding across her most sensitive button of arousal.

"Integrity?" he murmured between wet, languorous kisses into the valley between her breasts. "At the moment, *ku`uipo*, I'm not interested in your fucking *integrity*."

He made sure she thanked God for that at once.

Then again.

And again.

And again...

CHAPTER SIXTEEN

"Boom chaka laka!" Franz spun a full circle in the middle of Z's den. "Game, set, and match!"

"Yep. Guess it is. Good job, dude." Luke, standing a few feet away, shook his head—but by the time the kid's "sheepish" glance was visible past the flop of his trendy haircut, his jig was up. Not only was the teen an awful actor; he'd borrowed the expression right out of his mother's playbook, meaning Franz's victory had just turned into a fresh challenge. How *did* a guy hide a fresh erection, courtesy of the mother of the kid still delivering a fake smirk and finger-twirling a video game controller?

His skill at creative body language had never come in handy more. Shoving his empty hand in front of the stiffy, he quickly crossed the opposite on top and then rocked back, going for a mix of hip-hop star and casual suspicion that probably appeared more like an older dude being a complete dork-ass.

And sometimes, dork-ass had to be good enough from the neck down. He made up for the deficiency with a healthy dose of the dragon glare, flung at the kid with one brow ticked, menacing jaw jabbed.

"Yeah?" he added, going all-business with that too. "Good game? You really think so?"

Luke shuffled back by a step. Averted his gaze. "Totally. You been practicing on the backhand?"

"Have *you* been practicing on the window washing?" Chuffs were cute when teenagers tried them. "Huh?"

"You're as transparent as a Windex commercial."

"*Huh?*"

"Come on." He folded his arms. "Your mom told you to throw it, didn't she?"

"What?" Another shake of the shag. "*No.* Sheez."

From the recliner behind Luke, a girlish snicker swirled out. The chair was rotated by a foot in bright-pink socks, until Mia appeared. "Toss it in, Jedi. Don't you know when a senior's onto you?"

Franz exchanged a glance with Luke—as dudes newly united on the same side. There were cool ways to mitigate shit between dudes, none of them including cute nicknames. From the open pout on her face, he guessed Mia was aware of the rule and went there anyway. Part of him couldn't blame her. While he'd worked with Rayna to disguise the kids enough that they could go out for quick supervised walks with Z, the novelty of this experience had worn off on them after two days. It felt like prison, and he knew it. They were all feeling the strain.

Bitter as the conclusion was, it brought blaring justification about the plans he'd made for tonight—if that was what he could call them. What *would* he call them?

Another issue for another minute. Right now, Luke became priority again—looking like he wanted to throw Mia *and* the chair right through the window behind the drawn drapes. "Do *not* keep calling me that. *Please.*"

Mia rolled her eyes. "'Please' doesn't count when you don't mean it."

"*Shit.*"

"Not nice, Jedi!"

"How about the first hundred times I *did* ask you nice?"

"Okay. *Whoa.*" John hurled the controller to the couch—no hard-on to stress about anymore—and planted himself between the teens. "Back to your cages, heathens."

Luke flung his own controller the same direction. "*Life* is a cage, Franzen. Deal with it."

John chomped the inside of his cheek to keep from pummeling the kid's emo moment with a laugh. But hell, was he tempted. Strongly. Luke was a damn fine kid, but puberty as a politician's kid had to be the worst under *normal* conditions, especially without a father. And *there* was the ultimate clincher, dampening Franz enough to simply watch as Luke skulked out of the room. As he watched the boy disappear around the corner into the kitchen, all slumped shoulders and brooding angst, he relished the chance to finally indulge his chuckle...

Only to find it gone.

Every last trace.

Instead, Franz rubbed hard at his chest—and the anvil that had landed there instead.

Mia's tearful sigh thickened the *Les Miz* pathos in the air. "I'm really sorry," she whispered. "I—I didn't mean it."

Franz glanced back. The girl sat on the recliner now, head hunched into her hands. He ruffled the top of her blond curls. "Of course you didn't, *kaikamahine.*"

"This is just so *hard.* Why do we have to pay the price for the crazy crap of some spaz-natch terrorist?"

Franz exhaled hard, aiming for a Jon Val Jean vibe—gruff but gentle. "That, my girl, is the ten-million-dollar question."

Mia raised her head. Wet tracks etched her cheeks. "Are you going to talk to him?"

At that, he did smile—mostly for lack of anything more

confident. He wasn't on an inch of familiar ground right now. What *was* the etiquette of calming down two hormonal teenagers at once? Things were a hell of a lot easier when soldiers pulled this shit. They got told to suck it up and shut up, end of story. At least he had an excuse for checking in on Luke without setting off Mia again.

"Yeah." He palmed the top of her head again. "You okay with that?"

Well, hell. That almost came...*easily*. Maybe he *was* getting better at this communication shit.

"Totally," Mia replied. "I'm glad you are, actually."

He hitched a wider smile. "Cool."

"Hey." She rose, awkwardly twisting the fingers peeking out from beneath a baggy sweatshirt emblazoned with a barfing unicorn. "When you—*can* you—tell him I'm sorry for the nickname thing?"

Franz gave her the benefit of his quiet assessment for a long moment. In a matching tone, he responded, "I think it'll mean more coming from you."

Her pout returned. Not so much snark this time. "You're probably right."

"Tell you what? I'll let him know *you* want to play him a few matches next. Sneak it in between sets. It'll go a lot easier."

Her watery grin melted half the damn anvil. Franz smiled back, imagining he looked a lot like Pops after he or Lino had finally understood some important life lesson.

Okay...this communication shit was kind of cool.

He just hoped he still thought that after the showdown with Luke.

He found the kid slumped against the island in the middle of the kitchen, picking at the end of a banana and sulking like

Pompei had just fallen. Or his new video game was on delayed release. Same thing in the world of a fifteen-year-old.

Franz leaned elbows to the opposite side of the island. Waited another measured moment before murmuring, "Hey."

Luke glanced back up—the kid's eyes were so much like Tracy's, it was a bit freaky—before turning back to his banana picking. "Hey."

"You all right, man?"

A one-shouldered hitch. Gawky but defiant. "Sure. I will be, I guess."

"You guess?" He underlined it with a direct stare, not that the brat was paying attention. Again, so much like his mother. Defenses went up, and not even the fiercest infantry was breaching the barricades.

"Yeah, *I guess*." Luke tossed his head, a mutinous pony fighting his harness. "I mean, I'm not allowed to be anything else, right? That's what everyone expects, so—"

"I'm not everyone."

"You might as well be."

John pushed up. "Oh, fuck that shit."

Luke's eyes blew up to the size of quarters—then silver dollars—as Franz planted hands to his waist. He was dressed in his usual now, a black form-fitted T-shirt and black cargo pants, which probably played to his favor in the shock-and-awe department—as well as the special plans he'd made for Tracy tonight.

Stow it, asshole. Not the time for a fresh hard-on.

"Don't pretend your virgin ears are scalded, mister," he growled into the boy's stunned silence. "You've heard worse online—just like you know, in your gut, how awesome your life is compared to a lot of kids your age."

"Okay, okay." The defensive tone was mitigated by sullen shoulder hunches. "I know, I know." Another swift gray glance, accompanied by some twitchy teenager kicks at the floor. "Seriously, dude. I get it."

"And I believe you." Franz lowered his arms. Went on, while sidling around the island until they were diagonal from each other, "So don't go after yourself with a cat-o-nine about it either." He clapped the kid on the shoulder. "It's been an unusual week for everyone. Nobody's expecting you to handle it all with a rosy smile and a Bob Fosse show-stopper."

"A what? With who?"

He damn near groaned.

Holding him back? The look on Luke Rhodes's face.

Blasting awareness through him like a nuclear detonation.

This kid, so bright and perceptive and good-looking, would soon be the first son of the country. He'd already been the vice president's son for a year. He was surrounded by a small army of guys who'd take a bullet for him and another small army of his mom's staffers, advisors, and keepers.

But the look on his face right now only spoke one truth, loud and strong and strident.

He was beyond lonely.

"Never mind." The words rumbled out of him, awkward with the blast of emotion in his chest, as he shifted his hold to Luke's nape. "Not important."

Luke looked up—not fighting his hold one bit. The kid's mouth, broader and plusher than Tracy's elegant curves, quirked up at one end. "If it has anything to do with all that Broadway shit you and Mom are always talking about, you're right."

Franzen mock-growled. "That's close to sacrilege, man."

"You're from Hawaii. Your native religion promotes polytheism. Deal with it."

Had he been *admiring* the kid's intellect? "You been checking up on me, Lucas Levane?"

The teen leaned an elbow to the island. "Why yes, Keoni John, I have." He let only a few beats go by before blurting, "No offense, dude—but I'm performing due diligence. My mom's really into you."

And he'd thought shit like hostage extraction and dodging landmines was tricky. "That so?" Was that casual enough? Humble enough? Did he sound like a dick? Worse, like a douche? Did a kid like him know the difference? "So...uhhh... how'd you come by that intel? Did she tell you?"

Luke dropped his head. Slowly shook it. "Dude, she's my *mom*. I can tell when she's happier."

"Happier?" Forget dick and douche. He was certain the trophy for goofy idiot had his name fucking engraved on it. "You, uhhh, think so? She's happier?"

"Oh my *God*."

Or at least that was what the kid's moan sounded like. His face was enveloped by his cupped hands, muffling the syllables, meaning Franz had to pick from *Oh my God* or *Ah my crotch*. Obviously, the lesser of two evils got the high sign.

Luke himself wasn't about any clarification either. With a heavy huff, the kid jacked his posture straight back up. Reached to emulate John's move by reaching out and clapping his shoulder. John chuckled, though quick and painlessly. The teen earned himself instant bonus points by maintaining the hold despite noticing how his hand looked like a puppy pawing a Mastiff.

"Just don't make her cry, and you'll be cool. You make my

mom cry, I don't care how big you are. I'll come after you, and I'll hurt you. Feeling that, *Dragon*?"

Franz held up a fist, offering it for a bump with Luke's free hand. "Affirmative, Mr. Rhodes."

The teen nodded, apparently satisfied, before they sealed shit up with a solid bump. Immediately after, Luke shoved both hands into his pockets and kicked the floor again. "So, I heard you're taking her out tonight? Like, on a...date?"

Franz emulated the stance, sans the floor jabs. "Something like that, yeah." He deliberately kept things general. It was best not to let on, even to his own mind, what the itinerary for the evening really was. No point in believing everything was going to go exactly as he hoped, anyhow.

Generalizations or not, Luke opened up a new scowl. "So how's that going to happen?"

That, he *did* expect. "Easy, *kaikana*." And answered with a soothing tone, paired with raised hands. "We're not even leaving the building. Just thought it'd be nice to get your mom out of the condo for a little bit. She hasn't even gotten to have walks, like you and Mia."

The kid had the grace to look a chastised. "You're right." He jerked his chin up, diffident respect edging the action. "Probably took a lot of planning just to take her downstairs."

You have no idea, kid.

And he never would.

"Zeke's going to be with us." He could give up that much, at least. "My friend Max Brickham too. Don't worry; he's as bad-ass as Z. We're not going to let a damn thing happen to your mom."

Well. Nothing she didn't beg him for first.

Not now, jerk wad. Not. Now.

"Cool." Stars literally danced in Luke's eyes once Z was brought into the picture. Yeah, the Zeke Hayes fan club had officially grown by one this week.

"What's cool?"

As the source of the query appeared in the doorway and then moved to wrap arms around her son's waist, Franz focused on reminding his lungs to breathe. *Holy. Shit.* He'd been so used to having the Tigress in her most raw form, as a messy, moaning, panting lover, he'd forgotten how incredible she looked all sleek and cleaned-up.

No. It was more than that this time.

Oh, she was one fine, *fine* woman on a physical level; he wasn't taking exception to that—but her effect on him was so far beyond that, he was only able to identify it now, after having to tolerate an entire afternoon of her locked away in the guest room, strategizing with Ronnie and Gem about the hundreds of scenarios they might encounter when she finally returned to DC.

And the Oval Office.

Not a future he was going to think about tonight. Not for one fucking second.

Luke pivoted enough to hook his arm around Tracy's neck. "Hail to my parental unit."

"Well, hail to my sunshine." She smacked him softly on the cheek, leaving an imprint of soft lip gloss. Though Luke grimaced, he let the stuff stay where it was as he gave her a once-over.

"Wow, Mom. You look different. You look...nice."

Tracy bopped his shoulder, but her beam didn't falter. Clearly, the clinch meant more to her than the compliment—such as it was. "And *that's* what's cool?"

"Nah. That's a bonus. Good job, Mom."

A flush stained her cheeks, darkening as she glanced across to John—unleashing electrical bursts where every one of his nerve endings used to be. Yeah, to the point he had to suck in an audible breath because of it. She'd respected every one of his "firm requests" for her look tonight. Light makeup. No jewelry. Hair pulled completely off her face. She'd even worn the simple black sheath Rayna had helped him pick out from a local boutique's website. Thank fuck for the internet, which didn't pass judgment at a credit card used for the Bastille Kink Club in downtown Seattle. Thank fuck even more for Rayna Hayes, who'd gone out and picked up the dress *and* the new makeup.

Most of all, thank fuck for gorgeous little brunettes with soft, submissive eyes and sexual energy that could turn air into fire.

And make him see, for the very first time, maybe there *was* life after Special Forces.

So *much* life.

And excitement. And challenge. And feeling.

Had he ever thought he'd *feel* like this again?

And burn like this, blood flaring higher and hotter, as Luke finally went all independent cool dude again, freeing Tracy to step around the island. As she neared, Franz pulled in more air. Feigned a casual smile. He hated feeding her the lie of his poise, but the alternative was hiking her up on the counter, ramming her legs around his waist, and then kissing the rest of that lip gloss off her delectable mouth. *Not* quite an option at the moment.

"Okay." She leveled it while bouncing glances between Luke and him. "Do I have to keep guessing? What kind of wickedness *have* you gentlemen been up to in here?"

Annnnd there was the goddamned erection again. One mention of "wickedness" in her playful drawl, and he was hard as granite all over again.

Because tonight, he was going to blow her mind with wicked.

Christ. He'd really sworn off the dungeon for too long. After the disaster with Abbie and then the cluster fuck of Kaesong, he'd been thrown off the horse twice in a row. Brutally. The last thing he'd wanted was anything even reminding him of the saddle. No leather. No buckles. No riding crops. No thoughts of *riding* anything or anyone.

Now, he couldn't think of anything else.

Especially with this stunning woman. *His* stunning woman.

Who would, gods be begged, soon be his perfect submissive.

He battled the thoughts with his most rigid poker face, to no goddamned avail. His gave him away, burning with needs he could barely keep in check. He knew it because of the answering bursts in Tracy's gaze, igniting more as he moved around the island too, ensuring the bulge in his cargos got hidden from Luke and shown off to her.

Her gaze got bigger.

So did his smirk. Why the fuck not? And why the hell had he waited this long to learn good subterfuge didn't always involve spooks, assets, shadows, and night goggles? What a way to reassign his skill set—in the name of a much more enticing mission.

With a much more meaningful target to take out.

If Tracy would let him.

There was the huge elephant still in the room. He was just the only one who saw the damn thing at the moment.

Time to change that. As fast as possible.

"Everything's fine, *ku`uipo*." He swept a meaningful look down over her face. "We're just clearing the air."

She nonchalantly tapped at the end of a banana—giving the motions much more meaning than her son had. "Dare I ask about what?"

"Hmmm." Two could play at the easy-breezy act. "For starters, the issue about this young man purposely throwing a certain virtual tennis match."

"Do *not* look at me," Luke sputtered at Tracy's accusing gaze. "He figured it out, just like I told you he would."

"Smart kid." Franzen added a chuckle, using the relaxed moment to make things more *un*relaxed for the woman. His own discomfort was torture but so fucking worth it. So damn *right*, to be close enough to watch the thrumming pulse in her neck...to feel the new tension in her body...to soak up the new heat of her, all but shimmering the air like waves of rainforest humidity. She smelled that good too, the cream of her clean skin accented by a hint of perfume not her usual. Something fruity yet spicy, mixing so perfectly with her chemistry...

Tracy snapped him back to practicality with her sniff of bafflement. "Well, he lets *me* win all the time, and *I* can't tell."

"Because I *don't* do that?" Luke ticked a knowing glance at Franz. "Now *she* has the bad-ass backhand."

He chuckled again. "Somehow, I believe it."

"Mia's is killer too." The kid pivoted, leading with one dipped shoulder. "Which is as good an excuse as I have to get the hell out of here..." He subtly lifted the end into a question, hooking a look back to Tracy in the doing.

"Go." She made a shoo'ing motion. "Off with you, child."

"And off with *us*." Franz murmured it as soon as Luke vanished, underlining his growled command by wrapping a hand into one of hers. The responding pressure of her own, squeezing with such complete trust, sent a rush of incredible new sensation through him. Heat—there was *always* that—but also strength. Confidence. The driving certainty that every drop of his plans for this had been the right call.

Even if she might not think so at first.

If that bridge was going to be crossed, now was the time.

A message his whole body really got on board with—as soon as he had her in the elevator and the doors slid shut.

Sealing them completely in together.

Franz didn't wait a damn second longer to pin her down.

Her body up against the lift wall. Her legs high, clamped around his hips. Her mouth open, taking the hot plunge of his tongue. Her moan strident, echoing through every synapse of his senses. Her cleft hot, writhing to meet the fevered slide of his erection.

"You wanted wicked?" he finally snarled against her lips. "How's this for a start?"

His kitten's breath, panting and eager, was a sweet mix of toothpaste and lust. "Uh-huh." She nodded eagerly. "Yes...*yes*, Sir."

"Damn glad to hear that, *popoki*." Keeping her tacked against the wall with one hip, he kicked the other back and up, tagging the red stop button with his heel. Alert bells clanged all around them. The noise only seemed to feed Tracy's desire. As his leg came down, she gazed as if he'd just scaled the Great Wall of China instead of simply killing two birds with one stone.

Which brought him back to the task at hand.

He had a minute at best until Z and Max broke into the elevator shaft from the basement and started climbing to get them. Just to be sure he had her full attention during those seconds, he braced the curve of her jaw in the U of his hand.

"You took our little agreement to heart, Tracy Rhodes. I admit, it was fun getting to beat the kid at least once."

Her stare turned silken. So did her lips, parting as she licked them. "I'm glad to hear that, Captain Franzen."

Gods, how he craved to kiss her. But kissing wasn't a luxury for a deadline like this.

"Well, then. You'll be happy to hear *I* took things seriously too."

As he anticipated, her features pursed with confusion. If she didn't recall his end of the bargain, or *did* remember and tried to discern exactly what he'd done, the same result filtered through her body. His psyche gulped her apprehension like a quarterback downing Gatorade. *Yeah. Let me feel that fear, kitten. Melting it away will feel so fucking good for us both...*

"You challenged me to help with your stage fright... remember?"

A long swallow undulated her throat. She wetted her lips again—this time, darts of sheer nervousness. "I—I remember."

He slid in closer. Needing to fill her vision with him. Needing to fill his senses with her. She smelled so good. She felt so good. *So right.*

"Do you trust me to do that, *ku`uipo*?"

He rasped it in her ear as the bells continued blaring around them...as the world narrowed to nothing but them. He kept his lips there, hovering an inch above the throbbing pulse of her carotid, waiting...

Waiting for her form to soften.
Just like it did.
Waiting for her throat to exhale.
Just like it did.
Waiting for her to speak...

CHAPTER SEVENTEEN

"Yes."

It flowed from her with the dedication of rain down a waterfall...with the conviction of gravity to the earth. At the moment, she wondered how close to the truth the comparisons might truly be. She was already soaked with need for more of his body, his command—an obsession so consuming, her senses spun like weightless comets in space. He only heightened her sensual chaos by using his hold on her jaw to lock her head against the wall. Pressed in just tight enough to prevent her from moving.

Whoa.

Wow.

She'd never been handled by a man like this before. A treatment that should have started and ended in this moment—and probably would have, with any other man.

But John Franzen wasn't any other man.

To the point that she gazed at him now, angling his face over hers, and realized she didn't even see a *man*.

She saw a dragon.

A creature born of fire and brought by magic to save her life—in many more ways than one.

She saw thunder.

A force crackling the skies of her psyche, bringing back the lightning of her passion and the storm of her new awakening.

She saw her Dominant.

The lover—the partner—who'd exacted more from her body and mind than any male she'd known...

And given twice as much in return.

Who poured out the same fullness of that force now, coating her face in the burnished beauty of his stare as he rose up, filling her sights with nothing but him. He was dragon and slayer, sun and moon, give and take...her god and her apostle.

"Say. It. Again."

His lips barely moved.

Her heart hardly beat.

"I—I said yes." She reveled in the effect of it across his face, her supplication moving through him like an electrical charge through his thunder clouds. "I trust you...Sir."

The voltage in his presence intensified. His eyes flared wide enough to make her gasp. "Even if that means this might be...uncomfortable? A little unorthodox?"

"Moving past fear usually isn't a pleasure cruise. And as for unorthodox..." She took a turn at raising the expressive brows. "I think my experience with that one speaks for itself?"

His rough chuckle warmed the air but tensed her body. The laughter belonged to him but didn't. It was like everything else about him since they'd stepped into the lift. Sharper. Harder. Fiercer. There was a damn good chance she simply filtered it that way, that everything was going to look and feel different during her first few minutes of "freedom" in days, but the explanation was just a bunch of rhetoric to her nerve endings, refusing to let go of their sizzling anxiety. And to her lungs, constricting from bands of real fear.

And to her sex, throbbing with how much she liked it.

Which would have hurled her into a tailspin of what-the-hell-is-wrong-with-you, if the man didn't chop it short with everything that was right.

Everything that was *him*.

A floor-eating step, shaking the car with its force. A slam to the call button, ending the alarms—while he started a new chaos by hauling her close and kissing her again. Hard. Ramming open her lips with savage mastery. Taking her tongue in nasty swipes. At last pulling back so she beheld every bold, etched angle of his face—and the iron control over them all, despite the brutal hunger he'd just unleashed on her.

"Very well," he told her then. "I accept your trust and appreciate your honesty." He pulled her hands around, holding them in the scant space between their bodies. "You honor me with both." His kisses to her knuckles were warm but quick, laying groundwork for more steel in his composure. "And now, you'll honor me by confirming your safe word."

She swallowed so hard, she could feel the echoes in her ears. "Y-You're talking like—"

"I might actually be hearing it from you?"

Well, shit.

His fingers squeezed hers as his left eyebrow jumped. *That damn brow.* It had come to carry meaning for her, always making her pulse race and her grin spread. Now her system cooperated with the former—but she wouldn't know a smile from her own reflection right now. She was too busy scoping out the nearest exits.

An abandoned plan as soon as the lift doors whooshed open.

And she stood, motionless as an impaled martyr, at the sight before her.

She'd tried keeping her expectations open about Franz's "big plans" for their evening, but he *had* given her some tiny hints already in his "requests"—aka orders—for how to show up for the fun. She'd complied with everything except the one about ditching her underwear. Wasn't exactly a sucky plan; just not applicable to a situation with a sheath that stopped several inches above her knees. One careless whisper of a breeze, and her intimate bits would be clearly on display for whoever was helping him in this scheme—

In this case, Sergeant Zeke Hayes.

Along with another man to whom he now chatted quietly, dressed in the same head-to-toe black favored by her Sir and Zeke. Like them, the color enhanced the man's towering height, commanding posture, and prominent muscles. Also like them, he had thick hair the shade of a raven's wing, grown to a length somewhere between John's skull spikes and Z's Renaissance Faire waves. *Un*like them, the guy's eyes were a thousand shades of brilliant blue, reminding her of Lake Austin on a summer morning. When the man turned with Zeke to greet John and her, his whole aura seemed lighter as well—though once again, she had to set the impression against her experience of the last week. The only males with whom she'd had contact were her hormonal son and a gang of seasoned Special Forces professionals. She'd been all but bathing in growly testosterone for over a hundred hours.

"Gentlemen." Franz calmly intoned it while leading the way from the elevator. Just fine by her. Even with her underthings on, the air possessed a distinct chill. The thuds of their footsteps were absorbed by the walls instead of bounced back.

Were they underground?

She glanced up before exiting the elevator. Indeed, the overhead display glowed with a bright red *B*, for *Basement*.

Basement, she repeated inwardly. *Not Dungeon.*

Was she emphasizing the point out of celebration...or disappointment?

Zeke didn't give her long for contemplation. "The man of the hour," he greeted, holding up a hand as if to arm wrestle John. Dear God, to be a fly on the wall during *that* match. John accepted his clasp, and they pulled on each other for one of those "bro bump" things to the shoulder. The other man strolled forward too but only gave John a courtesy glance—on his way to zero in more closely on Tracy.

"Meh. Who cares about him?" Mr. Lake Austin Eyes bent over, lifting her free hand in both of his. "Let's get to the important part." Brushed her knuckles with his lips. "It is a pleasure, darling kitten, to meet you at last."

Darling kitten? At last? Tracy didn't know whether to curtsy, giggle, or attempt a glib return—though the latter would be a challenge, considering the potency of this rogue's flirtatious charm. His gaze was even more magnificent up close, and he smelled like cloves and bergamot.

Once again, not a lot of time for debate. Before her throat could fully function again, John jerked her back by the waist, rotating to loom protectively. "All right, scum chunk. Hands. Off."

The guy spread up his hands as if those words had been *Stick 'em up.* "All right, all right. Got it loud and clear, honey. Untwist your panties."

"Just keep your dick in yours." Irritation all but shot out from Franz's pores. "I mean it, man."

Tracy glanced back to the rogue, hoping he'd have a decent zinger for that, though was immediately stabbed by guilt. John was sincerely agitated, and all she could think was how much this beat old senators duking it out across shiny conference tables. But John and his fellow Dom—for that was the only certain conclusion she had about the guy so far—were only interested in battling over one thing.

Her.

Not as their vice president. Not even as Zeke's odd, intrusive houseguest.

As the only role she was here to fulfill tonight.

A desirable woman.

It was pretty damn nice.

"Well," Zeke butted in, laying on a layer of overly bright sarcasm. "Now that we have all the housekeeping notes taken care of, boys and girls..."

"*There's* your girl." Franz and the flirt stated it at once, trading pointing fingers. Tracy couldn't abstain her giggle any longer. This really *was* better than any committee meeting on the Hill.

Oddly—or maybe not so much—her laughter incited the same from the men. As they mellowed, Franz slipped his hand down, securing her hand in his once again. "*Popoki*, it's my honor to introduce you to the hugest asshole on the planet— and my dearest friend—Max Brickham."

She actually felt her eyes widen as Max flourished a new bow, sans the finger kissing. "At your service, kitten."

The words weren't just lip service. They hinted at a second meaning—one the man clearly thought she knew. When her blank gaze answered his raised gaze, Max scooted a questioning glance to John, who flung back a quelling glare.

Time for apprehension to make an encore. "At my service...for what?" she charged.

Max straightened, trading a secretive look with Zeke.

Ohhhh no, they didn't.

Tracy jolted forward by a step, brandishing her put-up-or-shut-up look. Just as swiftly, she was jerked back to Franz's side, his grip possessive steel around her middle.

"Well," Max finally murmured. "This just got a hell of a lot more fun."

Tracy tossed an open fume at all three of them—but especially the tight-lipped hulk at her side. Okay, *she* was more at *his* side, but semantics weren't key on the priorities list right now.

Addressing his imperious, but holy-effing-hell delicious, glower? Another story completely. But damn it, she'd addressed dour foreign leaders, self-important senators, and more ranting lobbyists than one person should in a lifetime. She had this.

"Fun?" she repeated, barely moving her lips. "Want to fill me in on what *that's* all about?"

Franz's gaze went heavy, sultry. His nostrils flared as his brood took on a new heat...sparking straight into the triangle between her thighs.

Shit, shit, shit.

Maybe she *didn't* have this.

"In due time."

Nope. Definitely not. How the man could turn three words into verbal arousal, she had no idea, nor was in any condition to ponder, as he pulled her toward a long hallway offering the same gray-walled bleakness as the elevator foyer. While his words had to be the most unacceptable basis for following him, Tracy did just that—battling a mix of dread and anticipation.

Why did this still feel like he led her for processing in a medieval prison? And why did *that* concept make her wetter in every intimate crevice? What the hell did that say about her? Was she out of her damn mind? Maybe it was best that Blake LeGrange just go on leading the free world. Maybe there *was* a serious crack in her psyche, and it was a better idea to—

"Tracy."

Though his low dictate refused to be ignored, his grip was the leash on her focus. Her head snapped up. Her senses refunneled on him. "*What?*" she retorted.

"Stop thinking."

"Excuse me?"

"Stop thinking." His accentuation, sharp but sleek, matched the double doors they approached. The portals were made of black steel. They had no handles and were bound at the middle by a key card panel made to look like a big silver padlock. "And start trusting."

She worked her hand tighter against his. "Trying, damn it." Though her shaky tone hardly backed up the point, even as Franz bussed the top of her head. Adding insult to injury, she swung a nervous glance back at the dim hall they'd just traversed—wondering why she felt like it was about to disappear in some treacherous fog. "Wh-Where *are* we?"

"We haven't left the building." He murmured it into her hair, spreading warmth across her scalp. Tenacious tendrils of the heat dripped down, past her neck, until pooling behind both her nipples. The man definitely noticed. Damn it, where was a padded bra when a girl needed one? "The complex has two parts," he went on to explain. "Residential and commercial. This corridor is one of the bypasses."

Max sidled up to stand on the other side of his friend. "When one owns a kink club, it's also nice to have a secret entrance for members who need discretion."

Unbelievably, *that* part of the explanation cracked her lips open on a smile—as many other parts of her were showered in shards of anticipation. "Oh?" she returned, giving the look an impish edge. "Is that what I am, now? A 'member' of discretion?"

John's chuckle was like island thunder, dominant but gentle. "Woman, you are more than a member tonight."

She let him gather her fully against him. The broad expanse of his chest was such an ideal snuggling zone. "That so, my Sir?"

"Hmmm. Yes."

"So what, exactly, am I?"

He didn't hum that time—though both Max and Zeke did, ending with sounds she couldn't identify. Were they snickering? Clearing their throats? Maybe both but attempting to be discreet? And why did she care—despite how the rejoinders made her think an orange jumpsuit was in her near future?

Focus on your Sir.

Trust your Sir.

Remember what you promised.

"You're the VIP attraction, kitten."

"*Huh?*"

Again, no time to process any other reaction—not that she'd even be able to form it—as Zeke pressed a key card on a chain up to the shiny padlock. Instantly, the doors parted with ominous blasts.

Z flashed a grin at John. "If anyone's checking, the log will tag my entrance, not yours."

"Outstanding."

Her Sir's approving growl affected her bloodstream like solar flares. She had no idea why but simply flowed with the incredible sensation.

What was wrong with her?

Every neuron in her brain screamed she should be shivering in trepidation, not burning up with arousal. This wasn't a fantasy novel or a scene in a play. This was real. She was letting a man pull her through those doors, into an oddly quiet hall now defined by leather-covered walls, dark-tiled floors, and air smelling of patchouli, smoke, latex—and sex.

She was turning, watching as Max wiggled his fingers at them, crooning, "You kids have fun"—before the doors slammed back shut.

She was standing, still trying to summon even one shudder, as Franzen—no, as Sir—pivoted so they again faced each other. Cupped her shoulders in his powerful, masterful hands. Tugged her so close, her aching nipples nearly brushed his wall of a chest. Summoned his voice in a rough, commanding inhalation.

"Kitten. Look at me."

She tilted her head up. Got down a gulp like a wrecking ball as his gaze affected her composure the same way. Her knees were dust. Her nerves were incinerated. Her pussy was a flooded, aching mess.

"You still trust me?"

Her senses surprised her with another smile. He was checking in, still conscious of her. Still caring about her. Still prioritizing her. Even if he handed her an orange jumpsuit right now, her response would be the same.

"Yes, Sir." She finished the whisper by standing on tiptoes to kiss him. "I do. I truly do."

He returned the pressure of her lips, though it was infused with fresh formality. The veneer toughened as he slid both hands beneath her short hemline—

Then encountered the barrier of her underwear. As his hand halted, she stiffened. In this new environment, with its new set of playing rules, what would ignoring his "request" mean for her?

To her shock, not much more than a mysterious hum.

At least at first.

"That means a lot to me, *ku`uipo*." He pulled away—but as he went, smoothly scooping up both hands, gathering more and more of her dress. When he finally settled his stance again, he'd pulled the whole thing over her head, off her body. "Because it means you won't have any trouble with me watching you strip the rest of the way."

She forced down a deep breath—and then on the exhalation, a dutiful "Yes, Sir." What other choice was there? Rebellious brat was just stupid, after knowingly snubbing his direction. And no way was she chickening out of the adventure now, when it was getting pretty damn interesting.

More than any of that, she wanted this.

Wanted.

This.

How many times, over the last few days alone, had she blatantly fantasized about the chance to have this man drag her off into a place just like this? To brook no argument about his commands? To openly demand to have his way with her?

An equal number of times, she'd set aside the dream as just that. The logistical details of making something like this happen, even during this interim in which she was a non-person to the rest of the world, sent her head spinning. On top of that, it was a Friday night—likely one of the most popular periods for everyone to get out and "get their kink on" in a place as luxurious as this—blowing new depths of her gray matter apart in gratitude. He'd worked damn hard to make this all happen...all for her.

So yeah—it was time to strip.

The bra was the easy part. The little black demi-cups already exposed just about everything the man wanted to see about her peaks, which certainly weren't anything special. Before Luke came along, they'd been...normal. Not too big, not too small. Now, they were normal but saggy—a truth not lending a shred of logic to the man's starving beast snarl as she unclasped the bra. But if she'd learned anything about John Franzen over the last few days, it was the man's insistence on enjoying what he referred to as her "juicy *hua*."

His rasp of the syllables now, caressing the air so thick with sensual promise, turned her nipples into points of acute, aching need. She gasped as her areolas puckered, making the nipples stand out even harder. Damn it. Wouldn't the man do anything more than stare at them?

No such luck. He had an agenda and was sticking to it. That much was obvious by the brace of his stance, hands fisted at his sides while air pumped his chest and a bulge strained the juncture of his thighs.

"Now the rest," he finally ordered. "Let me see your hot *kali*, woman."

Her blood raced as she bent over, hooking thumbs into the sides of the panties. She pushed them into a pool at her feet. As she rose back up, standing nude in the middle of the hallway, a shiver finally claimed her.

Why?

The man had seen every inch of her body, on a very intimate basis, many times over the last week...

Only right now, she was as nervous as a virgin.

In a kink play club.

In front of one of the most formidable, beautiful warriors she had ever met.

Looking across all his features, like the hardest, most delicious piece of human toffee, and knowing exactly what he planned for her naked body next.

Or...

Maybe not.

She'd expected him to reach for her once again—though not with anything *in* his hand as he did. Certainly not with a fistful of...what, exactly? She gawked at the formless black latex. Back up at Franzen. His expression was a dark, unreadable puzzle. His face had darkened and hardened after she took off her panties though never fully returned to its original cliffs of dedicated dominance.

What the hell was he up to?

"Come here." The bastard didn't clear up anything with his thick growl—except her body's overriding desire to obey him. As she inched closer to him, he raked her form with his ravenous eyes and stated, "It's time for the kitten to get into her play clothes."

Fresh scowl. Open confusion. "Kittens have play clothes?" And why did that make her think of nothing but those helpless felines on the internet, forced to wear dumb costumes for owners who thought "cowboy cat" and "superhero cat" were actually cute shit?

"Hmmm. *This* kitten does."

Why didn't *that* make her feel any better than cowboy cat?

Nevertheless, she stood patiently as he pulled the latex piece wider, stretching it between his hands. In a flash, recognition hit. The thing was a hood, made to go entirely over someone's head, with almond-shaped holes for the eyes, along with spaces for the nose and mouth. A pair of molded cat ears sprouted off the top.

For a long second, she just stared at the thing. Back up to him. Back at the hood. *Damn*. He really wanted her to wear it. To let him put it on her, erasing every discernible aspect of her face. The idea didn't bring on a ton of tranquility—though the alternative wasn't exactly fear. It was trepidation, uneasiness... and ohhhh yes, a new gush of unstoppable arousal.

What would it be like...to not be *her* anymore?

To become, in so many ways, his sexy submissive kitten?

"Let's try it on." While his voice was low command, his gaze formed a gentler question. He wouldn't do it without her consent.

Consent her lips couldn't seem to give. Her throat felt like a vise. Her lungs worked harder and harder for half as much air.

She prayed he'd get the message as she inched back toward him—and then dipped her head forward, almost nudging the hood like a real kitten.

With a rumble of low satisfaction, John slid the latex over her.

As the cool, tight plastic adhered to her like heavy glue, a string of reactions hit in frenetic succession.

So this was why he asked for the severe hair style.

How long does he want me to wear this thing?

It's kind of comfortable.

Oh my God, I must look fifteen kinds of silly.

My head must look smaller. That means my butt must seem huge.

What the hell am I doing this for?

"Holy. Fuck."

That. Growl.

That was what she'd done it for.

That...and the rest of the electricity firing off Franzen from the moment the hood dropped completely into place.

Turning her breaths into fire as his pumped harder in his wide chest.

Turning her skin into hot and cold fusion as his gaze devoured her body.

Turning all those words in her head into nothing but needy mewls in her throat as his posture became forceful lines. As hard as her mind clawed to maintain the hold, something about this new anonymity turned her into something else too. A creature, fully female. An animal, fully feral.

A submissive...fully his.

"Come here, kitten."

Her blood, still just a mass of white-hot currents, somehow powered her limbs enough to take a step. Then another. Every inch she closed in on Franzen, a force field seemed to crackle around him as well, extending spindles of pure energy toward hers.

Once her body was nearly flush with his again, the man stunned her once more, suddenly dropping to a knee. Before she could determine his purpose, he supplied it—by holding open a pair of black latex booty shorts. "Step in," he instructed, and she obeyed at once. If it occurred to her, for even half a second, to question why he'd made her strip before *re*dressing her, the design of her new "outfit" provided that answer now. The shorts had no crotch panels. The center seams, right and left, were masterfully designed to overlap each other but also to part ways from each other. *There* was a convenient fix for camel toe.

A fleeting human thought from her faraway human life.

The feral feline batted it away, especially as her Master began checking the fit of the shorts in all the key places. She whimpered louder with every stroke of his strong, hot touch, especially as he stood again. With their mouths just half a breath apart, she let out raw, rhythmic pleadings, shuttling her crotch against the blissful confidence of his fingers.

"Such a good little pussy." As he gifted her with the praise, he flattened his hand against her entire mound. "So hot. So compliant. So ready for me."

"Unnnnhh," Tracy cried, high and strident. "Mmmm hmmm."

He groaned, harsh and hard, before forming his lips to her slightly parted ones. The latex stretched, erotic and noisy, as he forced her to open wider, accepting the scalding flame of his tongue.

Several minutes later, when he pulled away, Franz's breath had taken over his body with as much erratic violence as hers. He set her back as if having to order himself to do so, before whirling for the wall shelf where he'd gotten her hood and shorts. There was one more item up there, waiting for him to use on her.

A roll of black electrical tape.

His eyes never leaving her, he peeled off a small length and cut it with his teeth. Repeated the motion three more times, until he had four equal lengths extending from corresponding fingers.

"The finishing touch before I take my pussy out to play."

In another time and place—as in, back out in the gray

hallway, no more than fifteen minutes ago—she would've already been analyzing his words backward and forward. Wondering what the hell he meant or didn't, had planned or didn't. Formulating what constituted a clever response, along with the proper attitude to back it up. But right now, in the confines of this space, she wasn't that person anymore. She was just an obedient stick of heat, gasping through more arousal as her Dom crisscrossed the tape lengths, X style, over both her nipples.

She was sealed in.

Tight.

Aching.

Wanting.

And now, following.

Letting him tug her to the end of a hall. Around a corner. Past rooms lit up in red and purple, with brighter spotlights on strange and frightening and erotic things. A "medical exam" room. An exotic harem with silks, leather swings, and a gilded cage with retractable pins. And yes, a "castle dungeon" reigned by a huge wooden table outfitted with everything from spreader bars to steel handcuffs. Relief swept her when they bypassed that last one—though she hadn't turned off so much of her brain to avoid the logical follow-up.

What if the room to which he pulled her was filled with worse?

A question she suddenly, violently didn't want the answer to...

Only to feel she already did, the moment her gaze lifted all the way back to his perfect face...

To find half of it covered by a mask of his own.

Her jaw fell. What the hell? Though the covering wasn't

a full hood like hers, it was just as jarring a change. The black leather was custom-molded for his face, recessed for both midnight-dark eyes, sloped out for his nose, and tapered at both sides to hug the upper edge of his jaw.

"Wh-What?" she managed to blurt. "*Wh-When—*"

He stopped her by yanking her close and kissing her deep. Though it wasn't the longest or most sweeping kiss they'd ever shared, there was a new energy from him...something turning the contact into something new and potent...

And unnerving.

When he let her drag free, she opened her gaze just inches from the intensity of his. Even with both their masks in the way, his focus was an unrelenting power drill. If the man hadn't made the point completely clear, she'd have guessed *he* was the one here to learn from *her*, not the other way around.

He drew in a significant breath. While setting it free, released one word for her too.

"Incredible." His palm nearly engulfed the back of her head. She always felt so tiny in his hold, but the compression from the latex only intensified the size contrast. "You are so fucking incredible, and we haven't even started yet."

Haven't started what?

Another question for which there'd likely be an unwanted answer—so she locked it tight despite the scream of her senses, even as Franz lowered his mouth to hers once more. This time, he took her as if he were kissing a spun-glass sculpture, brushing both hands to the bare curves of her shoulders, continuing the feathered strokes even after he lifted his face back up.

"*Ku`uipo.*"

The question mark wasn't inherent in his tone, but Tracy

whispered anyway. "Yes, my Sir?"

"Do you...still trust me?"

Despite the catch of her nerves during his purposeful pause, a smile readily brimmed across her lips. She felt it find completion in her eyes during her single, sweet nod of punctuation. "With all my body, Sir. And all my heart."

His whole body swelled, manifesting the pride in his own smile. "You have no idea how much that means to me, kitten."

Oh, but she did. At least a little. She wanted to bounce like a teenager, giddy from feeling as if she'd given him diamonds instead of words. After that, she'd fry once more into nothingness, happily letting his power, presence, and command take over again. Worth it. It would all be so damn worth it, if only to have known the profound recognition of this sparkling moment.

A moment she'd never forget, as long as she lived.

The moment she realized everything this man had come to mean to her.

The fire he'd brought back to her life. The magic he'd given back to her soul. And yes, the trust he'd instilled again to her heart...

Even as he led her across the hall and opened a new door.

Beyond which was a scene that really did fry away every sensation in her body—except one.

Fear.

Not the good kind anymore.

Not when she stared past the portal, across a shiny lacquered stage illuminated by a dozen bright spotlights. Not when she beheld the contraption at center stage, with its black leather cushions and thick matching straps. Not when she beheld the display rack next to that furniture, at the ready with everything from heavy leather floggers to wicked wooden paddles.

But especially not when her eyes adjusted enough to see that the stage came with an audience.

CHAPTER EIGHTEEN

"*No.*"

Not a single rocket scientist genius needed to anticipate that response. Knowing it was coming gave Franz the advantage, already shifting his hold to her wrist and his voice into a deep warning. "Kitten—"

"Do *not* with the 'kitten.'" Ironically, her hiss was ferocious and feline as she struggled like a cat dumped in a rain barrel. He'd expected that part too. *Not* expected? How much his accelerated pulse would feed his burgeoning erection. Abbie had always been so perfect and prim, never even raising her voice with him outside her orgasms. The few submissives he played with overseas were much the same way. Having to work for this Tigress's respect was a new game.

A conquest worth pursuing.

A wildcat worth taming.

"All right, *popoki*—"

"You can shove *popoki* up your ass too."

"Just calm down—"

"Are you freaking *kidding* me? Calm down? Calm d— *ahhh!*"

A wave of unexpected arousal hit, only John didn't know what surged his cock more: the sting of his hand against her ass or the spike of her shriek on the air. By the *gods*, how she made his blood roar and his instincts sing. How she reminded him of every reason he'd first craved Dominance—and added a few new items to the list too. How she doubled his desire to see this through with her, no matter how vehement her fight or strident her rage.

The resolve was all he needed to draw her close again, his clasp unforgiving but his voice unruffled. "Are you ready to discuss this?"

Her nostrils flared, sending puffs of heat onto the black latex. "Are *you* freaking kidding?"

"All right." He yanked her aside, into the shadows behind one of the stage doors. Behind him, a rustle of soft laughter trickled from the crowd of no more than twenty, comprised of Bastille's most elite members. Thanks to Max's and Z's tireless calls, they'd all dropped alternative plans for the night, showing up to be the witnesses for a "visiting Dom" needing to break his subbie of abject stage fright. "Back to square one, then."

In the narrow space between his body and the wall, Tracy squirmed. Fumed. Squirmed again. "You're at square zero, *mister*. This is—"

"Not your call, *missie*." He bent his arm and spread his legs, leaning deeper over her. His opposite hand cupped her chin, subjecting her gaze to the impact of his scrutiny. "Right over there, one damn minute ago, you proclaimed your trust in me, with your body and your heart, and I believed every word." He lifted her face higher. Locked her stare harder. "Was I wrong, *ku'uipo*? Did you not mean it?"

Her lips flattened. The latex beneath her nostrils fogged up again. "I meant it." She ended the rasp with an unsteady swallow. "Damn it...I did."

He pushed air out through his own nose. Jerked her close and kissed her slick forehead. "Then you're going to trust me now—as well as all those people in there, who have given up their time to encourage the personal growth of a subbie they don't even know. You're going to be sweet, you're going to be obedient, and you *are* going to try to like it."

He allowed her to a tiny but hysterical snort. Even let it slide when she added a defiant glower. But no way in hell did he back off until both elements slipped free from her composure and her body sagged beneath the weight of a resigned sigh. "Yes, Sir."

He released her chin. Slid that hand down until he gently palmed one of her breasts while dipping in to reward her with a kiss. "Thank you, kitten."

Her next breath, hotter and heavier, tasted like heaven. "Thank *you*, Sir."

One side of his mouth jerked up. From the eye on the same side, he dashed off a roguish wink. "Save it, woman. You'll need it for later."

But he might as well have told her she'd been crowned Queen of England too. As he led her back through the doorway, the glare of the stage lights had nothing on the you're-a-bastard glints in her bright silver eyes.

They were goddamn breathtaking.

She was so fucking exquisite.

And yeah, he was certainly the new envy of every man in the room—a mystery Dom pulling his creamy, lovely subbie up to be his sole property for the night.

His cock stabbed at his jeans.

Impatience crawled in his blood.

Desire burned beneath every step he took, gently pulling his adorable kitten across the stage.

When they reached the center, in front of the footlights, he stopped to sweep Tracy in front, fully facing the crowd. He braced himself behind her, hands atop her forearms, keeping them pinned to her trembling sides.

"My friends. Thank you all for coming tonight."

His voice boomed out over the crowd. Would some of the Doms recognize the bold baritone as that of their supposedly dead friend, John Franzen? Perhaps but not likely. This was his first time in the club in six months, and even before, Abbie's body-image issues had usually led them to favor private sessions. At the moment, he was almost beyond caring. Tracy's identity was completely protected, and that was his foremost concern.

"As you've been informed, my girl has been dealing with some nasty stage-fright issues. We all have them from time to time, of course, but she's about to accept a job in which this cannot be a stumbling block anymore. I'd like to thank you all in advance for assisting me in...exposing...her fears and then conquering them."

A round of polite applause answered his greeting. Tracy started, obviously surprised.

John tucked his lips against her ear and chuckled softly. "Relax, kitten. The catcalls don't come until later."

He could tell she considered a comeback, though speaking aloud could mean disastrous disclosure. Instead, with her posture tense and her lips clamped tight, she allowed him to lead her to the bondage bench. It was a modified horse, with only the back end angled up, though it still had knee and elbow pads where they would keep her most comfortable. After all, his goal wasn't to turn her body into a pretzel. Twisting the dough of her mind was going to be challenge—and enjoyment—enough.

"Up you go, pretty."

As he watched her comply with the direction, positioning her arms and spreading her knees, he clicked the remote to the house sound system, setting free a laid-back techno beat backing a woman who couldn't decide whether to moan, sigh, or sing. In short, the perfect music for this interesting "lesson."

He moved quickly through the next part, latching her down with the leather ankle and wrist restraints. As he finished with the latter, he wheeled the instruments rack over, enabling the woman before him to get a good look at it. "I won't use it all," he explained, "but will freely choose what treatment you'll take, unless any of this is a hard no."

Almost at once, she shook her head—once more as he had expected. This afternoon, when loading up the cart, he'd deliberately left off extreme implements like bullwhips, clamps, and electro-stim. That was shit for people who'd known each other a lot longer than six days, in much more private settings. The only thing he wanted tonight was to bring some of her useless walls down, inspiring her self-confidence to grow. There was more than enough here to get that job done.

Including his next step.

A necessary one.

The cart also contained drawers. He slid open one, removing the two contents within. Rotated back to Tracy with one in each hand.

"Necessary evil, kitten—and you know why—but I'll let you pick."

He hadn't been able to fathom which way she'd go on this one—though her open glare at the ball gag all but handed the default win to the bit gag. Though she glowered as he fastened it around the back of her head, Franz shot back nothing but his hooded, knowing gaze—as the crowd sent back a murmur of kinky-minded approval.

"If you really don't like it, I'm sure we'll find something else to keep you quiet for a bit."

"Not until we watch her drool for a bit." The comment, issued by a sultry female in one of the front rows, was seconded by a round of soft chuckles from everyone.

Franz used the pause for walking back, toy rack with him, to the V between his subbie's spread legs.

"I already know my kitten enjoys a good spanking," he announced, delivering a series of light but sharp smacks to both her ass cheeks, waking up the blood just below her skin. "But this is the first time she'll feel my flogging skills." He glanced at the half dozen instruments hanging nearby, all beautiful works of art in various forms of leather and rubber. "Suggestions?"

A male voice, British accented, called out, "Latigo and buffalo are always perfect for waking up my girl."

"Bullshit." The self-sure female again. "Use the rubber tails—or the braided strands with the spiked tips."

The crowd *oooh*ed and then laughed.

Tracy jerked and then moaned.

But only until Franz brought both hands down on her ass again.

He waited a few beats, stroking the heat from the blows over the skin beneath her shorts, before pulling the big buffalo-hide flogger out from the display. Tracy shivered, clearly interpreting the sound. He walked, carefully and slowly, back to the space in front of her face. Reached out, curling one hand around her head and bringing her close to him so he was certain she knew which instrument he'd picked. Not anything that was going to hurt her. Simply an instrument to, as the Brit had stated, wake her up.

And yeah, if he was being honest, it was a good excuse to stroke her head once more—an experience, he openly admitted, unlike any he'd ever known. The necessity of putting her in the hood was rapidly becoming the sight he couldn't do without. Everything about her raw sensuality was still there—her huge eyes, expressive nose, and sexy-as-hell mouth, especially with the bit parting her lips like that—but now, because everything else was literally blacked out, the force of her desire was refined into something more. Something so perfect. So potent...

Something ensnaring every inch of his dick as she let out a high, exigent moan.

"The buffalo hide." He needed to ensure her of it, despite looking at the direct line of her gaze on the flogger. "This is what I'm going to use, kitten. Now just take deep breaths and focus on the sensation of the leather against your skin. Let it jolt you...warm you. Let it soften you...send you soaring. Think about how hard I'm going to get, watching these strokes heat up your skin...each and every one branding you as wholly mine tonight. Think about how thoroughly that knowledge pleases me...and about how I'll dream of claiming you as my kitten alone tonight."

Not even Sadist Sally in the second row had a smartass snark for that.

The room was quiet, except for the incessant throb of the music.

Until Franzen swiveled the flogger high and swung it across her back with smacking force.

"Unnnnhh!"

The crowd was silent in the aftermath of her visceral wail. A scream and stillness. A fire against the dark. Her pain. His pleasure.

Damn. Yes.

Without hesitation, Franz whipped the falls back and then forward again.

Again.

Three more strokes followed those. Three more after that. For every strike, Tracy gave up a strained cry—stark sacrifices to his ruthless dragon. Though time didn't stand still, he damn well wished it could. He had no real idea how long it all took; only that through all nine blows, their audience was utterly mute—listening, as he did, to the symphony more beautiful than anything a standard conductor and orchestra could create. It was the honest, brutal music from the depths of this woman's throat. First, pitched with shock and fear...but soon, deepening with acceptance and awakening...

And finally, surcease and surrender.

"Christ." John reeled, sweating and stimulated, as he staggered to behold what magic the leather had evoked along her skin. The length of her spine was as pink as a branch of cherry blossoms, some blooms deeper pink than others. That branch rose and fell from the breeze she fanned via mindless undulations, fighting to manipulate her body tighter against the leather pad with coiled arms and rolling hips. But the reason he repeated the oath wasn't due to any of that.

"*Christ.*"

It was the cock-grabbing beauty of her face.

Yes, even under the hood.

Especially under the hood.

Because all he saw right now were the elements that mattered.

The animal inhalations of her nose. The wild stimulation in her eyes. And, as his female "friend" in the audience voiced,

"Mmmm. Drool."

The stuff reddened his subbie's spread lips. Dripped to the stage like mesmeric poetry, all but making John forget the ultimate plan for the rest of her lesson. How he yearned to toss the damn flogger behind him, yank that fucker of a bit off her lips, and then sink every inch of his dick into her soft, wet mouth and fuck her there while the crowd cheered.

But there was a better plan at work.

An even better use for that gorgeous liquid dripping from her.

Didn't mean he couldn't have some fun transporting it, though.

Perfect. Solution.

Driven by the decisiveness, he one-handed the fly on his cargos. The pants, constructed so a guy could easily accomplish business in the woods, gave his cock plenty of room to fly free. The damn thing leapt for his navel the moment he sprang it free from the zipper. He had to wrestle it into his fist in order to work the precome up and down the shaft, a struggle well-rewarded by the brilliant lightning of Tracy's gaze, following every inch of his movements.

"Not for you, kitten," he admonished. "Not yet." He channeled the energy into circling the flogger back in, swirling it in a Florentine figure eight before her eyes. "But *this* is for you—if you want more?"

"Mmmmm." She moaned it like a wildcat in heat, the pitch jacking higher as he teased just the tips of the falls along the valley of her back.

"What was that, pretty kitty?" He twisted the handle, waltzing the strands like kinky ballroom dancers. "Couldn't quite hear you."

"Me, neither," a faceless male called out from the crowd.

"Couldn't hear a thing here," another stated in an ominous bass.

Several more people chimed in, finally making him openly chuckle. When kinksters combined sarcasm and sadism, the result was one unique explosion of humor.

The woman in front of him clearly didn't agree. Eyes blazing and shoulders nearly up against her cute latex ears, she grunted soundly at him—eliciting a dark growl from his own throat. Her primitive sound was sure as fuck arousing but not effective for what he ultimately needed. Grunts didn't make saliva.

Screams did.

"Oh, come on, kitten." He threw some force into the taunt, smacking her skin a little harder. "If you want it, beg me for it."

"Mmmmppph!"

No translation degree needed for that one, thank fuck. Roughly, he estimated it fell somewhere between *fuck you* and *flog me, damn it.*

He was more than willing to assist with at least half that checklist.

With a whirl, he flung the flogger high.

With a crack, he landed the falls down her back.

The crowd burst with approving applause.

Tracy conveyed the same message with a fierce scream.

Perfect. So fucking perfect.

"More." He whipped the falls back again. "Louder."

He struck. She screamed.

Fuck. Yes.

His cock bobbed in front of him as he secured a stance closer to her. "Louder!"

One more blow, and her throat went hoarse.

And her lips started coating his dick with the evidence of her efforts.

"So good. So damn good, wildcat." John exalted her with growling reverence, kissing the top of her head while letting the flogger fall to the floor behind him. With tender fingers, he removed her gag for a brief moment, letting her suck some bottled water through a straw. He'd made sure to place the bottle into the kink cart earlier, anticipating she might need the rehydration after he was done with her.

But that was just the thing.

He *wasn't* done with her.

Not by a fucking long shot.

Thank. The. Gods.

Long shot or not, this was a lesson he'd never forget—for what it was enlightening in him as well as her. This had been about empowering Tracy, but somewhere on this wild, kinky ride, the universe had spread the cosmic love to his own spirit. The sleeping dragon had been roused—and now remembered what it was like to stretch its massive wings...

And fly.

No scrambling for the evidence to the conclusion. That shit jutted straight out from him, gleaming and erect, as he pushed the bit back between his kitten's luscious lips. With a groan, he watched as more of her saliva coated him, a shimmering bath over everything from balls to crown. He worked the juice up and down the red length, hissing as veins popped against his skin like a relief map from the land of turned-way-the-fuck-on. Still pumping, he paced back to the space behind her, frantic in his quest to use his next toy...

Waiting in his pocket, where he'd been stowing it since this afternoon.

Where it had been taunting him mercilessly through the hours, preparing for this consummate moment.

"Who's ready to see this girl truly become my kitten?"

A round of approving hums answered from the darkness beyond the stage. They swelled as he pulled the length of tapered metal out of his pocket—its wider end embellished with a length of virginal white cat fur. Immediately, he swiped the glass along his cock. Twirled it and then sent it back the same direction. When he was done, the two and a half inches of stylized metal were shiny, wet...and ready to meet the tight recesses of his subbie's hot body.

Now for the fun part.

Preparing her too.

He started by sweeping a spread hand down the pinkened slope of her back. As he expected, her skin was still striped with heat from the flogger but knotted with trembling tension. She watched, along with everyone else, as he readied the anal plug with his unique flourish. She knew what was coming next.

She knew—and wasn't happy about it.

Sure enough, he reached beneath the center flaps of her shorts, sliding a probing finger toward the rosette in her ass, and met a resistant pucker.

"Kitten." He modulated the word with gentle rebuke. "You know how this goes..."

"Relax, girl." The British Dom sent some aid for his argument. "Fighting only makes it worse."

But Tracy did just that, shoulders bunching as she blatantly resisted the urge to wield a full glare at the bloke. A moment before the temptation took over, another voice called out.

"You're doing so well, kitten."

Then another.

"Better than that. She's fucking gorgeous."

"Such a pretty, perfect thing."

"Magnificent."

Her body rolled as she pulled in a long breath. As she released it, everything softened for him. Not by a lot...but by enough. Franz angled his head toward the darkness, dipping a nod of gratitude to the supporters. Amazing, how a few words of praise went such a long way. If the whole world adopted such an outlook, they'd be retraining everyone on the team to harvest corn or herd goats instead of close-quarters battle and fast-roping into nests of hostiles.

Or wondering how the hell they'd gone through so much life before doing something like this.

Reveling in how it felt to peel back latex shorts, exposing their submissive's silken ass to a room full of growling admirers.

"Bastard," one of those devotees said, laughing it out.

"*Fucking* bastard," another interjected, also chuckling.

"Sure you don't want to bury your cock in that flower instead, man?" the ultra-low bass added to the argument.

To that, Franz swung back a meaningful look. *You have no damn idea, my friend.*

Really...the guy didn't. Franz wasn't even sure *he'd* steeled himself well enough for the sight, proved by his clenching fingers into the silky spheres of her ass before baring the crimson bloom at their center. Just beholding that sweet fissure made his dick seep new milk, joining the juice he hadn't spread on the plug yet, dripping into her hole like erotic nectar.

"God*damn*." His grate hit the air a second before he touched the plug to her anus. She writhed, and the force of it rocketed through the crowd. "Relax, kitten." He twisted the taper, pushing it past the sensitive ring at her entrance. "Breathe deep. Push back, and then accept it in. This is going to happen. Don't fight me."

"Oh, *pssshhh*," came the Domina's dour scold. "Let her fight. I *love* a good fight."

"No," the Brit argued. "Just give it to her direct, mate. You've got enough lube for that pretty and two more."

"He's right," said the Dom who'd first called him a bastard. "Plunge it in now. Nice and deep, so we hear her scream again."

"She has a beautiful scream," the Domina purred.

Franz let them debate, focusing only his steady penetration into her tight, rosy hole. With every new territory he gained, his Tigress snarled and keened harder. Her thighs clenched and shivered. Her body quaked and jerked. And yes, *oh yes*, her pussy leaked and glistened.

"Mmmmm." He moaned the approval before slicking two fingers between her intimate lips. With the cream he gathered, he re-lubed her back rim. "Such a naughty, gorgeous little kitty. Feel how hot you are to grow this new tail."

"It's almost in," observed his British friend. "Damn, that's hot."

"Damn right," someone else snarled. "Giving me a few new ideas for my own little girl, man."

Franz took a long moment to stroke praising hands up and down her back, reconfirming he was still listening to her and vice versa. Though his subbie's stunning head now lolled between her shoulders, everything from her neck down spoke a renewed vow of connection to him...fealty to him.

He was her master.

Her owner.

Her humbled, spellbound Dom.

"You like that," he finally murmured, the words turning his throat into a cactus garden. "You like that a lot, don't you, kitten? That soft fur, swishing. That hard spike, invading your ass..." He grabbed the base of the plug, determinedly twisting it. "Tell me, kitty. Good," he crooned as she mewled in faltering abandon. "Now show me—*and* them. Swish your ass like the shameless little pussy you are."

The crowd gasped, sucking out all the air in the room. Surely that was the reason why he couldn't find his own breath while watching her wave her incredible globes from side to side, hints of a smile appearing around her gag as everyone showered her with applause. *Gods in every firmament.* It had to be the most erotic thing Franz had ever witnessed, and he was the damn schmuck who'd orchestrated the whole thing.

No. Not a schmuck.

He was a fucking genius.

And a textbook idiot.

Now, every person in the theater wanted her. Even the sarcastic Domina. None of them kept it a secret. Franz knew the sounds of erections being adjusted or outright stroked—and, in at least five different corners, freed from zippers, as well. His subbie and her flawless ass, shaking that foofy tail in every damn direction, had affected the crowd so much, a bunch of them weren't willing to wait for the after-party.

His first response to that was a flash of irritation—replaced at once by a surge of possessive pride. Let every single one of them fantasize about fucking her. Only *one* Dominant in this room was going to put the exclamation point on this subbie's ultimate lesson.

Right. Now.

The resolve was a forest fire in his mind—and torturing

pressure up his cock. It was the fever in his fingers, digging a packet from his pocket, and the frenzied tear of his teeth through the foil. It was the feeling of her body tremoring beneath him, as he lined his erection up with her cleft and his lips against her ear.

"Showtime, kitten."

CHAPTER NINETEEN

He didn't order her to scream this time.

He got a scream anyway.

Emanating from everywhere yet nowhere; full of white heat but black ice; a sound of abject confusion but ultimate clarity...

It was everything.

He was everything.

Leveling her senses. Demolishing her resistance. Liquefying her limbs.

Destroying her.

Delivering her.

Into a fear so consuming, she could only surrender to it— and then fly through it. On the other side, she burst into a world where everything in the room was clearer. People were kissing, touching, discovering...inspired by her. They moved together, succumbing to their passion...because of John and her. They opened their desires and needs and bodies...because of what he'd demanded from her first.

Lusts swirled on the air, seductive as incense. Sighs broke those snake charmer patterns, more edicts for action instead of tantalization.

As her Sir thrust his hot length into her welcoming channel, other Doms did the same thing to their submissives.

They were beautiful.

Bodies twining. Moans growing. Skin smacking. Arousals climbing.

They were perfect.

Whispers exchanged. Orders growled. Cries released.

Exclamations of surrender...

Taking her higher.

So much higher.

Into a white-silver apex of heat and hunger, nakedness and wantonness, honesty and audacity, she wondered if the "stage" in this place even mattered anymore...

Because her fear sure as hell didn't.

It had fallen away. Far behind the barricades. In this new freedom, there were no worries about right or wrong, embarrassment or errors, what was "trending right" or "falling flat." There was only the rightness of feeling. Of accepting. Of taking more and more of him in, as his lunges grew longer, harder...

Then even longer.

Even harder.

Oh.

My.

God.

"That's right, kitty cat. Let it all out. Scream about it. No judgments here. Only pleasure. All the pleasure. Take it, kitten. Take *me*, my beauty."

"Mmmm. *Mmmm!*"

"Yes. *Yes.* As loud as you want." A deep chuckle—*bastard*—as he reached fingers under, ripping the *X*'s off her nipples. "Maybe even like that."

"*Unnnhhh.*"

"Just wait, pretty one. Just wait."

"Fuh you."

"I prefer fucking *you* right now, darling pussy."

"Mmmmm." And she was really back to that? The mindless moaning? *What the hell?* But she couldn't latch on to anything else to be, as the good part of "just wait" finally came. After the initial rush of blood back to the tips of her breasts, both mounds became sensitive, sizzling balls of electricity. With every new plunge of Franz's cock, her nipples slid along the leather pad—and then burst into brilliant spheres of sensation. She even wondered if she'd look down and see they resembled a pair of those purple plasma balls.

If so, then they were all about sharing the magic too.

Everything from her nipples to her knees was a network of light, lust, longing, need...and all of it got worse with every lunge her Dom took into her body. But Franz didn't stop. Her clenching limbs and pulsing pussy only compelled him to conquer her more. Deeper and deeper he fucked, inspiring the other Doms to do the same, until all over the room, growls of discipline were laced with moans of arousal...and juicy sounds of rising passions.

"That's it, girl. Take me deep."

"Pinch your nipples while I do this. Such a good little *querida*."

"Yes, boy. You may put your dick into your goddess's grotto."

"Your cunt is dripping for me, baby. Spread your legs; show me more."

"You enjoy my cock in your ass, angel? Good, because I'm going to come there."

It was so much.

Too much.

Freedom stripping her breath away.

A wash of joy, of inhibitions gone.

A completion she had to have. A flight starting low in her belly, firing sparks and heat and need, before swirling around the rocket of her ultimate pleasure...the final explosion of skin, magic, friction, fantasy, combustion...

Explosion.

She strained, head snapping back, as the cosmic force of it took her.

She screamed, lost to raw feeling, as it convulsed through her.

She surrendered, rocked to her core and taken to the stars, as John slammed into her and then froze, roaring with the force of his own blistering release. She shuddered, feeling the fire of his come even through the condom...feeling the intimacy of his lips on her neck, even in a room full of strangers. No. Not strangers. She knew none of their names or faces or even what they liked on their pizza, but they'd made room in their schedules, their lives, and even parts of their hearts for a completely faceless woman tonight. They'd shown up to lend support but done so much more, sharing their intimate selves with her...and then consummating one of the most beautiful parts of their humanity with her too.

She was humbled. Moved. And yeah, even floored to the point of having a punch-drunk silly moment, there in the confines of her sleek kitty mask.

"Imagining an audience in its underwear" just got a crazy new lens filter.

Talk about truth being way stranger than the coffee mug inspiration.

Stranger. And better.

If only...

So many things in her world hadn't also gotten brand-new filters.

If only she wasn't so obsessed with gazing through all those new lenses now...

Especially the one labeled *John Keoni Franzen.*

He moved like the same guy, his actions defined by quiet mastery as he pulled out, zipped up, and then discreetly disposed of the condom. He acted the same too, handling her like a dew drop while unbuckling her restraints, pulling out the bit, and gathering her close to his sweat-drenched chest. His heart throbbed with the same powerful rhythm, pounding at her ear even through his soaked T-shirt, confirming the impact of their passion on his own system.

But none of it was the same.

He wasn't the same.

He was more now.

So much more.

The hero daring enough to make this whole night happen for her. The Dom confident enough to keep pushing her through it. But the lover tender enough to cradle her tight now, murmuring soft encouragement, as she shook from the mental impact of processing all of it.

The man, vigilant and bold and beautiful and strong, who'd come to touch so much of her soul...and rule so much of her heart.

Who was so dangerously close to claiming even more.

No.

Wasn't going to happen.

Couldn't happen.

If he took anything more than what he'd demanded tonight, there would be bloodletting in having to let him go tomorrow. Or the next day. Perhaps the next. Did it matter? There were cosmic scissors in their future, plain and simple.

Disgusting jaws that, in one mighty snip, would send her back to DC and John back to the post-military relaxation he'd earned.

Shockingly, she managed to hold on to that resolve as Franzen rose, still clutching her close, and strode off the stage. Even in the shadows and cold beyond the floodlights, she was adamant about accepting his warmth and tenderness but nothing more. She even managed a lopsided grin when he carried her through another door, down a short hall with more leather-lined walls, and into the intimacy of—gasp—a normal bedroom. Well, at least what *appeared* normal. Who knew what kinds of things were stored in the drawers beneath the four-poster bed or in the huge chest against the wall? For that matter, *four-poster bed*. Hello, hidden bondage rig points?

She could only hope.

But even that thought was best tucked into another mental drawer, relinquished in the name of savoring only this moment. Maintaining this soft smile, even as John set her down on the cushy, ivory coverlet and then slowly peeled away the hood. He gazed at her for a long moment, pushing aside stray hairs his action had yanked free, before moving in to kiss her with lingering reverence.

Accept nothing more than this.

Believe nothing more than this.

But crossing the Pacific in a rowboat was beginning to seem easier.

Treasure the moment.

Only the moment.

Even as he finished the kiss and then guided her to turn over, stomach down, on the bed.

Even as he stretched his massive body alongside hers,

skating fingers like feathers down the curve of her body, until they brushed along the furry extension still lifting from her backside.

When he pulled the plug all the way free, an unthinking moan erupted up her throat.

"You okay?" His query was just as careful as his touch. He rested his head in the crook of his elbow, watching her with a stare that missed nothing.

Tracy nodded. Quirked up one corner of her mouth. "Fine...Sir. It just..."

"Just what?"

"It feels...empty now."

His lopsided smirk copied hers. "If that's a bad thing, *popoki*, I can certainly fix the issue."

"That so?" Her own voice wavered a little. Maybe a lot. After the intensity of what they'd just been through, could she handle even more new sexual territory now?

She only knew she wanted to find out.

With him.

Yeah, despite five kinds of anxiety and twice as many fears—maybe even because of them—she set her chin, met his gaze, cleared her throat, and said, "What...do I need to do?"

Franzen's nostrils flared. He continued to watch her, not even blinking, as he tossed the anal plug to the floor. At once, he returned his hand to the crevice of her ass. "Not a damn thing you don't want to." He reached in, softly stroking the rim of her hole, while going on, "But if you really want my cock here, roll to your side so I can get you ready."

"What if I already *am* ready?" She bantered it to ease her tension while positioning her body as he asked. Franz obliged with a soft laugh, though at the same time, he slid out a drawer in the headboard where a small bottle of lube was hidden.

"Wicked *wahine*." His tone was puma stealthy as he shoved aside the panels of her shorts, baring her backside. But his fingers...oh hell, his fingers were like cobras dancing on a snake charmer's song, swirling and teasing at the sensitive rim of her naughty hole. "We'll see about that. *Breathe*, kitten."

She'd been trying to do just that—but wondering about that lube was a mental path she hadn't anticipated. But why? They were still officially inside his kink club; it made complete sense—but even if it did, had he used that stuff on others? And if he had—because he probably *had*—why should it matter to her? And why should she care if there was plenty of liquid left in the bottle too? Why should she admit that it ached to think of him using that stuff on the submissives who'd be in here with him after tonight?

It shouldn't matter. It *didn't* matter.

But damn it, *damn it*, it did.

And just like that, the tears she'd reined back through the last hour took two seconds to prick her eyes.

She sniffed hard, ordering them back to the insecure corners they came from, but they assaulted again as another epiphany hit. A whopper this time.

She wanted to burn this bed down before thinking of anyone else in it with John.

Put it away. Put it away!

"*Ku'uipo*." His utterance, though coarse as gravel, was a salvation in her grief. "Fuck." He leaned in from behind, soaking up several of her tears with his lips. "You're crying. It already hurts?"

"Yes." It was pathetic and weepy, but she couldn't give the man a Rodgers and Hammerstein score right now. She refused to lie. Not to him. Not *ever* to him—about *any* of it. "Yes, it does—and damn it, don't you dare stop."

She needed the pain now more than ever.

Pain only he could give.

Agony only he could assuage.

With his sexy economy of motion, Franz nodded. With his perfect infusion of understanding, he grunted. With his wordless way of knowing exactly what she needed, he pushed her shorts to her thighs...

Then plunged two fingers into her ass.

"Oh!" There was *one* way of forgetting the self-pity. The word shot out again as the man anchored his digits and then spread them out. Turned into a whimper as he twisted his hand, opening her in painfully erotic new ways. Mellowed to a moan when he soothed the sting by pouring a generous amount of lube into the aperture he'd just created. Then the torment began all over again. His spiraling motions. His widening fingers. He was stretching her in impossible new ways, though she knew it was still just a prelude of what his cock would do to her.

How he'd decimate her.

Dominate the most illicit part of her body.

So she could, for just one blessed moment, forget the anguish of her heart.

"Ahhhh!" She gasped it as he drove his fingers in to the hilt. And damn, did the man have long fingers.

"Still hurts, kitten?" His lips returned to her ear, heating its shell with grating force.

"Y-Yes, Sir."

"That shouldn't turn me on." He bit into her lobe as he plunged in deep again. "But gods help me, it does."

If she needed any fuel for the fire of her next sharp mewl, that was sure as hell it. "Damn!"

"Tell me it hurts."

"It—it hurts, Sir."

"But you want to take it, don't you?"

"I—I want to take all of it, Sir."

"So you want me to hurt you more...by fucking my cock into this sweet hole instead?"

"God." She choked as his voice worked its wicked dark magic and his fingers plunged to newer, naughtier depths. "Ohhhh God..."

"Not what I asked, woman." His free hand backed up his crossbow of a tone, digging into her hip. He only let go once he'd scooted his own body closer, hurriedly jerking down his zipper once more. As his erection worked between her ass cheeks, he dictated, "I asked if you wanted *this*. Right *here*."

"Yes." It spilled with all the unthinking force of her lust... and the unmitigated magic of her surrender. "Yesssss."

"Then tell me." His command was even darker and dirtier, heating the column of her neck. "Tell me exactly what you want, kitten."

Her mind spiraled. Her senses swam. And her sex...Mack fucking truck, her sex...

Throbbing. Craving. Needing to let him take her...to claim her as no other man had before...

"I want your cock," she finally got out. "There. *Right there.* In my ass."

Another sound, rough as a grizzly but ruthless as a dragon, vibrated through him. He withdrew his fingers from her hole, using them to position the hot, wet crown of his length at the trembling rim of her entrance...

And there, he paused.

Stopping her heart.

Seizing her nerves.

Closing up her throat.

As she waited. *Waited*...

"Kitten?"

She swallowed hard. Focused on breathing. Like *that* was happening. "Y-Yes, Sir?"

"Am I the first one to fuck you like this?"

"Yes." At last a breath came. Shook like a damn raindrop on the wind, but it was there. "Yes, you are."

"Good."

And then...he did.

His thrusts were sharp and short at first. Every motion wasted nothing, as always. But soon, he took more savoring stabs, spending more time with each stroke. He rolled and flowed, learning the secrets of her back grotto. Teaching himself what made her soften for him...moan for him...and soon, unbelievably, writhe and push back at him.

It hurt. There was no denying that. But the stretch was so wicked and the invasion so complete, she had no room for anything other than the truth of what he brought.

That in the pain he delivered, there was freedom.

A flight to vistas she couldn't describe. An escape to a nothingness where she didn't have a persona to consider, a face to put on, or an act to take part in. She wasn't a symbol of anything or a spokesperson for anyone.

She was just *woman*.

She was simply his.

Opening for him. Gasping for him. Taking every inch of him, pushing even deeper, until his guttural groan filled her ears and his balls caressed the sensitive tissues between her ass and pussy...

Making her so aware...

So on fire...

Her folds weeping...

Her clit needing...

"Yeah." His growl morphed into an actual word in her ear, making her realize where her own fingers had strayed of their own instinct. "That's good, kitten. Stroke your clit. We're going to do it together."

For the first time since she'd balked on him outside the kink theater, a frisson of hesitation sneaked in. No. Worse. She was...embarrassed. Franz surely felt that too, since her blush did its usual global takeover from her neck up, but the cadence of his heated breaths didn't falter by one beat. Instead, the wicked, wicked man slipped his long, long fingers down, pressing them atop hers...and then helping her circle them in and up, massaging her most tender button with brazen surety...

"Together."

His echo was a rasp of lightning in her senses.

His fingers were the masters of lightning on her clit.

His cock was the bearer of lightning inside her body.

Her senses could no longer fight the storm. She let it jolt her. Singe her. Claim her.

Incinerate her.

"Fuck. *Fuck!*"

"Yeah, kitten. *Yeah.*"

"No," she protested. "*No.* I—this—I'll never..."

Survive this.

Survive you.

I'll never survive you, *John Franzen.*

Especially if the orgasm was what his fingers already promised...

"You *can*, wildcat. And you *will*."

"I—I—"

"Let it come, Tracy. *Fuck*, how I want to go off inside you, *ku`uipo*. You feel me? That come already at the tip of my dick? There's more than that. So much more...I promise. I'm going to give it to you...right here, in your naughtiest hole, kitten. I'm going to fuck my come into your ass, and you're going to take it, and you're going to love it...and you're going to scream..."

And she did.

As she'd never screamed before.

As she'd never come before.

Taking all of him, just as he'd promised. Loving it, also just as he'd promised.

But still not certain he'd made good on the other part.

Had she survived?

Did she even want to?

Or was surviving John Franzen just another one of the delusions she kept feeding herself lately? Yeah, like the one about returning to DC as the same woman who'd left last week. Or the real crackerjack, where she tried to determine the exact moment he started rewiring every circuit in her soul—only to realize it was a trick puzzle, because the answer was too damn simple.

From the moment he first laid eyes on her, the damn dragon started changing her.

In another life, she'd have called it destiny. Fate. Whatever.

Not in this one.

In this one, she could only long for the one wish she couldn't have.

Walking away from him and not regretting it.

No. Freaking. Luck.

The weight of it crashed over her as the girth of him slipped out of her. It made her grip the pillow like a life ring in a typhoon, grateful John wasn't looking as he lithely rolled from the bed and headed for a small attached bathroom. But even if he noticed, the pillow survival grip was better than succumbing to the tears again—no matter how badly they scalded everything behind her eyes.

She wouldn't set them free again. What was the damn point? None of this was a news flash. She'd known it, like an extra weight on her psyche, even from that soul-changing moment back in Vegas. But that was the thing about soul changes. They altered one's entire world—until the world forgot to read the memo. So it was up to someone to write the memo for themselves, as many times as they possibly could, praying the ink would seep in and the memories would last forever...

God, the memories.

And the lessons.

Ohhhh, yeah. Those too.

Perhaps...*especially* those.

It wasn't the world's funniest joke, but it led her brain back to a mindset that wouldn't have her bawling into the pillow. As the mirth grew, so did the smile quirking her lips as she turned, gazing up at the panels of the stamped metal ceiling...

At least until John slid back next to her.

"Do I dare ask what has the kitten looking like she swallowed the canary?"

"Wha—huh?" Her head hadn't hit the clouds, but one newly naked, hot-as-hell warrior had just gamboled onto her mattress. Same difference. He'd just have to understand.

Franz snickered. Leaned down, softly suckling her lips, while dipping the damp cloth in his hand into the space between her thighs. Tracy opened, giving him better access for the care. For a Dominant who knew how to screw a woman's ears off her head, he was stunningly incredible at the afterglow shit too. Just didn't seem fair that he'd hogged all the good genes in the Dom pool, but she sure as hell wasn't going to lodge a complaint.

"So what's going on, my little canary binger?"

She gave up a brief laugh while snuggling tighter back against him. "I was just realizing...how a joint session of Congress is going to be a cake walk compared to *your* crowd."

This time, Franzen beat her to the laughter. His full-throated version was as smooth and rich as the toffee his skin resembled, coating her in sensations just as warm and delicious, especially as he compelled her to roll over and face him again. Wasn't a horrid request to meet. A new sigh spilled out just from the sight of his face again, so exotic yet noble. She let a huskier sound interrupt it as she tucked a hand under his T-shirt. Holy gravy train, the man was well-made. From the defined slant of muscle bordering his hip to the sleek ridges of his abs to the broad beauty of his pecs, she'd never get tired of exploring his sculpted glory. He was like a relief map for the land of oh-my-fucking-God. If so, then she'd happily be his Lewis and Clark expedition. *To the west!* Though at this point, she wouldn't mind even staying in the east. Or the central valley. Really, anywhere on the grid was fine by her.

"Well." His gaze grew hooded as she kept exploring. A thoroughly male growl unfurled from him. "My work here is done."

He could have slammed an iceberg on her chest and impacted her less. But maybe that was exactly what she needed. This could never be their reality; he was just sucking shit up and accepting it faster than she. It was time to follow that lead. Put her big-girl panties on—or in this case, hike her latex shorts back up—and be grateful for the magic he *had* chosen to give her.

So much more than she'd ever dreamed of. Hoped for.

And it had to be enough.

Because no way could she ever offer *him* enough.

It was laughable, but so damn true. The White House? Sure—but what was a man like him going to do in an environment like that? Sit around and oil paint while she finished eighteen-hour work days? Get in putting practice on the East Lawn while she made trade policy and signed shit into law? Squirm in a tuxedo from time to time, as her "arm candy" at formal dinners?

He'd hate every second of it.

Then he'd hate her too.

"Tracy." His voice was rough as a rusted penny, betraying the million-dollar hit he'd landed on her thoughts. She lifted a hand to his face, spreading fingers into his dark stubble, grateful the hard part had already been said though sensing he still fought to dig deep for the prose. *Why?* She pressed the word into him with the force of her gaze. *Why are you doing this? Why are you making this harder?*

"John," she finally uttered, slowly shaking her head. "It's— it's all right. We both knew, going into this—"

"No." He all but snarled it. His gaze turned to flames as his fingers clawed into hers. "Don't you get it? I *didn't* know." His dimple became a violent tick. "I didn't know I'd..."

And just like that, the glacier was a waterfall. A flood of burning, blazing awakening...

Of realization...

Of *hope*...

For what, she had no damn idea. She only knew that if she didn't dive into the water, she'd never forgive herself.

Even if she ended up on a rock somewhere downstream, drowned by her own stupidity...

The jump was everything.

The jump was now.

"You didn't know you'd *what*, John?"

A hard breath entered and then left him. He closed his eyes...and when he opened the sienna depths to her again, the honesty in them was more stark, raw, and real than she'd ever seen or felt from him before. He was bared to her, far beyond the bronze magnificence of his body. His soul was naked now.

And his heart...

For one exquisite, perfect moment.

Right before the door back to the club was nearly pounded off its hinges.

Alarm crashed over Franz's face. He pushed up, instantly throwing his body in front of hers. "What the hell?"

"Franz!" The voice, deep and booming, wasn't Zeke's. Max? No. Not enough snark. Even after knowing the guy for all of a minute, Tracy knew Max Brickham had been born with a taunt in his eyes and a sneer on his lips. "Are you in here? *Franz!*"

Tracy's hands, now on his shoulders as she crouched behind him, were suddenly filled with rigid muscle—for the two seconds he stayed on the bed. As he cleared three strides to the door, one word spilled from him, just as urgent and ferocious.

"Shit."

Some versions of the word were easier to hear than others. This wasn't one of them. The waterfall gained new ice floes as Tracy scrambled, throwing a pillow around her middle, before John flung open the door. It was the best she could do since the man had obviously changed gears. The last time she'd seen him like this was five days ago, in the back of a speeding Escalade, with smoke billowing in the sky behind them. The same heat roared through his body now. Defined every terse move he made.

He was back in full battle mode.

Without repeating the word, he unlocked and then jerked open the door. At once a man stalked in, dressed in similar black cargo pants—though from the waist up, his look was radically different. A sand-colored T-shirt was mostly covered by a bulletproof vest, two loaded gun harnesses, and a small backpack with other paraphernalia worthy of a *GI Joe* plot. Looks-wise, the man was also Franz's polar opposite. With hay-colored hair, summer sky eyes, and even a few light freckles across his nose, the guy was an older, hunkier Tom Sawyer. In special ops gear. With a bad-ass swagger.

"Nessa Rose and the fucking red shoes." Every word dripped with John's shock.

Tom Sawyer smirked. "Great to see you too, Dragon."

"You're not supposed to be here, fucker. Thailand—"

"Shock of shocks, the op went easier than we anticipated. And maybe, I...errmm...texted Z to let him know."

"And *maybe* he texted back that we might be having some fun of our own up here," Franz growled.

"Maybe."

"Hell."

"Shit." That one blurted from Tracy. Dots finally connected in her brain. "Hawk," she stammered when the two men snapped their attention over. "For Hawkins, right? *Garrett* Hawkins? It took me a second to recognize you." But now she sure as hell had. Hawkins was the dashing SOF soldier the media couldn't get enough of a few years back, rocketing to fame when rescuing white slavery victims in an East Asia jungle, only to discover one of them was the fiancée he'd presumed dead. They'd planned a gorgeous wedding only to have it become the scene of more drama, if she remembered right. Something about twin bad guys and a quest for revenge taking ugly turns...

Not worth going into, especially as Hawkins returned her interested stare with riveted intensity. "Holy fuck. It's really—I mean, Zeke told me you and she were really—" He colored and then composed himself. "I mean—holy shit—it's, errr, *really* nice to meet you, Madam Vice President, and I'm sorry about this, but—"

"*Hawkins.*"

It was the only charge John needed to issue. The younger man snapped back to attention for the man who'd been his commanding officer for so long, reverting to all-business focus. With a nod of his own, all but confirming this wasn't the first time he'd seen the inside of this club, the soldier gave an answer that served as the second iceberg her bloodstream hit tonight.

CHAPTER TWENTY

"You're absolutely sure?"

What was he hoping to accomplish by saying it for the hundredth time? To turn it into some kind of *abra cadabra*, making Hawk's announcement less true? To rub it in like chafe balm, expecting it to erase the stab wounds altogether?

Gashes from an attack he'd even known to prepare for. A plan he'd prayed they'd never have to use.

Because the assets had never been more invaluable.

And who the fuck was he kidding with *that* platitude? *Assets? Invaluable?* If they genked this up, there wasn't any "sweating it off" with hours in the gym or "drinking it off" with hours in the bar. There'd be no erasing it, period. This time, the assets were the woman who'd given him back his spirit and the boy who'd given him back his smile.

But they were prepared. And preparedness was half the battle, yeah?

What the fuck moron had said that?

Because he sure as hell wasn't prepared for this. Yeah, the logistics were clicking. Yeah, the details were being handled— technically. But none of it eased the mounting dread in his gut, the relentless pressure on his chest. *On his heart.*

Yeah. There it was again. And right now, he didn't even try to deny it. He didn't even want to.

He pulled in a long breath. Several more. He could do this. He'd been under worse stress before and kept his shit together. Okay, maybe not—but maybe that all figured into the preparedness thing too. *That* was the shit the woman in the bathroom needed to hear, especially now. Tracy's anxiety was palpable, even through the closed door. The little huffs she made, hurrying to get back into the black dress along with the legging things Rayna sent along with Hawk, dug fresh gashes into his own composure—reminders of how high the stakes really were. The instant replay of Garrett's words, bringing fresh bile along with his recall, were another "convenient" cue.

Of course we're sure. You think Z would've called and told me to get my ass over here if we weren't? Ethan's been listening for an hour now. It's definite chatter, and it's absolutely not ours. They're referring to something called "Tigress's cave" and urging someone to "get the cub first."

That was all Tracy had needed to hear.

It was all *he'd* been able to do, forcing her to calm down, get dressed, and trust Zeke and Max were completely handling things upstairs.

Yeah. As in getting those two teenagers and her two best friends out of that condo as fast as they possibly could.

Because if something happened to Luke Rhodes, the country could go ahead and get used to Blake LeGrange in the Oval Office. There'd be nothing left of Tracy Rhodes to fly back to DC.

And if there was nothing left of Tracy Rhodes, there was nothing left of him.

Damn it.

It was the most dangerous mindset for approaching a mission. The hugest liability a soldier could strap to his psyche. Effective warriors cared about the objective but *not* about the asset. In the name of protecting humanity, they disavowed their own. When their focus strayed from the bigger picture of the horizon, they tripped over their own two feet. Began making decisions from places other than where it mattered the most. The cold, incisive surety of their mind.

Franzen was certain he wouldn't recognize his mind if it bit him in the ass right now.

A situation *not* helped by the rising panic of the woman behind the bathroom door.

"Shit!" Tracy bit it out seconds before a *thwump* rattled the door, followed by the sound of towels whizzing off the rack.

"Ma'am?" Hawkins yelled it, rushing to the door. "Are you all—"

"She's *fine*." Franz shouldered him aside, acknowledging and owning the overprotective ass factor of the move. "And don't call her ma'am."

He left Hawk behind, still smirking at him like a pretty boy wise-ass, as he rushed into the other room without knocking...

Nearly causing a second crash when he tripped over Tracy's prone form.

"*Shit*. Kitten."

"I'm all right." But her voice faltered like the tufts of towel lint on the air. "I—I just can't think. I can't even put these damn tights on. I can't think!"

Her desperate rasp brought him to his knees. "Ssshhh." He scooped her close, pulling her hair free of its pins and bands, letting the strands fall loose around his massaging fingers. "Ssshhh now. You need to breathe for me."

"Trying." She gripped his forearms, pulling at the hairs in her desperation. "Damn it, I'm trying."

"I know." He meant it. He felt how she quaked, wanting to lose her shit a lot worse than this, but if this was going down—if the chatter Archer picked up was real—he needed her buy-in on trusting him now more than ever. Yeah, even more than the moment he'd tugged her to the middle of a kink club stage dressed in nothing but a latex kitty hood and electrical tape.

"Luke—"

"Is going to be safe." He gave it as an order. No way would he let her think otherwise. "You want to know why? Zeke Hayes himself is upstairs, personally making *himself* the kid's body armor if it comes to that. He'll do the same for Mia, Gem, and Ronnie too. He isn't playing games with this shit, kitten. He even called in Hawkins to help—and that big ape doesn't ask for help easily."

As her body settled into longer intakes and exhalations, he tucked her even closer. "This is all probably nothing but a giant coincidence," he asserted. "But if it isn't, we'll handle it. Somehow, we will. We'll take care of Luke—*and* you."

He let his eyes close for just a moment—telling himself to savor this. Exactly this. The perfect weight of her in his lap. The exultation of her total trust, her full belief. Completion. Connection.

The perfect space.

The room he'd been looking for since walking into the kink mansion, all those years ago—though only now arriving at the atrium of epiphany in that place.

BDSM wasn't the key to his perfect room.

It had only been the door.

But he'd kept pounding on that door, for a dozen damn years...expecting it to magically open...

When he never had the key.

As if the universe really needed to pound that one into his gray matter, Tracy's soft chime of a laugh echoed through his whole body. Before he even asked, she explained, "You know, if word gets out that the bad-ass dragon was found cuddling on the bathroom floor with his mission target..."

A wry snort escaped. "Dragon's cover was blown long before we met, woman."

Weirdly, she reacted to that by pulling back by a few inches—and surprising him even more with her newly insightful gaze. "Because of the op you led in Kaesong?"

Okay, ditch surprised. Astonishment took over, hiking both his brows. "Whoa. That sit-rep made it all the way up the Hill, eh?" Just as swiftly, he let his expression tighten. "That's comforting, in a jacked-up way. Guess I went out a notorious man."

"Well, we weren't passing it around like the newest memes of the day," she countered. "And when I first heard you mention it, I wasn't sure *you* were *that* guy, from *that* mission—"

"But now you are."

Her lips hitched into one of her mysterious smiles. "Yeah." Her hand, pressed to the side of his neck, squeezed in. "I am."

Nothing about that smile, or the energy accompanying it, should have had his gut cranking out new acid. Nevertheless, the bite of it had him shifting on his haunches. "And now debating the best way to gracefully exit?"

He meant more than just the bathroom, and she sure as hell knew it. He'd seen a lot of rapid changes to her face over the last week, but nothing like the shadows falling over it now. "The hell?" she spat back.

"Don't pretend you didn't hear the juiciest parts," he countered. "I openly defied CentComm orders, Tracy."

"Yeah. To let three scientists defect, rather than return to a country who'd use their hard work for destruction and subjugation."

"And almost started a war."

"Against a disgusting dictatorship? Like CentComm shouldn't be behind *that*."

One patience-gathering breath. Another. "Some things aren't that black and white."

She snorted. "And some things are."

"Your friend Craig probably wouldn't have agreed with that." The sheepish aversion of her gaze confirmed that truth. "I'm wondering, if once you're filling his shoes, you won't change—"

He said nothing else because Tracy didn't let him. By slapping him.

His ears had barely cleared out the stinging ring when she seared them all over again. "You know what, Captain? Screw you." She shot to her feet, efficiently yanking on the leggings now. With a barely disguised grimace, John watched the black spandex cover her ass. He could've gazed at those perfect swells for hours—especially when they bore the dark-pink reminders of where he'd spanked her, flogged her, fucked her. He was pretty damn sure that wasn't what her present challenge represented, backed up when she reiterated, "Screw *you*—and every lachrymose delusion you're clearly *still* carrying about this bullshit."

Another adjustment on the haunches—though he finally pushed up, parking his ass on the closed toilet seat, fighting to process what unnerved him the most about her accusation. "Delusion?" he growled. "*Still?*" And what the hell did "lachrymose" even mean?

"You think I don't see it?" she retorted. "That I haven't seen it since that first day, when you moped in your milk with Dan and Shay about it? That I don't see your woe-is-me inner dialogue about it?"

He jolted to his feet too. His new height gain didn't change an inch of her defiance. And he'd really expected it to? "My *what*?"

"You heard me." She jogged up her chin. "You heard me loud and damn clear because it's true. Because it's easier for you to play misunderstood hero than take responsibility for what you did and know it was the right thing." With a lengthy huff, she curled a hand around one of his elbows. "You did the *right thing*, John—no matter what those asses in the big office think."

Air escaped his own lungs in harsh bursts, drawn out by the warmth of her confident grip. His sights tunneled on her, needing and hating her words at the same time. He looked down, dazed, as her fingers slid down to cover his white-knuckled fist.

"Not every hero gets the pomp and parades, Captain." Her voice moved over him like her touch, a river of empathy but encouragement, admonishing but acknowledging. "They have only the true north of their own compass, confirming they took the right path when it most mattered. And if they're lucky"—she wiggled his arm and flashed a winsome wink—"they also get a cute-as-fuck subbie to remind them about the *other* ways they can be heroes."

That was it. She was no longer a river. Franz pushed closer, letting himself drown in her breathtaking, beautiful ocean. Letting his gaze get lost in the gray foam of hers, as his fists unraveled...

So he could yank her even closer.

And breathe her in.

And all but feel her heartbeat, slamming as hard and

fast and brutal as his, as he considered just opening his damn mouth and telling her...

Just telling her...

I love being your hero.

Because I love you, *Tracy Rhodes.*

"Mrs. Rhodes?"

They broke apart, flustered as if they'd been trading more than moony-needy gazes with each other, when a distinctly female yell came through the door.

Franz stepped around Tracy to jerk back the portal. Rayna Hayes stood there, a glowing smile on her face and a pair of tennis shoes in her hands.

The sight of her was...weird. Yeah, he was more than aware of how she and Zeke had moved to the building for its proximity to Bastille, but the idea of her in this club, as a willing subbie to the guy he'd slept in jungles with... *No. Just no.*

As a matter of fact, after tonight, he wasn't certain he'd be able to see *any* other submissive in this place but the woman behind him—and now, thank fuck, stepping in next to him, tucking into the crook of his arm. He'd worry about how to deal with her kitten-sized ghost in this place later.

Rayna bit her bottom lip and held up the shoes. "Zeke sent me down. He thought you might need these. Just in case something happens, I mean. Which it won't, but..."

"Thanks." He fought to say it like he meant it, as Tracy actually accepted the shoes. But if Z was sending Rayna down here with a fucking *shoe* delivery...

He beat back the downhill of that conclusion—at least long enough to move around and stride toward Garrett, already modulating his voice so the women couldn't hear.

"Hawk." He hooked the guy's elbow, directing him even

farther away. "What are you hearing from upstairs?"

The guy's bearing, twice as rigid as two minutes ago, was a crappy prelude for the reply. "Not a damn thing."

"Fuck." He gritted it under his breath.

Hawk jabbed hands into his front pockets and rocked back on his heels. The bastard's call-sign should've been Opie. He was the king of hiding a thousand dark secrets under that aw-shucks exterior. "About sums it up."

"Who has the radio?"

"Zsycho."

"And you've hailed him?"

"Five times in the last minute."

"And he didn't respond?" Franz persisted. "Not even to give notice he was sending Rayna down?"

Hawkins ticked his head in a terse negative. "I almost shot her head off because of it too."

"*Fuck.*"

"Believe you covered that one already." The guy arched a meaningful glance at Tracy. "Likely in more ways than one tonight?"

He ignored that—also in more ways than one. First, no matter how many state secrets Garrett Hawkins would take to his grave, the guy didn't need to know what his old CO and his new president had been up to a few rooms over. Second, Tracy wasn't going to be *anyone's* next president if they sat here like the stupid people in a horror movie, waiting for their friends to get back from "checking out what was in the woods." Z didn't ignore radio hails. Ever.

And with that, a new realization.

Silence really could be sickening.

"Tracy." He skipped both the formal address and her

nickname in favor of snagging her attention as fast as possible. No time for anything else. If Z was holding off hostiles upstairs, whatever the hell *that* meant, they had a few minutes at most. If they'd already taken him out—Franz avoided even glancing at the guy's pregnant wife while thinking it—then they had only seconds.

Thank God for the woman's supernatural perception. All the apprehension he'd only sprinkled into the word was now on full display in her eyes, bright as quicksilver. "What is it?" she rasped.

"Tie them." He jerked his head at the shoes she'd pushed her feet into. "Fast."

Under any other circumstances, he'd have watched her do it with lingering pleasure. She was so damn cute, with that slinky cocktail dress now joined by the leggings and runners, he longed for even a second to watch her moving around in the funny outfit. Then another second more, to put his own brand on the look with a hot, deep kiss.

Seconds they didn't have.

Another horror movie trope feeling the necessity to prove itself, the second she rose and he grabbed her hand...

And the world hit an insanity he never thought he'd experience this side of the Pacific.

Resolve fought reality. Adrenaline battled gelatin. And no matter how desperately he craved to hit the hidden transporter button, to materialize at Point B from this disgusting Point A, it wasn't fucking happening.

The combat zone began now.

The ferocious face of his best friend, charging out of the connector tunnel at them, confirmed that fact with sickening surety.

"Z's right behind me." Max, looking every inch the marine he used to be, sounded as if he'd swallowed half a bunker's worth of dirt. Like Hawk, a gun holster bisected his torso—making Franz feel, for the first time all night, stark naked. Dilemma handled, as Max hefted over the MP5 hanging off his back.

Regrettably, it was a tiny umbrella in the shit storm he'd brought with him.

"And you're telling me he's not alone." Not a question. Franz already knew the nerve-singing answer.

"It's the whole goddamned Death Star," Max growled back. "Whoever or whatever gave us away did it really fucking well."

CHAPTER TWENTY-ONE

"Fuck."

It wasn't the version of the word she'd expected Franzen to be ending their night with. To be honest, even after Garrett showed up, it wasn't how she expected things to go at all.

As the reality set in, so did the terror. The nerve-stealing, mind-gripping, I-can't-think-anymore fear, driving only one thought up from her senses—the same word that bled, raw and full of pain, from her lips.

"Luke."

Franzen spun her around. Shook her, forcing her to meet his gaze. His eyes were the darkest she'd ever seen them. Ruthless as coal. Rimmed with smoke. "Listen to me. He'll be safe." His jaw turned to equal flint. "I promise you, Tracy. He'll be safe."

Somehow, her head wobbled in a pathetic semblance of a nod. "Okay," she rasped, only to stammer the next moment, "Please....John..."

He cupped the back of her neck. His stare searched hers now, all the fire and brimstone suddenly lost. In their place was a wash of what looked like wonder, perhaps even awe—and something else. A something echoed in the deepest reaches of her soul.

She swallowed hard. That something had a name.

But not right now.

The only name she cared about right now was *Luke*.

Nothing else mattered. Nothing else made sense. It also explained why John's shout of her name sounded as if he was on repetition three or four, to which she finally gave a mumbled, "Wha...?"

"I said, you need to go with Max. Right now."

"No." She gaped at him as sharply as the lucidity rushing back in. Was he nuts? She refused to acknowledge the answer that surged from her gut. He wasn't nuts. He was John. He was Sir. He was the one who saw her, who *knew* her—who made every damn decision with her happiness and confidence and well-being in mind. Who always made the *right* decision...

Yeah, well. Everyone was due an off night.

"No," she echoed, because now *he* hadn't heard *her*. They were still headed the wrong direction down the tunnel, down a strange side hall in which the gray bricks gave way drywall and paint and the air smelled of exhaust and gasoline—nowhere near the basement laundry room they'd passed before. "John, I'm not going to—"

"You sure as hell *are* going to." In any other time or circumstance, that succinct growl would've had her belly fluttering and her pussy clenching. Right now, it only made her yearn to yank away, turn heel, and run back into Bastille like the batshit brat he was making her feel. If only this were that simple. If only she really could lead him on a merry chase through a bunch of kink role play rooms, finally letting him catch up and punish her in any wicked way he saw fit...

But yeah, this was her off night too.

Because this nightmare was really happening.

Thoughts she had no damn time to process because hell was hitting too freaking fast. Even in Rayna's runners, she was breathless keeping up with John's wide, efficient strides. Even forcing her mind into crisis mode, she had to blink against disbelief when he whipped one of his burner phones out of a side pocket and barked five unfathomable words.

"It's Franzen. We've been made."

At the end of the hall, there was a wide glass door. Through the pane, she spotted rows of parked cars—beyond the cobalt-blue Hellcat and steel-gray Jag XKR-S idling in front of the lobby. Max and Garrett, having somehow disappeared during her brain's flight from sanity to panic to fear, paced in front of both front bumpers like textbook goons from a gangster movie. It was an improvement from the horror show comparison, at least—turning damn close to a joyous chick flick when she spotted Gem and Ronnie seated in the back of Garrett's Hellcat.

They both flashed her elated grins, while raising hands with two fingers up and two down, thumbs extended. Their version of love, the American Sign Language way. As thoroughly as Tracy longed to answer by dashing over, yanking open the door, and crushing them both into hugs, she was hyperconscious of the exact situation they faced right now.

We've been made.

It meant that at any moment now, some lunatic—perhaps the same one who'd set the explosives in the villa at the Bellagio—could jump out from anywhere, ready with even more of his fun fireworks. With Franz still on the phone, only Max and Garrett had eyes on the entire garage. The job usually required a Secret Service army of ten.

"You think I fucking know how it happened, Sol?" The fury in Franz's voice shot through his body, though when Tracy squeezed his hand in support, he returned the pressure. Such a strange, seemingly insignificant gesture—but as soon as her heart flipped twelve different directions because of it, curtains raised on a much bigger mental vista. Suddenly, it was like she balanced atop a hundred-foot flagpole at the edge of the Grand Canyon.

Was this what her life was going to be like until the next election? And beyond that, even if she decided not to submit for reelection? Would she always be hiding now? Always wondering if the next parking garage—or movie theater, or airport, or hotel villa—was hiding assassins in its shadows, waiting to toss a bomb into her belly or fire a bullet into her brain?

If so...how was she going to handle any of it without John?

No.

How was she going to handle even the *normal* days without him?

Yeah, even when he was like this. Perhaps *especially* like this, with his stance like a gladiator, his glare like a lion, and his voice—dear God, how his voice sizzled through her, even now—like an avenging angel from the wrong side of the celestial tracks.

"Tell you what, man," he sneered into the burner. "Why don't *you* tell *me* how it happened? You're determined to do it the right fucking way, after all. Come on; I'm interested to hear this. Tell me where I've genked up. Nothing I'm not used to hearing—but you know that too, don't you? Lend me thy great and powerful wisdom, Mr. Wrightman. I'm all fucking ears."

Tracy could tell he wanted to pace. She didn't dare let him go. He kept up his side of the grip, but maybe that was because he was so preoccupied. Damn. He berated Sol to the point of composing a full masters' thesis on the subject.

Wait.

What?

He really was berating Sol. A lot.

Taking the time to do it. Right now.

With his gaze glued to...

Max?

Who returned the scrutiny by rolling a finger in the air. Then added a new motion, as if pulling a zipper sideways—the universal television production symbol for drawing a conversation out.

What. The. Hell?

"Done there, sparky?" he gritted into the phone. "Don't let me harsh your groove, hot stuff. I mean, the great and powerful Sol Wrightman knows exactly how to do all this subterfuge shit, doesn't he?"

He finished that part by throwing his gaze down at her—though the incensed fire she expected to find in his gaze was nonexistent. She felt her lips fall open as he stared harder.

Looking as if Sol had just told him someone had died.

What the hell? Tracy repeated it by mouthing it now but once more came up against the Great Wall of Franzen. The flint in his jaw now defined his whole stature. The bizarre sheen continued in his eyes.

On the other side of the car, Max kept up the TV production hand signals. Suddenly, that changed. He nodded sharply then jabbed both thumbs into the air.

The second he did, John switched up the dialogue with Sol as well. "Hey. *Hey.* I don't have time for any of this, asshole."

Asshole?

Before she could funnel the shock into so much as a glance, he barreled on. "I'm taking her someplace safe—clearly safer than this. Don't expect to hear from me until it's publicly reported that you've caught the Vegas bomber."

Why she was dumbfounded that he ended the exchange there, using his thigh to help him break the burner in two before hurling it into a trashcan, was a mystery for unraveling another time. There were bigger issues here to tackle—namely, what the hell was going on upstairs, what the hell had just happened here, and *where the hell was her son*—than to worry about Franz's lack of social graces.

At the moment, she wasn't feeling fond of the bullshit herself—especially when the man let go of her hand, pushing at the small of her back toward Max's Jag. *Hell.* He chose *now* to roll out one of the best moves in the alpha male playbook? She wanted to enjoy it, damn it—not be struggling to accept this might be the last time she'd ever feel it. The last time he'd be touching her, period. She wanted him to be escorting her to this piece of automotive porn for a glamorous date involving booze and chocolate and sex, not as a getaway car to—

Where?

She stopped in the space between the open passenger door and the car itself. Looked at Max, his thunderous expression still the same, and then at Rayna, who'd already climbed in and buckled up in the Jag's back seat, worry glistening in her huge emerald eyes. Finally, she swung a new gaze back, at the other waiting car.

And came to a sudden, distinct recognition.

None of this had happened randomly.

This was a coordinated effort—as in, someone had worked out a plan, gone over it with the guys, and ensured it would all happen.

As in, someone had practically *expected* their hideout to get blown.

As in, the hulk now standing in front of her, due to the furious spin she executed on his hulking, scowling form. "*Franzen.*"

His hand, now at her hip because of her whiplash move, dug into her flesh like his fingers had turned to I-beams. "*Tracy.*"

"Uh-uh," she fired at his equally iron tone. "No way are you going dragon on me right now."

He splayed more I-beams against her other hip. "No way are *you* calling an inch of what happens right now."

"What the hell's going on?"

More flint etched its way over his face. "Not at liberty to discuss with you, ma'am."

Not at—

Ma'am?

Her jaw plummeted. "Are you shitting me?"

He didn't even blink. "Get in the car, Tracy."

Even as he ordered it, Max was already doing just that. The guy turned the engine over and revved it, as if deliberately adding a grating backup to his friend's logic.

Yes, damn it. *Logic.* She'd have readily accepted a root canal over admitting it, but Franz's urgency wasn't just smart. It was necessary. The longer she stood here trying to pull rank she didn't really have over him, in *any* version, the more precious seconds went by without him getting out of here and up to Zeke...

And Luke.

God. *God.* Her boy. Her sanity.

He'd be safest if she got the hell out of here. It was a brutal truth she couldn't rewrite—one Franz had already forced himself to confront.

But how? And when?

When he hadn't been between the sheets—and in the shower, and on the desk, and in the laundry room, and on the couch—with her, he'd been spending valuable time with Luke, hours she'd treasured as much as all their intimacy. So when had he carved out *more* hours in those days to develop this escape plan with the guys, *just in case*? And why did she glare harder at him now, only to be slammed by the most insane instinct for *that* effort? The feeling that he'd actually known *just in case* might become *just a matter of time*?

Holy shit.

The realization twisted in deeper, feeling like a corkscrew to her chest.

Had he known? Had he sensed—perhaps even gotten some intel to back it up—that this horrible shoe might really drop? Had he continued screwing her, charming her, *dominating* her, and consciously kept this from her? Had he seen her most terrified tears, fulfilled her most filthy fantasies, and demanded the most brutal honesty of her soul while holding back this vital information about the people trying to snuff her *life*?

And if so, why did he even *think* she wanted him near her now?

And damn it, why did he pick that exact moment to lean over, staring in and reading every shred of that fury across her quavering face? Why the hell did he make her feel like shit about it without even trying, with double daggers jabbing vertically between his eyebrows? Why was she even tempted to reach for him as the hurt stretched across his face, ticking his jaw and clenching his teeth?

She looked away. She had to. Like that did any good.

He loomed so close, every one of her viable sightlines was consumed by him—every one of her breaths was full of the potent command of him.

Damn him. *Damn him.*

"Tracy."

"*What?*"

"You have to trust me."

She swallowed heavily. Because she had to. Because if she didn't, the bile would invade her tone more than it already did. "I know."

What the hell. Maybe she'd still puke, just for the hell of it. Not inside Delphine, though technically Max was a culpable accomplice here and deserved the mess in his car—but hurling on John's boots was such a superior idea, in so many ways...

Also not an option. Not now.

Now, just like so many other times when just giving up and getting sick was a temptation better than chocolate mousse and Dwayne Johnson combined, it just wasn't a damn option.

Now, like those other times, she had to bracket her spine with steel, command her chin to lift, and grit back the tears until her teeth hurt. Her boy, hiding and horrified somewhere in this building, needed her strength.

Even the strength to leave him.

And damn it, the strength to trust this man with his life. This man who, despite hiding a vital truth from her, still somehow *had* her trust. That made less sense than refusing chocolate and Dwayne, but there was even less time for therapist shopping right now. And the last time she checked, dead women didn't need therapy.

She wanted to need therapy.

She wanted to live.

And she *had* to get out of this alive, if only for one damn, driving reason. She wanted it so badly, she spoke it into existence from between her locked teeth.

"I'm going to find a flogger and use it on *you* after this, Captain Franzen."

She braced herself for his just-try-it grin. Maybe even the preening arch of both his brows. She *hadn't* prepared for the meaningful heat turning his gaze to darker smoke—or for the touch he joined to it, a swift brush of knuckles over her cheek, accompanied by words he merely whispered but might as well have shot from the gun on his back.

"And I'll be looking forward to it, my love."

Nine seconds of his breath.

Nine bullets to her heart.

Nine explosions of shock. Of joy. Of elation. Of incredulity.

Of swearing she was going to flog him harder for pulling this shit on her in *this* damn moment.

This all wrong, but suddenly so right, moment...

Just before the world detonated around them.

Pop, pop, pop.

Blam, blam, blam.

Many times in the past, especially since she and Luke had moved in at Observatory Circle, she had heard fireworks in the summer and worried they were gunshots. She now knew the difference. She'd never have those summer skitters again, not after hearing the real thing. The shots blazed with sharp violence, echoing with sickening surety against the parking garage walls. Not after identifying the inevitable chaos latched to it. The frantic rush of racing boots. The acridity of fried lead. The spike of panic on the air. The bellows, deep and demanding, of soldiers jacked by adrenaline, dazed by explosions, and consumed by violence.

And one more sound.

One gutting her to the point of true, undeniable nausea.

The shouts of a fifteen-year-old, forced to grow up by years because terrorists were chasing him. Shooting at him.

Shooting to kill.

"No." It burned her throat, which felt as small and meaningless and helpless as the rest of her body. "Nnnooo." Now it was a moan, strangled by panic and horror. A sound that disgusted her. It was supposed to have been his name.

Luke.

Luke!

But she couldn't force the syllable out. Her tongue was made of rubber. Her lungs were useless blobs. She only knew she couldn't unclick the seat belt and bolt out of the car faster—

Only to be thrown back in.

Locked back in.

Chained back down.

By the monster she kicked at. Clawed at. Yearned to tear apart, limb by goddamn limb, and then squash the caramel mess of his body into a giant cosmic food processor. The bastard deserved worse. He tied her down. Pretended he did it to "help" her. Who stroked her cheek and called her his "love."

His *love*!

He didn't love her. Not after this. Not after planting his big, controlling hand in the middle of her sternum, glaring at her like a wild animal to be tamed, and ordering, "Goddamnit, Tracy! Stay!" Especially not after lifting the dual torches of his eyes, locking that glower into Max, and yelling, "Get them the fuck out of here. *Now.*"

"No." Her shriek unclamped her throat. "No, damn it.

Luke. *Luke!*"

He grabbed both her shoulders. Shook her until she looked directly at him again. "He'll be safe. I swear it, *ku`uipo*. I *swear* it." He breathed hard, pumping fresh blood to the gash down one of his cheeks. She seized a schism of comfort. Knowing she'd inflicted that damage. "Max is taking you someplace safe. They won't look for you there. I'll bring Luke to you at the same spot. You have to go!"

He didn't wait for her reply.

As usual, the dragon's orders were law.

And as Max stomped on the gas, peeling the Jag out of the garage and into the streets of midnight-drenched Seattle, Tracy forced her soul to sit down with her heart's warring factions over that damn edict.

She really, really hated him.

She totally, completely trusted him.

What the hell was she going to do without him?

★ ★ ★ ★ ★

The thought had definitely *not* been her plea for a trial run on that answer.

Life, in its disgustingly evil way, had delivered anyway.

Twelve and a half hours ago, she was riding in an elevator with the man, feeling as giddy as a college girl on her first date. Steel and concrete had been her confines; outside there'd been one of the world's largest cities, bustling and vrooming and chaotic in its nightlife rush.

Two hours after that, she'd looked up at the canopy of stars over Mount Rainier, while climbing into yet another sightseeing helicopter. Her mood had been as dark as the thunderheads sneaking over the back of the famous peak, as Sam Mackenna piloted the aircraft south...

Across Oregon...

Far into California...

Until sweeping in over the ocean, sparkling as brilliantly as those Rainier stars, and landing in the huge meadow over which she now peered.

There were two helos parked in the grass now. Their blades drooped, the engines long since silenced. Only thirty minutes had passed between the two landings, officially the longest half hour of her life. But as soon as Ethan Archer touched down the second helo and her very alive, very animated fifteen-year-old had bounded onto the grass, her agony melted into inconsequence. She hadn't even minded about barely understanding the kid, letting Mia and him jabber as if they'd ridden fifteen roller coasters in a row. Apparently, barely escaping from mystery terrorists in a hail of gunfire, followed by a hell-bent-for-leather ride through the streets of Seattle and then a midnight helicopter ride over two state lines and hundreds of miles, was second only to ziplining in the world of teenage cool.

Reeducating the kid—and that *would* happen—could come later. For now, knowing there was nothing or nobody here to harm him, aside from a few curious bunnies and squirrels in the meadow, brought a rush of peace she would *not* complain about. A serenity she didn't even know still existed... at least not for her.

What did that say about the path she'd chosen for her life?

About what she now subjected *Luke's* life to?

The rolling hills, glowing sage and amber in the burgeoning dawn, gave her no answers. They extended for miles, finally blending with the glimmering sea, an equal enigma for enlightenment. At the moment, she was beyond caring. The sun, finally breaking into full light, proved why they called this place the Golden State. The morning wind, whispering across the meadow, lulled her into enjoying a long breath in and then out. Then another.

She closed her eyes for the same peaceful moments. Her nostrils filled with pine and ocean, even a light tinge of coffee being brewed inside the rambling ranch house. The slight chill in the air gave her a tiny shiver, and she welcomed it. For six days, her world had been only twenty-five-hundred square feet of enclosed space, with occasional peeks at a patch of sky. Getting greedy about all this was her due.

And, God willing, her eraser.

Like that was going to happen, now that John sneaked into a corner of her mind. Then commandeered a bigger chunk. Stomped into the one next to that.

Shit.

Shit.

John Keoni Franzen.

He wasn't just the dragon slinking into her space anymore.

He was the knight who'd lowered her drawbridge and ridden right into her keep. Who commanded her desire and then taken her orgasms as his trophies of war.

Then went even farther.

Strutted into her damn throne room and walked up to the seat at the front.

Where he still ruled, whether she liked it or not.

Who the hell was she trying to fool?

She liked it. She liked it too damn much.

"It's pretty out here."

No. She hated it.

His murmur, quiet as the breeze in the oaks and sycamores, roped that truth in with perfect timing. So what if that dark-chocolate voice spread to the farthest reaches of her body, coating her like the most decadent dessert on the planet? So what if his footsteps, slow but steady on the wide stone veranda, reverberated through every nerve ending she possessed? So what if his presence, consuming more of the air as he moved, woke up her sex more sharply than the tang of the ocean on the air?

John moved up next to her. Stretched an arm up, bracing his forearm against one of the natural log support beams. She dared a glance over. While he was still dressed in his date night/Dominant/life-saving warrior clothes, he'd washed the grime off his face and arms and had even cleared the dust out of his dark hair—not helping her libido calm by one damn bit. *Biscuits and effing gravy.* The man's rugged beauty reached whole new heights in natural light. The sun, now reflecting off wispy peach clouds, mellowed his features and brightened the gold in his gaze. The wind, gusting a little stronger, flattened his T-shirt against his T-shaped torso.

Damn it.

She really needed to hate him right now.

She really longed to jump him right now.

More than that. She yearned to drag him off into the bushes and mount him.

There was a creative option for an uncomfortable silence. Definitely hadn't ever been an option she'd gone for on the Hill—though she doubted *any* man in those chambers even remembered the definition of silence.

She liked what Franz did with this one.

God, *God*, she didn't want to—but she did.

He simply let it rest. For a long minute and then two. Just let the morning surround them, as the dawn shifted from pastel to primary hues and the air warmed from chilled to pleasant, before he finally spoke again.

"Whole place belongs to Ethan," he said, actually attempting conversation. She added a craving to hug him, on top of the monkey sex. The man "enjoyed" chit-chat about as much as she once "enjoyed" trips to Cheesy Chuck Pizza Land with Luke. He was trying, though. It was a start. "Far as you can see, nearly to the Morro Bay city line."

"Oh." Before she could retract it, her surprise underlined the reply—though the revelation should've been anything but. The soon-to-be ex Sergeant Archer wasn't at ease discussing himself, but she at least learned he was one of *the* Archers, heir to a sizable fortune already. "Well, that makes sense, I suppose. He's about to become Hollywood royalty. This'll be a nice place to get away from all that stress."

"Stress." He flipped her expectations by echoing it on a chuckle. "It's just...ironic," he addressed to her open gape. "That you use that word."

"Why?"

"Because the guy's end goal isn't addressing *his* stress." He looked out over the horizon. "He wants to turn this all into a working ranch. Seriously. With dudes in Stetsons, horses, cows, chuck wagon barbecues on the weekends..." He pointed toward steeper slopes off in the distance. "He's even thinking of putting in a vineyard, somewhere over there. Grape-growing ju-ju's supposed to be great."

While she was glad for the distraction from gawking-but-not-gawking at him, her brows pushed together in deeper puzzlement. "So what does all of that have to do with the stress-that-isn't-his-own?"

"Because the place is going to welcome others, free-of-charge. It's going to be like a working retreat for former soldiers, and others who qualify, who are fighting PTSD."

"Oh." Her reiteration of the word was doubly stunned—but in all the best ways. "That's..."

"Pretty cool, right?"

"Better than cool." She meant it and hoped he could tell, before she turned and sobered once again. "Hopefully that'll also apply to survivors of the Oval Office." She tried to add a wry laugh, but it never materialized. They were talking, but the elephant on the porch wasn't listening. "If I ever get to the damn place."

Which, she was beginning to think, might not be such a tragedy...

"Okay." He stretched out the word a little, almost tilting it toward a question, before asserting, "That's fair subtext."

"*Subtext?*" Now she did laugh. Bitterly.

He hurled back a huff. Also bitterly. "Tracy—"

"*John.*" She was tempted to just end the bullshit there. A blunt middle-finger salute, a sharp turn right, and she'd be on her way toward the oak grove, ready to enjoy a peaceful morning's walk. When was the last time she'd done something like that? When was the last time she'd been able to enjoy *anything* normal, stable?

The answer actually hit right away. It had been a little over a year ago. After the meeting in which Craig declared his intention about her appointment, she'd taken Luke home for the weekend, to Corpus Christi. Nobody but Norene, Luke, and the appropriate staff members knew, and she had a couple of days before her world blew up. She'd talked to Dad a lot, walking along the bay, skipping stones, and throwing sticks for his two dogs.

After two days, she'd nearly lost her mind.

Even Dad had noticed. He'd chuckled heartily over Sunday morning coffee, muttering words laced with love—but, right now, felt like some bloody cosmic curse.

You're not wired for normal, Trace. Never have been, never will be.

And over the last week, for the first time in a long time, the man in front of her made that okay. Showed her that sometimes, *many* times, alternative wiring could be exactly what the world needed. She believed him too. Trusted him.

Right up to the instant she realized he'd been keeping shit from her.

So no, there wouldn't be a middle finger for him. There'd be this. Her stare, full of her hurt and raging tears. Her words, full of the challenge she stabbed at the high-and-mighty Franzen in his beautiful, brooding throne.

"Look at me," she dictated, moving to lock herself directly in front of him. "*Look at me*, damn it, and tell me why." Her lungs burned, getting in the air to keep speaking, but she imposed mind over matter, forcing them to keep functioning. "*Why* did you know there was a crack in our cover and not *tell me*—"

"Because I *didn't* know." He shoved off the pole so violently, she almost checked for the spear clearly skewering him through the back. "Because I didn't know, Tracy. Not for sure, at least."

She pivoted, narrowing her gaze. "What the hell does that mean?"

"I was only running on a hunch." His hands lifted, dragging in tandem across his skull. "A really crazy one."

"All right," she said slowly. "A hunch you *couldn't* share with me?"

"No."

"Why not?"

His hands lowered. His whole frame became unnaturally still. He was, in really trite terms, like a glorious statue just added to the ambiance of the ranch. "Because if it was right," he finally returned, voice filled with just as much stone, "you would have given it away...when you were talking to Sol."

"Sol?" For a second, it felt as if the wind had stolen the word before it even got to him. That was the moment before she knew her gut had beaten it to the punch.

The really huge punch.

She slumped to the stoop, legs giving out, as the blow fully hit.

"*Sol.*" Vaguely, she felt her head shaking. Her mind fighting. "You—you think *Sol* gave us away?" But that same mind filled with a flashback of Franz seething into that burner phone, back in the garage. Ranting at Sol. Calling him an asshole. John wasn't exactly a Ps and Qs kind of guy, but that was beyond stretching the norms. It had snapped them.

Somewhere in the middle of the mini movie replay, Franz turned back to her. Gazed now, as if reliving that exact scene with her. "It was only an instinct," he muttered. "But the more I turned details over and over, the more shit didn't feel right—a feeling that got worse every time I got on the line with the guy."

Tracy hugged both arms around her middle. She compelled herself to keep listening, no matter how huge the boulders got in her belly. The man had logged eleven years in Special Operations. That was over four thousand days of reading people purely on vocal cues and wonky-strange evidence. His "hunches" were better than most people's hard facts. "Wh-What kind of a feeling?" she finally managed to stammer.

"Plain and simple?" John volleyed. "The feeling we were being played. Started back in Vegas, even before the explosion at the villa. What the hell was with his *huge technical glitch* at the Vegas Convention Center? You want to tell me that army of trained audio technicians hadn't backed up the sound settings for that presentation?"

"That...*is* odd." She said it while a family of rabbits sought the shade beneath one of the helicopters. Had *she* been like one of those clueless creatures? Looking only at the grass, when larger things were happening right over her head?

"Well, that was only the beginning," John persisted in a tight growl. "Didn't come close to the alarms that went off when I talked to him after the blast."

She focused a stare up at him. "I remember. He was baffling the hell out of you. At the time, *I* was still so rattled, I didn't think..."

"And why did you think you had to?" He lowered to the step, sitting next to her. "You've always trusted him."

Tracy said nothing, though that didn't negate a reaction. She kept it to herself, choosing to contemplate how he gritted the word *trust* harder than the rest. *Trust.* To his warrior's spirit, the word meant so much. To his Dominant's soul, it meant everything. No matter what, he'd never taken the word lightly. Deciding to hide all this from her... It had been a shitty burden on him. A lie of omission, in order to honor the trust she'd given him.

"He was adamant that I not tell him where I took you—but as the days went on, I began to wonder if he didn't already know."

She clutched her stomach, now aching to the point of a hard throb, tighter. Dreaded blurting the one word on her lips. "Why?"

John looked out toward the oaks. His jaw hardened and then jutted. "Nothing glaring. Like I said, just enough for a hunch. One night, I called him around eleven. That would have been around two a.m. in Washington, but the guy was wide awake."

She sent a scoffing huff. "Nobody sleeps a lot in DC, John."

"With a local news feed on in the background? Talking about all the cranberry harvest festivals?"

"Oh." The trend was getting ridiculous. But when the syllable fit...

"Later the next day, you were on the line with him, joking about forgetting what the sky looked like. His response surprised even you for a second."

She unfurled her arms. Pushed them to the cool stones as she jolted, recalling the same exchange. "Because he joked back that I could stand in the shower and get the same result." She jerked her stare at John. "I figured he was just referring to the weather in DC."

"Even though it'd been pouring all day in Seattle?"

"Oh my God." She shoved all the way to her feet. Stumbled a couple of steps, hands cupping her face. "Oh my God. He—he *did* know." Stopped, wheeling back to fire the dispute taking over her mind. "But...how?" Freezing panic set in. "Did I say something by accident? Give something away?"

Franz rose too. Swept over, reaching her after one

powerful stride, and hauled her close. "And why would that have been so awful? Your safety has been in the palm of that man's hand. Your *life*. And Luke's. *Fuck*."

The man's wrath, however quietly gritted and tightly coiled, was as welcome as the sun to her psyche. And his body, wrapping around her and against her... *Yes. Oh, yes. This*. He *was* her sun right now. Burning into her. Sustaining her. Huge and brilliant and strong for her as she started shivering from the inescapable truth of this. The truth her own gut confirmed. All the stress *she'd* heard in Sol's voice. All the cryptic subtexts she'd wondered about, only to write them off as ramblings due to helping on a worldwide manhunt.

A search for terrorists *he* already knew about?

Criminals *he* was helping?

"Was that why you laid into him?" she finally whispered. "During that call, in the garage last night, when you went all Hamilton on his Burr?"

"Burr? Sir?"

It was all the permission she needed for two seconds of a necessary laugh. He joined her, indulging an inhalation of the new day's air, holding it for several telling seconds before it came back out with leaden meaning.

"I had to string out the call," he clarified, his voice once more a taut steel cable. "And pounding him was the only realistic choice, given I didn't have him there to actually take down."

She supplied the obvious conclusion to that. "Because Ethan was still upstairs, trying to reverse trace the call."

He slid in a hand, delivering praise in a squeeze to her neck. "My smart, sexy *popoki*."

"Was he successful?"

He pushed another breath out—ten times more brutal than the first. "Sort of. We locked the device down to somewhere in the northwest."

All hail the *Titanic* of her bloodstream. New iceberg of dread, straight ahead. "So he not only knew where we were but led that crew to us."

John gathered her even closer. Muttered with dark resignation, "Yeah. Seems that way, beautiful."

"*Asshole.*"

"Seems that way too."

She no longer wondered how or why he'd brandished the word in the garage. She could've spat it twenty more times and not be done spewing her wrath. Instead she stepped back, kicked violently at the grass, and sputtered, "But—I still don't get it. I mean...how? *How* did he know?"

John grunted. "Better question is, how could he not know? Not with the technological resources at his disposal— the FBI, CIA, NSA, DHS—all firing at full thrusters and all likely crashing into each other because of the global manhunt for these bastards, whoever they are. Nobody would have noticed him performing some extra 'side searches,' even if they weren't approved or validated." His spine stiffened, and he looked ready to jab a new hole of his own into the grass. "And since he'd already checked out my background before I even hit the ground in Vegas, he likely narrowed his searches to all the homes of the guys in the battalion."

The explanation made sense—but no way in hell did it comfort her. The opposite effect began with a grenade to her heart and then shot panicked shrapnel along her extremities. "*Shit.* That means he'll follow us here too."

Franz shook his head. "Archer made the purchase through

a third-party broker, using the name of the nonprofit he already set up. Nothing but a deep paperwork search will trace any of it back to him." His lips twisted in a wry grimace. "And right now, I don't think Sol has time for deeply doing anything. He knows we're onto him. *He's* the one running now."

She let out a whoosh of relief but only halfway. "For now," she uttered, truly wondering if this was all going to end up like bad experimental theater, with no clear ending ever supplied. What happened when one couldn't leave the show and hash out plot opinions over cocktails with their friends? What happened when the plot loop was one's freaking life? "So... what do we do now?" she asked anyway, hoping he had a much better metaphor for an answer.

"We figure out the rest of the story." His obstinate tone, joined by his arrogant soldier stance, already had her ditching the off-Broadway experiment for his in-your-face Lloyd Webber overture. "We dig up not only Sol Wrightman's role in this insanity but what the hell the insanity *is*."

"*Yeah*." She borrowed some of Luke's post-fifteen-roller-coasters energy, mellowing to a sheepish grin when Franz stopped her fist pump with his enveloping grip. "Yeah," she repeated past her growing blush. "Good plan."

She lowered her fist. His hand descended with it.

She unfurled her fingers. John meshed his with them.

Just like that, reconnecting all their circuits. Retying all their knots. Reigniting every flame of their cosmic combustion... the inescapable, indelible force that was uniquely, beautifully *them*...

For one perfect second, she surrendered to it once more. Gave herself to *him* once again. Showed him so by dipping her forehead to the middle of his chest and then leaning closer to him. Leaning *against* him. Letting him accept her whole weight and all the racing emotions of her spirit. Giving him all her confusion and fear, her weariness and apprehension, her trepidation...but her *trust*.

He knew it too. She heard the confirmation in the deep, thundering breaths consuming his lungs.

He accepted it. She felt it in the mighty pull of his arms, wrapping her like giant ti leaves around a tiny flower.

And yes, he treasured it. Just like he always had. Just like her own soul confirmed now, emboldened once more by his strength, humbled once more by his devotion.

And yeah...sizzling once more at just two of his guttural, growly words.

"Thank you," he murmured into her hair. "*Mahalo*, my sweet *popoki*."

She sighed into his chest. He skimmed fingertips up and down her spine.

Just one moment more...

"I'm the one who should be *mahalo*ing." She lifted her head as he bent his, tugging him down closer, breathing all of him in. Holy hell, how could one man turn his own sweat into such an erotic scent? His salty, earthy essence mixed with the morning wind and her own. "John," she whispered. "*Sir*. I jumped to awful conclusions about you. Judged you..."

"And didn't trust me?" He raised one black knife of a brow.

"I *always* trusted you." She let her own brows take on a touch of coy. "I just didn't like you very much as I did."

She expected the jibe to sink in and his soft laughter to roll out, but her tease didn't even get him to a smirk. As she glared, trying to decipher his scowl, he pulled away and marched into the oak grove.

"John?"

"*Sir* is fine for now, madam." His voice had chilled along with the air as she followed him beneath the trees. Though the area was dappled in sun, it would be a long time before the warmth came along with the light.

"Madam?" Tracy kicked up leaves and dirt as she came to a mutinous stop. "So that's the way it's going to be? Because I was honest with you?"

He whipped back around. Ducked in time to keep from clocking himself on a low-lying branch. A shaft of dawn broke through, glinting in the piercing gold flecks of his angry stare. "Your honesty was very much appreciated, ma'am. After all, I'm not here for your adulation, right?"

Like an even sharper slice of sun, understanding stabbed in. Her arms plummeted. Her throat went dry.

He cared.

He cared.

Enough to be this butt-hurt that she'd even made fun of "hating" him. Enough that he tried masking the shit under fury that worked as well as dollar-store sunscreen. Enough that he actually thought she wouldn't see the burn, though he was already toasted on all sides with it.

So damn adorable with it.

So irresistibly sexy.

"John. *Sir.*" Even his visible rise from her slip made her want to do it again, though she didn't want to be his deliberate brat right now. She wanted to be his worshiping kitten. His loyal subject. For just a little while longer, she wanted to be *his*, period. "I *do*...adulate you."

The words spilled without thought—and felt so right, she let the same inspiration guide her actions.

Plummeting her down.

Down.

Down.

Until she gazed up at him from her knees.

Offered everything to him with her eyes.

Finally pressed closer to him, warming the magnificent swell of his crotch with her hot, needy exhalation.

Franzen hissed his own breath in. Released it in shaky spurts. Tunneled a hand into her hair, twisting deeper into the strands, keeping her head locked right where it was, riveting her with the stark need in his own gaze.

"And fuck, kitten, how I adulate you."

She slid her eyes shut for just a moment, letting the perfect rasp of his voice shower over her, through her. The last of its warmth was carried away on a new gust of wind, lifting leaves around them. She reopened her gaze to watch sunlight flowing across his stature, caressing his body in fingers of adoring gold. She was instantly, intensely jealous.

And refused to wait any longer to show him.

With her stare still fixed on his face, she unbuttoned him. Unzipped him.

Flowed her breath—*only* her breath—over him again.

He hissed again. Hard.

She dipped closer. Questioning.

"Let me adulate you like this, Sir. Please?"

CHAPTER TWENTY-TWO

Adulate.

He never really had a lot of use for that damn word.

Always thought it was pretty fucking stupid.

Never again.

Never.

Again.

Words tattooing his spirit as she parted her lips and took him into her warmth. A vow in every cell of his blood as his aching crown fitted in the cradle of her throat. And a promise in the depths of his heart, humbled by this incredible, open expression of hers.

Awareness he could examine and explore later.

Much later.

After she assuaged the violent beast between his legs. After he fed the beast to her, inch by glorious inch, watching it rage at the walls of her mouth. After he nearly retreated only to plunge back in, over and over and over, fucking those elegant lips of hers.

No. Elegant no more. They were his filthy playthings. His to violate and dominate, to ruthlessly rule...

Until he couldn't.

Until suddenly, the control was no longer his. His cock was at her mercy, like a candy stick she couldn't get enough of, feeding her voraciousness. She slammed her mouth up and down, harder and harder, greedier and greedier, until he had to release her and grab an overhead tree branch just to keep his feet under him. His knees were water. His thighs were fire. And dear fuck, the magic she worked over his sex, even working a hand over his balls and squeezing with purpose.

"Christ!" he rasped. "*Christ*, my sweet kitten..." His pants dropped to his ankles, baring his ass for the kiss of the cool breeze. The sensation contrasted with the searing brand of her tongue, lavishing her candy with starving moans. Driving him half-mad with lust...

Half?

Maybe a little more than half.

Maybe a lot more.

He was aware of everything and nothing at once. The earthy scent of the trees. The tangy hint of her arousal. The golden drops of the sun. The burnished brilliance of her hair. More sighs of the wind, blending with the soft moans from her throat.

Her throat.

Jesus *fuck*, her throat.

Taking him so far down...even clamping in with every new lunge he took, making his tip weep and his body quake. By the gods, she was good at this. Really, *really* good at this. His vision swam. His dick ached. His balls screamed, already sizzling with the fire, so inevitable and brilliant, he longed to enflame her with...to flood her with...

No. *No*. He had hold back. Had to lay her flat in this bed of leaves and take her hard. Rut on her in the dirt, like the mindless animal taking over his senses, his body...

But the fantasy made his cock swell more. Made his slit start to pulse, swimming in the wet, tight cavern of her sweet, hot hole.

No. *No.*

"I can't—" He clenched his ass, trying to pull back. Tracy gripped his thigh, clawing him hard, commanding him to keep taking her wanton torment. "*Popoki.* I won't be able to—*shit!*"

He froze, watching her cheeks hollow, adding even more excruciating, amazing pressure.

She groaned harder.

Swept her thick lashes up, exposing his gawk to the knowing sensuality of her stare...

And the sight of her free hand, rubbing feverishly between her legs.

And he was done.

Done, in a deluge of heat and release, spilling from him in white-hot, silken-wet ropes.

Done, in replacing her very breath with his essential life, branding her with his cream, filling her with his fire.

Done, in feeling her own climax hit, turning her mouth into a tunnel all but glowing around him, ordering his balls to give up yet another explosion, falling out of him on a rambling, breathless groan. "Yes. Oh yes, beauty. *Ale ko'u kai.* All of it. Take all of it from me. Swallow my life...swallow my flames..."

Many long minutes later, he let go of the branch—and plummeted to his knees beside her. The movement unseated him from her mouth, now getting bracketed by both his hands, for the longest, most adoring kiss he could summon from his tapped-out, sucked-out body.

As soon as he tasted her, he wanted more.

By every god he found holy...

She was an ambrosia. Redolent. Decadent. Naughty. Nasty.

His.

Fuck the sweet breeze, the chirpy birds, and the dreamy sunbeams. He embraced the clanging, five-alarm certainty of that single, perfect word...and its violent, virulent call to every eager servant of his spirit and soul.

His.

He kissed her again, needing her to know it too. Needing her to *feel* it—as well as his commitment to it.

No.

Needing her to hear it too.

"Tracy." With hands still framing her face, he lowered his forehead against hers. "*Tracy.*" His sweet, smart, passionate, headstrong warrioress of a woman...

He was hers too.

I'm yours...

"John?" Her gaze thickened to mist as concern laced her voice, only to soften as his fingers gripped into her hair and his lips sought hers yet again. The kiss was different this time. A brush. A seal. A promise. "Oh, *John*," she whispered.

"For as long as you'll have me." He uttered it knowing the rest wasn't necessary. Absolute in the truth her soul already heard, her heart already knew. "For as long as you need me."

She swallowed. Pulled away just enough so he was pierced by her beautiful gaze again, consuming his focus as she dipped a silent nod. "Okay," she finally rasped, lifting a hand to trace the edge of his own face. "Okay."

They let out long breaths together.

Pulled them back in as the wind blew, loosening leaves from the oak boughs around them. Such an irony, Franz thought. As symbols of expired growth fluttered the air around him, seedlings of new feeling began sprouting in his spirit.

But that was just the start of his curiosity in this moment.

Another inquisition knocked at his brain like a cosmic bill collector. He wasn't letting her get away without helping him pay the debt, either.

"*Ku'uipo?*"

Her lips lifted into a tiny smile. "Yes, Sir?"

"Before we hit the road on figuring out all this bullshit with Sol, I need to know something."

"Hmm?"

His mouth opened, but nothing came out. Well, shit. How did he pay the collector without making her gasp at the invoice?

"YouTube."

Though apparently, she'd already glanced at the bill. Or just read his damn mind again. Or, door number three, misunderstood his silent stammer and lame blush and thought he was going somewhere completely different with this.

"You were wondering how a thirty-five-year-old widow, who's had more sex in the last week than the last four years of her life combined, knew how to give you a BJ that had you cracking tree branches."

He didn't know whether to laugh or snarl. "I—wasn't—"

"Branches cracked, Sir." She smirked. "You're welcome."

He huffed. Again. Maybe flipping the tables was in order. "YouTube?"

"A girl has to learn new things." She shrugged. "I got curious one night." Then flushed—to the roots of her hair. "Okay, maybe more than one."

He decided the laugh was a better idea. Indulged it with chest-deep fullness before dipping in again to taste her with long sweeps of his tongue and ardent nips of his teeth. He switched and went for the snarl as soon as she opened fully, accepting his passion with beautiful little mewls.

"My curious little kitten," he murmured once they were done, between his labored breaths—though at last he cleared his throat, re-tucked his cock, and forced his legs to work again, stating, "Who's going to become a screaming little pussy if we don't stop right now."

"Oh, dear." Tracy's tone was a purring mock as she accepted his outstretched hand. "We can't have *that*, can we?" Once she gained her feet, she tilted a newly curious stare. "Especially because we're...how did you say it...*hitting the road on figuring out this bullshit?*"

He scooped her hand beneath his bent elbow as they began walking out of the grove. "Affirmative."

"Okay." She lingered her pace and then finally stopped altogether. Signs of conscious life had started to rustle inside the ranch house, now only ten feet away. The smells of coffee and bacon cozied the air. "So...hitting the road where?"

He stopped along with her. Faced her directly. He owed her that, even before what she'd just done for him. These plans weren't just some mission she was weighing in on as VP. This was his next step in ensuring she stayed alive. So yeah, direct was best.

"You won't like the first part."

Her face quirked. "Does it involve fast-roping or skydiving? Though if push came to shove, I *might* be talked into the fast-roping..."

"It involves leaving Luke."

Her mirth melted away. Slowly, she responded, "Leaving him...where?"

"Here," he clarified. "With Ethan, Ava, and their staff." He wrapped both his hands around hers. "Mia would stay too. I think the kid already likes it here."

He watched as she took a breath, though he couldn't determine if she still considered his suggestion or had moved on to debating white verses whole wheat bread for the kid's morning toast. The woman was involved in nearly every aspect of her kid's life, so it would come as no surprise to learn she'd YouTubed breakfast breads too.

"I see the wisdom of the thinking," she finally said, so adorably Disney Channel mom about it. The impression, joined with a memory flash of her kneeling before him in the grove, nearly had him dropping his grip to hide a fresh erection. Thank fuck she kept shit on target, querying, "I think it depends on where you plan on *us* going."

"I see the wisdom of the thinking." He gave her a few more props with a fast wink. "And the answer to that entails two steps."

"First step being..." she prompted.

"Twenty minutes east," he supplied. "Which will get us to the tarmac at San Luis Obispo Airport."

Her head rocked back. Her gaze narrowed. "Because...?"

"That's where Ethan has his private jet being fueled for us."

"To take us...?"

"The one place I can get access to the same technology and man power Sol is using to track you." Because he could, he added a swift wink. "It's time to bounce that Judas shit right back on that bastard's ass."

As he hit the word "bounce," Tracy's energy began to do the same. Like a kitten taunted with a feather, her whole body hummed with energy and her gaze flitted with undisguised pleasure. "Okay, I'm going to bite."

He waggled his eyebrows. "Really?"

She smacked his chest. "By asking you where this epic Judas-chasing location actually *is*."

He prefaced his response by letting a full grin flash through. "Home turf, kitten." Then quickly but soundly kissing her. "Hommmme tuuuurf."

★ ★ ★ ★ ★

"Captain Franzen?"

He smiled before even answering. To be honest, he hadn't stopped smiling since they left the California coastline behind, but this moment was worthy of an even bigger smirk.

The awe in Tracy's voice, as she gazed at the gentle waves, azure sky, and tawny shore of Barking Sands Beach, was already the perfect start for a Kaua'i-style twilight. She looked more incredible than he'd anticipated in one of the light cotton dresses he'd asked Lino to pick up on the way to the base, with a few adorable freckles already appearing across her nose.

By the gods, she belonged here.

All right, maybe not *right* here. Though the base was, as bases went, pretty damn cool with its oceanfront cottages, it was still a military facility, offering the navy's barest fundamentals for operating the globe's largest missile training and testing range. And there *was* the whole thing with being around so many squids, but he had to overlook that sand in his oyster at this point as well.

Right now, only two priorities mattered.

Keeping Tracy alive. And learning why Sol Wrightman had been in on the plans to achieve the opposite.

A protective growl climbed his throat as he responded,

"Yes, Madam President?"

Her lips pursed, but her eyes smiled. In the setting sun, their gray irises were as bright as the silver foam atop the waves. "I'm enjoying your home turf advantage so much, I'm not even going to glare you down about that."

He let the growl become a low laugh, hooking an arm over her shoulder before smashing a kiss to her temple. "And the nap you got in on Ethan's private plane has nothing to do with it?"

"The nap *you* interrupted?"

"By repaying your 'adulation' from the oak grove?" He tossed down a skeptical side-eye. "Didn't hear a lot of complaining, kitten—unless that shit suddenly sounds a lot like 'Oh yes, Sir. *Yes*, Sir. Fuck me harder with your tongue! *Harder.*'"

She giggled to the point of snorting, retaliating with a fierce scratch across his back. "Hey. While the kid is away, Mom needs to play."

"Outstanding motto." It finished on a lusty snarl as the wind tossed a bunch of her auburn waves into his face. They smelled like the vanilla shampoo she'd used during her shower at the ranch, bringing back every moment of what she'd done to him in the oak grove right before it—as if he needed a reminder, after recalling what *he'd* done for "repayment." Good times. *Fucking* good times. *Amazing* times. He missed them as if eight months had passed instead of eight hours. Craved them. Craved *her.* Hungered for her screams in his ears, her taste on his lips, her heat in his soul...

His body readily agreed. His senses were alive with her. His heartbeat practically matched their steps. His dick throbbed, more than ready to support a tromp to one of the palm trees on the berm, where he could hike her dress around her waist, her legs around *his* waist, and get inside her until the moon was high and the stars caught fire from their passion...

"Glad you approve, *ku'uipo*." They strolled a few more steps, their feet mushing into the sand as the rising tide rushed the shore. "So...not missing Luke as much?"

"Of course I miss him." She tempered it with a tiny laugh. "Half my soul is gone." Then sobered it with a sigh. "But he's safe and happy at the ranch with Ethan and Ava—and Sam is personally flying in Mia's parents to reunite with her too. It's a win-win for all."

"Except momma bear," he pointed out.

"Yeah." She sniffed, clearly fighting back tears. "But momma bears learn to deal with this kind of shit."

He tugged her a little closer, as much for his own comfort as hers. Watching how this separation—if only for a few days from a son who was happy and alive—affected Tracy gouged him with remorse for what his beautiful *makuahine* must be enduring. To this very minute, the woman who'd given him life, in more senses of the word than one, still thought she'd memorialized her eldest son three days ago. She wasn't dealing with it well, either. Lino's minimal words on the subject, when he'd finally gotten around to saying anything at all, were blatant as blood on rice paper about it.

He steeled his jaw.

He couldn't mourn the unchangeable circumstances right now.

Forward.

Move forward. Focus on what you can *change.*

That meant no more playing *South Pacific* with his adorable *wahine*. Time to get his ass back up to the cottage, where Lino was working to transform the living room into a miniature command center capable of helping him comb out every speck of cyberspace lice there was about Sol Wrightman.

Wasn't going to be just a two-man job, thanks to Tait Bommer and Kellan Rush. The attached-at-the-hip comrades, once his ace sniper team for missions, had expanded their skill set considerably since joining SHRC, an ultra-elite team of covert operatives made up of the most tenacious bastards from all the branches of Special Forces. Franz had hated signing the pair's transfer requests to the Sharks but was still happy as hell for them, since the opportunity allowed them to stay in Hawaii, where they both found personal fulfillment. The fact that they found it with the same woman, who had been like a third little sister since he and she were kids, had definitely been the harder "paperwork" to "approve"—but when Lani Kail arrived with the guys a few hours ago, Franz admitted he'd never seen her look happier. She'd found her unique version of true happiness—and who was he to call bullshit if that involved two lovers instead of one? Hadn't he been closer to heaven than ever just a day ago, getting to fill up his subbie as an audience of dozens approved?

A person didn't get to pick how they were hard-wired. Hell, the wires were usually the easiest part.

The hard part?

Finding the one with the circuit board that didn't short yours out.

Circuit boards feeling as right as the woman under his arm.

Wires as awesome as her hand roaming under his tank and then skating fingernails up and down his back. Connections inspiring his contented sigh as he rubbed his cheek against the top of her head. "At least you'll have some good girl time tonight. Gem and Ronnie already seem to like Lani."

"What's there *not* to like?" She swirled fingers across his lower back, teasing at the top of his board shorts. "Besides, I'm looking forward to plying the woman with wine and hearing a few stories from the childhood annals of the Franzen family."

He groaned. Halted. Circled her around into a deep, wet, tangle of a kiss. Her answering moan came with her bolder touch, slipping beneath the shorts to cup his ass. He groaned in return. *Fuck*, this work attire was way better than BDUs, body plates, and eighty pounds of weapons and survival equipment. Thank the gods for brothers like Tait, who brought spare clothes along with a six-pack for the evening's fun.

Borrowed clothes. Borrowed jets. Borrowed condos. Borrowed time. The wild boys of his battalion, as well as the amazing females they'd chosen for their lives, were literally giving everything they could to help him figure out this insanity, all while pretending his ass was still a cremated pile of ash at the Bellagio villas. They astounded him. Humbled him. Came through like true brothers, without any questions. Without any doubts. With complete trust.

The same trust resonating through his woman's deep sigh now...

Just before she moved back from him by a small step.

Just before she tried mitigating that meaning with a soft smile.

A smile never making it to her eyes.

An anomaly she obviously hoped he'd catch.

A smile kicked up his lips too. She was so easy to understand. Even easier to adore. But best of all, to really help, beyond being her bodyguard or hired gun. This was the job description he liked best of all. Being her *heart's* hero too.

"*Popoki.*" He gave her hips a pair of gentle tugs, itching for her hands to find their way to his ass again. No dice, but that was okay too. As her palms flattened to his chest, more new details betrayed her changing mood. The hesitant twitches at the corners of her mouth. The drop of her gaze to the tips of her fingers, jabbing a little against his heartbeat. "Hey. What is it?"

She sneaked her tongue across her lips. "John."

"Tracy?"

"I've been thinking."

"Gods help me."

She didn't take his humorous bait. Shit. Maybe the gods really did need to get their asses down here.

"When this is all over...I'm going to be out a Director of Security."

His pulse revved but then skidded to a stop. That was usually what pulses did when the gigantic writing on the wall was revealed, right?

"Yes," he murmured with deliberation. "I imagine you will be."

Her kitten tongue jutted again. Enticing him, even now. Captivating him, as she visibly fidgeted for what to say next. "I was hoping—well, after everything that's happened and how perfectly suited you are for the position—"

He cut her short with his sizable grunt. She was really going to make him read the wall out loud, wasn't she? "You want me to consider the job."

Her head jerked back up. No more lip wetting. She was too busy blinking, an open broadcast of bafflement. "Don't be overly thrilled on *my* account."

"No worries there." His snark was drier than hers, but it worked for the point. The forest she was still missing through a *lot* of damn trees—none of which got in her way as she flattened her hands and pushed off, stumbling back by two big steps.

"What the hell? I thought you'd jump at this."

"Jump? Like a shiny new pony?" Again, more wry control—instantly earning a new chunk of self-hate. Yeah, hating himself. Fucking *flogging* himself for defaulting to this sarcasm instead of summoning the balls to order all the bullshit out of his soul's cellar—out to where she'd see it. Know it. Understand it.

"Okay, murder the bee in that bonnet." She tossed her head impatiently, as the wind whipped a glistening brown chunk into her face. Throughout it all, her gaze never lost its incensed fire. "Is that what you really think? That I'm offering this to you as my token stud pony? *Payment for services rendered?*"

He dipped his own head. Unbelievably, he didn't have a comeback. For the first time since their hands had first clasped, this wasn't a reaction he'd expected from her.

For this first time since they'd met...he had no damn idea what she was thinking.

"Turn the camera around," he finally leveled, folding his arms. "If *you* were looking through the lens, what would *you* see? How would you feel?"

Her hands braced to her hips. "Grateful," she spat. "I'd feel completely, overwhelmingly *thankful*, damn it." The tops of her shoulders trembled with ire—a move that, in any other time or place, would've had him dying to soothe that tension with the flat of his tongue. Right now, his whole mouth was school paste as she kept going. "I'd feel like a well-qualified, highly skilled soldier, newly shafted by the brass who were always supposed to have his back, now offered a chance to serve at the pleasure of the president of the United States."

"Ahhh, yes. Serving at your pleasure." He added a laugh to the drawl, unable to help himself—probably having to do with the inescapable bitterness behind the sound. Shittiest thing? Most of it was self-directed. She was right. He should be grateful. He had exactly what he'd been asking the universe for. A direction. A purpose. But all he could fixate on was the metaphorical bridle around his head, along with the saddle on his back. "Gotten the pony to the water, haven't you?" Annnd why not go totally for the asshole factor, as long as he was at it? "But will he drink?"

Yep. Asshole. Her face crumpled in, confirming it in spades, before she wrestled her composure back into place with a tigress mode glower. "I'm not swimming in your metaphorical mess this time. John." Her eyes flared, battling tears, to no avail. "Because I'm already drowning here, okay? I'm—" Her hands dropped to her sides. Fisted to the point of tremoring. "I'm trying to figure out something here. Something...*anything* to..."

The tiny chokes between her words were massive stabs to his soul—and his control. He surged to her, fiercely sweeping her close once more. To his joy *and* sorrow, she melted into him. Wrapped her arms around him, twisting both hands into the back of his shirt. "I'm...sorry," he grated into her hair. "I'm so fucking sorry. It's not my intention to...drown you. *Ever.*"

She sniffed against his chest. "So what's the issue, you big *kanapapiki?*"

He groaned and then laughed—though this eruption contained true amusement. "Just a few hours after meeting

Lani, and she already knows the dirty stuff."

She returned a light giggle. "Damn right, *okole puka*."

"All right, all right," he groused. "So I deserve that."

"And you'll accept the job?"

He hated—*hated*—deflating her shining joy with his somber, steady gaze. Didn't matter. *Couldn't* matter. He had to say this. He had to make her see all the moss on the stones she walked—before either of them slipped and fell on the treacherous shit.

"My beautiful *ku'uipo*. I *am* grateful for your offer. But we need to stop and think. If we really started singing this song, what would it sound like? Are the notes going to make people rise up and cheer—or cover their ears and flee the show?"

She huffed. "The *show*? Who the hell says it's—"

"It's a show, Tracy." He stamped a growl beneath it. "We both know it. Hiding in the dressing room isn't going to stop this curtain from rising. That means we have to think about what the scene looks like, even from the nosebleed balcony seats. Translated into street side terms, that means the whole fucking world will be watching."

Her chin jutted and her eyes flashed. "I'm well aware of what that means."

"Good. So you know you no longer get to be Tracy, and I no longer get to be John. You become the president, and I get to be the guy with the dark glasses and don't-fuck-with-her scowl. I'll be invisible—which means I have to *stay* invisible."

Her face jerked up even higher. Her gaze anxiously crisscrossed his face. "Which means...what?"

He pulled down a measured swallow. "That if you let me accept this job, you'll no longer get me in your bed."

Her breath audibly hitched. She blinked, dazed as if he'd

belted her with a two-by-four. "That's ridiculous."

He cupped her shoulders. "No. That's necessary."

She squirmed against him. Stopped when she realized he wasn't about to release her. Not by a goddamn long shot.

"*John.*"

"Tracy?"

He jumped a brow. She thrusted a pout. "We—we'll be discreet."

"*Fuck* discreet."

Her scowl intensified. The two-by-four changed from splinter board to ironwood, and he was glad of it. No. He was elated. Maybe this time, she got it. *Really* got it.

Shit.

Damn.

No.

It was time for *him* to get it. Like a shiv of lightning through his heart. Like a blast of thunder inside his soul.

"Fuck. Discreet." He forced it out through tight teeth, if only to test if it'd bring on the storm again. Christ. *Christ.* It was a fucking Cat Five disaster. An intergalactic cataclysm. The Death Star, Krypton, Alderaan, and the Borg cube detonating inside him at once. Every pore in his body started sweating. Every molecule of air left his lungs. His heart, heaving hard, kept him going.

His heart.

His heart.

Pushing him closer to her. Tightening his arms around her. Pushing him...pushing him...

Until he was taking her mouth under his. Parting her lips with his. Sweeping his tongue inside, attempting to consume her just like she'd taken over him. Over *all* of him. His body.

His spirit. His soul.

His heart.

When he finally thought he could attempt it, he dragged away. Even then, with just an inch of space between his face and hers, it felt like miles. How did guys do this when they had to actually leave for months at a time on missions? How the hell was *he* going to do this, just to get his ass back into the cottage to join Lino, Tait, and Kell?

But first things first.

And the answer he had to give her—*had* to give her—sure as fuck came first.

"I'm done hiding, Tracy." One of his hands splayed across her back. He lifted the other to her face, pressing his fingers to her gorgeous skin, telling himself to memorize the shape and feel and warmth of her, only to realize he already had. Days ago. Days that now all seemed but minutes. Minutes he'd sacrifice his goddamn soul to get back. Why had he taken them all for granted? Why hadn't he *known*?

Known exactly what his lips now confessed.

"I'm in love with you, Tracy Livia Rhodes." His voice was a rusty sawblade of stark emotion, and he didn't care. He cared about nothing but the woman in his arms. The miracle the goddamn universe had finally given to him. And yeah, he cared about telling her exactly that, in his clunky way. "I'm in love with you, and I don't want to be *discreet* about it. *Ssshhh.*" He emphasized the dictate by shoving his fingertips into her hair and yanking hard. "I know this is a shitty thing to lay on you right now. I know the timing couldn't be worse and that neither of us can do a goddamned thing about it. I know you can't offer me anything more than what we've had this last week...which has been more than what I ever dreamed of."

He only took a pause because he had to. Because getting the words out meant letting the feelings spill too. *All* the feelings. So many. Too many. They rushed him like an army of cosmic insurgents, hell-bent on killing him with bullets bearing her name. Exploding with her magic, her life, her light, her passion...

And now, her tears. Streaming down her upturned face, each of them searing a hot, wet trail through his soul before hovering on her parted, quavering lips. "John...oh *God*...I don't know..."

"But I do." He stroked down her jaw and took her lips again, simply brushing them this time. "I *do* know, kitten." With a thumb, he swiped the salty wetness off her upper lip. "And because I do...I'm turning your offer down. But I'll still be watching, okay? Whatever bastard *does* get lucky enough to preserve your safety, he'd better be ready to answer to me for every fucking move he makes—keeping you safe, for me."

A halting breath entered her. Exited her on a wet, sparse sob. "Wh-What...d-do you..."

"I'll be waiting, Tracy." He lifted his other hand, treasuring her face like a diamond in the setting of his palms. "You tell me you want me there, and I'll be waiting the second you leave the White House. I'll be waiting, ready to love you just as deeply and completely as I do right now."

Her mouth fell open again. Not a single sound spilled out, which was probably a damn good thing. Right now, as he dropped his hands and turned away, only the endless crashes of the waves and the empty whisper of the wind felt like fitting music for the resigned decision of his soul—and the fucking eternity of torture he'd just agreed to put it through.

CHAPTER TWENTY-THREE

"Margarita for your thoughts?"

The question, coming at her in alpha male stereo, startled Tracy enough to lurch up from the sand. Not that she missed the spot. She'd shed so many tears, the ground was becoming mud beneath her. As she shook more sand out of her dress, she nervously eyed the pair who'd come bearing a tumbler full of liquid gold comfort.

Tait Bommer and Kellan Rush were both nearly as tall as Franz, with muscles on top of their muscles—okay, there was a trend here, and she should've been used to it—but unlike the other guys she'd met from the battalion, this pair was different. They were like Kaua'i itself. Edging on untamed. Breathtakingly beautiful. Unapologetically sensual. No wonder Lani Kail decided she'd take them both instead of choosing.

Lani wasn't here now, having to leave the base to pick up her little brother from wrestling practice, but her timing two hours earlier had been tragically perfect. As John had returned to the cottage, she'd been stepping out—just in time to watch Tracy lose it for the first time. As the shock wore into confusion and the amazement became anguish, Lani's shoulder became the safe haven for all her unhindered tears— and unending remorse.

Why the hell had she let him walk away?

Why the hell hadn't she confessed her truth too?

Told him how completely she'd fallen in love with him in return?

Fresh tears welled along with the glaring answer to that.

She was going to be taking over the Oval Office soon.

As a single female.

After coming back from the dead.

After tossing the head of her Secret Service detail into prison.

No way would the American public, let alone the supporters she was going to need on the Hill and in the stock markets, be able to deal with a surprise fiancé on top of all that. And no way in hell could he stand by her side as anything *but* a fiancé.

No. That wasn't it.

She *wanted* him as her fiancé. Oh God, she did. With every desire in her heart and thread of her soul. How she craved his smile every morning and his kisses every night. How she yearned for his wisdom about leading men and his insight about taming her. How she longed for his strength on the air she breathed and his passion in the breaths he stole...

She was so screwed.

So yeah, she'd take the damn margarita.

Two seconds after accepting the tumbler, she chugged the drink like it was lemonade in July.

Whoa. Not lemonade.

After her vision cleared and her throat wasn't on fire anymore, she narrowed a watery glare at the boys. "Damn. You might as well have brought the salt and lime to finish that one off."

"He mixed it." They quipped it in unison, each pointing a finger at the other.

Tracy smiled. A little. Gingerly took another sip. "Well, I'll give you both the credit. And, in gratitude for the beginning of this buzz, a free tour of the White House."

"*Score.*" Kellan fist-bumped the air.

Tait rocked back on his heels, sending her a sideways smirk. "Well, ma'am, you're all right."

She eyed him over the rim of her glass. "You're all right too. But call me *ma'am* again, and I'll take up the issue with body parts you don't want me messing with."

Kellan lurched forward, almost spewing a mouthful of the water he'd just chugged. "*Bam.* And T-Bomb's owned by the tigress."

Tait glowered. "Douche nozzle."

Kellan returned the jibe with a smirk and a middle finger though hunched his shoulders with bashful guilt when realizing Tracy had caught every second of it. If her heart was more capable, she would've laughed again. Boys would be boys in so many ways. Some things never changed.

And some things—so many things—changed too damn fast.

She ran from that thought by taking another huge chug of her "margarita." Grimaced from the alcohol burn, despite expecting it this time. The men traded discomfited glances. Looked like she wasn't the only perceptive one around here. She just prayed their protective dragon modes didn't run as deep as Franz's and they'd really just let the cocktail be their offering to the TLC gods for now.

"So." Kellan broadened his stance, burrowing both feet into the sand for extra support. "Speaking of douche nozzles..."

Tait really spat water now. "Really, man? *That's* your lead?"

Kellan glowered. "What? When the boot fits, it fits."

"And there are times when boots aren't necessary at all."

"So I'm supposed to pretend Franz wears glass slippers?"

As Kellan punctuated it with a *pssshh* and a grunt, Tracy gave in to flinging a tighter glare at them both. "What the living *hell* are you two talking about?" Or was she that bad at handling her tequila now?

Both soldiers froze. Blinked long and hard at her.

"You mean *who* we're talking about," Tait stated.

"Not that we're talking *about* him, about him—like behind his back or shit," Kellan added.

"Aw, hell no." Tait snorted. "I'd say all this right to the big jerk's face, only he's a little busy right now."

Tracy took a turn at the puzzled blinks. "Huh?"

"Damn." Kellan's shoulders sagged. He pinched his nose. "We're making scrambled eggs out of this, dude."

"And burning them," Tait muttered.

"Well, I can't even taste them yet," Tracy intervened. "What...are you two..."

Before she could finish, Kellan heaved a huge sigh. Pushed his feet back together, raising his height by a couple of considerable inches again. "Look. We may not be the most eloquent ambassadors on the planet...but the upshot here is..." He stopped, chomping on his lower lip. "Hell. What's the upshot, T?"

Tait rubbed both hands on his to-the-knee board shorts. "Fine. I'll just say it. So, Franzen—"

Tracy started. "What about him?"

Tait whooshed out a long breath. "Well, the deal is..."

"Oh, fuck it all," Kellan muttered. "He can be a pain in the ass sometimes, okay?"

Tait helped him finish it off with a definitive nod—but after that, they both looked supremely relieved to let no sound pass except a new night breeze.

Only after the better part of a minute did Tracy sense they waited for *her* to say something. *Shit, shit, shit.*

"I—" she finally got out. "I don't know what to—Oh, *God.*" The backs of her eyes burned again, feeding on the kindling of her composure, now toasty-dry due to the booze. A headache throbbed, but she still fought them with every force of will she still had. "No," she choked. "You—you don't understand. You... don't..."

The only pain I crave is from him. To take for him. To please him...so that I can know him, and let him know me...

Don't you see? Don't either of you see?

It's not him.

It's not him.

It's not him.

"No." Tait stepped a little closer. Hesitated for one more second before enveloping her in a heartfelt hug. "We *do* understand. We do, okay?"

Kellan shuffled closer, joining the comfort fest with awkward pats on her shoulder. She almost shrieked out loud. They were taking the wrong side! Pushing their big, solacing shoulders at the wrong damn person! But even starting to envision their big dudes' version of "Kleenex and Häagen-Dazs," applied in force to her John sent a high, hysterical giggle up her throat.

"We know it's hard to believe," Tait went on, "but you need to believe us. Under the hard-ass dragon, there really is a great guy with a huge heart and an incredible spirit."

"What he said." Kellan added a few more pats in emphasis.

"Because I sure as hell can't add anything to it."

"We'd have you here all night if we started on the stories." Though Tait's step back was steady, his statement ended on a tremor. His tawny eyes gleamed with a discernible sheen. "I'd be a Skid Row bum with a shriveled liver right now if not for him." He visibly swallowed. "Still mourning a hell of a lot of ghosts. But Franzen—John—he gave me back my life."

"And, because of that, gave *me* back my brother." Kellan moved over, clapping his friend's shoulder.

Tait's nostrils flared. The soldier was so far out of his wise-cracking, surfer god comfort zone, it was almost cute. "So we hope you can understand..." he finally murmured. "We're not here to ram anything down your throat. We just hope to help you understand..."

"He's worth it," Kellan filled in. "Really worth it. Trust us."

Well.

That was that.

The rest of her soul's kindling, fed by a rush of remorse, went up in three seconds.

I dreamed a dream in times gone by...

There was no point in fighting it.

When hope was high and life worth living...

No point in pretending she wouldn't live another day without wanting him. Without remembering him.

He slept a summer by my side...

Without needing him.

He filled my days with endless wonder...

Her shoulders shuddered. Her throat constricted. The agony set in. The sobs spilled out.

But then...

For one perfect, crashing moment...

The impossible.

She wasn't just the vessel for the emotion anymore. She *was* it. Blinded, obliterated, consumed. The fire swelled and pushed and screamed and stretched and *filled*, until even her grief became the exact miracle she was seeking.

She disappeared.

"Shit. Mrs. Rhodes...errr, Madam Vice President...are you—"

"Damn. I knew that margarita was too hefty."

"Maybe you should get Franz."

"*No*." She thrust her brain back into her body. Even made it compel her arm up, a visual executive order. *See, John? I was listening.*

Brand-new heartache found fresh kindling. How it was possible, she had no idea, but she managed to grit back the breakdown long enough to speak again.

"C-Can I just be alone now?"

A long moment went by. She glanced up long enough to watch the guys swap unsure glances. Kellan was the first to capitulate, sending his friend an erudite nod with one arched, knowing brow—

Making the margarita fall from her numb fingers.

Tequila-soaked sand spattered her ankles, but she barely noticed past the fresh shrapnel in her chest. *Damn it.* Kell could've only learned that look from one source. The man belonging to the only face she could still see. The toffee skin and dazzling smile from which her heart screamed for release, as she wheeled and headed across the sand.

Alone.

Feeling, for the first time this week, truly afraid.

But somehow, forcing one foot in front of the other.

Trudging into the darkness toward the vast, black sea beneath the dark amber moon...its liquid magic reminding her so much of his perfect, knowing eyes...

Her soul seeking solace in his beautiful, incredible words...

Instead of wallowing in the fear, you chose to turn and face it.

Scared is a good thing, remember?

I'm scared all the time, woman. We all are. What turns the experience into triumph is what a person does with their fear...

"But I don't know what to do with it now, Sir." She whispered it to the wind and waves and stars, only to listen as if he'd actually use them to respond. "I don't know how to make this a triumph..."

I don't know how to be strong anymore.

Because if strength comes from our vulnerability...and you're *my greatest vulnerability...*

"Tracy?"

The hail was so faint, she first imagined it as a trick of the wind. She slowed, listening, but didn't hear it again. As her feet hit the flatter sand near to the water, she quickened her pace. Maybe just a few seconds of direct contact with the sea would reconnect her to the force she desperately needed. The will to push past the fear again.

"Tracy."

Not imagined. Not this time.

She spun...

And instantly wished this *was* the tequila playing tricks.

Just as immediately, the icy snakes in her bloodstream confirmed otherwise. And the scorpions clamped to every nerve ending. And the cockroaches of dread, taking over her lungs.

Do not panic. Do not panic.

Easier said than done, when the man she'd often called her dervish now paced the ground in front of her. The man who'd been a dervish for *her*. Who she'd trusted with her life...

Who'd conspired to take her life.

Somehow, the true horror of it only fully slammed her now. Maybe her head had comprehended it, but her heart had hesitated. No more wavering now—not with the awful truth gleaming at her from Sol's frantic, furtive stare.

She backed up. Sol matched her, step for step. Would be able to easily overtake her. He was built like a giraffe, all spindly legs.

Shit. Double Shit.

The buzz was completely gone. All her synapses fired at full throttle, ordering her past all the insects of fear. *No wallowing. Turn and face it. What turns the experience into triumph...*

"Sol." She dashed a hand up, as gawky as Luke. "Hey."

"Tracy." For an awful second, he eyed her hand as if to grab it. Instead, his lean features dissolving, he sobbed, "Oh, *Tracy.*"

"It's all right." *Breathe*, she ordered her lungs. *Breathe, damn it.* "It's—going to be all right." *Listen to yourself. That's for you as much as him. Breathe!*

He turned, pushing out a bitter laugh. Meshed both hands across the back of his head—lifting his sweat-soaked golf shirt high enough to expose the handgun in the waistband of his khaki shorts.

Triple shit.

"Wh-What are you—" While he wasn't looking, she scooted back by a shaky step. "I mean, how did you get—"

He laughed harder, spinning back around. "Please, Trace. Give me *some* credit. I figured Franzen would end up somewhere in the neighborhood—though I have to give him credit for finagling something here on the base and not going straight home. It's been kind of amusing, watching his family crying their way through the days and nights. I really thought the mighty John Franzen would cave to that kind of pressure. The man has a will of iron." He paused long enough to drop a heavy-lidded stare down the length of her body. "About *some* things."

Tracy barely disguised her shiver from the new bugs he brought, skittering from her scalp to her toes. It was time for another tactic. *Now.* Gee-buddy-nice-to-see-ya-again clearly wasn't the black and white safety zone it once was between them.

A lot of things weren't the same between them.

Especially that safety zone.

Had it ever really been there at all?

Nothing but a black hole opened in her heart as her answer—the dark space once occupied by her warm affection for this man. This friend who hadn't been one at all. This person she hadn't known at all.

What the hell had she missed? And when? Or had Sol's mask been that good, that polished? And for how long? When had his betrayal begun? And why?

The queries bombarded. Fed the insects. Gave them wings. They ate into her like locusts in a corn field, making her shake again.

In fury.

"I don't think you're in a position to make a quality call about anyone's willpower, Mr. Wrightman." She emphasized the last of it with gritted teeth, letting him know how close she'd been to substitute another name entirely.

At once, his own locked teeth appeared from his sneering lips. "Oh, for fuck's sake, Tracy." The expression exploded into a caustic bark. "Are you *kidding* me? Willpower?" His hands clawed at his head again. "You want to know about willpower? My whole fucking life, for the last fifteen years, has been about nothing *but* willpower."

That thudded the air between them like a four-foot-wide cannonball. Tracy shook her head. "That's really all you're going to give me?" she snapped back. "All you feel you owe me, Sol? I find out you've helped the monsters who murdered nearly every leader in the free world, and this is all—"

"No."

She jogged her chin up. It wasn't hard now. Anger sure felt a hell of a lot better than fear. "No *what*?"

"No." He diminished the space she'd gained with two hard stomps. "It wasn't murder."

She almost laughed. Raw grief, spurred by the memories of Craig and Norene Nichols, turned it into a jagged choke. "Fine. You prefer assassination? Execution? Slaughter? Multiple homicide?"

"Cleansing." He growled the word with such virulence, she again wondered if she'd imagined it—until he jabbed a glare to join it, just inches from her face. She jerked back, breathing hard. Sol yanked her back, shackling her upper arm in his grip. "I *prefer* cleansing, because that was exactly what we did."

No more hard breaths. No more breathing, period. Her heart and lungs collided, racing toward each other in disbelieving horror.

"S-Sol," she stuttered. "You—you aren't—you can't be serious."

He rolled his eyes. The casual move was a bizarre contrast with his vicious snarl. "Fuck. *Why* does everyone *always* say that? You think I'm just kidding about this? That I'd *joke* about something like the future of our world...our entire goddamned planet?"

Deep gulp. Then compelling the breaths in, one by one, until words finally emerged again. "Okay. All right," she murmured. "You're not joking. So—so help me understand, then. Help me see—"

"But you see already." His fingers closed in tighter, pinching until she had to clench against a wince. "You *see*, Tracy, don't you?" His stare intensified, starting to remind her of a religious martyr from some medieval painting. "You see the beauty of it. All of it. The world...*our* world...it has cancer, right? And to cure the cancer, you have to cut out the tumors. Rip them out...at their sources."

"Oh, God." It blurted from her, compelled by nauseated shock, before she could think twice. Who the hell was she kidding? She *wasn't* thinking. She was only reacting. Struggling like hell to wrap her mind around what she was hearing. That Sol, her vibrant and responsible and frenetic and fervent Sol, was actually a lunatic who bought into this insanity... "Rip out...their sources..."

"Exactly!" He lifted his free hand, snapping his fingers hard enough to sound like a whip. Tracy's whole body coiled as if he'd wielded the latter. "And filling all that blackness with new light. New energy..."

"A unified world regime." She could hardly believe she was saying this. That this idea existed outside badly written sci-fi, much less been a fantasy coup in secret development, across multiple countries and continents, for what Sol claimed to be fifteen years.

"A new day." Sol nodded, once more appearing like the crazed martyr—about to have his eyes gouged out. "A new order." His head ticked, clicking his weird focus straight back at her. "You *do* get it, don't you? Oh, *Tracy*." He clutched her by the other shoulder, using the hold to yank her against him. "I knew you did. I knew you *would*."

Quadruple shit.

And was it even working keeping track now? If she even could. Panic, hideous and hot, rushed her veins. It collided with a new freeze of fear, spinning her senses and faltering her balance, as she scrambled for what to do. Sol wasn't spouting the credo of a typical political coup. This was his declaration, proud and bold, of membership in a worldwide cult. A sect of insanity.

"Right?" His eyes, wild and wide, confirmed every drop of her dread. "You see it now. All of it. This is what *we* saw, fifteen years ago. What we all committed ourselves to achieving."

"All of us...who?"

How she got it out evenly, she had no damn idea. Despite that, Sol's head jerked as if she'd slapped him. He stabbed her with an irritated glance before snapping, "All of us, damn it. *All of us.* We—we were in the same battalion. We were together, hating the senseless terror of it all. The same monsters fighting each other—in the name of what? *Of what?* Innocent lives paid for their quests. Cities were burned. Families were torn. Planes came down. Malls were bombed. Destruction. Death. Atrocities even the US ignored..." He flinched again, interrupting the mournful trail-off. "We made the resolve then. Promised each other...that we'd spread across the world, infiltrating from back doors...where nobody would notice. We kept recruiting. Revising. Rededicating. Doing whatever was necessary to make all the pages fall into place. To recalibrate it all, in one perfect swoop of decision. *All* the pages *had* to fall in place." One corner of his mouth jogged up. "They almost didn't, you know."

"Do I?" It was the bare minimum to keep him talking. The time she needed to buy, still scouring her brain for some way to make him let go. But when a man was clinging to a cliff, even one he'd climbed to, prying his hands free was up to the wind and his resolve. And right now, Sol Wrightman's resolve was very fixed on her.

To the point of dragging his heated perusal down to her toes again.

All the way back up to her face, where he lingered over her features for unnerving seconds, before restarting his account with a murmur so arrogant, it belonged more on a Hollywood red carpet than the middle of a Kaua'i shore. "So interesting," he remarked, "that so many were so willing to believe Duane Sanford just keeled over in the middle of the golf course that day. Bet he didn't even think it would happen." He *tsk*ed, setting the stage for the knowing angle of his lips. "And just three days after his cardiologist gave him the all-clear for another year."

Once again, breaths were rusty blades in and out of her chest. "I—I don't want to hear this, Sol. Damn it, why are you telling me this?"

"Because you have to see all the rest, Tracy." He pushed in closer, the whites of his eyes and the grit of his teeth turning his face ghoulish. "You have to *know* the rest. How important it was...that they all were taken and you were spared."

Her throat closed up. Her stomach roiled.

"Sp-Spared?"

He nodded with slow deliberation. "Given back your life, beautiful woman. By me. *Because* of me."

And there it was. The cuckoo in his nest she'd suspected... dreaded. Still, she forced herself to blurt, "Wh-Why?"

He rushed out a breath. "Come on, Tracy. Connect the dots, baby. They eliminated Sanford when he balked at following through with the recalibration. But LeGrange was already on board, and the golden boy for the VP nod—until the president defied everyone in DC by appointing you." He snorted, pushing at once into a quirked smirk. "And just to throw an extra twist into things, you refused to back out of the gig for Dan Colton in Las Vegas—right on the day we were scheduled for global recalibration."

A new need to retch swelled but churned at once into rage. "If you're looking for an apology, you can kiss my ass." *Global recalibration.* He declared it like some tech sector guru unveiling a software trend, not the annihilation of the free world's infrastructure.

Shockingly, that only caused the monster to laugh. "Nah. You just made everything a little more interesting, that was all. We all scrambled a little to pull off the last-minute fireworks show, but as you know, we made it happen."

"You—you mean finding someone to plant that bomb at the Bellagio." As the words tumbled out, her composure finally dissolved. Her head throbbed with horror. Her chest crumpled in like an acid-dipped soda can. "A bomb...intended to kill me. And my friends. *Oh God.*" A sob spilled out. "And my son. Oh God!"

Fool. You have been such a damn fool.

She'd been holding out, even now, to somehow find the scrap of humanity Sol still had left—to discover where the monster could be breeched and then redeemed. And if he could be redeemed, then there was a hope of her escape.

But there'd be no redemption. Insanity had taken over her friend.

Meaning she had to fight now.

With everything she had.

She wrenched. Bucked. Squirmed. Kicked. But Sol, with his wiry stamina and vicious zeal, was stronger. *Damn it*, so much stronger.

"But it *didn't* blow you up, Tracy." His voice was as savage as his hold, sliding down to manacle her wrists. "It didn't, damn it—because I didn't let it." He hauled her in, forcing her tight, until his mouth was at her ear, shoving his hot, greedy breath into her. "Because I love you, Tracy. Fuck, how I love you."

The chaos in her stomach threatened to become the mess all over his shirt. Holy crap, how she wanted to give in to the urge but held back, battling to trade the bile for words. "You— you l-love me?"

He let out a long snarl, squeezing thumbs into the hollows of her wrists. "I haven't told anyone that. You're the first— and the only. They all suspect now, of course—which is why they've sent me now. I'm supposed to prove my loyalty to the movement. Turn you...or kill you."

A new ice storm raged through her senses. Her nerve endings were its brittle icicles, snapping off and shooting away from her consciousness.

Icicles aren't options. Burn them. Turn them into steam. Power them into daggers. Push through the fear, Tracy. Transform it. Use it as new energy. Think. Think. Think!

"Or set me free." She steeled her will, ordering her stare to lift and meet his. Making him see the open plea in her eyes.

"Option number three, Sol. *Prove you love me.* Let me go!"

His features pinched in, aging him ten years in ten seconds. "Not an option, Trace."

"And *that's* not true," she countered. "You can make it an option. You can give Luke back his mother. Return the country's hand of leadership to its rightful owner. Reach inside and find the humanity you thought you sacrificed in those trenches with your battalion—"

He cut her off with a seething snort. "Humanity? *That's* what you think I've lost? I've thought of nothing but humanity for the last fifteen years, Tracy. Humanity has been my goddamned Dominatrix. My unforgiving *bitch* of a mistress."

"Then take back the control! All you have to do is choo—"

A gasp of pain took the place of her conclusion. For a moment, she couldn't figure out why—pieces snapped into place as the sting of Sol's slap echoed in her right ear.

"It's time for you to shut up."

"No, Wrightman. It's time for *you* to give up."

Pain had never become joy with such mach speed. Even the clanging in her ear turned into bells of elation, greeting the booming baritone from across the sand. *That* baritone. The voice that had curled her toes from its first stroke on her blood. The growling dominance in her soul. The dragon's song in her heart.

He materialized like a fantasy, his broad, elegant form backlit by the cottage's porch light—a black handgun braced at the end of his straight, coiled arms. His exotic features were defined by severe, stark lines and utter, violent focus—warrior mode as Tracy had never witnessed in the man before. Even as Sol whipped her around, using her as his shield with his arm clamped against her sternum, she was oddly more afraid for *him.*

"John."

Her voice came as another shock. How did she suddenly sound serene as a swan on a glassy lake instead of a hostage in the hands of a lunatic? She only had to gaze through the night, to the man with the eyes of night, to know that answer. She had her strength again. He was here. *He was here.* As long as her dragon was by her side, she could be as mighty as freaking Xena the Warrior.

"John." She underlined it more firmly. "It's all right."

She heard his harsh breath though his massive form hardly faltered. "With all due respect, ma'am, that's not an assurance I'm banking on right now."

"Ma'am." Sol snorted it into the ear he hadn't knocked a few decibels from. "Who's he trying to rattle here, me or you? Or do you just take it from him because the dick is good?"

Tracy drove a heel back into his shin. Though he only grunted and clamped her tighter, she'd gotten her satisfaction—especially when noticing it bought Franz a few seconds to sprint closer.

A short-lived victory.

Triumph replaced by instant terror.

Such a huge sluice of the stuff, she could only react in one way.

"John!" she screamed. "He has a gun!"

A freakish stillness engulfed the air. Even the wind and waves went eerily silent, stepping back to acknowledge the new shift in power along the shadowed sand.

"Thank you, *ku'uipo*. I'm well aware of that fact."

"Awwww." Sol's derision emerged as a nasal mewl. "Isn't that just the sweetest? A nickname. What does that one mean, island boy? 'Piece of sweet Texas ass'? 'Little bitty fuck toy'?

'Darling Johnnie dick lover'?"

"Keep going, asshole. Just give me one more reason to really do this." The growl in John's comeback gave new meaning to his call-sign. It reverberated through Tracy's blood, and she eagerly soaked up its force—only to have it all drained by a maniacal laugh from the man at her back.

"Ha! You forget, fancy pants, that I've researched you? You're a good shot, Franzen, but not that good." He raised his hand, brutally squeezing Tracy by the chin. "And no way in hell are you going to risk putting a bullet through my little piece of insurance out of here."

John solidified his stance. "There *is* no way out of here, Sol. No final act left for you to play, man."

Sol grunted. "Bullshit. They're going to take care of me. They told me—"

"There *is* no 'they.'"

Sol's entire frame went stiff. "That's bullshit too. You're handing me *bullshit*!"

"And I'd do that...why?" Franz countered. "Because I want to piss you off further, while you've a gun in your hand and the woman I love in your arms? Because this is really the way I want to spend a Saturday night?" His head ticked to the side, a sarcastic move in any other circumstance. "Come on, man. Buy a clue here. This isn't bullshit. My boys finally got a nice, hard cyber-hammer into your club's fun little black 'net site. Those files are making some fun weekend reading for the kids at the FBI and CIA. In short, the curtain's down, dude. Take your bow now, and I can ensure you won't get the death penalty."

A vibration spiraled through Sol. Tracy winced, feeling his violence by osmosis. "Fuck you, Franzen! *Fuck* you."

His fingers twisted harder into her jaw. She fought the pain. Scratched desperately at his forearm. Clawed a hand toward his head. A cacophony filled her ears again and then her senses. More bells, first like alarm clangs but suddenly a beautiful sound, like cathedral gongs—sliced by a scream. *Who was screaming?*

Her.

It was her.

Screaming in pain as Sol yanked her like a rag doll, dragging her into the darkness, toward the water.

Screaming in hope as Franzen's bellow was layered by others. Tait? Kellan? *Who?*

Screaming in shock as orange bursts flared in the night. Then pops from phantom guns—aimed at them.

Returning *pow-pow-pows* from Sol's gun, spraying bullets toward all the soldier silhouettes...

Toward the distinct form with the hulking shoulders, tapered torso, and beautifully carved legs—

"No! Nooooo!"

Then screaming in slow motion, the sound unstopping in her throat, as she stumbled from the man with the suddenly slack grip—and the dead eyes straddling a flawless crimson head shot.

Then pleading, choking, and trying to breathe past her sobs while lurching toward the fallen man in front of her.

Then...

No screaming.

No sobbing.

No breathing.

Her throat incapable. Her senses stopped. Her heart shattering.

As she dropped to her knees beside Franz, fisting his shirt. Ripping it as she desperately shook him. Scoring the beautiful bronze pectorals beneath, longing to tear in deeper and breathe her own air into the eerily still cavity underneath.

"John. *John.* Damn you. *Damn you.*"

Scraping her hands up to his shoulders, over his parted but still lips.

"Wake up. Wake up! John Keoni Franzen, don't you dare—don't you dare—"

Rolling her fingers higher, over the crimson-drenched planes of his beloved face. His strong blade of a nose. His prominent, proud cheeks. His right eye, closed so terrifyingly tight.

And the bleeding gash where his left eye had once been.

CHAPTER TWENTY-FOUR

For two damn weeks, Franzen searched for the gratitude.

Stretched for it so damn hard, his psyche could've touched fucking China.

Force-fed himself every one-liner he'd given so many others, for so many years.

It could have been much worse.

You're lucky to be alive.

Shot could've taken your brain along with your eye.

You'll get used to it. Your mind will compensate. Your body will heal.

Give it time.

Give it time.

Give it time.

Time.

Goddamnit.

All he had was fucking time.

Days of it, seeing half the world he once did. Months of it, adjusting to that new reality. Rediscovering how to function. Relearning how to live.

Then the years of it to come...

Of a life without her in it.

But *with* her in it too.

Fuck.

With nothing *but* her in it.

Taunting him every time he turned on the TV, internet

405

news, or any other outlet providing half a coherent concept of what was going on in the world. There his wildcat would be, at the center of it all, guiding the world back to normalcy, security, happiness. Hell, she'd already started. As soon as the FBI and CIA directors received and read the files he uncovered with Lino, Tait, and Kell's help, "President" Blake LeGrange had been arrested—and Tracy Livia Rhodes, miraculously back from the dead, been named as the next president of the country.

And, because of it, had been ordered back to DC within hours after he'd woken up from surgery. She'd had time to kiss him. To whisper that she loved him too. To tell him she wasn't letting go that easily.

And then she was gone.

A move for the better.

He told himself that as he watched her emergency swearing-in from his hospital bed, his chest swelling from pride and his sinuses burning from fighting back tears.

Told himself again as she proudly marched to the podium to deliver her first speech as the nation's leader, wearing a new one of those suits she liked bitching about—instantly fantasizing about ripping every thread of the fucker off her body.

Forced himself to remember it, over and over and over again, every time another nurse rushed in to tell him President Rhodes was on the phone—before he invented a new excuse for refusing to take it.

It's for the better.

The theme was common rote by now, nearly as comforting as the slosh of the waves through the twilight painting the Kaua'i shore in peach and amber hues. Over the horizon, far beyond where Lino, Maki, and Nani tossed a Frisbee in the shallows, the sky was an explosion of orange and purple ribbons. Nearby, on the lanai, Pops sat with his ukulele, picking out a peaceful rendition of "What a Wonderful World." Mom hummed along in the kitchen, her voice still bright with my-son's-not-really-dead joy, finishing final preparations for dinner. In honor of the guys from the battalion, all of whom had found excuses to "come visit" over the last week, she was prepping a soldier's Sunday dream dinner: slow-roasted pork ribs, honey-fried chicken, beef tri-tip, corn on the cob, homemade bread, and plenty of fresh-picked pineapple from the local groves.

"Yo, Franz."

He barely looked up from where he was parked in the sand, glaring at the world through one eye. "Yo, crap waffles."

While Rebel Stafford chuckled, Rhett Lange glared. The two buddies, who'd been his best recon and intel team, were among the earlier arrivals of the week—obviously eager to make up for lost time since missing all the action in Vegas, Seattle, and Barking Sands. While their lives certainly hadn't been boring since leaving the Big Green machine, the stress of missions replaced by the whirlwind of comanaging their woman's dance career, "the mavericks" had arrived at the house looking like fanboys who'd missed the opening weekend of a *Star Wars* episode. Didn't take them long to stow the self-pity, however. Not with a much more nuanced role to bite right into. *Let's take care of Franzen but pretend we're doing something else.*

Surprise, surprise. It was such a fun part, everyone else wanted a crack at it too. The whole fucking gang of them were here, as well as their women. Joking with him. Drinking with him. For Christ's sake, even rallying for bullshit like poker games and movie nights.

Movie nights.

Who the hell flew all the way to the northernmost end of Hawaii just to watch Indiana Jones for the twentieth time?

Idiots like them.

Friends like them.

He'd been nothing but an ass to them all, for nearly seven days straight, because of the one factor they couldn't change.

The only person who hadn't gone in on the let's-pretend-we're all-just-having-fun act was Tracy Rhodes.

Worst part about it?

All these bastards saw right through it. Especially the two who'd damn near invented this particular part of the game.

And, judging by the whip of a glance they exchanged, held back from the group microbrew stock-up trip into Port Allen for the purpose of calling him on his bullshit.

Fine by him. He was ready for the double whammy of a speech, ropes of tension down his shoulders as proof—but he was also ready as hell with the comeback to silence them.

"Well." Rhett dove in first.

"Deep subject," Franz rejoined.

Neither of them tossed out a groan, let alone fake laughs. "In some cases," Rebel huffed instead.

"Guess it depends on how far you want to bury the body," Rhett added.

Rebel jumped on that one. "You mean like the choad bucket that was supposed to be buried under our asses right now?"

"Thank you very much, Mister Moonstormer." Rhett's return was as artificially sweet as his smile. "That's *exactly* what I meant."

As the guy added a sarcastic finish of rapid-fire flirty blinks, comprehension power-blasted in. "Shit," he growled. "*Kanapapkis.*"

Oh, they laughed at *that.*

He didn't.

They led with *his* lead. Popped the ammunition out of his goddamn gun, slammed it into theirs, and then teamed up as the elite stealth team they were damn near famous for.

"So now that we're all in agreement"—Rhett's drawl was edged with the lazy snark from the Bayou in which he'd been raised—"that playing the better-bitter-than-dead card is off the table now, let's see what you're really ready to ante up, Dragon Man."

Franz didn't say a word. Pretended to swat at a bug. "What the living fuck are you talking about?"

Rhett chuffed. Shoulder-butted Rebel. "Isn't that adorable? He looks just like a constipated gorilla."

"I was thinking more a bad cos play pirate." Rebel's eyes flared. "*Merde*, Franz. You going to ask to switch call-signs now? You'd be a good Moonstormer. The original wore a tricorn, though. You like tricorns?"

Franz shook his head and shot to his feet. "Eat shit."

"Not a problem," Rhett jumped in smoothly. "Just as soon as we hash a few things out."

Damn it. The guy's equally unique accent, a combination of highbrow British and hardcore New Yorker, was smooth as a knowing criminal—because he damn near was. Fucker had known exactly where this conversation would go, didn't he?

Franz grimaced, unsettled. No. Horrified. Since when did his own guys pull a psychological wedgie on *him*? It was *his* job to know *them* better. Always.

Always.

He jammed both hands in his pockets.

And, for the first time in his entire life, began to pace.

Fuck. Fuck. Fuck.

His world was so goddamned off-balance—a chaos having nothing to do with losing his eye. This shit went deeper. So much deeper. Half his breaths weren't worth taking anymore. Half his thoughts weren't worth completing. At the top of every minute, he all but screamed at time to hurry the fuck up and get on with the next—only to realize the exact same experience waited for him in the next sixty seconds.

Every one of those sensations was even worse now—not helped a goddamned bit as he wheeled on the smug sonofabitches, openly gritting his teeth. "Just a few things. huh?" Raging defensiveness cut into the words. He heard it and hated it—and forced himself to just live with it. If this was what Head Shrink Lange wanted, this was what the bastard was going to get. "Out*standing*. Let's go, doc dickwad. What you got for me?"

The guy pushed to his feet too. Almost assumed a full attention stance, which flattened Franz's instinct once more. How the hell was he supposed to stay pissed at the *po'o 'olohaka* when he was playing the half prince of politeness in return?

"This isn't about what *I've* got for *you*, Captain." He lifted his head a little higher, causing the sun to ignite the red tints in his light-brown hair. "And I think you know that, as well."

"Oh, by God's massive cock." Rebel rolled upright, heaving a labored sigh. "And they say we French beat around the bush."

Rhett swung a pissed glower. "Maybe I'm attempting a little bloody respect? We're talking about the president of the country, asshole."

"Who's also a human being," Rebel rebutted. "A *femme magnifique*, I might add—one who is, perhaps, a woman at last worthy of this *homme incroyable*." His stare sharpened as he dipped a nod toward Franzen. "Question is, does this guy still agree?"

His jaw clamped so hard, his teeth hurt. Didn't come close to the agony of the vital organ beating at the inside of Franz's ribs. "What this one agrees or disagrees to isn't part of the equation." When Reb just blinked blankly, he snarled, "Reminder of the day? In your boy toy's own words? *President of the country*, Stafford. Let me translate that one a little clearer. A woman who's now being called on to help redefine a brand-new world. To restore some semblance of security for our whole land. To take on a job that will be, on most if not all days, overwhelming—"

"And you think she doesn't want help with that burden?" Rhett stepped in, firing the charge—making Franz notice, for the first time, that both he and Rebel wore long white cargo pants with their basic white polos, instead of shorts. "That she doesn't long for someone to be there, helping with all those crazy days and decisions?"

"And suddenly *I'm* that guy?" Franz spat. And why the hell were they having it out about this, right now? If Mom was demanding everyone fancy their shit up for Sunday dinner, these two bozos *were* smart enough to realize she'd be livid about the "appetizer course" being a vicious dust-up, yeah? Because this shit was turning into *that* shit pretty fast. "And what happened to you being on my side about this? Understanding exactly who the hell we're talking about here?"

"Which is why I'm still standing over here—" Shrink Lange swept both hands toward his feet—"not lunging over there, trying to strangle some fucking sense into you."

Franzen spread his own arms—wide and violently. "I *can't help her*." The bellow turned his torso into a volcano, his mind into bursting lava, his composure into a black wasteland. "Do you not think I *crave* that, Lange? Do you—*any* of you—not see it's what I spend every other goddamn minute thinking about, grieving about, praying to any power out there about? Do you not really know that I wake up every fucking morning, begging—God, *pleading*—that I'd been smarter out at Barking Sands? That I'd told Kellan to take his shot at Wrightman sooner that night? Hell, that *I'd* taken the damn shot at the fucker myself, back in Vegas?"

His hands had twisted into fists. With vehement resolve, he uncurled one pointer finger out and then slowly raised the quivering spear toward his face. "Does *this* fucked-up shit see better than all of you boxes of rocks put together?"

"Maybe it does." The interjection wasn't Rhett's—or Rebel's. Only one guy belonged to that Dark Knight baritone, with the enormous physique to match. "So enlighten us, fucker," Zeke intoned, striding onto the sand in nearly identical clothes to his battalion mates. Garrett appeared behind him, also adhering to the all-white theme.

"I'm on board with that." Ethan. Scowling. Also all-whiting. "Show us the light, Franz."

He narrowed a glare. *What the hell?* Show them the light? But what if *they'd* already showed *him*? Had Wrightman really taken him all the way out at Barking Sands, and were the last few weeks just a strange Purgatory? Was he actually resting *under* the ground beneath these palms, being visited by weird angel versions of the guys? Or maybe this was just one hell of a crazy-ass dream...

No matter what the explanation, it brought one defining conclusion.

They wanted the truth that bad?

They could sure as hell have it.

"Okay." He folded his arms, running an assessing gaze along the semicircle of their attentive faces. "You want the light on? *Here's* your goddamn light, kids."

So starting was easier than continuing—but he tightened his gut, ordering the words back the right direction. Words that had haunted his psyche for all these agonizing, endless weeks. Had pushed at the confines of his heart like words to a poet, music to a minstrel...purpose to a warrior.

"I'm in love with Tracy Livia Rhodes. Pretty damn sure I have been since the moment I met her."

He looked up as another movement caught his eye. Quirked one side of his mouth, saying to the new arrival to their circle, "You all think I'm the one who kept her alive after that explosion and then the bullshit in Seattle—but the truth is, *she* saved *me*. All of me."

He trailed off, knowing he didn't need to say more—confronting the understanding of that in every inch of Garrett's brotherly smile.

"And though I'm the one who locked the handcuffs on her, *she* was the beauty who locked *my* sorry-ass beast down."

Zeke nodded hard, his gaze glassy, his formidable jaw jutted. He was joined by the Bommer brothers, Shay and Tait, who added emphatic nods of approval.

"And yeah, it was the best high in the fucking world, watching her finally embrace the beauty of her submission... just for me. Because she trusted...*me*."

Ethan's face, such a famous sight the world over now but

set in the smirk he reserved for his battalion brothers only, widened in a commiserating smile.

"She was my gift from the gods. The treasure that showed me the way again. Proved my life could still have purpose, when I truly thought I'd lost anything like it."

Christ. Cornier words had never spilled off his lips, but every damn syllable of them was true. So indelibly, breathtakingly, true. Every corner of his soul resounded with that truth. Sang with it. Ached from it. He looked up, squeezing stinging moisture from his eye, to witness the same sheen in Kellan Rush's gaze. Kell scooted in closer, clapping a hand around Tait's shoulder.

"She sees my scars but believes in my perfection. She knows my violence but calls it passion. She peers into my darkness and doesn't try to change it or heal it—but because she dives into it with me, she *does* change it. She *has* changed it."

For that, he received a pair of appreciative grunts from yet two more arrivals to the circle: Sam Mackenna and Dan Colton.

"Awww, fuck it," he muttered then. Let himself drop back into the sand, his head low, his mushed-up vision trying to focus on the tops of his doubled-over knees. "She's changed *me*. She's changed me forever. Forever..."

He didn't even waste thoughts on everyone's angel garb, or why Pop's ukulele music was suddenly silent, or why the air was so thick and quiet and expectant. He only knew the breeze smelled like Tracy, citrus and ginger and jasmine colliding with the tang from the sea and the salt from his tears, twisting his heart into a bigger, messier, stupid-ass knot. He only knew that for once, he would accept every goddamn branch of support his men offered to him right now. He'd readily let them grow a fucking tree under him if they wanted, lifting him up with the incredible, unbreakable, bond of their brotherhood.

Until the circle parted once again.

Opened with the discernible rustle of warriors' feet...and the tangible energy of their collective honor.

To let one more into their energy.

One more with tiny footsteps...preceded by the scent of citrus and jasmine.

An angel disguised as a kitten.

The core of his soul...contained in the most gorgeous female on this planet.

The woman who plummeted onto the ground in front of him. Wrapping her small, urgent hands around his. Holding him as if she'd plunged all those sweet fingers into his chest, yanked out his heart, and now held it in the center of her palms.

Because she pretty much did.

"Forever sounds damn good to me, soldier."

John blinked. Again. Swallowed hard but realized inhaling the whole damn ocean wasn't going to help his dry, tight throat. Every drop of liquid in his body, now packed with every joyous, merciless, careening, disbelieving, detonating emotion in his soul, began exiting him through one orifice only. His one goddamn eye.

Finally, his vocal chords snapped into line again, working themselves around rasped syllables.

"Tracy?"

Her sweet kitten mouth turned up in a tiny smirk. "Yes, Sir?"

"What the hell are you doing here?"

All the guys laughed.

He didn't.

"You're the president, damn it." He didn't wait for the mirth to fade. This was too damn important. He showed her so by securing their hands tighter, twining his fingers between hers. The move had absolutely nothing to do with how fucking good it felt to touch her again. With what a miracle he once more held...and already dreaded having to let go. "You can't just be flitting to the Hawaiian Islands on a whim, just to—"

Her sharp jerk back sure got him to shut up. "Flitting?" she retorted. "On a *whim*? Is that really your argument here, asshole?"

He was conscious, vaguely, of the guys chuckling again—though mostly he dealt with his fresh irritation. Why was she so bent out of shape? And why the hell did she have to look so magnificent about it? All he wanted to do was order everyone to go back inside and demolish Mom's dinner so he could flatten her in the sand, hike up the embroidered skirt of her filmy white sundress, and bury his body inside hers for hours.

But even that wasn't an option anymore, since here was Mom, suddenly appearing behind the woman. Even she'd changed into white, with a matching hibiscus blossom in her hair and bright tears brimming her eyes.

What. The. Hell?

Tracy consumed his attention again, rising on her knees to plant hands on her hips. "Let's set a couple of things straight, mister. I wouldn't have to be 'flitting' if you'd come to the damn phone even once when I'd called. Do *not* even *think* of dreaming up another excuse on that. Second, this isn't some damn 'whim.'" She traced a broad circle on the air with the top of her head, including the guys and Mom—and now Dad, showing up behind *her*—with the motion. "You should be buying at least half a clue on that one by now, right?"

He scowled. Hard. And yeah, it probably did turn him into the goddamned pirate of Rebel's reference, but it was better than admitting he didn't comprehend even half her precious "clue." Stumbling in the dark wasn't something he handled well on normal days—and this was sure as hell *not* a normal day.

"Tracy. *Fuck*." He topped off the growl by dragging a hand across his head. "I—I don't know what the hell you're looking for here."

She lowered again. Scraped her own fingers across the length of his jaw. "For starters, how about repeating the good shit?"

Deep scowl. "The *what*?"

She grinned. "Okay, maybe not all of it. Just the part about me being your beauty and taming your hot ass down. Oh, and that gift-from-the-gods stuff too. Definitely that."

He swore beneath his breath but ended on a caustic laugh. So she'd been eavesdropping. What the hell did it matter? "I'd be thrilled to repeat *all* of it with you sitting right here, *ku`uipo*, but what's it going to accomplish? You sure as hell can't reopen that job offer"—pointing out his Bluebeard patch would've insulted even the seagulls' intelligence, so he didn't—"so there's no talking about being your Secret Service fling anymore—"

"Oh my God." She muttered it so fiercely, he expected a chest whack to follow. No such luck. She smacked him with the reproof in her eyes instead. *Christ*, her eyes. How had he lived a day, let alone weeks, without those dove wing depths? "I knew you were stubborn, but this is ridiculous."

"Excuse the hell out of me?" Enough was enough. He

pushed all the way up to his feet again. "No, don't excuse me. I'll do it myself—because clearly, I'm *not* stubborn. Just really fucking dense." He spun a glare around the wide circle of his friends. "You all look like a bunch of penises. And *you*," he gritted, pointing at the woman who'd matched his jolt with a rise of her own, "are too goddamned gorgeous for even this beach."

Tracy's chin, already jutted at him, tightened just a degree more. In a second, she went from gorgeous to outright hot. "Even if I came to this beach to get married?"

And from confusing to outright baffling.

"Married?" Franz shot back. "Now? Tonight?"

As she rolled her eyes, she was joined by her two best friends. Gemini Vann, looking more like Tracy's sister due to her silky white jumper, folded her arms and imitated the chin toss. "Is he always this quick on the uptake?"

"If so, I'm worried." The chime, along with a giggle and wink, came from a similarly dressed Veronica Gallo. The small plumeria bouquet in her hands didn't miss his attention. Gem swept an identical bunch from behind her back before handing Tracy a larger arrangement.

Well...*shit*.

Pretty as all the blooms were, they didn't touch Tracy's laughing beauty as she murmured, "That's usually the plan when two people are crazy for each other, Captain."

Still...this crap didn't compute. It sucked, but he wasn't such a douche he couldn't cop to hitting the weeds. "You—you can't get married, Tracy. You need the people's confidence. The markets need to be—"

"The markets will do just fine." She tilted her head, kicking up one side of her mouth. "Maybe even a little better, if I've got a ring on my finger and a hot military hunk on my arm."

He went still. Really fucking still. Hundreds, maybe thousands, of stealth missions under his belt, and he didn't remember concentrating this hard on not moving a damn muscle or taking a single breath. Simply put, he didn't want to let the moment go. This diamond of an instant, surrounded by his men and basking in an island sunset, in which he hoped—believed—this goddess of a woman was actually standing before him, speaking the words of his craziest fantasies...

Until the instant was gone.

And she didn't stand next to him anymore.

She knelt in front of him.

As she dropped, slipped her hand into his once more. From that connection, spread her warmth through every inch of him...a sizzling, permeating awareness eclipsed only by the radiance of her upturned face. Her eyes were like sunlight through mist. Her smile held the mystery of a knowing but naughty angel.

His angel.

By the gods. Could it really become truth? Was this really happening? If it all still really *was* a dream, maybe he didn't want to know anymore. Because damn, it was the best dream he'd ever had. Most detailed too. Maki, Nani, Lino, and Luke had even populated the scene, along with an older man looking so much like Tracy, he had no doubt about the guy's role here.

Which had him freaking about *his* role here...

Especially as Tracy took a deep breath and started speaking again.

"Keoni John Franzen," she whispered. "You know that I love you, more than—"

"No."

Her brow furrowed. Her chin quivered. "No?"

He pulled his hand free. "This isn't right."

The guys weren't laughing anymore.

Tracy blinked rapidly. Swallowed hard.

Her dad looked ready to rip Franz's balls out.

He didn't care. *This had to be right.*

With his hands bracing both sides of her waist, he reversed their positions with one commanding sweep. Though taking a knee before her was easy, gazing up into her face simply wasn't.

"Damn." He was unable to summon any other word for a long moment. Finally, after getting air back in, he rasped, "Will it ever be possible to look at you and not consider myself the luckiest man on the planet?"

Tracy took her own turn to go motionless. She stole his breath with the stillness as much as she did in tigress or kitten mode. "Wh-What?" she stammered at last.

John slid his hands around hers—without wavering his gaze from her incredible face. "I'm saying that whatever I did to deserve you, whether it was another life or some shift of karma in this one, I'm ordering the universe to pay the hell up, here and now." He lifted her fingers, crushing their curled knuckles against his fervent lips. "I'm saying that I love you too, Tracy Livia Rhodes. Desperately. Illogically. Completely."

Tears continued out of her eyes—accompanied by a much different glow from their quicksilver depths. "John. *John.*"

Her sweet whisper crushed his chest—in all the best ways. He still squared his shoulders and maintained his grip on her. "If you really want to give this shit a go with a guy who knows a bit about service, a lot about honor, and craves to learn every incredible detail about *you*, then I'm the guy dropping to my knees for the chance." He hauled in a huge breath, fighting the heat in his head and losing miserably. "I'll drop to my knees every damn day for it," he uttered between his own tears—though crazily, they didn't rob him of any control. They gave it back to him. In Franzen's surrender to love, he finally found the dominion he'd been seeking over his life. A new purpose, a new meaning, under new rules...

For which he was ready.

"I promise, I *promise*, that if you'll love this dragon with the one eye, the snarly temper, and the dumb jokes, he'll spread his wings every day to keep your body pleased, your heart happy...and your soul completely filled."

Tracy jerked their joined hands up to *her* lips. Drenched his fingers in the salt of her tears and the passion of her kisses. "The tigress says yes to the dragon."

"Then I guess we'd better make this thing official." The declaration was made by yet another new arrival to the throng: the only one in their group besides him who hadn't gotten the memo about the white wedding motif. Or maybe Max *had* gotten it and just decided he liked his powder blue cutaway tux better.

Right now, the guy could've been in a gorilla suit for all Franz cared. His skin felt three sizes too small as quick introductions were made—Mom and Pop quickly making plans to show Tracy's dad around the island tomorrow—and everyone moved into place. The sole break he got from the nervousness came courtesy of Luke, who pulled him into a fierce, wordless bearhug—

Before Max dove right in.

"Dearly beloved...we are gathered here today..."

Simple rote phrases—that were somehow, stunningly, perfect.

"To have and to hold, from this day forward..."

Forward. The word he never thought he'd say with joy again.

"To love and to cherish..."

Cherish. The commitment he never thought he'd know with such completion.

"As long as we both shall live..."

Living.

The concept he never thought he could fully embrace.

The happiness this woman had given him with her insights, her honesty, her fire, her passion, her submission...

Her love.

Even after seeing all the darkness and wildness in him...

Her love.

Wasn't that what any wild beast really craved?

Because, as all those wild things knew, sunsets were pretty, but midnights took commitment.

"Ever after" was poetic, but "happy" depended on understanding.

And while dragons were beautiful, their fires demanded the most exceptional princesses.

Warrioresses with untamed hearts of their own.

Women destined to run with the wild boys.

Not to tame them.

Simply to love them.

Simply to know...

Wildness defined the fiercest heroes.

And heroines.

And always, *always*, turned love into an adventure.

ALSO BY ANGEL PAYNE

Honor Bound:
Saved
Cuffed
Seduced
Wild
Wet
Hot
Masked
Mastered
Conquered
Ruled

The Bolt Saga:
Bolt
Ignite
Pulse
Fuse
Surge
Light

Secrets of Stone Series:
No Prince Charming
No More Masquerade
No Perfect Princess
No Magic Moment
No Lucky Number
No Simple Sacrifice
No Broken Bond
No White Knight

**For a full list of Angel's other titles,
visit her at AngelPayne.com**

ACKNOWLEDGMENTS

Dear readers,

Four years ago, I began this crazy, wilder-than-wild journey, inspired by my love of military heroes and a kernel of an idea based on a real-life couple I'd met at a Los Angeles book signing. That Dom and his wife became Garrett and Sage, the first lovers of the Honor Bound series.

Now the series is at ten books and counting, and I couldn't be more thrilled that so many people have not only found my "Wild Boys," but loved them enough to want more.

Number ten definitely felt like the right book to bring you all the story of Keoni John Franzen and Tracy Rhodes, his epic tigress of a leading lady—though I'm going to be honest, the idea of telling John's story was originally so daunting, I originally thought I'd dash off a fast and dirty novella just to get him to shut up. You can all stop laughing about that one now.

I first thought that John and Tracy's story was going to be my goodbye to the Honor Bound boys—but am so excited to say that I've signed a contract to write two more for you. While book eleven will likely be Max Brickham's story, I'm open to ideas about whom you'd all like to see for book twelve! Drop me a line at any of my socials and share your views!

I look forward to hearing from you, just as I am excited about the idea of telling you how grateful I am that you love and believe in the guys. Never in a billion years did I think that I could write in the world of military romance for this long, but

I'm so grateful that the passionate, pulsing thrill ride hasn't stopped yet!

From the bottom of my heart, *thank you* to all of the original core readers (you know who you are!) for believing in these books and in the stories my spirit needed to tell with them. When I think of how far we've all come, from the original WILD Boys to now, with the Honor Bound guys, I'm simply blown away. How thankful I am for every single one of you for believing in these amazing, beautiful heroes of my heart.

I hope John and Tracy's story has been a fantastic reading adventure for you. As always, I have no words after this point— for my gratitude to all of you is beyond bounds, as well.

~Angel

With special, incredible thanks to the editing team, from the beginning and through this edition who have given so much of themselves and cut their damn veins open to make the Honor Bound boys shine:

Meredith Bowery, Riane Holt, Jacy Mackin, Ellie McLove, Rory Olsen, Melisande Scott, Jenny Rarden, Jeanne De Vita, and my editing hero: Scott Saunders!

With more gratitude in my heart than I can ever express... The one who's held my hand through it all...

The Tracy with heart, beauty, brains, and spirit putting even this fictional one to shame...

Tracy Roelle, you are such a gift to me from above.

And as long as I'm bawling my eyes out... Victoria Blue, you are the touch point in my days... the keel who keeps me even...

the friend I don't deserve...

but the goddess for whom I am so damn grateful, each and every day.

Thank you for seeing my wildness and loving me anyway!

The Honor Bound boys have only been as good as their betas—and goddesses, I have no words (None!) to express how you have helped these stories—and the writing overall—become the absolute best they can be! Thank you from the bottom of my heart:

Angela Barrett, Ceej Chargualaf, Kimberly Hellmers, Amy Rudolph, Carey Sabala, Victoria Blue, and Lisa Simo-Kinzer.

To every single blogger and review team who took time out of your days and nights to not just read the books but give them honest words of appraisal from your hearts...I am so indebted and grateful to you all. What you do is amazing—and so much harder than it looks! If I tried naming everyone, it'd be a disaster and I'd feel awful about leaving some folks off. I just want you to know that I know how hard you work, and the time you've carved out for Honor Bound has never, ever gone unappreciated.

So many hugs, and a few thousand cups of coffee I'll never be able to repay, to the beautiful (inside and out!) Shannon Hunt, and the entire Once Upon an Alpha team. No way would I have kept my sanity without you—in so many more ways than one. I am so deeply indebted to you...for everything.

An incredible, engulfing hug of thanks to the whole Waterhouse Press team, especially Meredith, Jon, and David, for believing enough in these books to revitalize them—and to ask for two more!

The most special thanks of all...

To the men and women heroically serving in all branches of our nation's armed forces.

Your sacrifices are never forgotten.

ABOUT ANGEL PAYNE

USA Today bestselling romance author Angel Payne loves to focus on high-heat romance starring memorable alpha men and the women who love them. She has numerous book series to her credit, including the action-packed Bolt Saga and Honor Bound series, Secrets of Stone series (with Victoria Blue), the intertwined Cimarron and Temptation Court series, the Suited for Sin series, and the Lords of Sin historicals, as well as several standalone titles.

Angel is a native Southern Californian, leading to her love of being in the outdoors, where she often reads and writes. She still lives in Southern California with her soul-mate husband and beautiful daughter, to whom she is a proud cosplay/ culture con mom. Her passions also include whisky tasting, shoe shopping, and travel.

Visit her at AngelPayne.com